MW01128380

BOOKS FROM THE LAND OF LYRE

ALL NOVELS BY PHILIP RANGEL CAN BE FOUND IN AMAZON BOOKS

THE WIZARD AND THE WHITE WOLF SAGA

Through The Eyes Of Children

BOOK I

PHILIP RANGEL

Copyright © 2023 Philip Rangel.

All rights reserved. No part of this book may be used or reproduced by any means, graphic, electronic, or mechanical, including photocopying, recording, taping or by any information storage retrieval system without the written permission of the author except in the case of brief quotations embodied in critical articles and reviews.

This is a work of fiction. All of the characters, names, incidents, organizations, and dialogue in this novel are either the products of the author's imagination or are used fictitiously.

Archway Publishing books may be ordered through booksellers or by contacting:

Archway Publishing
1663 Liberty Drive
Bloomington, IN 47403
www.archwaypublishing.com
844-669-3957

Because of the dynamic nature of the Internet, any web addresses or links contained in this book may have changed since publication and may no longer be valid. The views expressed in this work are solely those of the author and do not necessarily reflect the views of the publisher, and the publisher hereby disclaims any responsibility for them.

Any people depicted in stock imagery provided by Getty Images are models, and such images are being used for illustrative purposes only. Certain stock imagery © Getty Images.

ISBN: 978-1-6657-4050-0 (sc)
ISBN: 978-1-6657-4051-7 (hc)
ISBN: 978-1-6657-4052-4 (e)

Library of Congress Control Number: 2023905012

Print information available on the last page.

Archway Publishing rev. date: 07/10/2023

FOR MY CHILDREN...

Contents

ACKNOWLEDGMENTS

Patricia A McKillip, Stephen R Donaldson, Frank Herbert, Hickman & Weis, Tanith Lee, Michael Moorcock, Anne McCaffery, Heinlein, Terry Brooks, Marion Zimmer Bradley, Jean M Auel, Jo Clayton, Janet Kagan (My Tailkinker), JK Rowling, and of course, JRR Tolkien—thank you.

Recently, my wife and daughters have introduced me to a new addiction. I would like to add Nora Roberts, Seanan McGuire, my homegirl Patricia Briggs, and the incomparable Sarah J Maas.

I don't know what I would do without you.

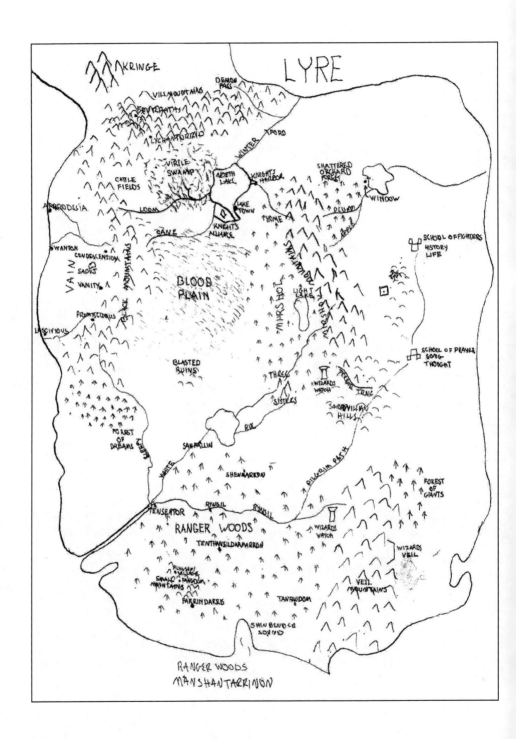

PROLOGUE

927TH SEASON OF THE REIGN OF THE KINGS

The bonfire cast fourteen shadows on the dust-coated plain. Benjamin, Seer of Lake Town, He Who Sees All, stared in silence at the figures before him. Thirteen children whispered among themselves as a single figure entered the circle of light. Benjamin's dark blue eyes widened in surprise. A white wolf pulled an impossibly huge bundle of sticks to the fire and came to a panting halt.

Moonlight calmed her nerves and changed shape. The snapping of bones and the crackle of fire, oddly similar in sound, silenced the whispered laughter and derogatory comments of the other children. She finished *the change* and added her contribution of wood to the fire. Ignoring the other children, she turned and approached He Who Sees All. In total awe of the only human present, Moonlight stared at his feet and nervously offered a respectful bow.

Benjamin watched as the skinny albino *wereling* turned and walked away. She did not join the others. Taking a place to one side, she turned back to him and crossed her slim white arms across her flat chest. Her expressionless gaze changed not at all as crude comments and laughter were cast in her direction. Benjamin sighed and shook his head. Human or were, it did not matter, kids would be kids.

The werelings quieted as He Who Sees All gazed up at the full moon. His memory played over his past. This was the thirty-seventh time he had made this journey. However, the ancient memory of his ancestors held 958 midwinter nights on the lifeless dust of Blood Plain. Almost one thousand seasons ago, his direct antecedent, the Seer of the North, had been blessed by Myril the White. The high cleric had instilled his own countless seasons of memory into the old seer. Knowing his own mind and being personally familiar with *the gift of sight*, he charged Benjamin's lineage with the duty of *witness* to the Vow of Blood Plain.

Benjamin blinked away from the lure of exploring picture memories of the past. He faced the werelings and raised his right hand. "Nine hundred and fifty-eight seasons have passed since your forefathers first spoke the Vow of Blood Plain. I am He Who Sees All. I am your witness. I stand before the Creator and acknowledge with pride that the were are faithful. In almost one thousand seasons, not a single were has reached puberty and failed to take the Vow."

Benjamin held his left hand forward and beckoned to the children. One at a time, they came to him and knelt. One at a time, he accepted their vows. Benjamin noticed as he listened to the verses that the small albino girl waited in the background as the rest of the children stood before him.

Moonlight watched the other whelps as they took the Vow. When they were all finished, she approached He Who Sees All. As she came to a stop and trembled before him, her father's words came back to her: *Take the Vow very seriously, daughter. In a few hundred seasons, we devastated humankind in the northlands. The great wizards could have destroyed us. The* were *could be but a fairy tale to scare little children. They did not. For whatever reason, the wizards found good in us. They took from us the horrible curse that almost destroyed us. We no longer change shape from human to demon. Our natural change is now human to wolf. For the grace that we have been given, we now swear to protect humankind.*

For over nine hundred seasons, our people have stood guard over the evils of Vain. Prophesy says that, one day, our probation will be over. One day, the Creator will not require our vows. One day, we will be accepted into his fold as one of his own. Who knows? Perhaps you, my Moonlight, will play a part in the salvation of our people.

Benjamin watched the white wereling tremble as she dropped to her knees. He nodded approval and listened to her words.

"I will go,
I will fight,
I will die—"

Without warning, the *sight* came full upon him. Benjamin watched this small child of the were in a battle with a woman dressed in red silk wraps. This young albino werewoman, in perhaps four seasons, fought with an ancient ivory staff. Her opponent wielded a staff capped with a razor-sharp, platinum disk. Their skill was so great Benjamin could barely discern the staves as they blurred through the air. Cut, bruised, and bleeding, both women staggered in exhaustion.

A man dressed in black silks with a ruby-studded armband stood in the background. He was being restrained by a huge she-bear. Green eyes glittering, he too watched in helpless frustration as the duel continued.

Moonlight recited the words of the Vow. She glanced up at He Who Sees All and almost faltered as his eyes turned bright yellow. She squeezed her eyes closed, suddenly terrified, and desperately fought to control her trembling. Voice quaking, she clasped her hands to her thighs and spoke her vow.

Benjamin watched this child of the were stand back. Both women circled as they took each other's measure. As the scene circled, the small albino woman attacked. Her ivory staff blurred through the air and knocked the staff from her opponent's hands.

Benjamin's perspective changed until he viewed the scene as if he stood behind the woman dressed in red. In his vision he gazed directly into the werewoman's bright magenta eyes. He could see that she had been crying. She answered the red-clad woman and turned her head. Benjamin followed her line of sight and saw what he had missed before.

Moonlight spoke the final words of the Vow of Blood Plain. She hesitantly looked back up. He Who Sees All now looked down at her with a gentle smile. His eyes were back to their normal dark blue. Sniffing his scent, she found he was feeling pride. His scent was not general or all encompassing. It was directed only at her. Goose bumps covered her skin as he reached down and set his hand on her head.

Benjamin had been told by his father that, sooner or later, he would have this vision. Sooner or later, this moment would be foretold. In his lineage, it was a trait to warn the seer. A warning always heeded so the line would not fail.

He was now fifty-six seasons old. He had never taken a mate. Benjamin was the last of his line. He ruffled the shaggy mass of white hair, and said kindly, "Rise, daughter. Go forth and remain true."

The midwinter air finally penetrated his heavy cloak. Turning to the bonfire for warmth, Benjamin once again beheld the final scene from the vision. His own lifeless body lay still in the grass.

January

928TH SEASON OF THE REIGN OF THE KINGS

January stood at the edge of the Shattered Orchard Forest and gazed back toward the city of Window. A cold chill prickled the hair on the nape of his neck. Last night had been one more close call—one more strike. He had already been caught twice. One more offense, and he would lose his right hand. He sighed and laughed to himself. Good thing he was left-handed.

January had raced through the dark streets as four market guards had tried to catch him. One was old, and one was fat. The two younger guards had been his main concern. He'd run around a corner and slipped on a pile of table scraps next to the innkeeper's back door. Luckily, the two younger guards had done the same thing. After literally swimming through a heap of old, nasty garbage, January had crawled on hands and knees and dove through a cellar window. Jumping up to his feet, he had slipped again as one bare foot landed in a mop bucket. The guard behind him had cursed. January had looked up and grinned. The guard's sword belt had gotten caught between two steel spikes that were supposed to keep thieves out. January had pulled his foot out of the bucket and laughed.

January had raced up the stairs and out the front door. He'd headed straight to Lake Side, where the other street urchins spent their summers. When he'd reached the edge of town, he'd slowed and finally taken a long, deep breath. With a heavy sigh, he'd made his way back to the grove of oak trees and emptied his pockets for the three children who were still too young to steal for themselves.

The guards must have realized where he was headed. Later that night, a great noise of shouting and cursing had startled him from sleep. He'd peered through the trees and watched as they'd drawn near. Cursing his own body, he'd silently pondered the twist of fate that had caused him to grow almost a foot in six moons. His equilibrium just hadn't caught up to him! Well, that's what the barge captain had said. All he knew was that, six moons ago, no guard had ever caught him. Now he had three strikes against him in a few short moons.

January turned back to the edge of the forest and took a deep breath. *I ain't goin' back. I'll learn to live out here, or I'll die tryin'.* Resolution firmed his fears as he stepped onto the forest trail and passed beneath the trees.

Sunder, the Mythit, stared at the fawn. Glowing purple eyes held the young deer hypnotized. He wondered, as he had many times, how the wizards had created the spell that surrounded the enchanted Forest of Mirshol. All the animals were capable of reason. Every creature that passed the borders of the forest gained the ability. This fawn was as dumb as a rock. Then again, he was not in Mirshol. Orange furry fingers reached out to stroke the fawn's neck. The snap of a branch drew Sunder's gaze away from the young deer. The fawn shook its head, took a step back, and leapt away.

Loud, stomping feet approached Sunder. He turned his head as the young human cursed at a tree root. The boy had tripped over a root crossing his path and was climbing slowly to his feet. Sunder grinned.

January got to his feet and wearily continued up the path. Four days into the Shattered Orchard Forest, and he was only now reaching the feet of the Mirshol Mountains. He was sure the mountain range would have been closer. He thought he would have been *here* on the first day. His stomach rumbled as he stopped to listen for the sound of water. *Shoulda brought a water skin. This is ridiculous!*

Sunder listened to the human as he thought. The boy was looking rather worn. There was a stream off to the left, but from this point on the trail, it was at least a hundred yards out of earshot.

Then the most amazing thing happened. The boy looked directly at him.

January was worn to the bone. As he stared straight ahead, not really seeing anything, something in front of him moved. He blinked and looked again. No, there was nothing there, but he could have sworn an orange blur had passed before his eyes.

Sunder's jaw dropped open in shock. He gathered his wits and started jumping up and down. Could this boy be the one? No human had seen a

Mythit in over nine hundred seasons. Still, the prophecy of the Seer of the North had spoken of a boy. Sunder frowned. *This* boy standing in front of him was at least six feet tall. The yellow spiked crown of his own head barely reached this young man's waist. Boy indeed! A bumbling colt was more like it!

January sighed and continued up the path. He needed water, and he had no idea how to find it. He could picture himself reaching the mountains and looking back down. From that vantage point, he hoped he could see a stream. With that thought in mind, he looked up and cursed. A low-hanging tree limb had smacked him right across the forehead.

Sunder burst into outrageous laughter as the young human landed flat on his back. He jumped up on the boy's chest and laughed down into his face. Laughter died in an instant. Ice-blue eyes gazed up at him, and this time Sunder knew the boy had seen something.

January lay perfectly still. For a brief moment, a pair of slanted, glowing purple eyes had been staring straight down at him. He could have sworn the eyes were laughing.

Sunder took a deep breath and calmed his racing heart. *You are the one. You really are the one!*

"I'm the what?" Jan blurted out. He thought he'd heard something. Maybe he was losing his mind. He shook his head and sat up. "Yeah, that's all I need. I'll go back to Window and walk around talking to myself. Then people will throw coins and food, and I won't have to steal!" Laughter welled up inside him as he thought about the old beggars and crazy people from Window. He sobered as he thought. They had been beggars and thieves all their lives. He wasn't going to be like that! He would not end up old and useless, wandering around cities at night.

Sunder gasped as the boy sat up. Long blond hair flew right through his face. Sunder rolled his eyes at the ethereal sensation. *Only in the presence of humans.* Mythits were corporeal just like any other creature on the face of Lyre. Only when humans were present did they fade. It was part of the spell that surrounded Mirshol. No matter where in Lyre any Mythit was, they would fade in the presence of a human. Only the Young One spoken of in the prophecy could change that. Sunder knew that human was sitting right here before him. Sunder turned and frowned. The boy was digging one finger in his ear, trying to extricate wax.

January sighed and climbed to his feet. No, he wasn't going to die old and poor in a city. He was probably going to die of thirst in a forest full of fruit trees!

Head off to your left and walk two hundred steps.

January turned his head. "What?" He gazed around as he turned in a circle. "Is someone here?"

Sunder frowned as he wondered what it would take to knock the boy into the proper frame of mind to perceive him. He grinned. That tree branch had been a good start!

January shrugged and headed off the trail. It couldn't hurt, could it? The trail was getting thinner and less worn with every passing hour. He might as well make his own trail, right? As he passed through the trees, he snatched an apple out of his pack. Three days and nothing but apples. Oh well. He had lived on apples before. He had even tried to sell apples.

Window was the source of fresh and bottled fruit for the entire northern region of Lyre. Every spring, traders from both schools would come to Window and buy wagonloads of fresh and bottled fruit. With the help of the other street urchins, January had tried to pick and sell apples. They quickly learned that the market was closed to them. The city vendors had paid the market guards to protect their interests. Two weeks of hard work had ended up in the lake. January scowled through the trees as he remembered the way the guards had laughed as they'd destroyed their little booth on the edge of town. The apple core January held whizzed through the trees as he sighed in frustration.

Water. He stopped all motion and listened. He heard a stream! Suddenly parched to the point of misery, he took off running through the trees. Ducking and dodging branches, he listened as the splashing of water drew closer.

Sunder faded in and out behind the boy as he followed. They were almost to the water. He watched the lad toss his pack to the ground as they reached a small waterfall. Sunder grinned as the boy simply fell face-first into the pool.

January gulped water as he floated facedown beneath the fall. Slowly gaining his feet, he dug his toes into the pebble bed and luxuriated in the cold mountain stream. As his mind and body calmed, he rolled his head, trying to ease the muscles in the back of his neck. Eyes closed, he listened to sounds of the forest. Then he went completely still.

How many times had he been in the market and known a guard was watching? He was gifted with the ability to know when someone was studying him. He knew it right now. Very slowly, he turned and nonchalantly passed his gaze through the trees. From the corner of his eye, he saw movement. Something small and orange blurred before his eyes as he turned to look. Heart racing, he wondered what it could be.

Sunder felt himself fade as the eye path of the boy touched him. What was it going to take?

January watched a fish jump and forgot all about seeing things. He climbed the bank and rummaged through his pack. With a hook and line, he rolled a rock and found a grub. Tying the line to a tree, he slung the hook into the water and went back to the clearing to start a fire. The thought of fish would usually make his stomach turn. He was absolutely sure he had eaten more fish than any other person alive. Right now, a fish would taste wonderful. Anything but apples!

Sunder sat down and watched. Maybe it would just take time. The boy was piling sticks for his fire. Even as the boy began the task of striking flint and steel, Sunder felt himself materialize. The Mythit realized that starting a fire must be second nature to the boy. The mind behind those bright blue eyes must be lost in thought.

January glanced up and shouted in surprise. An orange, furry creature that couldn't have been more than three feet tall was sitting on a rock. A shock of bright yellow hair that spiked to all angles grew from the crown of the little round head. Glowing purple eyes blinked back in surprise. Almost as quickly as he saw it, the creature vanished. "Wait! What are you?"

He didn't need to ask. He knew now what it was that he had seen. A Mythit! There was a Mythit right here in this clearing! He thought about all of the funny stories he'd heard about Mythits. Tricksters, pranksters, they were said to live for the fun of playing practical jokes. But they were a myth! Surely no one had ever seen a Mythit before. If his stomach wasn't rumbling, and if he didn't feel so dead tired, he would have wondered if he were dreaming.

Mythits, dragons, werewolves, wizards. Myths! They couldn't be real, could they? He'd heard fantastic stories of dragons and gold and wizards and magic. He'd heard many stories about wizards fighting demons. It was said that Blood Plain used to be the greatest forest in Lyre until it was destroyed by the magical battles between the wizards of Lyre and the demons of Kringe. Mythits were supposed to be able to show wizards how to be more powerful. He wondered if there really were Mythit-trained wizards.

That, young human, is impossible. A wizard hasn't seen a Mythit in over nine hundred seasons.

January turned around, watched the creature disappear, and asked, "What? Why?"

Look at the ground.

"What?" Jan shook his head. "Are you talking in my mind?"

Yes, you big bumbling oaf! Look at the ground.

January blushed at the tone of the thought. Rolling his eyes, he stared at the ground. Almost immediately, the creature appeared off to one side. January glance at him, and he disappeared again. Focusing his gaze back at the ground, he watched as the little orange figure returned. Very slowly, he ran his gaze across the ground until he was staring at a rock in front of one orange, fur-covered foot.

"Can you hear me now?"

January tried to stay calm as his own excitement seemed to make the foot vanish. Taking deep breaths, he calmed, and the foot became clear. "Yes, I hear you now."

"Good. Now very slowly let your gaze defocus into a blur and look up."

January tried to stay calm. As his eyes raised, the orange body kept trying to fade from his sight. Very slowly, he took deep breaths and raised his eyes some more. The hands and feet of the Mythit were darker orange than the body—almost red. He counted three fingers and toes. As his eyes finally reached the face, he gasped. Purple, slanted, glowing eyes blinked as the Mythit grinned from ear to ear. "Guess what?"

January was afraid to move. "What?"

"You got a fish!"

January turned his head. Sure enough, his line was taut and trailing back and forth in the pool. When he turned back, the creature was gone. Sighing, he went to his line and gave it a tug. A huge pull yanked it back out of his hand. *Must be a salmon going upstream to spawn.*

You know something, you're probably right. Why else would it be here?

Jan scowled as his mind filled with laughter. He found a stick and started winding the line around one end. As he tried to pull it in, he realized his line would probably break. With another heavy sigh he jumped into the water and reeled the fish up to his chest. Grabbing the salmon by both gill slits, he swung it up and out of the water.

After he climbed the bank, he went and searched his pack for his one and only knife. He noticed that the Mythit was once again sitting on the rock. He found his knife and cleaned the fish as the Mythit watched in silence. With one long stick and two short sticks, he made a double-armed cross. After he shoved the stick into the ground and leaned the salmon over the fire, he sat and glanced at the Mythit. "Why are you being so quiet?"

"You're learning. I'm teaching."

"What? What am I learning?"

"How to pay attention."

"I already know how to pay attention."

"Really? Then why didn't you see me before?"

"I don't know, maybe—"

"Maybe you weren't paying attention."

January allowed his gaze to slowly approach the Mythit. Once again, he beheld those strange glowing purple eyes—no whites, no pupils, just slanted orbs of liquid purple color. "Why do they glow?"

"Because I can see farther than you."

"Oh? How far can you see?"

"I can see fourteen thousand seasons."

"What? How can ... You mean you've ... Uh, how old are you?"

Sunder burst into laughter. "Very good! I am impressed! I have watched the changing of the seasons fourteen thousand times."

"Fourt— No way! How could you live that long?"

Sunder smiled at the innocent naivete of this very young man. No explanation would suffice for his unopened mind. *Well, the lessons start now.* "I remember the land of Lyre before humans even walked on it. I have seen wonders, and I am going to teach them to you."

January caught his breath. "Me? Why me?"

"I have been waiting for you for over nine hundred seasons."

Goose bumps covered January's arms and neck. Suddenly frightened, he watched as the Mythit started to fade from view. Taking a deep breath, he calmed his racing heart and watched the figure solidify. "That is impossible."

"So is seeing a Mythit. No other human on the face of Lyre could do it. Not one. Only you."

January blinked as tiny bits of information he'd gleaned from stories started to form a picture. Diverging from what he really wanted to know, he asked, "Did you ever meet any wizards?"

Sunder burst into such a fit of laughter he fell off of the rock. *Oh, Blue! This boy is precious!* Finally getting the better of his mirth, Sunder answered, "Yes, boy, I've met a few wizards. The most powerful wizard ever to walk the land of Lyre was my best friend."

January thought about that. Like everyone, he had heard the legends of the Red Wizard, the Blue Wizard, and the White Wizard. Everyone seemed to believe that, if there really were wizards, then the Blue Wizard was the greatest. Curiosity could not be held in check today. "Do you mean the Blue Wizard?"

Sunder looked him straight in the eye. "Yes. The Blue Wizard was my *companion*. We walked the land together for almost thirteen thousand seasons."

"Then the legends are true?"

"Yes, they are true."

January could hardly believe he had the nerve to ask, but he did. "Think you can teach me magic?"

Sunder grinned. "I'm glad you're a fast thinker. I don't *think* anything. I *know* I'm going to teach you *about* magic."

Jan could hardly believe his ears. "Really? Why?"

Sunder raised an eyebrow. He thought about it before he said it. Then he just decided to say it. "Because the Dark Lord will be freed from his prison, and you need to know how to fight him."

Sunder stood up and walked to the boy's side. Smiling kindly, he gazed down at the very young face. If he said anything else right now, it would not be heard. The boy had passed out cold next to his fish.

2

MOONLIGHT

930TH SEASON OF THE REIGN OF THE KINGS

Moonlight stalked through the mountain pass. Shaggy, snow-white hair bounced around her face as she padded on bare feet toward her foster father's hut. The time had come. Today was the day. Dead or alive, she would no longer be subject in any way to the clan of the bitch, Sambra. The *change of the were* almost came on her as she thought about killing her foster mother. Hair began to sprout on her shoulders and back. Taking a deep breath, she regained a measure of self-control. The white hair on her shoulders receded as she continued down the rocky, dirt trail.

A rough circle of huts came into view as she rounded the last bend. The were of Sha's pack paused to watch as she padded straight to the center of their summer camp. The white skinned, magenta-eyed maiden threw down a bundle of fur and began to etch a rough circle in the packed dirt of the canyon floor. Many of them started to laugh and snicker among themselves. A few of them remained silent. Nevertheless, every single one of them knew this day would come. The few who were wise enough to smell her scent before they laughed at the young werewoman, considered whether or not she had a chance. No one had seen Moonlight in almost two whole seasons. Who knew what trials had tested her mettle? Perhaps she was now Sambra's equal.

Moonlight glanced sideways as Fluffy stepped up to her side. She didn't want to give in to emotion, but Fluffy might make this hard on her. Her eight-season old foster sister was the only member of Sha's clan she'd ever cared for. She watched the skinny little naked wereling push tangled hair out of her face. Moonlight reached out and wiped a smudge of dirt from the girl's nose. "You're so big. Pretty soon you will take the journey to find your ram."

Fluffy frowned. The only time she had ever heard her father speak of Moonlight with pride was when he told the story about how he'd found her beaten, shredded body by a small pool. She had been covered with blood, and much of it had been her own. Still, she had survived. At only six seasons of age, Moonlight had walked the path to become a warrior. Sha had said she'd killed a mountain ram with only her teeth.

Moonlight sighed as she studied Fluffy's gray eyes. "Tell Sha that I am preparing the Circle of Challenge."

Fluffy, not understanding, said, "Moonlight, my mother isn't here. She is on a hunt."

Moonlight's face lost all expression. She grasped the girl's hand and then let it go. "Foster Sister, I draw this circle for Sha. Please, go get him."

Fluffy stepped into her father's hut. Sha glanced up from cleaning his sword and smelled his daughter's scent. Curious, he met her eyes. "What is it?"

Fluffy bowed her head in respect. "Moonlight has returned from the mountains. She is outside at this moment drawing the Circle of Challenge."

Sha raised one eyebrow. "Is she going to kill your mother?"

Fluffy swallowed the lump that formed in her throat. She almost wished it were that simple. "No, Father. She is drawing the circle for you."

The surprise he'd felt before was nothing to the shock he felt now. As he rose to his feet and stepped out of his hut, he wondered what Moonlight must be thinking. She couldn't take his pack. Only a male could be pack leader. Then it dawned on him. She must want to follow in the steps of her true father. If Moonlight could beat him in single combat, then she could become One Who Walks Alone.

Sha blinked as he watched his whole clan gather for the fight. *This can't be happening! Does she really think she can beat me in the circle?* Sha watched the skinny little albino as she finished drawing the ring. By the Vow! The top of her head barely reached his chin. With a show of quiet dignity, she stepped out from the circle and began to strip. He raised his hands for silence as males and females started laughing. If he were forced to kill her, he would not want it to become a spectacle.

Silence spread across the clearing, but it was not due to Sha's upraised hands. Surprise and even fear filled Sha's nose as Those Who Walk Alone stepped out of the marsh. Lindon, the true father of Moonlight, walked to Sha's side as the rest of the elite fighters passed through the assembled were and stopped in front of the small albino girl. Sha watched as Swiftfoot

Who Walks Alone offered a respectful bow and picked up her pouch of rendered fat.

Moonlight looked up into the huge were's eyes and sniffed his scent. With a quick smile that vanished immediately, she raised her arms and spread her feet. It was almost disconcerting for Sha as he watched the big burly weremale kneel at the feet of the tiny young woman. Dipping both hands into the pouch, Swiftfoot began to smear the rendered fat all over her pale, naked body.

Lindon Who Walks Alone stopped at Sha's side, stared up into the cloudless sky, and whispered, "It is a good day to die."

Sha studied the older were looking for some kind of response. Lindon turned to watch his daughter being prepared for the circle. "Lindon, is this really happening?"

Lindon turned back to Sha, and this time the old were's gray eyes could have frozen water. "Need you ask? She is *my* daughter. Your pack has fostered her, but she never really belonged here. If she can't become One Who Walks Alone, then she will take her own life. It is better for her to die by the blade. Suicide is the coward's way."

Sha sniffed Lindon's scent and once again felt surprise. Lindon actually believed there was a chance Moonlight would walk from the circle victorious. "I could let her win. I would not like to kill her."

Lindon's eyes narrowed to slits. "If you do not take this seriously, I will kill you myself."

Moonlight wiped her hands on an old piece of deer skin.

Swiftfoot whispered, "'Ware his weight and his feet. You have a longer reach with your staff. Take that advantage and use it well."

Magenta eyes landed on her foster father as she stepped into the circle. Her true father was even now helping to grease the pack leader for the Challenge. Sniffing the air, she found Sha's scent. It made her smile. Sha had no idea she was truly prepared for this challenge. For two whole seasons she had been training with Those Who Walk Alone. She could beat any one of the elite two times out of three. Except for her father. She knew no other were would ever be the match of Lindon in the circle. Sha was about to drop to one knee, and he didn't even know it.

Sha stepped into the circle and studied those disconcerting magenta eyes. Sambra called them "demon eyes." Sha had to admit that Moonlight could chill your heart with her direct stare. Unlike the mother of his children, Sha knew the reasons for that ability. What child, raised by a ruthless bitch like Sambra, could enter adulthood with a shred of humanity? Sha had always regretted Sambra's treatment of Moonlight. Many times, he had wanted to stop Sambra from her cruel treatment of the little bitch. The problem was, he knew his interference would fuel Sambra's hatred. Any kindness he might show Moonlight could very well have meant her death. He shook his head and wondered. Was he about to pay the price of his mate's abuse?

Moonlight had been waiting for this moment for moons. Lindon had finally given in and offered a father's blessing. She had waited for his blessing, and he knew it. Calm settled on her shoulders as she sniffed the scents coming from her former clan. They thought they were about to watch her die. A slight smile touched her lips as she realized she no longer cared what they thought. After today, one way or another, there would be no more abuse—no names; no beatings; no mocking, stinking, filthy member of Sha's clan would ever touch her again.

Sha was taken aback as his nose found nothing but resolution and calm. There was absolutely no fear in her. Either she really thought she was going to beat him, or she simply did not care. Either way, a person in her state of mind was the worst kind of opponent to face. There would be no holding back. As he started to circle, broadsword in hand, he studied her style. Eyes narrowing, she stopped dead in her tracks and waited for him to make the first move.

Moonlight cast her gaze toward Sha without narrowing her perspective to any single part of his body. She watched him stiffen as she stopped. Her oak staff spun in her right hand as she waited for him to attack. Her blatant offer, allowing him the first attack, was an insult and everyone knew it. Curses from the onlookers were cast in her direction. Who did she think she was anyway? Moonlight grinned, which made them hiss worse. She was about to show them who she thought she was.

Sha stepped in and tried to knock the staff from her grasp. Moonlight ducked and rolled so fast he had to jump back. Then he realized she had set him up. In midair, Moonlight whipped her staff at his feet and knocked him off balance. He landed at an angle and had to back step to keep from falling down. He realized that, if she could truly put on a good show, he wouldn't have to kill her. He could let her win, and no one would question it. He wondered if he could pull it off.

Moonlight rolled up to her feet and allowed Sha to get his balance. She didn't really want to kill him. Studying his eyes as he started to circle, she almost missed his scent. Almost. Sniffing the air, she found his signature. He really thought he was going to let her win!

Sha blinked as Moonlight's magenta eyes widened. Then they narrowed to slits. By the Vow! He didn't even see it coming. One moment, he was standing up; the next moment, he was flat on his back! His broadsword was hammered from his grasp as he tried to get up. Her staff whipped across his shoulder blades and then across the backs of his thighs as he tried to stand. He was able to roll toward his sword, but his hand was smacked away from the hilt even as he reached out to grasp it.

Moonlight stepped back and paused to listen to the silence around her. A single rumble of laughter was the only sound in the clearing. She grinned as she recognized Lindon's chuckles. Many of the were thought that he was getting old and a little insane. This would probably reinforce the rumor.

Sha snatched his sword hilt and jumped to his feet. He eyed Lindon over the top of Moonlight's head and frowned. He momentarily wondered if Lindon knew how well he had trained this little werebitch. It was a fleeting thought. Of course Lindon knew. He was One Who Walks Alone.

Moonlight stepped in, faked right, stepped left, and rolled forward. Sha's blade passed through the space she had been standing in. She felt the wind pass over the top of her head. Reaching out with her staff, she swung sideways and pulled back. Her staff caught Sha behind the calves and knocked him forward to his knees. His blade came around to block as she reversed. Her staff stopped a bare two inches short of the tip of his nose. A quick reversal, which he couldn't counter, thumped him on the back of his head. Spinning up from one knee, she stood over him as he tried to rise.

Sha felt Moonlight's staff tap the side of his head. She was right behind him, and he couldn't do anything about it. He tried to stand. Her staff came across his right shoulder and snapped his collarbone like a twig. She could kill him right now. He knew it. She knew it. Everybody in the clearing knew it.

Sha threw down his sword and sighed. "Will you take my clan?"

Moonlight felt sudden tears come out of nowhere. Just like that, the dread and fear of the last two seasons was over. "No, I will not."

Sha turned so he could face her. In his own way, he was proud of her. Lindon would understand that, while she would not. "Moonlight, I release you from name and clan. If there is any here who would challenge Moonlight, let them come forward now."

Moonlight turned in a slow circle and studied the faces of the males and females who had fed her nightmares ever since she could remember. With the single exception of her foster sister Fluffy, there wasn't one face before her she didn't have resentment for. None of them had ever even tried to stop Sambra from beating her. Where was the cowardly bitch anyway?

Sha's eyes widened as he smelled their fear. He wondered how many of the young males would call Challenge against him since Moonlight had beaten him so easily. Well, it would happen in its own time. When no one spoke, he stood up. "Moonlight, you are free to follow the path of your heart. You may start your own pack, or you may walk alone." He paused for a moment and then said very seriously, "You won't understand this, but I must speak it. Foster daughter, this day you have made me proud."

Moonlight scowled. He was right. She didn't understand. If it weren't for the absolute honesty of his scent, she would call him a liar, but his scent said he spoke the truth. Her eyes narrowed as she shrugged. "What is that to me? Sha, maybe I don't understand. Why would you be proud? Never mind." She glanced at the faces surrounding her and said with absolute sincerity, "I will not form a pack—even if there was a man who would have me. I am glad to leave this clan forever. Let it be known. If Sambra crosses my path, I will kill her. Standing before you now, I say openly, her life is in my hands. If she lives or dies, it is because of my whim. Tell her this. Tell her I spoke before her entire clan. Let it be known that I am Moonlight Who Walks Alone!"

BENJAMIN

932ND SEASON OF THE REIGN OF THE KINGS

Benjamin dreamed of his past. He saw himself climb the mayor's steps and hammer on the screen. A maid answered and then jumped out of the way as Benjamin rushed through the door and hurried down the hall. Storming into the study, he told the mayor to clear the house and call the fire watch.

Mayor Storis gave an order to the maid. He gazed at Benjamin and asked, "What is it?"

Benjamin stated, "The tree in your yard will be hit by lightning. It will fall on the side of the house and destroy the servants' quarters. This house will burn to the ground."

The mayor walked out of the study, down the hall, and into the court-yard. He rang a bell that would sound an alarm.

The dream changed. Benjamin was galloping down a dirt road. He came to a farm and spied a field-worker standing by the gate. Benjamin reined in and told the worker to call his master. The worker ran down the path to the farm. The caretaker of south field came to the door. Benjamin told him to open all of the canals.

"Why?" the caretaker asked.

"A flood will wash away the spring harvest. If you open the canals and drain the reservoir before the floods, the damage will be greatly reduced."

The caretaker cursed but gave the order. The field-worker ran to the barn to fetch a mount. The caretaker gazed at the clear sky and then glanced back to Benjamin. "I hope you're right about this."

Benjamin said simply, "I hope I am not."

The dream changed. Benjamin found himself standing before two ancient oak trees. They were dead. Their lifeless branches intertwined and formed a canopy over dull brown earth. The space between them was a path. He turned in a circle and realized where he was. He was standing at the border of Mirshol—the greatest forest in the land. There was enchantment here. No human had ever entered Mirshol and remained sane. Benjamin walked up to the path and looked in. A thought struck him. *I'm dreaming!*

He walked through the arch of lifeless branches. Streams of light danced through the leaves and dappled the ground. He could smell the richness of the forest, the earthy, loam fragrance of the soil. All of the plants and trees played in a symphony of health and life. The only flaw seemed to be the two trees that watched the path. Yet, as he gazed around, he realized that Mirshol paid them a quiet respect.

Benjamin found himself floating down the path. He came to a sunlit clearing. A ring of mighty oaks surrounded a circular altar of black marble. Thin, spidery veins of gold shot through the rock. A chill ran down his spine as he thrashed in sleep. The altar had a thick, filthy aura that Benjamin recognized as pure evil.

A doe and a fawn walked through the trees and approached the stone. In sleep, Benjamin screamed, "*No!*" He watched helplessly as they stepped up onto the altar and turned to dust. A wolf stalked into the clearing and jumped lightly to the stone's center. It began to change. Long clawed fingers grew out from the paws. The wolf's back hunched and cracked. Arms and legs contorted and lengthened. It stood up, shaking its head, and snarled as fangs warped and curled. Screaming in agony, it leapt off of the black marble and stood panting. Sniffing the air, it turned and seemed to look right at him. Drooling jaws split into a wide grin. Hideous laughter filled his mind.

He woke up.

Benjamin was the Seer of Lake Town—eighty seventh in a direct line of descent. Long hours of meditation had helped him stay the insanity of being able to see. Benjamin would never forget the terror and agony of the two seasons that followed the opening of his mind. Many nights had been spent in his father's arms. The word *nightmare* had taken on new proportions.

The first sights he had witnessed were visions of the past. Dreams of wizards and black sorcerers raged through his mind. Werewolves of the Old Curse prowled the mountains in the north. Dragons, flying high in formation. Demons, and war. He saw the story of Lyre's history, the incarnate evil that the mightiest wizards of the land had fought countless battles against.

After two seasons of anguish, the nightmares ceased. Dream and meditation taught new lessons. His mind became his right hand—his most prized possession. He learned that the power of sight was a two-edged sword. Benjamin must remain true of heart and mind in order to detect what was false.

I don't want to go to Mirshol, but I don't have a choice. Mirshol was a bane to the human mind, and he knew it well. *I have never had a dream that hinted at such a potent evil. How can this be true?*

Benjamin did not question the truth of the dream. He knew it could come to pass if he didn't act. He knew it could even if he did. *I thought that kind of evil died with the passing of the wizards.*

With a great sigh, he rose from bed. As he watched himself shave in the mirror, he felt dislocated from his body. An old man peered back at him—six feet tall, iron gray hair, still strong and lean. At the moment, his eyes were a very dark shade of blue.

Well, I do not feel old.

Sixty seasons suddenly felt like a very short time.

Shan, the keeper of his estate, served him breakfast in the dining room.

"Shan, you look radiant this morning!"

Shan glanced at him sideways. "What do you want?"

Benjamin allowed himself a rare chuckle. "My, what extraordinary perception you have, my lady. Where do you get it from?"

"Give me a break, my lord. I've known you for thirty seasons."

"Don't call me my lord. My name is Benjamin. I want you to fix up some food for me. I need ten days of rations, and I do not want to have to eat any of that nasty cornmeal stuff they feed to soldiers on the trail! I want—"

"Hold it right there!" Shan interrupted. "Why the formal speech?" Then she saw the pained look in his eyes. "Where are you going, my lord?"

Benjamin, the Seer of Lake Town, sighed. "Shan, I am going to walk a trail that I cannot *see*. I do not believe I will return to this house." The statement did not ring true in his mind. "To stay," he finished.

Shan heard the stress on the word *see*. What, if anything, could he not *see*?

"Shan, there is money in my room. Take it. This will be your house now."

He paused, and she fairly shouted, "But, my lord, can't you send someone else? If what you're doing is so dangerous, then take some knights with you! There's a whole legion of them across the lake who would gladly go with you." Shan paused for a moment.

Benjamin smiled at her.

She hated that smile! The first time he'd given her that look, she'd thought it too cynical for a man so young. She knew better now. "OK," she asked, "where, exactly, are you going?"

Benjamin answered, very quietly, "Mirshol."

Shan watched him ride down the path. She saw his face in her mind. *Don't call me, my lord.* She wasn't sure, but she would bet he had said that to her every day for thirty seasons. She smiled warmly at his back, and whispered, "I love you, my lord."

She knew he couldn't hear her. A tear rolled down her cheek. It was a tear for a child that would never be born, a tear for an ancient line that had failed. She finally accepted this. He had come to terms with it long ago.

A three-day ride from Lake Town brought him to the edge of Mirshol. He stopped to watch a group of deer on the plain. They watched him, too. A dark brown horse stepped out of the trees. It beat the air with its hooves as it whinnied. Still watching Benjamin, the deer made their way back to the forest. Both of his horses felt compelled to follow. Only with a tight grip on the reins and lead line did he manage to keep them still. "Patience," he said firmly. "We will enter Mirshol soon enough."

Benjamin rode south down the western edge of the enchanted forest. Both horses constantly veered toward the trees. Elm and oak bordered the plain. The plains and hills would soon turn barren. The beginning of Blood Plain was an hour's ride away.

Nothing grew on the plain of blood. Many people thought nothing lived there. It was said that many battles of magic had been waged between Lyre's wizards and the demon lords of Kringe.

It was said that the *were* would go there and dance with the moon. The northern wolf people would go and howl a song of pain and longing so intense that any who heard would weep in anguish. Even now, humans feared the were. The were dwelt in the Vile Mountains north of Lake Town. They hurt no one and kept to themselves. Many could not understand them. Benjamin knew that the were and Blood Plain were bound together. To the were, Benjamin's title was He Who Sees All. Their name for Blood Plain, was the Plain of Hope.

As Benjamin rode forward lost in thought, the horses once again veered toward the trees. He was startled into the present when they came to a halt. He looked up to see two giant oaks. They were dead.

Benjamin stepped down from the saddle. This was compulsion! The horses started walking away. For a moment he thought about going after them. Only for a moment.

He walked toward the trees. Vision erupted behind his eyes. Half-blinded by dual realities, he stepped forward and set both hands against one of the trees. Instantly, both trees burst into brilliant green flames. *Tree fire!* The only being that could awaken them from their slumber had come. They rejoiced in his touch. As they held each other by branch and root, so could Benjamin feel them both. They were warm and loving. He could distinguish their personalities as if they were two different people.

They spoke in the language of earth and wind. They told him of children, animals, and birds. In a moment's time, Benjamin watched a family of birds hatching in their branches. A hundred times the children came back to nest before the line failed.

Line failed …

The greatest pain Benjamin had ever known came suddenly and overwhelmingly back to haunt him. Eighty-seven times, from father to son, Lyre's only true seers had renewed themselves. With a special blessing from the cleric called Myril the White, the past had been given to them. The seers witnessed memories of the past as their bodies changed from boys to men. This was power, but it was not magic.

Benjamin was the last of his line. His father had shown him that he would bear no heir. The anguish and fear in this choice came to him now. Tears streamed down his face; racking sobs shook his body.

Be at peace.

He was startled by the compassion and soothing well-being that emanated from the trees. They gave him something else, the one explanation his father would never give.

He watched in awe as his father approached these same two trees. He watched the dream his father beheld. He *saw,* as his father had *seen,* himself, walking toward a young man. The youth stood up; waist-length blond hair hung straight off of his shoulders. Ice-blue eyes were open wide as the young man exclaimed, "I have seen you in my dreams!"

Benjamin finally understood with a surety that his father had done the right thing. The trees gave him something else, a memory altogether unexpected. The only true seer in Lyre watched three wizards sing. They wove a melody, a tune that Benjamin could feel, around their staves. With quiet humility, they removed their power gems from gold and platinum crowns and placed them in a gold and ivory box. The Blue Wizard silenced a globe of light and whispered, "It is done."

He watched the Red Wizard shut and seal a stone door on the face of a cliff. The White Wizard placed a stone pot by the door. Two seedling oaks grew within the pot. The Blue Wizard passed his hand over them and the seedlings fell into dormancy. The Three changed shape. The hawk watched as the falcon and the eagle flew away. Then, the hawk leapt from the cliff and soared over the mighty Forest of Mirshol. It dove to the ground and changed back. The Blue Wizard paced the last few steps to the two oak trees and then placed both palms flat against one. Benjamin felt the tree's memories play this over. They, too, fell into dormancy as the Blue Wizard sang his song.

With great reluctance, Benjamin stepped back and opened his eyes. The trees still blazed with luminous, green tree fire. His horses were off to one side seemingly intent on some curiosity. He laughed and shouted, "All right, come on. We're going into the forest!"

Three figures Benjamin could not see spoke to them. The willow-slender figure in shimmering blues, smiled. "Go now with your master. He has need of you."

The horses laughed; Benjamin heard them whinny.

Benjamin stepped between the trees and gasped. The aura of the magical binding surged toward him. Aural rainbows splashed against his human thought. The buzzing of a thousand bees threatened to consume his mind. Wild, angry chimes seemed to surround him. All at once, a blinding white light sprang from his forehead. His own aura slapped a barrier between himself and the forest glamour. The chimes quit their angry tones and became curious. A tiny major chord sounded next to him. Other major chords joined and quickly tuned the discordant song.

Benjamin beheld melody. The prismatic rainbows of music, incorporated into the wizard's spell, recognized the very nature of his mind. The pure white light—the foundation the ancient cleric, Myril the White had used to create the *blessing* that gave the seers the ability to see—was recognized by the blanket of magic that covered Mirshol.

In a thousand seasons, only two others had walked into Mirshol and remained sane. He turned and watched his horses walk between the trees. He blinked in surprise as an aura of shadow fell away from them. Both horses came to a stop and turned around. Benjamin witnessed something only one other man had ever seen. Upon entering Mirshol, the horses had been gifted with thought and the ability to reason.

They came to him, prancing. He watched their auras and saw the complexities that made them capable of learning a language. Nevertheless, they were physically unable to speak.

He did not know what to do! Benjamin felt as though he should now ask them to carry him and his pack. His mount decided the issue by nudging and urging him into the saddle. As they walked the path, Benjamin spoke to them. They became friends.

Night came on swiftly. Benjamin dismounted and removed packs and saddle. The horses stood still, watching him expectantly. He opened the grain sacks and set them down. Still, they stood, watching him. "I see, I would like to leave at dawn."

During their ride, he had spoken to them of clouds, rain, the sun, the moon, and the stars. These were things he thought they would easily understand. His mount nodded as though he did understand. In truth, Benjamin did not doubt that he had. The packhorse walked forward and set his nose against Benjamin's shoulder. Benjamin smiled as he stroked the horse's cheek. "Go on. I've been alone all my life."

The packhorse nickered softly in his ear. Then, with tentative, backward glances, they both went in search of the sweet grasses they had smelled all day long.

Benjamin slept. He dreamed of the School of Prayer. He walked down the main corridor of the House of Song. A woman's voice came sweet and clear to his dreaming mind. He approached the door the singing was coming from and stopped to listen. The voice was singing a solo in a light alto. She sang of the Mirshol Mountains. As he listened, it seemed to him she sang nonsense, something about Father Mountain chasing away his three daughters.

A figure shimmered above him. White clerical robes billowed in an ethereal wind. White glowing eyes, within a halo of white hair, watched the Seer of Lake Town turn in his sleep. Her lips formed a tight line as she motioned to a jay in the trees. "Follow him. Let me know when he reaches the mountains."

She settled to the ground and knelt at his side. Curiously, she watched him smile in a dream. He opened his eyes. She watched him sit up and look around. He sat still for a moment and then lay back down. "Such beautiful singing," he said to no one.

She smiled as she set an ethereal hand on his forehead. The memory of his dream made her laugh.

"Ah, High Cleric, we meet again!"

She glanced back at the jay. "Let no harm come to him." Gazing up at the stars, she raised her pale arms, gathered their light, and faded away.

With the appearance of the horses, Benjamin resumed his journey. They traveled a fairly straight path toward the mountains and came to a stop in the early evening. He thought about the mountains. *That is where I need to go. What am I looking for? Father Mountain?* His dream came back to him, and he remembered the song. "Father Mountain. Where are your three daughters?" He mused on this for a moment and then nodded and spoke to the air. "The Three Sisters. Of course! Which mountain is the father?"

He was not much concerned. Benjamin knew the answer would come to him in time. Long hours of careful thinking had taught him great patience. He glanced around and listened to the sounds of the forest. *It is so peaceful here.*

A bird burst into song above his head. He looked up and saw a blue jay. It suddenly occurred to him he had yet to see any kind of animal life. He instinctively realized the animals knew he was here and that they were keeping away from his path. As he gazed at the jay, it flew down to the ground and hopped about at his feet. He laughed, and exclaimed, "My, aren't we full of energy today!"

The bird chirped and flew back into the trees.

The sun set and the stars came out. Benjamin lay by a small fire and watched as a falling star raced across the sky. It was unusually large and did not fade as he lost sight of its trail through the trees. Benjamin smiled as he thought about the people of Lake Town. He knew that, to some of them, this would be a sign, an omen. Something bad was sure to happen! He never did understand why people were so superstitious. No one could understand better than he about premonition. He knew it was *always* a personal thing, *never* something a whole city would see. That was nature. It had nothing to do with a sign, premonition, or forewarning.

A huge yawn stretched his jaw. Gazing around at Mirshol, he blinked heavy lids and closed them to sleep.

A figure wearing light and dark blue silks appeared on the ground by his feet. A lion of the mountains approached as she beckoned. In a ring around the sleeping seer was a rabbit, a doe and a fawn, a bear, and a hawk. Four horses stood on the trail. A chipmunk jumped on the lion's back and peered over its head.

"This man is in your charge. We have traveled far this day and learned much. Feed him well and treat him with respect. Now go. He would not think it a kindness to wake and see you watching him."

Without a sound, the animals melted into the forest. The figure dressed in shades of blue looked to the jay. "Thank you, my little friend. Now come. You have a Mythit to find and a story to tell!"

4

CALKING CO YOURSELF

S under sat on a rock in the shade. Eyes closed, he created illusions and set them in January's mind. Warriors appeared wielding swords and staves. One after another, he set them in motion.

January stood barefoot in the sun. He wore violet Mythit silks that wrapped him from his lower stomach to just above his knees. An ancient long sword cut and flashed through the air as he danced.

"Tell me another story about the Blue Wizard."

Be quiet! Pay attention to your big feet! Keep your elbows in. There's someone behind you and to your left. Strike!

Jan whirled, steel flashing at an illusionary foe. Sunder whistled under his breath as he watched the speed with which Jan moved.

Too slow!

"What!" Jan protested. "You furry little tyrant! I'll give you too slow!"

He jumped at the Mythit. Sunder vanished. Jan cleared his mind and felt the air for the yellow and orange Mythit. Tendrils of feeling spread from his aura like fine spider silk. *I got you now,* Jan thought.

I doubt it.

Jan turned to his left and put one foot forward, *I got you where I want you!* With swift agility, January rolled backward, took one step, and snatched the Mythit from thin air.

"Ha!" Jan yelled in triumph.

Sunder laughed, and for the first time in a day, spoke out loud. "I let you catch me."

Jan cocked his head, caught the falseness in the statement, and smiled.

"Yes," Sunder said approvingly, "you have traveled far since we met four seasons ago. Are you ready to go back?"

"What?" Jan was surprised. He had not seen another human in four seasons. He had lived with the Mythits at Home, the northern tip of the Mirshol Mountains. Jan gazed at Sunder and saw that he was serious. "I don't know."

Sunder watched him think. January was ready to play his part. He knew the weight of Lyre would soon settle on this young human's shoulders. *I have waited for over nine hundred seasons,* Sunder thought to himself. *That is a long time even for me. You are the first mortal able to perceive a Mythit since the wizards blessed the forest. You are now ready to help change all that. What more can I do?*

"Yes," Jan said.

"Hmm?"

"Yes, I would like to go back. To visit anyway." He gazed into Sunder's glowing purple eyes and said, very seriously, "I do not belong there any more than you do."

Sunder smiled up at him. *Indeed. Go tell Jasmine and Flower that we are leaving. I feel someone calling my name.*

"Are they coming with us?"

No, I think it will just be you and me.

"OK. Sunder, I'm hungry."

Sunder laughed, *You're always hungry!*

Jan went to the edge of the clearing, picked up his scabbard, and sheathed his long sword. Walking through the trees toward the stream, he untied his wrap and pulled it off. He had made a dam when he'd first arrived in Mirshol. Carrying logs and rocks that he scavenged from the surrounding area, he made a decent pool for swimming. As he waded into the water to bathe, he considered returning to Window.

Meat. I haven't eaten anything but fruits, nuts, and fish since I got here!

He thought about his trips into the depths of the forest with Sunder, Jasmine, and his foster sister, Flower. Even if he wanted to, he could not hunt here. The cats, bears, and other meat-eating predators of Mirshol didn't even eat meat.

The Mythits were a marvel and amazing. They had taught him many mental and physical powers, but the animals in Mirshol were enchanted. *That was magic. It just didn't feel the same as mental abilities. Well, I guess it takes mental abilities to make a spell. But that's just it; it was or is a spell. I can taste the difference. Why? Sunder says when we go back, other humans still won't be able to see him. He can control their emotions though. I sure know that's true! He used to play me like a harp!*

Jan laughed quietly to himself. Exaggerated and overplayed—first experiences should be that way. Forever be blessed the wonder and awe of a child's delight in learning something new! A child could take so much pleasure from the simple act of tying his laces for the first time.

"I guess I grew up when my father died. I didn't have much time to be a child. Sunder has given me that and a lot more!"

Jan dressed and walked to the area called Home. A ring of huge trees stood in a rough circle, spreading their branches toward a common center. Woven limbs created a roof that nothing could penetrate. Moss-layered, leaf-covered areas called *nests* became cozy little dwellings high up in the branches. Jan used ropes to climb with. Mythits didn't need them. They could fade out from the ground and fade in, into a nest.

Jasmine, his foster mother, taught him to weave. She was so skilled at the art, he swore she could make silks out of wire. As he approached, he heard Jasmine, Flower, and Snow talking inside of Flower's nest. Stepping up to the woven silk rope, he heard his name mentioned. He didn't like to listen in on their conversations without their knowing, but he just couldn't help himself.

Snow said, "I don't like it! That old fool is turning him into a warrior."

Jasmine spoke firmly. "Jan must be able to protect himself. You are too young to remember, but I tell you there are all kinds of evil men who travel the roads. In the old days, humans had to travel with armed escorts for the sake of simple safety. Only a fool would walk the face of Lyre as though it were a bright spring morning on the shore of Light Lake!"

Snow said, grudgingly, "Jasmine, I know you're right, I just don't like it! Have you seen Jan *dance* with that sword? He already has the grace and strength of the old knights. You tell us they used to train for ten seasons before the Knights Alliance would even consider taking them. Sunder would have us believe Jan could go to the School of Fighters or the Knights Alliance and teach them more than they could teach him. What really bothers me is that Sunder is right!"

Flower's singsong voice laughed in delight. "You speak highly of my little brother!"

"Little!" Snow exclaimed. "He's three and a half feet taller than any of us. Besides, how can I not speak highly of him. He has the lightest, purest *personality* I've ever witnessed."

Aura, Jan thought. *Personality* was the Mythit word for aura. He had been taught by Sunder to see his own aura reflected from anything he gazed at. *It isn't any different than theirs.* "Hmm." *I wonder what she means.*

Jan cleared his throat and climbed up the rope. He kissed Jasmine on the forehead, ruffled Snow's top-not, and put his arm around Flower as he sat.

"That's not fair!" Flower pouted. "I want a kiss!"

Jan favored her with his sideways, lopsided grin. "Flower, if I were a Mythit, I'd marry you!"

Flower giggled as she set her cheek against Jan's chest. "I guess that's good enough."

Jan thought, as he had many times, about just how different every Mythit was. They were all about the same size, almost three feet tall and slender, with glowing eyes. Flower had yellow and orange fur that was striped from top left to bottom right. Her eyes were pale pink. Jasmine, Flower's mother, was two shades of pink and red with white splotches thrown in at random. Her mushroomed topknot, like Flower's, was red, but Jasmine's eyes were bright red—florescent red. All Mythit eyes glowed in the dark, but he could pick Jasmine out of a hundred on a moonless night. Snow's fur was snow-white, the Mythit equivalent of an albino. Her eyes were magenta, a shade of pink-red that generally seemed soft and gentle.

"Sunder and I are going to Window," Jan said quietly.

Jasmine looked up from her weaving. She thought, *Are you ready to* see *humans through our eyes?*

Through our eyes said much. She meant, could he control his thought and emotion and not be disturbed by the auras of others? He smiled fondly at her. *Yes, my little mother, I think I'm ready.*

"Ready or not, it will have to wait."

They all turned to see Sunder standing in the mouth of the nest. He said, looking at Jan but speaking to Jasmine, "The Guardians are awake. They have allowed a human to enter Mirshol."

Jasmine tilted her head inquiringly. "What are you going to do?"

Snow said sourly, "Get ready to move."

Flower glanced around her nest with gloomy pink eyes. "I sure did like this place."

Jan pulled her close and held her tight. "You're not going anywhere if I can help it!"

"Oh, for the sake of *Song*, will you all quit!" Sunder exclaimed in exasperation.

Jan had to smile at Sunder's weary tone. Flower and Snow giggled.

Jasmine said, smiling, "Well, what in the name of Song are you going to do about it?"

"I'm not going to do anything, but I think Jan is."

"Who has the power to wake the Guardians?" Snow asked reasonably.

"I don't know," Sunder answered. "I thought Jan would be the one to do it."

Jasmine's eyes narrowed. "What made you think that?"

A secret smile, reserved for Sunder alone, crept across Jan's face. "The Blue Wizard."

Jasmine gazed at Jan long and hard. Sunder raised one brow. Snow nodded. "Makes sense to me. We all knew you were both crazy."

Flower said to no one in particular, "I wish I could see a wizard."

Sunder turned purple glowing eyes on his daughter. *Child of my mind,* Sunder thought only to himself, *don't look now, but* your *wizard has his arm around you.*

In the 932nd season of the reign of the Kings of Wizards Veil, Sunder and January rode away from Mythit Home. Sunder summoned a herd of horses, and two agreed to carry them. They traveled light. Jan carried some food, a blanket, and his sword.

Sunder rarely spoke out loud. They communicated mostly in thought. At first, Jan would listen and answer vocally. Sunder allowed this until they had formed a link.

Listening is easier than speaking, Sunder had said. *Nevertheless, you must learn the mind speech. There will be times around humans when you won't want to appear as though you're talking to yourself.*

For some reason, that had been so funny Jan couldn't quit laughing. Even weeks later, he would laugh at the mental images that statement had invoked. He thought about some of the old beggars in Window who walked around talking to themselves and wondered if they had ever seen Mythits. Sunder had said no. Mythits have been unable to appear before human sight for almost a thousand seasons. Well, now at least, Jan could mentally speak and listen easily with all of the Mythits.

That night they camped on the western face of the Mirshol Mountain Range. January and the horses were eager to keep traveling, but Sunder wouldn't listen. *We have traveled farther today than you think. We will be where we need to be by tomorrow evening.*

Sunder, tell me about the Guardians.

Sunder considered the request for a moment and then spoke. "The Guardians are two oak trees on the edge of the forest. They stand parallel to the northernmost point of Blood Plain, which is about fifteen leagues from the city of Lake Town."

"Why are they called the Guardians?"

"The Blue Wizard put them to sleep," Sunder explained. "Those two trees are one of the keys into Mirshol. Because of the spell on them, humans have been kept out of the forest. Blue told me only one person could awaken them. I asked him if it would be you. He only smiled at me and said, 'When the day comes, he will be there.' I guess he led me to believe it would be you."

Sunder stood up and looked to the stars. He smiled at a private thought. He felt Jan's gaze touch here and there but was still startled when Jan's emotion of surprise bombarded his aura. Jan's emotions and his empathy were so strong! Sunder wondered, *Have I trained him well enough to keep his feelings under control?* He glanced toward January and then followed his eye path. *Yes, that blue jay has been following us all day.*

"Do you know why?"

Sunder grinned. *Yes, I do. Now, go to sleep. Tomorrow will be a long day. I'm going for a walk.* With that said, Sunder walked into the night.

"But," Jan stammered as he watched Sunder fade out. "Well! Sunder thinks wizards are closemouthed and misleading. If they're more frustrating than Mythits, I'd sure hate to talk to one!"

Sunder sat on a rock and beckoned to the horses. He spoke with them and learned that the animals of Mirshol had already spread the news about the Guardians. He could not figure out how. These animals were capable of reason. That had been a gift from the White Wizard. Blue had made sure no humans could enter Mirshol. Since the Mythits were restrained from teaching them language, it should be impossible for them to pass news on this scale. Yet, somehow, they had learned.

I don't understand.

He allowed his gaze to hypnotize the horses. He probed their minds. Sunder's purple, glowing eyes widened as he came across something no other Mythit had ever thought to look for. A closed door! *I'll bet all of the animals in Mirshol have this place in their minds!* He tried to approach the mental block, but the horses instantly shook off the effects of Mythit sight. They stood very still, watching him. *OK,* Sunder thought, *once again you have it your way, Blue. I wish you were here. I miss you!*

He allowed calm to spread over the horses. Another thought came to him and he sighed. *I have to tell him tomorrow. It's time for him to understand.*

They left camp at sunrise and rode until noon. They stopped at a quiet little clearing surrounded by pines that hugged the mountains. Jan glanced askance. "Out with it. I know when you have something to say, so say it!"

Sunder was so surprised by Jan's tone of voice that he threw up barriers and disappeared.

Jan smiled to himself. "That bad?" he asked the empty air. He cleared his mind and felt for Sunder. Involuntarily catching his breath, he turned. Sunder's aura was flowing misery like a lantern. He reached out with tendrils of feeling and wrapped soothing peace around his little friend. Very gently Jan pulled him from the ethers of Mythit thought.

Sunder let Jan's strength flow into him. As Jan held him, Sunder looked up at the young human's face. *He doesn't even have a staff or any other focus of power. The Voice of Command is a natural ability with him.*

To Jan, he said, "I have something that needs saying. I have to say this now because you must know before you meet this human. What I have to say is very important. It is also the shame and guilt for all of the Mythits you already know."

Jan stood Sunder on his feet. He sat on the ground and watched Sunder intently. He had never seen a Mythit this serious before—especially not *this* Mythit.

Sunder looked away. Jan didn't speak, but he allowed his own aura to wash calm around the clearing. Sunder received the gesture gratefully. He looked up and met Jan's eyes. "There are evil Mythits in Lyre."

"What!"

Sunder looked at the ground. "They live in the Black Mountains. They hardly even resemble us anymore. Their foul spirits have turned their fur black and their eyes, bloodred."

"Well, it's not your fault!" Jan exclaimed. "How could it be?"

Sunder looked back up into Jan's ice-blue eyes. "It *is* our fault. I am very old even to Mythits. I was the first Mythit ever bound to a human. I was old even when the wizards brought us into the sight of men for the first time. That didn't last long, but the second time they performed the binding was when this happened. Many Mythits became accustomed and used to the human ways, pleasures, and desires. Before the Three Wizards went to their deaths, they made sure we understood that, in defeating the Dark Lord, all Mythits would return to their spirit state.

Even though we are solid in our own eyes, humans cannot touch us, see us, or hear us. They can only sense us with their empathy. Let me tell you, humans in general have very little empathy! You might not yet understand this, but it is because humans only care for personal, singular things.

The only humans who can truly feel us are the clerics and teachers in the School of Prayer. Yet, they think our presence to be that of the Creator of life and light. They are mistaken. Every Mythit knows that the Creator, which we name Song, sits in his heavens. He will not come among us and interfere with the destinies of his different peoples.

It is our fault that we did not teach this to our children during that time. We lived for thousands of seasons in the sight of men. We increase slowly; we do not bear children in the same manner as humans. Only Flower, Snow, and a few others have been *made* since the second veiling of Mirshol. Nevertheless, during the time before the second binding, many Mythits were made." Sunder looked away sadly. "Almost all of them are lost to us now."

January did not know how to comfort him, but he tried. He reached out with all of the love and care the Mythits of Home had given him. He stood up, went to Sunder, picked him up, and held him in his strong arms. *I am your son—even more than my true father's son. I am not lost to you.*

Jan could feel Sunder's spirit lighten. He thought to his innermost self, *I will find a way to make it right. I swear it!*

A figure in red wraps and a fighter's vest stood at the edge of the clearing. She set one ethereal, red-skinned hand on the pommel of her sword. *I believe you will.*

They rode for the rest of the afternoon and stopped just before nightfall. January saw that Sunder was once again his old self. The Mythit turned and looked up at Father Mountain. *Our visitor will be here tomorrow. We will wait.*

"I wonder who he is."

Are you talking to yourself?

Jan laughed. "I guess I am." He laughed again.

Shortly after sunrise, two large mountain cats padded into the clearing. Jan watched them stalk the area and then return to the path and settle down. A few moments later, a buck, a doe, and a fawn appeared from the path and walked up to him. He recognized the doe. She stopped by his side, while the fawn laid down at their feet. A half dozen squirrels swarmed out of the trees.

They pounced around for a few moments and then settled on the two cats' backs. Jan heard the clip of horse hooves before he saw them. He realized they were shod. He stared down the path and saw a large figure emerge from the shadows. It was a huge bear. Right behind her rode an old man wearing a brown, travel-stained cloak.

As he entered the clearing, Sunder gasped. *I know him! That is Benjamin the Seer! Jan, this is good fortune indeed!*

Jan registered the name, but that was all. He had jumped up without realizing it.

Benjamin came into the clearing and saw the young man the Guardians had shown him. He wore a simple purple skirt that Benjamin thought must be pure silk. Long blond hair hung straight and loose almost to his rump. Ice-blue eyes looked at him with an expression he knew well.

Jan walked toward him. "I've seen you in my dreams!"

"Indeed," said Benjamin.

I should have known, thought Sunder.

Jan snapped back to the present and turned. "What?"

You're talking to yourself.

Jan turned back to Benjamin, who was looking him over with great curiosity. "Your name is Benjamin?"

Benjamin gave Jan a startled smile. "Yes, yes it is. Who are you?"

Jan said simply. "My name is January."

A line of an ancient song came into the old seer's mind—*January, the beginning and the end.*

Jan and Sunder both heard the thought. Sunder smirked. *In the name of Song.*

Jan couldn't help it; he laughed out loud.

Benjamin watched him carefully. Those ice-blue eyes were almost unreal. He was just over six feet tall, which allowed them to see eye to eye. He was very muscular but not large. Benjamin was reminded of the sleek grace of a stalking panther. It was the best likening he could come up with.

He also noticed the sword strapped across January's back. The sword had an ivory grip inlaid with gold. It was a very old long sword, and Benjamin knew it was an artifact of ancient times. It seemed to suit this young man very well. "Where have you seen me?"

Jan gave him a tentative smile. "Only in my dreams."

Benjamin smiled kindly. "*The sight* is a gift I know well. Names do not usually come with it. Surely you have seen me somewhere before."

Jan tilted his head to one side. "I didn't know your name until you walked into this clearing."

Benjamin *knew* truth. He raised an eyebrow. The young man's words chimed true.

Jan asked, "Why have you come to Mirshol?"

"To find Father Mountain."

Sunder walked around Jan and stood between them. *It's the mountain right behind us.*

Jan looked back and pointed. "That's Father Mountain." He turned back to see Sunder jumping up and down waving his hands in Benjamin's face. Trying not to laugh, Jan asked, "Why do you seek a mountain?"

Benjamin watched as Jan tried very hard to suppress laughter. He wondered at it. *Maybe he's crazy. Is this what happens when humans enter Mirshol?*

Sunder's eyes opened wide and then narrowed. *Crazy indeed!*

Jan couldn't help himself. He burst into laughter. After a few moments, he caught his breath. "Are the two horses yours?"

Benjamin glanced back at the mounts. "They were once, but not anymore. I think, perhaps, they are now my friends."

Jan felt the fond affection from the two horses. "I think you're right."

"Why are you here?" Benjamin asked this out loud, not really expecting a response. He was surprised when January answered.

"You woke the Guardians. We ..." He didn't know how to finish.

"We?" Benjamin inquired.

Jan looked to Sunder. Sunder just shrugged. Jan looked back to Benjamin. He said cautiously, "Many creatures know that the Guardians let you into Mirshol."

Benjamin was a wise old man. He knew when someone was trying to hide something. His trust in this young man was instinctive. He gazed around the clearing at all of the animals and smiled. "I see."

Sunder did a double take at the words *I see.* He thought only to himself, *I believe you do, old man, I believe you do.* To Jan he thought, *Ask again why he seeks Father Mountain.*

Jan asked.

The Seer of Lake Town responded, "A cave."

Sunder yelled, "Yes!"

Jan and all of the animals started.

Benjamin saw the reaction to the word but had heard not a sound.

5

A Piece of Past: 1

When men first arrived in Lyre, the old races witnessed the human ability to adapt. They multiplied quickly. The domination of Lyre by men became inevitable. Even as the first few demon spawn of the Dark Lord were created, they were instructed to slay humankind. The Mythits, through inherent luck and natural skill, found a realm between light and dark, sight and touch, life and death and willingly led their people through. Mythits, within a hundred seasons, became legends to men. Within a thousand seasons—after the wars of men, wizards, and a handful of black dragons, against the combined forces of the Dark Lord's might—the Mythit race became legends to all. When the bitter fighting between the races came to an uneasy truce, very few of the old races remained.

Of the mighty, three wizards stood among men. Seven wizards stood among the hordes and legions of demons. The Dark Lord could still walk among them, but they did not know him. The Three Wizards knew he must exist. However, they had no clue as to how to find him.

The High Wizard Binban, in the Forest of Life, chanced upon a mathematical equation that explained the disappearance of the Mythits. The Mythits had not realized the many variations of the equation. Nevertheless, being who he was, Binban was quick to understand the possibilities.

The Dark Lord stood in the essence of his own making as the High Wizard appeared in front of him. Binban knew immediately that his power had been stripped. A cage of black iron appeared around him. The Dark Lord laughed and jeered. "You will pay a thousand deaths for your sins against me!"

The High Wizard laughed back. It was the music of life in that lightless place. The scent of flowers and trees assaulted the Dark Lord in a way he could not comprehend.

The Dark Lord raged at the High Wizard in a fit of fury. He placed lightning in the cage of iron and watched gleefully as the High Wizard was struck again and again.

With his great store of knowledge, Binban lessened the assault. Still, he knew his death was near. He had witnessed it long ago. With the last of his strength, he composed a thought to his brother and hurled it out of the darkness.

The Dark Lord watched, amazed, as the thought came at him and passed through. He gathered his senses and reached with his mind, but it was too late; the thought had been received. Once again, the Dark Lord raged, but this time he used his hands. Clawed fingers ripped open the cage as if it were a woven grass basket. As he grabbed for the body, it vanished.

For the first time in his very long life, he realized he was not the greatest force in this world of another's creation.

6

The Black

A sensual, black-skinned woman stood in the middle of a huge cavern. The clothing she wore in the cities of Vain had been discarded at the door. Bushy silver hair; pupilless, bloodred eyes; and her lithe five-foot height bore witness to her Mythit blood. She always walked unclothed in the presence of the black creatures that surrounded her. It inspired their lust to gaze upon her. She stretched and moaned in ecstasy as she was wrapped in the thick, liquid heat of their auras. No male could ever satisfy her in this way.

Her name was Melody the Black. She was the last true cleric of the Dark Lord. Her father, Dagdor the Black, was now dead. He had been the greatest of the seven evil Mythit-bound wizards, known collectively as the Seven. Her mother was an evil Mythit.

Poison, her mother, walked toward her. She smiled sweetly at her daughter. "The time has come. The Guardians are awake."

"Yes," hissed Melody, "I feel power in the air." Her slim, perfect hands worked. No building of power came. "Damn!" Gazing at the glowing, bloody eyes of the black Mythits around her, she screamed. "I want a guard around Mirshol! When the veil lifts, I want a party waiting." Her eyes flickered with inner fire. She smiled to herself and continued in a soft, caressing tone. "I don't want one of those furry little rainbows left alive." She paused and then whispered, "If Jasmine and Sunder are found, let Jasmine watch as you kill him. Then bind her mind and bring her to me."

Poison turned and started giving orders. Melody walked past them and headed down a long corridor. Every fifty or a hundred strides brought her to a new intersection in the intricate network of the Lince Posh tunnel system. She followed the main walk that ran as true as an arrow straight into the heart of the mountain.

At the tunnel's end, she came to an iron-bound, black oak door. Melody placed her black widow amulet against the like symbol in the center of the door. With a soft push, tumblers clicked, and the heavy door opened silently inward. She moved to the center of the room and stopped at the foot of a circular, black marble altar. She gazed at the spidery veins of gold that shot through the marble. "Soon," she hissed. "When the Forest of Dreams loses its veil, I will make them pay." Bloodred eyes burned bright with a sudden, baleful intensity. "The whole of Lyre will swim in a sea of death!"

7

FOLLOWING FOOTPRINTS

Benjamin and January sat at the foot of Father Mountain. Jan had asked Sunder what they might find in this cave, but all Sunder would say is, *You'll find out when we get there.*

Jan stood up and started to pace. "Benjamin, there are a lot of things I apparently don't understand about what's going on here." Jan stopped and looked into the old seer's eye. "Tell me why you were called to come here."

"I don't know. Perhaps to find you."

Jan started pacing again. "If I'm going to be around you for very long, there are things I want to tell you. I, uh—" Jan stopped and looked back into Benjamin's eyes. "I know you can see personality when you look at others. I also know you have truth sense."

"Personality?"

"The colors of light that are the truth of a person," Jan explained. "Auras."

Benjamin smiled. "I see. Tell me, young January, how do you know that about me?"

Jan thought for a moment and then said, "Your eyes tell me."

"What else do they tell you."

Jan tuned himself to Benjamin's mind. "You're wondering where I learned to see." Jan turned suddenly away. "You also wish to know who taught me."

Benjamin was startled by his words but mistook his reaction. He said softly, "You should not be ashamed to have that ability."

January stood stock-still. Then he whirled and shouted, "That's it!" His mind began to reel. Memories flooded into focus—assessments made from his mental abilities seasons before he walked from Window. He had always assumed Sunder had taught him the mind powers. It came clearly to him now. The Mythits had only brought them to his attention. They had only taught him to use what was already there.

He looked for Sunder and found him at Benjamin's side. He watched their first meeting play through his mind. He had looked into Sunder's eyes, felt the pull of Mythit sight, and looked away. No other creature could have looked away from the nature of a Mythit's gaze. He remembered the ambiguous looks Sunder had given him.

Jan laughed long and well. The look on Benjamin's face was that of utter confusion. Benjamin was aware of the fact that the young man had just received a very personal revelation. Benjamin had gone through enough self-awareness experiences to know what he was looking at. What he was having a hard time understanding was why January kept whispering, "You furry little tyrant, you furry little tyrant!"

They spent the rest of the day at the foot of the mountain and talked. Benjamin asked questions January would invariably shy away from. So, after a few attempts at deeper answers, he gave up. Perhaps it would just take a little time.

Benjamin woke to see January practicing swordplay. Having had a fair amount of training himself, he watched Jan's style with interest. He saw a style of fighting that was half-familiar and half-unique. What was strange was that he couldn't quite remember where he had seen that style of fighting before.

The young man's flaunting gestures and varied facial expressions made Benjamin realize that January's seeming inexperience was a lure to draw an attack. He would then fade back to await the mistake of his opponent and lunge when it came. This was the training of a very seasoned instructor.

In a flash of sight, it suddenly came clear to him where he had seen this kind of fighting. His memories played back. A teacher at the School of Fighters had left the house. The man had been angry at the two schools for not being able to settle their differences.

The man had gone to the edge of North Lake and formed the Knights Alliance. He had five sons, who he trained from the cradle. One of his sons was named Corillion. Corillion had led the entire force on Blood Plain the day the Three Wizards passed away. Benjamin fairly leapt out of his bedroll as he realized that January was holding Corillion's long sword.

Jan turned to see Benjamin jump up. He looked cautiously around the clearing, both hands on hilt, sword up and ready. No apparent threat was in sight, so he looked back at Benjamin. "What is it?"

"Do you know whose sword that is?"

Jan turned and watched Sunder's eyes narrow. *He can't possibly know where I got that sword!*

Benjamin said. "That sword belonged to a man named Corillion."

In the name of Song!

Jan blinked. "Do you think he wants it back?"

Benjamin and Sunder both laughed. Sunder thought, *I doubt it. Corillion has been dead for over nine hundred seasons.*

"Oh."

"January, who gave that sword to you?"

Jan caught Sunder's eye. Sunder grinned, *Go ahead and tell him.*

Benjamin saw Jan look away. He was about to say, "Never mind. Don't tell me." But Jan's piercing, ice-blue eyes stopped all his thoughts.

Jan said, "A Mythit gave it to me."

Benjamin knew truth, but he didn't even need to hear it. He would have come to that conclusion given enough time. A Mythit would explain all of the questions in his mind concerning a young man walking free in Mirshol. Benjamin felt the sight take him. An ancient prophesy, in the words of one of his ancestors, rang clearly in his mind:

> *Seek the sword, greet the trees,*
> *swim in crystal, find a light.*
> *Embrace the moonlight, far she sees,*
> *kiss the sun, mind of right.*
> *Do not fear, man of Vain.*

"Why doesn't the last verse rhyme?"

"I don't know. I—" Benjamin looked up with a start.

Jan looked abashed. "Uh, I uh, well …"

Benjamin raised one eyebrow and put on his best no-commitment expression. "*I see.*"

Sunder, who was completely worn out with all of this idle conversation, yelled, "Let's go find that cave!"

Benjamin heard nothing. But for a moment, he thought he saw a little round glow between himself and January. He was overcome with a sudden urge to jump up and move. He gazed at Jan curiously. "Is your friend in a hurry?"

Jan was surprised at the question but said quickly. "As a matter of fact, he's ranting and raving about the cave and saying we don't have all day."

Sunder glared at Jan, and thought, in pure indignation, *Ranting and raving indeed!*

Sunder led Jan to the cliff. It was twice as high as the tallest pines in the area. Sunder had brought him here a season ago and told him this was a place of great beginnings. The Mythit walked to the cliff and knelt down. He tried clearing the dirt away from a rock, but in Benjamin's presence, he was ethereal and unable to grasp it.

Sunder gazed at Benjamin. *Old man, clear the dirt away from this rock and pick it up!*

Jan watched Sunder trying to clear the dirt away. When Sunder looked at Benjamin, January felt power wash through him.

Benjamin, who was standing still, gazing at the cliff, suddenly noticed the rock and went to it. He knelt and started brushing at the dirt. After a moment, he pushed on the rock and felt it give. Setting his shoulders, he lifted. It came straight up out of the ground.

Benjamin looked puzzled as Jan walked to his side.

A rod of crystal protruded from the cliff wall at an angle inside the hole. Benjamin reached for it. As soon as his fingers touched it, it started to glow. He pulled it from the wall and stared at it in awe.

Jan saw the cliff sparkle and light from top to bottom. A glowing hole was spaced every foot length from the ground to the top. "A ladder!"

Benjamin stood up and stared at the wall. "We can't climb it. The holes are filled with this crystal."

"I see that," Jan said unperturbed. "Do you have a knife? I'll try to pry them out."

Benjamin gave him a dagger and Jan set to work. Try as he might, he couldn't even chip them. "No way," Jan said at last. "we need a different idea."

Sunder watched all of this and said nothing. He wouldn't always be there for Jan, and he knew it. The spell was as clear as day. If only Jan would just close his eyes and feel for it. Sunder thought about the way Jan had pulled him from *squaring* two days ago. Finding a faded Mythit was one thing.

Holding a mind while it was squared was another thing entirely. *Wizards can't even do that!* The Three could, but even they had to have their staves to focus power. Sunder couldn't figure it. It was as though January had Mythit blood. That was impossible. Wasn't it?

January gazed at the crystal. *This is magic. Magic has to deal with it. If the wizards put this here for Benjamin, they would know he was a seer. They would know he was without any power to solve this problem. They had to have set some kind of key to allow the holes to be cleared.*

He stopped his thought and let silence flow from his mind. The power of the crystal became an image in his thoughts. He focused on it and realized it was in recognition of Benjamin's aura—*personality. The crystal recognizes him.* He could see clearly that the rod would not have come to life for either Sunder or himself. Then Jan realized that the rod was now waiting for him! It seemed to call him.

He let his mind settle back in place while he walked to Benjamin's side. Jan smiled up at the old seer. "Watch this." He plucked the rod from Benjamin's hand and allowed his aura to touch the personality of the crystal. A deluge of water drenched them as the crystal filling the foot holes turned to water. Shaking his head, Jan asked, "Are you ready to climb the cliff?"

Benjamin felt suddenly very young as he peered upward and blinked water from his eyelashes. He grinned as excitement welled up inside of him. "Yes."

A set of stairs began at the top of the cliff. They were made from the finest marble Benjamin had ever seen—pristine white shot through with veins of pure platinum. He was amazed at their condition. Knowing his history as only he could, he had a fair understanding of just how old they were. Thousands of seasons and not a sign of wear or use.

They walked the stairs all day, stopping for bare moments at a time to rest. Jan worried about Benjamin's stamina but quickly realized the old seer was in very good health and just as eager to reach the top as he was. They reached the top at dusk. They turned, as they had done many times, and enjoyed the view. The Forest of Mirshol seemed endless. Jan estimated that they had climbed a quarter league of stairs, and even from this perspective, Mirshol had no apparent boundaries.

They could see they were standing on the highest mountain in the Mirshol Range. They walked across Father Mountain's bald, flat head to the far side and looked down on the southern point of the Shattered Orchard Forest. Everything was dark as the sun began to set. Far to the southeast, a light burned strong and clear.

"The School of Prayer," Benjamin said. "Even as we watch, they sing the song of days ending." Benjamin bowed to the school and held up one hand in a gesture of respect. "Of all six houses, for I do not recognize the separation of the two schools, I give my love to the House of Song. It is an amazing place. Fountains and flowers and a strong feeling of ancient power. If I had a choice, I would like to die there."

Jan looked quizzically at Benjamin and noticed Sunder nodding in agreement. He looked back down at the light. "I would like to go there some day."

Benjamin sighed. "I think that day will be soon."

Jan looked back to Benjamin and started. His dark blue eyes were now bright green. Red flecks burned as though the seer's mind was in flames. He was about to speak when he noticed a white glow coming from the far edge of the plateau. "Look!" Jan pointed.

Benjamin and Sunder both turned. "What is it?"

He walked forward as Sunder ran ahead. They came to the edge of a large pool of water. Jan bent down to touch it, but Sunder yelled, "Wait!"

Jan sensed the water calling his name. He couldn't understand it. The water *knew* him. Energy flowed strongly here. Something, or some things, very powerful lay beneath this place.

Benjamin caught his breath. He was being compelled to reach out. He had wondered about this moment. He had known he had to find a way to explain *the gift,* but this was too soon! "January, stand up!"

With great effort, Jan pulled away from the call of the water.

"Give me your right hand!"

January felt Benjamin's aura reach out and surround him.

"January, it seems it is your birthright to receive *the gift of sight.* I do not have time to explain this to you!"

Jan looked straight into the Seer of Lake Town's fiery red eyes. Dancing flames seemed to be reaching into his mind.

"Will you accept this gift?"

January took a deep breath as the seer's aura embraced him. "Yes."

Benjamin nodded approval. "Then I stand open. Through me is the path. If the land of Lyre finds you worthy, receive this gift!"

January watched as a ray of light pierced Benjamin's personality. It flowed through the seer and into him. His head snapped back as vision filled him.

Benjamin stepped back. He beheld the blank look in the young man's eyes. Just like that, it was done.

January stilled as doors opened in his mind.

Benjamin knew it would be some time before January came back to the present. He looked at the crystal pool with great curiosity and bent down to touch it. Light appeared! He slid his fingers across the surface. A stream of light followed his fingers and dimmed, right up to the point where his finger now rested. He placed his palm flat against the surface and let the light appear. Drawing his hand away, he watched as the print dimmed to opaque.

Sunder couldn't resist. He jumped out as far as he could and turned to watch the old seer's expression. Sunder laughed in delight as Benjamin gasped. Still laughing, he walked in a circle and then stood still.

Benjamin was in awe. The Mythit! He saw the small footprints walk in a circle and then stop. Two handprints appeared. The handprints walked in a circle. Benjamin burst into laughter. The handprints faded as the footprints reappeared. Benjamin watched a point of light trace a pattern. He caught his breath as he realized the Mythit was tracing runes.

"I am called Sunder."

"Sunder," Benjamin repeated. He had heard that name before … Sunder …

January turned. He didn't see Benjamin or Sunder. He took one step and then another. As he stepped into the pool, he sank. He wouldn't drown, and he knew it. He drifted to the bottom and looked around.

Benjamin and Sunder were shocked as Jan stepped into the pool and vanished. Benjamin stared at the pool, while Sunder jumped up and down yelling, "January! January!"

It was full dark. Benjamin didn't know where to look for the mouth of the cave. He was at a total loss. With a sudden thought, he jumped out onto the crystal, hoping to follow. Solid! The Mythit's footprints were frantically appearing from place to place with no sense of order. "Where is the mouth of the cave? I can open the door if you show me where it is."

The point of light started tracing as the feet came to a stop. "I do not know!"

Benjamin thought for a moment and then said, "You check east. I'll check west!"

The footprints dashed away. Benjamin turned and ran to the west edge of the plateau and made a hasty search. He even backtracked the stairs a few dozen steps looking for a path. Nothing! Benjamin ran back to the pool. The Mythit was already there. "Any luck?"

"No!"

"Go north!" Without waiting to see if the Mythit went, he turned and ran to the south edge. He walked the edge of a sheer cliff and could not find a trail. Finally, he ran back to the crystal pool. The Mythit's footprints were waiting for him. As he approached, runes formed.

"This way."

Benjamin gathered his strength and followed the footprints. Sure enough, as he reached the edge, a set of stairs led down and out of sight. Hurrying down the path, he hoped he wouldn't or couldn't trample the Mythit in his haste. He came to the end of the stairs and then hurriedly walked the length of the cliff. There, in the corner, was a pot that contained the two seedling oaks. Taking a deep breath, he knelt down and set his fingers against the tiny trunks of the two little trees.

Immediately, luminous green tree fire burst from the tiny branches. Benjamin heard a crack. The outline of the cave door began to glow. Benjamin leapt to his feet and worked his fingers into the seam. Slowly, he pried the door open.

Sunder ran in the opening as soon as it was big enough to allow his small body through. He felt the change come over him as he crossed the threshold. He materialized as Benjamin's gaze fell on the room.

Benjamin stepped through the door and stopped. Sunder stood in front of a doorway at the far end of the chamber. The Mythit set his hands against it and pushed, but all it did was glow. A wall of crystal *was* the door. Benjamin walked to his side and tried to look in. Nothing. They both pushed against the crystal. Again, all it did was glow.

"Well, I guess we're supposed to sit here and wait."

Benjamin looked down at Sunder. "I believe you are correct."

He turned all of his attention to the Mythit and found himself staring at an absolutely remarkable creature. The Mythit was covered in short orange fur that almost became red at the hands and feet. A loud yellow topknot arrayed the crown of his head like the cap of a mushroom. He looked down into fathomless, glowing purple eyes. No pupil, no whites, just purple. The luminous glow brightened as Sunder smiled. All told, the top of Sunder's head barely came to Benjamin's waist.

Sunder grinned. "It looks like our young friend will have to find his own way out of there. Sit. We might be here for a while." Sunder walked to a table and jumped up on a chair. "This room is only for 'sunshine and sitting.' Anything we might find here that's useful is in there with Jan."

Benjamin glanced askance. "How do you know that?"

Sunder shrugged. "Nothing in here but a table, three chairs, and a box of gold."

Benjamin turned his head and saw the box sitting by the door. "How do you know there's gold in that box?"

Sunder tapped the side of his nose. "I can smell it."

Benjamin missed little. The Mythit had been here before. *Why didn't he know about the stairs?*

Sunder answered his thought. "I've only been here twice. The wizards used to think they needed some place of privacy." He grinned. "I wouldn't know why. Besides, I came on the back of a giant hawk. It made me keep my eyes closed."

Benjamin would have been startled by the way the Mythit read his mind, but he was too tired. "I think I will not, soon, get used to you two reading my mind." He saw in his mind's eye, January, sword in hand, head cocked at a jaunty angle. The youth fairly dripped self-confidence. "Where did you get that sword?"

A smug smile crossed Sunder's face. "Oh, I asked Corillion for it. He had the displeasure of my acquaintance, but he knew I was close to the Blue Wizard. In fact, Blue suggested I ask for it. Corillion promised it to me before the final battle on Blood Plain. He told me that if the Three didn't win that fight, one more sword wasn't going to matter anyway. I think it would. Corillion was one of the best sword dancers I ever had the pleasure to watch practicing the art."

Benjamin thought of just how old this particular Mythit could be, and asked, "Who was the best? The Sword Dancers of Lispin Shark?"

Sunder laughed at that. "Old seer, the Sword Dancers of Lispin Shark are a legend even the Knights of The Alliance don't believe in. The best sword dancer I've ever seen is also a man of legend. Even now he swims in a pool of crystal."

"Is he really that good?" Benjamin asked. "He is so young!"

Sunder grinned so brightly the glow from his eyes lit the small room. "January went from a gangly colt to a sword dancer in one season. I have refined him for three. Never have I witnessed such determination! I have a link with his mind. I have created illusions of the best dancers I've known. Mythits, as you well know, are prone to brag, but I tell you *my* illusions can have great initiative. He has been trained by, and beaten, Lyre's best. He *is* that good!

"I was taking him, in a roundabout way, to both schools when you woke the Guardians. As you said up there, I also see fate carrying him faster than I would have liked, but he is well prepared."

Benjamin nodded in understanding. He believed *this* Mythit, even though Jan was seemingly so very young. He hung his head. "I am worn to the bone. If we cannot help him, and I see now that we cannot, I need to sleep."

Benjamin got wearily to his feet and unrolled his blanket. He lay down and yawned fit to kill. As he drifted off, he thought of something he wanted to ask. "Did you send the animals to guide me through Mirshol?"

Sunder looked sharply at him. After a pause, he said, "No."

"Oh?" was the last thing Benjamin said before sleep took him.

Sunder gazed down at the Seer of Lake Town for a long time. Finally, he went to the cave door and walked through. Perching himself on the ledge, he turned his orange-furred face upward and watched the stars.

8

Three Gems

January turned his head. The crystal tickled his nose and ears as it flowed around his face. He opened his mouth to breath and felt the air pocket bend inward as air passed through the liquid. He breathed out, trying to make a bubble and found that the liquid crystal absorbed it faster than he could blow. It was strange, fascinating. He waved his arms and watched the liquid glow.

His eyes registered nothing but hand-hewn walls. The round room was empty. Yet, if he closed his eyes and used his senses, objects seemed to crowd around him. Jan cleared his mind and allowed tendrils of feeling to probe the chamber.

Three objects came instantly into focus. He opened his eyes and saw a bow and quiver, a large iron-bound chest, and a tripod.

January reached out to the tripod, realizing as he touched it, that it was three staves. Each staff was carved with intricate runes from heel to head. He ran his fingers up the length of the closest staff and let them rest at its setting. A large gem had obviously been set in the golden crown, but now it stood empty.

He glanced at the bow and quiver. However, the lure of a closed chest on a curious young mind was far too strong. Jan walked the distance to the chest and opened the lid. A gold and ivory box sat on top of a king's ransom of coin and jewels.

Steady fingers picked up the box and slowly removed the ivory catch. The ice-blue eyes of a very young man beheld three Mythit-made gems. Their lives sparkled in his eyes, and they were ancient! Even the red gem, fashioned thousands of seasons after the white and blue, gave him a feeling of timeless age. January reached inside and touched the large blue gem.

Eyes!

January had always known the feeling of eyes watching him. Jan turned his head and gasped. A willow-slender woman in flowing blue robes stood before him. Her skin was light, and her hair was dark, yet they, too, were blue. Dark blue eyes, glowing like Mythit eyes, crinkled at the corners as she met his gaze. She radiated a warm gentleness that Jan felt flowing from the center of her being.

"How are you called?"

January blinked as tendrils of feeling reached from her aura and touched the edge of his personality. He answered, "January."

"January, these staves are of the past"—she motioned to the tripod—"and no use to you. I am instructed to tell you that the moment you bring all three gems to life, many things will occur throughout the land. Anything magic created by them will awaken so long as it remains whole. The Mythits will once again be required to use their inherent abilities to remain unseen by men. The veil that holds the Dark Lord will give him warning the gems no longer sleep. The heart of the king's palace at Wizards Veil will give warning that magic has come back to life.

"I must warn you that the black Mythits will work fast when they can once again appear before humans. Even now, they hold the land of Vain in their power. There will be war. The land of the king is ill prepared for war, so you must speed them to readiness.

"January, you must make your own staff and place all three gems in its crown. They will teach you the meaning of power. Soon, however, you must create your own jewel and give the three gems their final peace.

"Before I go, there is something you need to know. A force of black Mythits march toward us as we speak. They will wait on the border of Mirshol until you *open* the forest. The great Forest of Mirshol will lose its protection as you take control of the gems. When your new staff is complete, the gems will help you replace the spell, but that will take a small amount of time. You must go now to confront the band of Mythit fighters. You will not be alone for Those Who Hold Vigil will be there on the Plain of Blood. Understand me—if the evil Mythits enter the forest, they will kill every Mythit of Light they can find. I will have a horse waiting at the foot of the mountain."

January nodded as he soaked up all of her words. After a time, he looked back up. "What's your name?"

"Sapphire."

As Jan watched, Sapphire faded away.

9

A Piece of Past: 2

January walked through the crystal wall with the gold and ivory box under one arm. In his other hand, he held the bow and quiver and a small pouch of gold and jewels. Benjamin awoke as he entered the outer cave. Sunder, feeling Jan's personality, walked in from the ledge, trailing sunshine like a shadow.

"How long have I been in there?"

"All night and half the morning," Sunder answered. "It's two hours until noon."

January sat down and told them most of what he had seen in the room. He said nothing about Sapphire. They knew he was holding something back, but they both understood not to ask. Then he hesitated.

Sunder grinned at Jan's indecision. "Just tell me what you need to."

Jan looked gratefully at the Mythit. "Sunder, take Benjamin and go to Home. The Mythits will have need of you. There's a band of, uh, enemies marching on Mirshol right now. I'm going to ride out and slow them."

"Forget it," Sunder said knowingly. "I'm coming with you."

"So am I," Benjamin put in.

"No. I am going alone. The Mythits must be warned, and you're the only one who can do it."

Sunder knew he was right. He just didn't like it. He wanted to be there for Jan. He realized how much January had grown and knew he could take care of himself. "OK," Sunder said. "But as soon as I see to their safety, I'm coming back to check on you."

Jan turned to Benjamin. He paused, wondering how to express how he felt. "In a way you play the role of father to me. I want you to know that I understand what you gave to me last night. I see our roads part for a while."

Benjamin looked into Jan's eyes. "What do you see?"

Jan watched Benjamin in his mind's eye. "I see a woman singing"—Jan hesitated and then understood what he saw—"about the Three Sisters." Jan laughed. "Go find her. I will meet you in the School of Prayer."

Benjamin bowed his head. "So be it."

Sunder walked to Jan and set his hands on the young human's knees. "You must know that you will make a staff of power. The seedlings at the door should do fine."

Benjamin picked up his blanket and rolled it. "That seems wise. The Three have touched them."

Jan stood up and walked to the door. He gazed down at the two seedling oaks. A slow smile spread across his face.

They walked down the mountain and reached the bottom just after sunset. Both of Benjamin's horses were waiting, along with a huge black stallion. Benjamin tied his bedroll onto his mount's back and turned. "I will travel south around the mountains. If you do not reach the School of Prayer within ten days of my arrival, I will return the same way."

Sunder spoke in thought. *If a creature all in black is with them, destroy it first and the rest will flee!* Sunder looked angry as he thought, but he continued with a sudden sarcastic smile, *'It' is a she, and her name is Melody. I don't really believe she would be there. But remember my words.'*

Jan nodded and leapt lightly onto the stallion's back. "I will see you at the School of Prayer." With that said, he turned and galloped away.

Jan rode through the night. He changed horses three times. The second time he changed horses, he set the bow and the box in a clearing next to an ancient oak. By noon, he was falling asleep. Jan opened his eyes with a start. The horse was watching him, standing over his body as if he were a colt in need of protection. He lay on the border of Mirshol and Blood Plain. He didn't remember getting there.

Hunger filled his thoughts. He realized it was the horse's sensations adding to his own that made his stomach rumble in need. He gestured for the horse to go. The stallion stared down at him for a moment and then quickly trotted away. Jan unbuckled the sword belt and laid it at his side. He blinked.

Lying next to him was a pile of fruits and nuts. He ate it all and remembered Sunder's words. *You're always hungry!*

Jan woke again late in the evening and stared across the lifeless dust of Blood Plain. Many wars had been fought on its once fertile soil. Jan drew his sword and gazed at it with great curiosity. His senses spread and calmed the area surrounding him. *Corillion*. He stood in one fluid motion, startled by the swiftness of *the sight...*

The Blue Wizard was standing on a hill, his long white hair and beard flowing in the wind. On his right was the White Wizard. And on his left, Red. They were surrounded by a sea of darkness. Warped, vile mockeries of human life charged them from three sides.

The Red Wizard wielded a golden long sword, slashing as he danced. White leveled a gold-crowned, steel-shod staff. It bucked and kicked as he beat down power shields with grim determination. The shields he methodically crushed protected the mental chaos that drove the horde. Blue worked his hands, enforcing the power of Red and White. As White destroyed a shield, Red's illusions shone through. The horde would behold an army of red clad dancers. Each dancer was armed with a bright sword that sent chills of dread into the very heart of the horde.

The swarming horde could, in no way, stand against the Three. The evil spawned creatures threw down their weapons and fled. The Three would then advance, slowly working their way toward the center of the enemy army.

Two full leagues behind the Three, the men of Lyre fought. And died. Corillion watched and directed his army of fighters and knights. The day had barely reached noon, yet a thousand of his men were already out of the battle. His thoughts ran ahead to the Three. The king had sent him and ten thousand men to protect them. Corillion could now barely discern, far in the distance, an occasional blast of white fire that could have only originated from the staff of the White Wizard.

They said they needed no help. They had argued time and time again, telling him to take his men and go home. They knew he would not. The king of Lyre had sent Corillion, the weapons master, vow maker, and sword dancer. Nothing would sway his determination.

Corillion glared to the north and remembered the Blue Wizard's words.

"We will not return. This is our final battle. When the end comes, you will know it. Save your men. Leave Blood Plain."

"But why?" Corillion had asked. "Why won't you come back? My men will protect you!"

Blue had smiled. He'd set his hand on Corillion's shoulder and gazed directly into his eyes. The brilliant blue glow in the pupilless eyes of the ancient wizard filled the warrior with a quiet awe. "What we will face, your men cannot fight. Although I do not wish to die a physical death, I will do so gladly if it will achieve our purpose. Ah, my friend, you have fought long and hard for all of your short life. You are a warrior tried and true. Can you even imagine Lyre in peace? Understand this—the battle is ours. I assure you we will not return. Nevertheless, the victory will be ours."

Corillion held Blue's gaze, trying to understand. After a long moment, he asked, "What can I do to help?"

The Red Wizard motioned toward the camp. "Save your men. It's not their fight."

A sudden wind forced itself onto the battlefield. The Dark Lord's minions and the king's men stopped their fighting as they were all slammed to the ground. Like leaves in a whirlwind, shields, tents, and supplies scattered across the plain.

Corillion raised his head and watched terrible black clouds roar in from the north. Continuous bolts of baleful power shattered the ground, crisping anything in reach. Yet, there was a light. A spot of white light far ahead remained untouched. Corillion saw white-hot bolts firing back at the mass of black clouds, and he knew the Three still lived. Against the storm they fought, there seemed no hope. Still, the white light held. Not only did it hold, it grew. He knew he was a witness to a battle of power the likes of which Lyre had never before seen.

Blue was being attacked on all sides. The Red Wizard was awed that White could gather all of this hate and blind fury and channel it back into its natural state. Blue gathered this cleansed, wholesome energy and turned it back on the animate evil that drove the storm.

By all accounts, they should be dead. Even now their physical state did not allow for this massive use of power. They were here to end this; they knew what they were doing. This sacrifice, their deaths, would *bind* this abuse of power.

Red slowly lifted his platinum-edged, golden long sword and aimed it at the clouds. A sudden feral grin split his lips. With a nod from Blue, he spoke a single *word*. Blue put one hand on Red's shoulder. The personality around White was blinding.

Blue was the tool, White was the channel, and Red, the weapon. The Dark Lord had overstepped his bounds. He would be defeated. A crystal tear came to Blue's eye as he placed his other hand on the shoulder of his soul's brother, the White Wizard.

Corillion watched as the force rose to challenge the storm. One blinding red flash, and then it was over. A soundless blast of power leveled the field and then died away. Quiet! The warped, vaguely human shapes fled. Corillion raised himself and stood motionless. Sunlight covered the plain in a rainbow of hue.

He heard a victorious yell and then another. His men were calling to each other in exited, wonder-filled voices. Corillion's second in command came forward, hand on hilt in salute. Corillion turned back to the last place he had seen the White Wizard's fire. He said softly, humbly, "The wizards are gone."

January snapped away from the vision and hit the ground. As he lay on his back, he held up the Sword of Corillion and grinned like a fool. The drain of energy faded quickly. Jan stood back up and gave the air a few one handed strokes, laughing at the whistle.

He called his horse and found the answer to a long-wondered-at question. The horse retained his intelligence even out of Mirshol. He knew it was Sapphire's doing that this last mount was a huge white stallion. "I'm ready," he stated. "I go to fight. Will you carry me?"

The stallion reared, hooves slashing air, and then pranced to his side. Jan mounted, and the horse fairly leapt at the plains, running like the wind.

10

Chose Who hold Vigil

January saw the glow of personality in the darkness and came to a halt. At first glance he did not understand what he was seeing. *Surely that is no normal aura.* He dismounted and walked toward it. As he approached, he realized it was two separate groups; the personality of one group was superimposed over the aura of the other. He stepped closer and then started to run. A single, chilling howl rent the air. As he approached, he realized a pack of wolves was faced off against a force that sent a chill down his spine.

He saw Mythits with black fur and bloodred eyes, and they were beautiful. Nevertheless, their filthy auras were a sickening stench of dirty, thick colors. *How can something so evil be so beautiful?*

A few of them heard his thought. They immediately assaulted his personality with thick tendrils of fear. Jan threw up a mental barrier and filled himself with calm. He realized the combined emotional force of the black Mythits' personality was being inflicted on the wolves. The pack was close to being overcome. The two youngest wolves were cowering; one started to whimper.

Jan walked up and through the pack. With exaggerated hand motions, he slammed a wall of quiet between them. A slow smile crossed his face as he raised his sword and held it level across his chest. The wolves' reaction to him was a pleasant surprise. They quickly formed a half circle around him to protect his back. *Those Who Hold Vigil*, Jan thought. He saw his effect on the aura of the evil Mythits and laughed.

The show of self-assurance made them pause. The fact that he was human was a bad omen. The fact that he understood and so easily blocked their combined personality was a worse one. The leader of the band shouted, "Find the were and kill it."

Jan realized that the speaker was human. He watched as the man walked through the group. Something about him caused his sense of correctness to buzz. *This isn't right.*

The man spoke. "It is said of the one who will come that he will come to battle too soon and cut off his right arm." The man was dressed in black leather and silver. It was the common fighting wear of Vainian soldiers. Dark, lanky hair hung ragged on his shoulders. The man drew a two-handed broadsword and spoke again. "I will test this prophesy of My Lovely Lady."

Jan held his sword ready and motioned him forward. "Indeed? I am left-handed."

The Vainian attacked. Sure, strong strokes pounded Jan backward. Jan watched, as he had been taught, to find the flaws in his opponent's style. *So, you lead with your feet!*

Jan blocked and stooped. The man jumped back as Jan swiped at his ankles. Rising, Jan attacked with upward, crosswise strokes. This took the Vainian by surprise. He was forced to block with downstrokes. Jan stepped in, set his shoulders, and started an upswing. The fighter had to put extra effort into his block to compensate for the force Jan seemed to be using.

Just before swords clashed, Jan sidestepped, watched the Vainian connect with the ground, and lose his balance. With a swift kick, Jan helped gravity. The man sprawled on his face.

The Vainian quickly rolled and got to his feet. Jan stood still, sword level across his chest.

Sword strokes sent sparks flying as the man attacked. Jan lured him in by exposing his left side. The black-leathered fighter took the bait. Jan stepped in instead of away. Ducking the swing, January hooked one foot behind the man's ankle and simply watched as the heavy broadsword forced the Vainian back and over.

The man jumped up in a rage and charged. Jan feigned right, stepped left, and brought the Sword of Corillion down.

The Vainian crumpled, split from shoulder to hip, and fell to the ground.

January turned to the Mythits. "You will not go to Mirshol. I will fight you every step of the way."

Two Mythits faded. Jan reached with his mind and wrenched them back into corporeality. They became visible, gasping for breath. After a moment, Jan released them. They backed up, personalities glowing with fear.

The black Mythit leader had never even heard of a human this strong.

The bright, clear aura of this youth caused him to *wilt*. As one, the Mythit band started backing away. To his shame, his little voice quavered as he hissed, "We'll meet again."

Jan watched them go. It had been too easy. The wolves gave sudden growls. He turned. Two Mythits stood on opposite sides of a white wolf. Teeth bare, it stood waiting. Jan followed the wolves as they padded toward it. The white wolf growled at the pack as if saying, *This is my fight.*

Jan realized that two Mythits could never get on opposite sides of a wolf if it didn't want them there. As the Mythits lunged, the white wolf pushed up with hind legs, swiped claws across the face of one, and pounced on the other. They rolled once. The wolf came out on top, teeth clamped on the black Mythit's throat. With calculated intent, it waited for the other Mythit to wipe the blood out of its eyes. When it looked up, the white wolf ripped the captured Mythit's head completely off and tossed it at the other creature.

The white wolf didn't attack. The black Mythit took a step backward— and then another and another. Finally, it turned and bolted in the direction of the others.

Even as Jan turned back to gaze at the white wolf, he was suddenly drenched in terrible, overwhelming pain. Blinding pain sparkled around the white wolf's personality. Jan blinked watering eyes and gasped in shock. It was changing shape! Slowly and painfully, it took human shape. He set up walls and felt his heart pound in sympathy as bones broke and reformed. Jan's empathy was great. He felt the pain as surely as the were. He wanted to reach out and take the pain away, but all he could do was watch.

When it finished the change, Jan's heart fluttered and started pounding again. This time, it wasn't in sympathy. The white wolf was a girl, and she was beautiful! Shaggy white hair hung in wild disarray down to the small of her back. She stood before him unclothed and seemingly unaware of her nakedness. She stretched, leaned toward him sniffing the air, and then shook her head in an obvious display of disbelief.

Jan's blood was boiling. *In the name of Song!* His lack of control made him suddenly angry with himself. He could see she was instantly aware of first his desire and then his anger.

Moonlight blinked bright magenta eyes and then hung her head. "Sorry."

Jan took a step closer, empathy requiring him to try to comfort. "What do you have to be sorry for?"

Moonlight looked up in confusion. January caught a bare flash of her sparkling eyes beneath her thick, unruly bangs. "You're not angry with me?"

"*No!*" Jan exclaimed in surprise. "I, uh …" he floundered. "Uh, where are your clothes?"

She jumped back as if slapped. Then her head drooped in what Jan sensed to be shame. "You *don't* like the way I look."

"No!" Jan blurted out. He wasn't handling this well at all. "That's not it. I, well, I was angry with myself."

Moonlight glared at him in doubt, assessing the statement. Then her eyes opened wide as she leaned close and sniffed his scent. "For what?"

She stood before him. The top of her head barely reached his shoulders. Her head was now tilted at a questioning angle. Her hair and skin were snow-white. She was albino, Jan knew. He had seen albino animals before, white fur and reddish pink eyes. However, this was a beautiful young woman—an exotically gorgeous, perfectly carved, young woman. By appearance, he guessed she was no more than sixteen seasons old. The simple nearness of her lithe body caused feelings in him that were totally new.

As he stood there thinking without answering her question, she seemed to make up her own mind at what he had been angry about. She tried, unsuccessfully, to cover herself with hair and hands. Jan saw her discomfiture, took off his outer wrap, and handed it to her.

Moonlight glared at him. Then with a look of great distaste, she snatched the silk wrap out of his hand. Her expression changed instantly. She ran it through her fingers and actually smiled. Rubbing it against her cheek, she closed her eyes and sighed. She breathed in deep, smelling his masculine, sweaty scent. She liked his scent. The incredibly soft material felt good against her skin! She knew humans wore clothes. If they wore things like this, then maybe it wasn't such a bad idea. The were used pelts and skins, but they were for winter, not for warm spring nights.

Hearing a moan, they both turned. The Vainian was trying to crawl away. "I thought he was dead," Jan said to himself. He walked back and saw a trail of blood. The man in black leather was desperately trying to flee.

Jan stopped him and rolled him over. The slash from shoulder to hip was not as deep as he had thought. The Vainian moaned again and Jan quickly decided he did not want this man to die. Ripping strips from the man's leggings, he wrapped the wound.

"Why do you help him?!"

Jan looked up. "I have to get him to Mirshol."

She glared down at the man and spat. "He tried to kill you!"

"Why did you let the other Mythit live?"

"It must live to tell its story," she answered. "They must fear to come on *my* land again! There is no purpose to let this *human* live." She paused and then said in quiet fury, "He killed two of my *children*!"

"I am human."

That made her pause. She had wondered about that. A human coming from Mirshol on a white horse. She liked him for that. By the Vow! She would like him for simply giving her the time of day! When she'd first seen him, she had somehow felt a part of him. Her actions, even though she wouldn't even admit it to herself, were calculated to gain his favor. Her pack treated her with no kindness. She had ugly white fur and red eyes. She was different, and they always found cruel ways to remind her of it. Still, this human rode a white horse to battle. He had come *alone* even as she had. Was he One Who Walks Alone? Did humans *walk*? She didn't think so.

She had counted forty of those sickening black creatures. When her children had almost bolted at the terror of those evil things, he had walked to the front to protect them.

Moonlight said slowly, "You are different. You care for the pack."

He turned and looked at the wolves. One of the youngest whelps groveled up to him and licked his hand. She felt a warm glow spread through her body as he smiled and ruffled its scruffy head. The wonderful sensation left as quickly as it had come. There was no use pretending; she would never be a mother.

"Why don't they change shape?"

She blinked in surprise. "They are wolves, not were."

"You called them your children."

She smiled. "All were call wolves children." Then she frowned. Jan felt a miserable hurt burning in the breast of the young werewoman, as she whispered, "I'll never have children."

"Then why are they here?" Jan asked. "This is no concern of theirs."

For the first time since they'd met, she gave him a level look and stated flatly, "You know nothing of the were."

"Yeah, I see that." He turned back to the Vainian. "Will you help me get him on the horse?"

She suddenly looked thoroughly disgusted, but she nodded agreement. "I will let him live. This time."

After they got the man on the white stallion, Jan gazed down at her. "What's your name?"

Moonlight thought fast. *Never let a human know your name!* She thought of her father and answered, "Lyndsy."

"Lyndsy." He smiled to himself. "A beautiful name. Can you tell your pack to watch for more of those, uh, creatures?" Calling them Mythits left a bad taste in his mouth.

"Yes, we always watch, but …"

"What?" Jan asked. He looked down at the man lying across his lap. "I've already wasted too much time."

Lyndsy looked at Jan for a long moment and then hung her head. "Go."

11

STAFF

Jan held the Vainian firmly as his steed sped across the plain. The man was losing blood, and Jan feared he would not make it. He didn't have a clue as to why he had decided to save this evil consort of Melody the Black. It was just something he felt he had to do.

Mirshol loomed into view at sunrise. The clearing where he had slept seemed to welcome him as he dismounted and pulled the man from the horse. He laid the man down and used his other wrap to tie off the bleeding. He could do nothing else. A thought occurred to him. If he could reach the clearing where the potted seedlings from the cave and the gold and ivory box lay, he might be able to save him. He knew the gems in the gold and ivory box must be the key to greater magic.

Sapphire, Jan thought, *have a relay of horses waiting.* It was just a thought. He didn't expect an answer, but he got one.

Yes, my lord.

Jan finally reached the clearing and ran to the box. Hurriedly opening it, he plucked the blue gem from its cushion. The blue-clad forest wraith named Sapphire appeared. "Can you help the man I left on the border of the forest?"

Sapphire bowed her head. She had been created to serve the one who awoke the gem. She had two sisters, Star and Rose. They were the Keepers of the Forest. They had been *designed* to accomplish a purpose, but many seasons ago, changes had occurred. They were capable of learning and found they had to make decisions that were not a part of their *design*. They had learned to think for themselves.

This was how the animals of Mirshol gained their ability to comprehend speech and to reason. A private joke of the Three—they had indeed created three Mothers of Nature. Like many works of magic, it had caused something of a side effect that the Three hadn't anticipate. Each had her own store of knowledge. This, the wizards thought, would cover any situation that might arise. However, the three sisters discovered they could also learn from each other.

This had started a game of intuition. Searching the forest, they'd hunted for bits and pieces of information that were not accounted for within their frame of reference. Indeed, there was a whole world within the mighty Forest of Mirshol that had no place in their original design.

Sapphire gazed through the distance and saw the man lying in the clearing. "Yes, I can help him. I need the help of the red and white gems. But when you touch them, the spell of protection surrounding the Forest of Mirshol will open. Are you ready to make a staff?"

Jan thought about the wolves, in particular the white one. They would chase the evil back to Vain. "When I make the staff, you said I could put the spell back around Mirshol. Will I know if someone slips through during the time that it's open?"

Sapphire nodded curiously. "Yes, you will know."

"Then I'm ready."

"Lift the other stones from the box."

Jan obeyed. He watched two figures materialize in front of him. One woman was tall and seemingly more solid than the other two. Her skin, hair, and long robes were white. She gazed at him through narrowed glowing white eyes as if she were watching him walk out of a dream. The other figure, in shades of red, wore the vest, knee-high leather sandals, and belted skirts of a warrior. Her eyes sparkled with a knowing smile as she leaned close and inspected the inlay on the hilt of the Sword of Corillion.

Sapphire spoke. "We will care for the man, but first you must be instructed in the art of staff making."

In what seemed only a few moments, they spoke to Jan's mind in the language of trees. Trees were the greatest of all plants growing on the face of Lyre. Trees knew the language of wind, rain, fire, and soil.

Human aura, the illumination describing the personality of the individual, was the heart of magic. Personality was light. Trees turned light into energy, which, in the right hands, could be shaped into anything the mind conceived. They were participants in the seasons. They traded life-giving oxygen for the waste of Lyre's animals. A *power focus* bound to a wooden staff would give a Magic User access to, and control over, all of these things.

Jan learned the reason wizards made their own staves. No Magic User could completely control a power tool created by the hands of another. The tree and maker, during the *shaping* of a staff, became bound to the aura of one another. Therefore, only the maker could fully control it.

January walked to the two seedling oaks within the stone pot. Kneeling before them, he set his fingers to the base of each tree. The three gems rolled out of his hand and into the pot.

Sapphire picked up the three gems and sighed. She turned to her sisters, holding the gems in her open palms. They gathered around her and silently gazed at them. Sapphire looked to Star and Rose. Star and Rose put their arms around their sister and wept. Linked arm in arm, they finally turned to January. He was already deep in contact with the two seedlings. Sapphire said sadly, "We have had long, full lives."

Rose saw the anguish in Sapphire's blue face and raised an eyebrow to Star. "It seems our better third is in need of her own medicine!"

Sapphire looked up. She blinked away tears and knelt at Jan's side. Smiling a sad smile, she let the gems roll out of her hands and back into the pot. "We chose long ago to do what we have just done." Then she stood, and all of her doubts were gone. She smiled a radiant smile. Birds sang her joy as a soft breeze danced through the trees. "Come!" she exclaimed, laughing to her sisters. "We have a life to save."

The seedlings began to grow. They came together and twined, reaching for the sun. Without realizing it, Jan reached for the water gourd and poured some into the pot. He *watched* as cells split and doubled.

With the illumination of his own aura, he fed the trees. One was stronger than the other. Following his lead, the stronger wrapped around the weaker, lending it strength. January spoke to them in thought and heard them respond. He lit the roots, bark, trunk, stems, and the buds that would soon leaf. He poured his personality into them and became one with them.

The trees grew.

He retarded the growth of the stronger to keep it from branching. He allowed the weaker to grow three slender stalks. He felt the trees suck the water from the pot and reached for the gourd. When the time was right, he reached for the gems.

He picked up the blue gem and held it to one of the three branches. Like a snake coiling in slow motion, it wrapped around the gem. Slowly, oh so slowly, he touched the gem with his mind and unlocked its power. Energy coursed through both trees. He picked up the red gem and repeated the process. He felt their power square as the two gems harmonized their pitch.

Stroking the branches, he caused the blue and red gems to sit side by side with a finger-breadth space between. He picked up the white gem. The third branch he coaxed into growing straight upward. With two fingers, Jan set the white stone against the branch and smiled as it wrapped around. With a gentle caress, he bowed the branch over so it was turned down, resting above the blue and the red. The white gem settled a hand span above the other two.

Jan felt his strength draining and pulled the newly made staff from the soil. Utilizing the power of itself, he formed the roots into a hard knot. Dizziness swept across his vision, and he dropped to his knees. His last memory was dumping the pot and running his fingers through the soil.

12

CULTURE CLASH

Jan woke with the sun full in his face. He tried to lift his hand. "Stop that! Here. Drink this. Slowly."

Water trickled into his mouth. He swallowed. Disobeying orders, he grabbed the gourd and gulped down half of the water. It came back up.

"Slowly! You don't want to drown, do you?"

He tried another small mouthful. It stayed down. Another. Then another.

"Are you hungry?"

He nodded. His head was lowered to the ground. He drank some more. The trees over his head swam in a blur as he opened his eyes. After a few blinks, they began to come clear. Lyndsy padded into his line of vision and knelt by his side. She reached out and dropped a berry into his mouth.

"Chew it slowly."

This time, he followed orders. He bit into it and swallowed the juice. Chewing the pulp, he swallowed again. "More."

Lyndsy dropped two into his mouth.

He chewed them up and swallowed. "More."

She fed him two handfuls, carefully watching his color.

Jan looked up into wide-set, liquid magenta eyes. "Woman, you're beautiful!"

Lyndsy scowled. "You're sick. You don't know what you say."

In a sudden panic, he tried to sit up. "Where's the staff?"

"Stop that!" she commanded. Then, almost quietly, "It's in your hand."

Jan rolled his head and looked down the length of his body. The staff was in his hand. He felt an intense wash of relief flood over him. Then he flinched and blushed. *I wasn't wearing anything yesterday! Now I'm dressed. Did she see me?* Jan looked back down. Sure enough, his silk was tied in the front, not on the side. *She dressed me!*

Sitting down, Moonlight raised his head and slid over. It was a liberty, but she knew he was too weak to do anything about it. Her hair fell across his face, so she tossed it to one side and glanced down. She blinked in wonder when she once again smelled his desire. *Never* had a man of the were desired her. She gazed into his ice-blue eyes and was awed. Then, just as swiftly as the glorious scent filled her mind, it was gone. His scent disappeared! Lyndsy leaned down, sniffing, almost touching nose to nose. She wondered if she had imagined it.

Jan steadied his breathing and let his senses flow outward. Tendrils of feeling surrounded him, blocking out Lyndsy's personality. She was looking at him with a strange, glowing aura. He didn't stop to puzzle it out. "Did you see the man? I left him at the edge of the forest."

She looked back into his eyes, and this time her expression was unfathomable. "I saw him. He was walking the edge of Mirshol looking in. I followed him all day, that night, and all the next day. He kept going north, not even hurt. You're a powerful wizard!"

Jan blinked up at her. "How long have I been out?"

Her bare breast swelled with pride. "It's been seven days since we fought together on the Plain of Blood."

"I've been out for seven days?"

"No. Three days ago I got here and saw you pull the staff from the holder. That's when you passed out."

Three days ago? It couldn't have taken four days to make the staff, could it? "No wonder I'm so hungry."

Lyndsy fed him again at sunset. This time, he ate ravenously. He watched her very closely but tried not to be obvious. She kept rearranging the single bottom wrap he had given her. He got the impression she was only wearing it because he had made an issue of her nakedness. She would gaze at him from time to time. Sometimes she was grinning fit to burst, and sometimes her scowl almost made him cringe. He tried to keep his eyes off of her, but she was so graceful and wonderful to look at that he just couldn't seem to help himself.

Lyndsy knew Jan was watching her every move. When she looked his way, he was always smiling! She didn't know how to act. She wanted, badly, for him to like her. That made her nervous and angry. She kept searching the air for his scent, but she couldn't seem to pinpoint it. Sometimes it was as though he wasn't even there. She glanced over one shoulder, just to make sure, just to prove to herself she wasn't dreaming. A swelling of passion that rushed from toenails to hair roots almost took her breath. He was still smiling!

They sat under a tree that night and gazed up through the leaves at the stars. Jan controlled his breathing to quiet his hammering heart when she sat down next to him, shoulder to shoulder. He could feel her eye path run along his jaw as she gazed sideways through her shaggy white hair. The touch of her skin on his shoulder was comforting. Her personality emanated concern for his physical state and something else he couldn't quite define. She had a strong personality; at the moment it was a soft red and very warm.

He glanced up at the full moon and thought about the changing of the were. He had always thought that they changed shape during the full of the moon. Right now, she was sitting at his side as though she didn't have a care in all of Lyre. "Do you control the change?"

She acted as though he had slapped her. She jumped up, glaring, and started backward. "Why?"

She looks like she's about to run away. "Uh, I'm sorry. If you don't want to talk about it ..." Jan trailed off, not wanting to say the wrong thing. She was still glaring at him, and it made him wonder what she was thinking. "Lyndsy, please sit back down. I won't ask again."

She seemed to consider him, and then he watched the anger drain right out of her.

She didn't understand humans and had always been told *never* to talk to one about these things. Lindon, her true father, had taken her to Lake Town, but she couldn't bear all of the people talking about her when they thought she couldn't hear. She had never gone back. Lyndsy had no experience with humans. The only human she had ever even talked to was He Who Sees All. But like the rest of the were, she was in awe of him and answered his polite queries with whispered single syllables. Yet, she knew instinctively that January was different. He had willingly put his own life in danger to save her pack. When she thought about that, she was suddenly ashamed that she had been distrustful and angry.

Lyndsy sat back down. "We have control as you mean control, but it's something we learn. Our pups change with the moon or when they get excited." She paused and then, "We—"

"Lyndsy," Jan interrupted, "really, if you don't want to talk about it, I understand. I've lived in Mirshol for four seasons. If I came to a town and someone asked me about Mirshol, I don't think I would want to talk about it either."

"You lived here for four seasons? Alone?" she asked incredulously. "If I had to live all alone, I would kill myself!"

The passion in her words made him blink, but he knew how she felt. He was afraid to say too much. Should he tell her he lived with Mythits? Could he really trust her? "No. I haven't exactly lived alone, but I haven't seen another human in four seasons."

She was watching him, waiting for him to say more.

He paused for a moment and then said, "I understand why you hesitate to answer questions of a stranger."

He looked over at her, and to his surprise, she laughed. Her laughter was throaty and delightful. *She's so beautiful!* He pictured her in his mind as a white wolf and then as this exotic young woman. "I wish I could be a wolf."

Lyndsy gazed at him sidelong and smiled. "Do you really?"

"Yes," Jan said seriously. "I really do." He froze. Her personality was reaching out to him and he totally misunderstood. Trying to appear casual, he leaned away from her.

Lyndsy burst into laughter. *He thinks I'm going to bite him!* His scent, for once, gave him away so completely she couldn't help but laugh.

"Weren't you?"

"No! It doesn't work that way."

Jan stilled. He had read her mind and spoken out of turn. He needed to be more careful! She'd apparently missed it because she was still talking.

"That's the reason humans are so afraid of us. They think we want to steal their children or something just as bad!" She looked up through her bangs and met his eyes. "No human can be *were*. You're a powerful wizard. It is known by the were that wizards are shape-shifters. Can't you change yourself?"

"I don't know." He knew that the Three had been able to take any shape they wished. "Maybe if I watch you, I could understand how you do it."

Lyndsy reached over and set one hand on his shoulder. She asked, with very real concern, "Are you too weak for this? How do you feel?"

She didn't know it, but her concerned direct gaze pierced through January's aura. January felt a fire at her unintentional mental touch. Her breath smelled like strawberries. If he had been feeling weak, the sudden rush of adrenaline pushed it far, far away. "I feel fine."

Lyndsy stood up, untied her wrap, and held the ends with two fingers. She gazed into Jan's eyes and let go. A very pleased look flashed in her wide-set magenta eyes.

Jan blushed crimson and quickly turned his head.

"Aren't you gonna watch?"

It was a challenge. Jan calmed himself and let his aura wrap around her before he looked back. She was afraid! Jan turned back and examined her personality. She was scared of something, and Jan couldn't figure it. Her eyes studied him carefully but showed no emotion at all. Only by inspecting her personality could he discern her fear. *What's she afraid of?*

Before he had a chance to think anything else, she started the change. Her face was the first place he felt pain. The crunching bones sounded bad, but with his senses wrapped so intimately around her, her pain was his. He felt the way her face was changing, and he *understood*. Lyndsy's backbone came into the play and told a story all its own. Fur shot through her pores like acid in an open cut. Jan steadied his breathing. He touched her mind and realized she felt far less pain than he was experiencing. Somehow, her mind and body were conditioned to this change, where his was not. It hurt her, yes, but it was bearable. When he finally thought he could control his own empathy, all four limbs started to snap. Jan kept his personality around her but was forced to look away.

A quick cooling feeling covered his body, and he gasped as the pain vanished. He raised his head and saw Lyndsy sitting on her haunches directly in front of him. She leaned forward and licked his nose. Jan smiled in relief as he looked her over. Oh, she was beautiful! "In the name of Song, Lyndsy! In the name of Song!"

Jan reached for the staff and watched the three sisters appear. They stood silently behind Lyndsy and simply watched him. Jan felt the power of the gems course through his body. Thinking of the change, he realized with great clarity how very simple it was. In the blink of an eye, he shifted from human to wolf. An overwhelming collage of smells assaulted him from all sides.

Lyndsy came closer to look him over. She licked his nose, paced around him, and growled. With a quick nip at his tail, she bolted to the trees. Jan grinned like a wolf and chased after her.

They ran through the trees exploring everything their noses led them to. Jan realized wolves saw a strange kind of personality. It was a form of heat seeing. They played and chased each other for hours. As the moon set, they returned to their camp by following their own mixed-up path through the trees. They reached the clearing and changed back. This time, Jan kept his senses away. Too tired to even talk, he lay back and fell instantly into sleep.

Lyndsy crawled to his side. She sat back on her heels and gazed at his naked body. He looked so perfect, strong, handsome. She reached down and picked up a fistful of his long blond hair. Closing her eyes, she rubbed the ends against her cheek and sighed. When she opened her eyes, the Red One was standing close, watching her.

Rose gazed at the petite werewoman as she jumped to her feet. The guilty wash of personality that permeated her aura vanished as a hot jealousy took over. Eyes blazing, the werewoman stood over Jan's waist. Fists clenched, she silently dared Rose to do or say something.

Sapphire appeared between them. Tranquil blue in blue eyes met the sudden uncertainty in the werewoman's glare. She nodded a greeting and bent over Jan's body. One hand outstretched, she ran her fingers through the hue of Jan's aura. She nodded again, this time to herself, and stood back up.

Now Lyndsy didn't know what to do. Her understanding of social life among the were led her to believe the Blue One was January's *first*. Hadn't the Red One stayed back when the Blue One appeared? She wondered if she could beat the Blue One in combat. Powerful magic was on the Blue One's side, so she would probably lose. *Magic be damned! I would try!* She decided to wait. If she could gain his favor, receive his kiss, then she would make the Circle of Challenge.

A terrible feeling of dread suddenly made her young heart ache. He wouldn't want her. She was ugly, loathsome; he probably only felt sorry for her. Yes, that why he hadn't run her off. He pitied her. She bowed her head and stepped away from Jan's sleeping body. The Blue One would want her place. Feeling wretched, she glanced around the clearing for a place to sleep.

"Wait."

Lyndsy turned as the Blue One spoke. She was very surprised to see a gentle smile.

She thinks you are January's first. A first is the mate of a pack leader.

Sapphire's eyes twinkled in good humor. *Sister, I too have been versed in the lore of the were.* Taking a single step backwards Sapphire motioned to the ground at Jan's side. "Do me this honor. Stay by his side."

Lyndsy's jaw dropped open. His first was asking her to sleep next to him! As quick as she could, before the Blue One changed her mind, she dropped to the ground and snuggled up to Jan's side. When she looked up, both figures were gone. Hardly daring to breath, Lyndsy wiggled closer and very slowly laid her head on his shoulder.

January rolled over, threw one leg across her thighs, grabbed her, and pulled her up against his chest. His hand came up and pushed her shaggy hair out of his face. He set his chin on the top of her head. Mumbling in sleep, he said something that sounded like, "Flower, your head's like a cactus."

Lyndsy didn't try to figure it out. All of her senses were pinging in passion. His masculine scent, which she could now finally smell, flooded her until she thought she would melt. Her face was pressed up against his chest, a rock was digging into the small of her back, and a tuft of grass was tickling her feet. She didn't care. She wouldn't have moved if the forest caught on fire.

Of a sudden, she yawned. How she could be tired, wrapped in the arms of a man, she really didn't know. She decided to close her eyes and revel in his warmth. She didn't want to sleep. She wanted to remember this sensation for as long as she lived. She knew good and well that no were would ever want her. If his companionship was a gesture made in pity, she might never get this close to a man again. Surely, the Blue One wouldn't spend another night away from such a strong, brave man. Another yawn stretched her face, and then she smiled.

They woke at the same moment nose to nose. For a split second, they looked into each other's eyes. Then they rolled apart, hurriedly searching for their wraps. Jan had Lyndsy at a disadvantage. Her white skin made her blush so obvious he had to laugh.

She whirled and stomped up to him. Hands on hips, feet spread, she yelled in outrage, "What are you laughing at!"

The top of her shaggy, tumbled hair barely reached his chin. Fuming in fury, she just made him laugh harder. She stopped herself and, realizing what she probably looked like, ruefully smiled.

Impulsively, Jan reached for her hand and led her toward a stream. As they walked, he thought about leaving Mirshol. He had to go and meet Benjamin. He didn't want to go, not now, but he knew he had to. The last thing he wanted to do was leave her. He had learned more about her in wolf shape than he could have ever learned about her in her human form.

As Jan went into thought, Lyndsy could feel the sudden absence of his attention. She had learned not to care what other were thought about her. She preferred solitude, but this man was beyond her. She was already beginning to crave his attention. The easy way he had reached for her hand, and still held it, made her feel cared for and maybe even special. She watched him frown as he thought. "What's wrong?"

He looked down at her and gave her a rueful grin. Then he stated seriously, "I have to leave Mirshol. Someone I know will come looking for me if I don't." Jan looked off into the distance. "Lyndsy, those evil creatures we fought will come again. I have to fight them." January gazed back down at her. "I will not let them destroy the heart and spirit of this forest. There are things I really want to say to you, but I can't."

Lyndsy glanced up, one eyebrow raised. "Then I will go with you. You might need help."

Jan shook his head. "Lyndsy, it's not that simple. You could be in danger if you're with me."

Lyndsy looked up at him with narrowed eyes. For the first time January beheld a look of complete confidence. Very quietly, as if instructing a small child, she said, "It *is* simple. I go with you." She folded her arms beneath her breasts in a gesture that said clearly the matter was settled.

January searched her gaze and then said slowly, "Lyndsy, I do want you with me."

She smirked. "See, it is simple."

Jan hadn't realized they were still naked until she picked up her wrap, looked at it through narrowed eyes, and put it on. Without a backward glance, she climbed the bank, and walked off into the trees. He didn't know what she was looking for, but he could see that she was intent on some particular thing.

Smiling at the image of her slim, curved figure, he climbed the bank and headed for the staff. A pile of wraps and other things sat next to it. He gazed around the clearing for Sunder but didn't see him anywhere. *Strange,* he thought.

Shrugging his shoulders, he picked up the staff. At its thickest diameter, Jan could hold it and touch thumb to forefinger. He realized he could remember every cell, every grain that made the staff whole. He closed his eyes and felt for the spell around Mirshol. He was surprised to find it to be a seemingly very simple, basic spell. It attacked any mind capable of realizing it. Any human could consider the spell. That was enough to bring on the mental assault.

A shimmer of light sprang up around the spell as he watched it with his mind's eye. This he could not understand. He tried, as Sunder had taught him, to reason it out, but he found he could not come up with any explanation for the clear-white illumination. It were as though a ball of light held the spell together. He gave up, puzzled, realizing he didn't like searching for an answer and not being able to find it.

Lyndsy came back into the clearing with a long, straight oak branch. She went to the pile of wraps and found a dagger. She sat down and set to work scraping the bark.

Jan looked from her to the branch and down to the pile of *things*. "Did you see who brought this?"

She gave him a hard glare. "Don't tease me."

OK, Jan thought. He turned again and looked for Sunder. After a few moments, he quit. Jan hunkered down by the wraps and assessed what was there—the dagger Lyndsy was using, two water gourds, and some of Jasmine's homemade soap. He glanced over to the bow and wondered why he had decided to bring it. Jan shook his head and turned back to see what Lyndsy was doing.

She had finished skinning it and produced a handful of assorted leaves and roots. She went to the stream and found a flat rock. Sitting, feet in the water, she started to pound the roots and leaves to pulp. She was so intent on what she was doing that Jan decided not to ask any *stupid* questions.

His thoughts wandered back to the staff. Actually, it had never been out of his mind. He picked it up again and thought about shape changing.

He realized quickly that the staff gave him an acute awareness of anything he chose to think about. He thought about being a bird. A memory from the white gem flooded his mind. A falcon! He felt the rapid heartbeat, claws, beak, wings, and feathers. Jan knew that, with a thought, he could fly away.

Other animals were present within the memories of the stones. Almost all the animals he could think of were there. No rabbit was present in the red gem. The Red Wizard had never utilized the power of his gem to help him turn into a rabbit. He grinned to himself as he jokingly thought of another shape. His blood ran cold! He could almost feel the ivory crown of horns on his head. He could almost feel the texture of scales as they covered his body. The shape was there within the blue gem!

Jan broke contact with the gem and rubbed his arms. Chilled to the bone, he closed his eyes and let the sun warm him. He finally opened his eyes and saw Lyndsy scrubbing the staff with a thick mush. He walked over to stand beside her. As he watched, he wondered if she ought to tell her people that she was safe. Somehow, he knew if he asked that she would probably bite his head off. Maybe he could use a different approach. "What were you doing on Blood Plain? Do your people know you were out there?"

Wrong approach!

Lyndsy glared up at him through thick, bushy bangs. She couldn't trust his scent; she knew that much. Right now, he smelled of concern. Fiery magenta chips softened at the piercing intelligence in those ice-blue eyes. He even looked concerned. Well, maybe he was worried that she was in danger. Perhaps she shouldn't let him worry. That thought startled her. Never before did it matter what someone else felt toward her. The were's general scorn and loathing of her appearance had long ago hardened her to anyone's concerns but her own. A weary sigh escaped her lips. No. She didn't want him to worry. She wanted him to smell like desire. At that stray thought, she smiled.

Jan watched Lyndsy's emotions change her personality. He wondered what thoughts were running through her head. Since she wasn't broadcasting loud enough to be overheard, he figured there wasn't a lot of method to her thoughts. Musing—that's what Sunder called it. *She's just musing. I wonder about what?*

"Don't worry. I Walk Alone."

Walk alone? He knew from her poise and tone of voice that her declaration was meant to answer his question. Walk alone? "What does that mean?"

Lyndsy scowled. "It means I don't need protecting. I'm not a stupid, soft human!"

Jan was getting used to her changing moods. He simply raised an eyebrow, remembering her actions on Blood Plain "No," he whispered, "you are very brave."

Lyndsy's anger vanished in an instant as pride swelled within her. She hadn't felt so suddenly elated since her foster father had looked up from one knee and conceded her the victory. Shoulders back, chin in the air, she folded her arms beneath bare breasts. Perhaps she could impress his some more and make him smell like desire again. By the Vow! Where were these stray thoughts coming from? Still, it was a rather good idea.

January watched her chin tilt back down. Her magenta eyes seemed to glow beneath her snow-white brows. He watched as her personality reached out to embrace him. The look in her eyes made him feel like she was sizing him up for dinner. Nervous, he turned away, trying to think of something to say. Rich, husky laughter rippled across his personality like heat waves from a fire. With a quick glance back, he saw her mischievous grin and once again wondered what in the name of Song she was thinking. "Uh, are you hungry?"

Wrong!

Lyndsy licked her lips and growled. "Starved!"

Jan turned away to fetch the fruit she had gathered for lunch. Lyndsy's laughter followed behind. When he turned back toward her, he was vastly relieved to see her attention back on the staff.

Jan set the fruit by her side. He watched her heft the staff and test its weight. Finally, realizing she was making a weapon, he remembered the bow. "There's a bow. I don't know why I brought it. Can you use it?"

She looked dumbfounded. "That bow?" she asked, pointing at it.

Not again! "Uh, yeah."

Instant anger filled her eyes. "No! I can't use *that* bow?" She looked away again and didn't say anything else.

She was angry again, but Jan realized that, for some reason, her feelings were hurt. Why? "Lyndsy, I—"

"No!" she yelled. "I can't use *that* bow!"

He wanted to say something. He didn't have the slightest idea about what had upset her. He took a step back and whispered, "I'm sorry I hurt your feelings. I want you to understand that I would never do that to you on purpose." Turning away, he walked to the pile of wraps and absently looked through them. Three extra wraps. *How are we going to carry this stuff?*

"January!"

Jan whirled, hand on hilt. "What? What is it?"

She ran to him and threw her arms around his waist. Jan dropped everything and held her close. Oh! Did she smell and feel good! Then, he realized with a shock that she was crying.

"Lyndsy, tell me what's wrong."

"Don't leave me!"

Leave you? He quickly understood that she had seen him packing and, for some reason, thought he was mad or upset or something. But why? Even as he asked himself that question, her unconscious thought process sent images running through her mind. Mythit trained, he found it an easy thing to see what she was thinking.

He saw that, in the last two days, he had shown her more affection and kindness than any were had ever given her. He saw himself through her eyes, walking to the front of her pack on Blood Plain. He was protecting her pack. He watched again as Lyndsy, calculatingly, ripped the head off of the evil Mythit. True, she had wanted the other black Mythits to fear her, but that had not been her main intent. She had been trying to prove herself to him. Why, he didn't know, but she wanted him to think her brave. She was showing him that she was willing to put her life on the line for the good of the pack.

"Lyndsy," Jan whispered, "look at me." He turned her head up and their eyes met. "I want you with me."

Jan blinked as the fear of loneliness in her personality faded away. *She's so emotional,* Jan thought. *I read her like a scroll.* "I want you to realize, from time to time, I will say things that might offend you. I don't do it on purpose. When I do, I want you to tell me why I said it wrong, OK?"

Lyndsy flushed with what Jan took to be embarrassment. "You really don't know about the bow?"

Jan could see it took effort to make that a question and not a challenge. "No, Lyndsy. I really don't."

"*That* bow belongs to *the* cleric."

Jan missed the emphasis on her words as sudden flashes of memory ran behind his eyes. He saw pictures of a time long past. The bow was a holy weapon, created by the Blue Wizard and wielded by Myril, Lyre's first High Cleric. The vision faded as quickly as it had come. Jan wondered how she had known. He didn't ask. She was smiling again and had her arms wrapped around his waist. He stroked her shaggy, white hair and set his chin on the top of her head. All was once again right with the world.

They gathered their things and started walking. "This is going to take too long," Jan said thoughtfully. "Can you ride a horse?"

She gave him a scathing glare that disappeared instantly. The change was so fast, he wasn't even sure he had seen it. She said, straight-faced, "A wolf travels just as fast as a horse." She made the words a statement, a question, and a suggestion that she obviously preferred.

Jan laughed. "You're right, of course. I know. Let's wrap this stuff up. I'll change to a horse. You put the pack on me. Then you change, and off we go."

Lyndsy gazed up at him with narrowed eyes. "A horse?"

"Yes. When you put the pack on my back, be careful not to touch the staff." Jan wrapped the various objects and left a long wrap he thought would wrap around the belly of a horse. With a self-conscious glance at Lyndsy, he turned away and stripped.

Lyndsy watched Jan turn his back and strip. She knew he wasn't trying to be offensive, but it still hurt. She was sixteen and still a virgin. Her shame was doubled by the cruel jests of the young bitches in her foster father's pack. If she had not become She Who Walks Alone, she would have killed herself. Jan had said to tell him if he said something wrong. Should she say something about his actions?

She had worked herself up to speak when Jan suddenly vanished. A large sorrel stallion appeared in his place. "January?" She leaned forward and sniffed his scent. "January!" Lyndsy leaned back and ran her hand along his powerful shoulder and side. With a mischievous grin, she caressed his rump and laughed as Jan blew and awkwardly backed away.

Still laughing, she picked up the pack and strapped it around him. She felt him watching her and smelled what seemed to be disapproval. Her smile vanished. Her head hung in rejection. *He would never want me*, she thought with great sadness. *At least he isn't mean to me.* She thought about his words when he was holding her. *He said he wants me with him.*

Lyndsy stripped and shoved her wrap beneath the ties of the pack. Looking at Jan through narrowed eyes, she thought, *Maybe I'm doing something wrong. How would I know?*

Jan heard her thoughts and puzzled over her words. Before he got very far, she started the change. He forgot all about it, as he was forced to mind his senses.

They traveled all day and far into the night. Chasing each other became a wonderful game they played with equal fervor. They finally stopped by a stream and made a camp. Jan found that, this time, her change did not scream at his senses quite as badly as before. He wondered if he was just getting used to it. Too tired to realize any sexual innuendoes, they lay side by side next to their little fire and fell asleep.

They reached the northern shore of Light Lake at noon. It was a lovely scene. The pine trees that circled her girth stopped at her white, sandy shore. The Mirshol Mountains rose over their pointed tops creating a wall of cliffs in the background. The overall aura of the smooth, glassy lake was bright and tranquil.

Jan changed shape and caught the pack as it fell. For once he didn't jump to put on his wrap. Instead, he pulled the staff from the pack and headed out into the water. A quick look showed him that Lyndsy sat on the beach, still in wolf shape, watching him.

He felt power! There was a store of strength here that he didn't understand. The last time he had visited the lake was a season ago with Jasmine and Flower. He hadn't noticed the sensation at the time. Now, his hair tingled as the clear, fluorescent water lapped at his body. Once again, he saw that strange aura of white light that held no meaning for him. He realized it was a part of the forest. He instinctively knew that it played a binding role in the weaving of the spell, but he had no reference for it.

The gems in the staff came to life as the Three Sisters appeared. They stood on the surface of the water in front of him. He asked about the strange white aura. Sapphire was about to speak when Star put up a hand to silence her.

"January, this is a sacred thing. It is something you must realize without being told."

Sapphire winked at Jan and turned to Star. "You speak well, sister." She looked back to Jan and smiled. "Do not let it worry you. Indeed, the answer to that question resides within you. You simply need to find the right question."

What?!? He spoke with mock sarcasm. "Wizards and Mythits have contests in speaking in riddles. You should join them. I see great possibilities!"

Rose did a startled double take. Star frowned and gazed at him uncertainly. Sapphire burst into joyful laughter.

Star shook her head and looked toward the shore. With another quick glance at January, she floated away. Sapphire smiled brilliantly, leaned forward, and cupped Jan's cheek with one hand. She gazed into his eyes for a moment and then turned and followed after Star.

Rose moved forward and stood directly in front of him. Her expression was hard. Because of her stern appearance, her words startled him. "You do well to choose a companion as true as the lady were. I'm sure you do not realize this yet, but she and I are warriors by nature. I see in her an ability of good judgment. Also, she is a Werewoman Who Walks Alone. She is as fine a staff to have at your back as a dozen trained fighters." Rose paused and looked straight into his ice-blue eyes. She nodded approvingly. "And she is swiftly falling in love with you."

Rose floated off toward the shore, leaving Jan standing waist-deep in the water. *She loves me?* Jan let his thoughts run. He closed his eyes and felt the warm sunshine on his shoulders. Oh! It's good to be alive!

He finally turned and made his way back to shore. He saw that Lyndsy was standing out of the water's reach, waiting. She had changed shape and dressed. As Jan started up the beach, she came to him and tied his wrap around his waist.

"I don't know why you want to wear this except that it feels so soft—specially with *your* body!"

Jan was about to speak, but he caught the underlying seriousness of her expression and decided against it.

After she tied his wrap, she said, in a stern voice. "Now, you are going to tell me everything."

Jan stepped back. "What?"

"Sapphire said—"

"Sapphire? When did you see Sapphire?"

"Just now while you were talking to the Red One."

"Have you seen them before?"

Lyndsy looked down as though she had just been caught hunting rabbits instead of standing guard. "Yes."

She looks guilty of something, Jan realized. "OK. This is one of those times. There's nothing wrong with being able to see them."

Lyndsy was suddenly furious. "I thought she was your *first!* I didn't understand until she told me!" Her glare softened, but her tone was acid. "Never mind. I guess it's just one of those *woman* things." Lyndsy kicked some sand and finished in frustration. "*I* really wouldn't know!"

"My first?"

"Don't change the subject!" She turned, and with a saucy sway of hips, walked into the shade. Pointing at the ground with one slim, white finger, she yelled, "Come here!"

January meekly obeyed, not knowing what else to do. She pointed again as he drew near. "Sit!"

Jan knew by her tone of voice that this was the way that she would talk to a pup, but he still didn't know what else to do, so he sat.

"Now, you will tell me of the Mythits—the ones you know, not those stinking, nasty, filthy, evil creatures on the Plain of Blood. Then you will tell me where we are going and why." She folded her arms beneath her breasts and started tapping her foot.

"Lyndsy, why are you so angry?" He raised a hand as she started to rant and rave. "I'll tell you everything. I promise. First, tell me why you're so angry."

"January, I'm not mad at you. I'm angry at myself. *Now talk!*"

Women! "All right. I came to Mirshol about four seasons ago …"

"That's better," she stated.

He knew there was something else on her mind. She seemed to be weighing decisions.

"Now tell me where we go."

"The School of Prayer."

She looked instantly frightened and excited at the same time. "Why?" she almost shouted.

She wanted a certain answer, but Jan couldn't figure it. Then something snapped into place. Sapphire and Star had said something to her. What? "To meet a woman in the House of Song, a cleric."

Lyndsy clapped her hands and caught her breath. January watched, amazed, as her personality turned clear white. A huge tear welled in her eye and rolled down her cheek. Her aura blasted right through him, and he could not stop it. Jan rose to his feet and pulled her into his embrace. He held her as though he would never let her go. She raised her face to look into his eyes and reached up to wrap her arms around his neck. Her sudden peace of mind made Jan realize that something had been building in her since they'd met. Now, at least, the tension was gone. She was radiant! Jan looked deep into her wide-set magenta eyes. "Lyndsy, you are so beautiful it's hard to believe you're real."

She gave him a sidelong look of great disbelief. "Do you *really* like the way I look?"

"I wouldn't want you any other way."

Lyndsy laid her cheek against Jan's chest and smiled. She was on her tiptoes, trying to get as close as possible. Jan held her tighter and, stooping ever so slightly, rested his chin on the top of her head.

They left Light Lake after dark. The trees around Light Lake reminded Jan of the Shattered Orchard Forest. Fruit trees grew in abundance, and before long they had a good supply of food.

"I know it would be wrong to hunt here, but I *crave* red meat!"

Jan laughed. "I know what you mean. I haven't eaten anything but fruits, nuts, and fish since I got here."

They pressed on all night. Jan swiftly realized that Lyndsy was now in a bigger hurry than he was.

They reached the southern tip of the Mirshol Mountain Range at dawn. Jan knew, from reading various maps, that they had traveled over thirty leagues. That was a long way, and even as young as they both were, they were weary. They found a pool surrounded by elm and oaks and wasted little time changing shape and jumping in.

Jan groaned. "Oh, my feet are sore."

"Yours," Lyndsy exclaimed. "A wolf takes twice as many steps as a horse! I think my feet are gonna fall off!"

Jan laughed and splashed water in her direction. "Come on, my footsore little wolf, let's get some sleep."

Lyndsy turned around and pushed herself up and out of the water. She stood up and arched her back in a luxurious stretch. Feet slightly spread, hands on hips, she leaned back farther and shook the water from her shaggy white hair.

Jan stopped to watch her. She stalked to the trees and picked up both of their wraps. Turning on one heel, she came back to the water and jumped in. Jan shook his head and shivered. The goose bumps on his skin had nothing to do with the cold.

He watched the sunrise over the trees and finally climbed out of the water. An idea made him smile. He quickly went into the trees in search of some flowers that Lyndsy had been particularly fond of. He gathered two handfuls and came back to their camp. She was just finishing washing the wraps and once again climbed the bank. Jan stashed the flowers and lay down. He stilled his breathing and let his senses spread. He insinuated himself into the fine web of the peaceful, still morning.

Lyndsy glanced at his still form as she hung the wraps on a low, thin branch. When she had them spread, she walked to his side and knelt down. His even breathing and lack of conscious scent made her think he was already asleep. She leaned closer and sniffed at his long blond hair. *By the Vow! You smell so good! You fine man, do you really like me? Would you ever want to do that with me? I'm were, not good enough for a human. At least let me stay by you. That's all I ask.*

He kept his eyes closed and listened as she lay by his side. Once again, her breath tickled his ear, and then she kissed him on the cheek. All of Sunder's illusions were nothing compared to the battle he fought at that moment.

He waited until he heard the even breathing of sleep. Then he got up, found the flowers, and started a simple extraction—something Jasmine had shown him.

Jan woke late in the afternoon. He rolled onto his side and watched Lyndsy sleep. She looked so small! With her like this, Jan felt an overwhelming urge to protect her. He remembered Rose's words. *She and I are warriors by*

nature. What had Rose meant when she'd said, *This is a Werewoman Who Walks Alone?* It had almost sounded like a title.

He stood, stretched, and walked over to the tree to put on his wrap. With a huge grin, he walked back to her side. "Wake up Lyndsy."

Her eyes popped open. "Where?" She flushed scarlet. "Oh, I was dreaming!"

"Oh?" Jan asked. "Was it about me?"

"Yes," she said, surprised. "How did you know?"

He gave her a closed look and grinned mischievously. "You were saying, 'Oh, January, kiss me again!'"

Jan couldn't suppress his laughter. He had come close to the mark, and he knew it. Lyndsy got up in a huff, but Jan saw that she was smiling.

She walked to the trees and stopped. Sniffing the air, she reached out and grabbed the wrap. Lyndsy bunched it up and put it to her face as she breathed in the rich scent of forest wildflowers that January had rewashed her wrap in. She turned back to him, and he could see that it was well worth the effort. She was emanating so much affection he caught his breath.

Lyndsy tied on her wrap and fairly jumped into his arms. "Oh January, thank you for being so kind to me!"

13

TERROR TRAIL

Be it curse or blessing, it made no difference. As the Three removed the gems from their settings, the action caused all of Lyre's magic to fall into sleep. Even as Lyndsy found January in the clearing with his newly made stave, they once again became animate. Tendrils of suggestion ran far and wide, searching for victims. So it was with Terror Trail.

Dagdor the Black cursed the path from the One School to the Blood Plain Wizards Watch. Dagdor was the most powerful of the Seven, Lord of Demons, and father to Melody the Black. During the dark of the moon on a midwinter night, he bestowed the path with a guardian. The waking of the gems allowed the guardian to renew his vigil.

January and Lyndsy reached Terror Trail in the hour of sunset. They traveled the last half hour in growing apprehension. Jan had insisted they travel in human form. If they had not, things might have turned out far worse.

Jan could not suppress his growing dread. When he caught his first glimpse of the trail, he fell to his knees. He could not understand what was happening to him. Lyndsy appeared to feel nothing except concern for him. *Can't she see that?*

The trail was a stench of thick, filthy colors that screamed at his nerves. "I think I'm going to be sick."

Lyndsy helped him as he tried to get back up. Once on his feet, he staggered and fell back down. *Sapphire?* Nothing—no response came. Sweat beaded his brow. He opened his eyes and saw a wicked, clawed hand reaching for him.

The staff didn't even come to mind. January gathered his thoughts and slammed a wall of silence around himself. Paying strict attention to his own aura, he created a mental shield around his personality. The apparition instantly vanished. The thick colors and feelings of terror faded. Leaping to his feet, he walked to the edge of the trail and stood still, glaring at the dirt. He glanced at Lyndsy and wondered why nothing seemed to be happening to her. Very slowly, he allowed his barriers to dissipate.

He could still feel a presence, but now it seemed very distant. He got the impression that whatever *it* was, *it* was now hiding from him. "Come on. Let's get out of here."

They walked the edge of Terror Trail and came to its end at midnight. The Serrinillin Hills rolled out before them. A scream rent the air just as Jan let out a sigh of relief. They started running when they heard another. The red glow of fire led them to a large crest. As they reached the top, they looked down on the last swings of a pitched battle. Eight or nine men wearing old leather jerkins and rusty armor had just ambushed a group of initiates traveling from the School of Prayer.

A huge, burly bandit walked up to an initiate, caught her by the hair, and ripped off her robes with one quick jerk. Lyndsy gave a bloodcurdling scream and charged.

"Damn!" Jan threw down his pack. He caught up to and passed Lyndsy as he drew his sword.

The bandits were startled, but they were ready. Jan leapt at the closest man and attacked. The bandit blocked two strokes before he fell. Turning left, Jan brought his sword around and blocked a stroke that would have taken off the top of his head. This second man was joined by another and then another.

As he blocked and sized up his opponents, he watched from the corner of his eye as Lyndsy came across from the hip and smashed a jaw. Teeth flew. She reversed with a blur of brown staff, and another bandit lost the use of his sword arm.

Jan lunged and caught one bandit between the ribs. Sidestepping, he pushed the body toward one and attacked the other. The Sword of Corillion flashed. Spinning on the ball of one foot, he started a volley of downstrokes. As the man caught the rhythm of Jan's swings, he changed his pace and reversed. The leather-clad fighter crumpled as his guts spilled to the ground.

Jan brought up his sword and held it level across his chest. Smiling at his opponent, he took a step forward.

The last man fled.

Lyndsy heard footsteps and whirled. In one fluid motion, she recognized Jan, made a complete circle, and once again faced the two men. As he stepped up to her side, she stated flatly, "The big one is mine."

The other man glanced from Jan to his downed companions. "Ain't no way!" he also fled. Jan considered going after him, but these people were in immediate need of help.

Lyndsy faked an upthrust. The man brought his sword down to block. Lyndsy reversed, clipping the side of his head. He staggered backward. Lyndsy dropped to one knee and hammered the big man's shin. Jan raised an eyebrow as he heard an audible crunch. Then, hooking her staff behind his other knee, she dropped him to the ground.

Lyndsy rose to her feet and watched him for a brief moment. She waited for him to look at her, and then, with a flick of her wrist, she smashed his nose. Dropping to one knee again, she grabbed him by the hair and made him look in her eyes. "You filthy, stinking animal!" she whispered. "I think I'll rip your heart out and drink your blood!" She smiled down at him. Her teeth were pointed, mouth and nose starting the change.

Jan swallowed hard. "Lyndsy."

As Jan's scent of disgust filled her nose, the anger drained right out of her. Did he really think she was serious? Her jaw muscles bunched and smoothed to normal. She turned to Jan and said carefully, "January, I just wanted him to squirm like he did to her." She felt a rage coming, but she kept her voice quiet. "He would have raped her!"

Lyndsy turned and walked to the initiate cleric. With tentative glances to gauge Jan's reaction, she knelt down and held the frightened woman as she wept. "It's OK now," Lyndsy whispered reassuringly, "I promise. No one is going to hurt you."

Jan glanced back down at the bandit.

"She's a demon!"

Jan smiled tightly. "Oh? You stay here and don't move. If she goes after you alone, I won't be able to stop her. Uh"—Jan looked back to Lyndsy and blew breath between his teeth—"do you understand?"

"Yes!"

Lyndsy felt a flood of relief as January turned to look at her and nodded approval. He wasn't disgusted with her anymore.

January walked back to the top of the hill and picked up his pack. It scared him to think he had just dropped his staff and run off. Just how far could someone get without touching it? He knew that, if someone else did touch it, he would know.

Gazing over the burning wagons, he counted twelve dead guards. They looked too young to be of any worth as guards. It didn't even occur to him that Lyndsy was only sixteen seasons; nor did he think about himself. *It's probably just a formality to have an honor guard between Sanfallin and the school.'*

Jan walked back down the hill and reached Lyndsy's side as she was looking over the survivors. "Are you all right?"

Lyndsy looked down at the blood splattered across her bare breasts. "That's their blood."

That's not what I meant, Jan thought.

Lyndsy heard a moan and glanced at the man still lying on the ground. As she stood and started toward him, he screamed, "Keep her away from me. You promised!"

Lyndsy gave Jan a questioning look.

"I'll tell you later." He turned to the man. "Get up."

"Get her away!"

"Coward!" Lyndsy spat. "Raping defenseless women!" Turning on one heel, she stalked away.

"I never raped a woman before," the man said brokenly. "I don't even know why I'm here!"

Jan thought of the clawed hand reaching down Terror Trail. *I think I do.*

14

A Good Spirit

There was the set number of nine initiates. They were travelling with two families. All of the guards were dead. Only one wagon remained usable. They settled everyone as well as they could and headed back toward the School of Prayer.

Jan and Lyndsy were filthy. Both of them were covered in sweat and blood. The water barrels had been dumped or broken, and what little water remained was needed for drinking. She came to his side as he walked by the wagon. "I know it's probably over, but I'm going ahead to scout the trail."

"Change shape? These people will see you."

Lyndsy looked around and shrugged. "It can't be helped."

Jan called the gems in his staff to life. He wondered what it would take to make Lyndsy invisible. All three gems were well able to supply the power needed, but he had to implement a spell. As he thought, a ray of morning sunlight struck a dewdrop. It sparkled, magnifying the light that touched it.

That might work!

January allowed tendrils of feeling to spread from his mind and cover Lyndsy in a skintight web. With the help of the white gem, he touched the webbing with power and made it opaque. Light couldn't touch her. She faded. "Lyndsy," he whispered, "look at yourself!"

He heard her gasp.

"I think it will last until you're finished looking, but I can't be sure." He glanced around and saw a young boy pulling at his mother's skirts. Jan caught his eye and set a finger to his lips. The boy thought about it for a moment and then grinned back. Jan winked and motioned for him to come and walk by his side.

Lyndsy was a long way off when she started the change. Jan was still very much aware of it. He felt the cooling sensation as she finished and then felt her senses fade away. When she was gone from the area, he looked around to see if anyone else had missed her presence. Caught up in their own misery, still in shock from the bloodbath they had witnessed, they plodded a weary path back to the school, heads drooping. No one had.

❦

They stopped at sunset. January watched the initiates feed the horses and turned to scan the horizon.

"January."

Jan turned in surprise and heard Lyndsy snicker.

"Are you ready to come back?"

Jan felt Lyndsy wrap her arms around his neck and pull him down. She pressed herself against him and gave him a kiss he wouldn't soon forget. After she squeezed him again, she let go and stepped back. "Now I'm ready."

"Come on." They walked away from the camp. Jan removed the spell. "Where's your wrap?"

"In the bundle with the water gourds. Bring two. I guess I should wear a top to cover my breasts. I overheard two women talking about me, and I really don't want to offend them."

He started away and then turned back. "You know, you don't have to sneak up on me just to kiss me."

For some reason, she took that very seriously. Her personality turned pale pink with just a hint of that strange white outline. Jan had the feeling he had just said something entirely different.

"I don't?"

He raised an eyebrow and smiled. "No, you don't. You can kiss me anytime you want to."

Jan watched an aura do something he had never seen before. He blinked as her inner light turned to pastel rainbows. He shook his head and blinked. Turning away, he went to get the wraps. When he came back, he was instantly kissed. She stepped back, caught the corner of the first wrap, and started to put it on. That's when Jan noticed what he had missed before. "You're clean!"

She grinned up at him. "Help's on the way."

"Don't change the subject! Where's the water?"

"I went all the way to the School of Prayer." She gave him a mischievous grin. "I had to wash, or they would have smelled me."

It registered. He gave her a sideways look. "What, exactly, did you do?"

"Well, there was … I mean … Uh, promise you won't get mad."

"Lyndsy, what did you do?"

She looked down at her toes and mumbled, "I went into the temple. There was a woman kneeling at the altar. I …"

"What?"

"I whispered in her ear. I told her I was a good spirit and that I had seen a wagon train ambushed and that she should send help." Hesitantly, she looked back up.

"You're kidding."

She shook her head.

Jan burst into laughter. He hadn't laughed that hard since the last time the Mythits had held him down and tickled him.

Lyndsy grinned. "I couldn't quit laughing either. I almost cracked up inside the temple. I barely made it out, but I think I scared some people in the courtyard."

"That's great! I can't wait to see the look on Sunder's face when I tell him this one!"

"He already knows."

Lyndsy was surprised when Jan just raised an eyebrow at her statement and said, "Tell me how it happened."

"When I walked through the outer gate, he appeared in front of me. He said he followed me into the temple. Jan, he said if he died tomorrow, he would be happy because now he's seen everything!" Lyndsy waited for Jan to quit laughing again, and continued, "January, you didn't tell me *who* Benjamin is."

Lyndsy's tone of voice made Jan wonder. He said, "Seer, Benjamin is the Seer of Lake Town."

"January, my people *know* him. To us he is He Who Sees All. He is our witness. The were have a legend that, when we have paid the price of Lyre's trust, He Who Sees All will help to free us from the Vow. January," Lyndsy said pleadingly, "Sapphire told me I would help to free the were from the Vow of Blood Plain. To us, it is called the Plain of Hope. January, he has to go to the land of my people with the high cleric. Please, let it be!"

January caught her up in his arms, compelled by her longing, and held her close. "Lyndsy, if I can make it happen I will."

"Give me the bow."

"What? I thought you couldn't use it."

"I can't, but it needs to belong to me."

"Why?"

"You'll see."

15

SAMANTHA

They continued their march at sunrise. Before they had traveled very far, a group of riders came into view. Jan called a halt, and they simply waited for the riders to approach. Twenty fighters led a train of supplies and extra horses. With swift efficiency, they comforted those in need.

The troop leader called January to his side and asked for details of the ambush. Jan told him everything he could. As he spoke, the leader's gaze returned again and again to the Sword of Corillion. He was sure the man recognized the description of the inlay on the hilt. By the time they were finished speaking, the man emanated so much distrust toward him that January wanted to laugh. Still trying to keep a straight face, he led the leader to the captured bandit.

"You will pay dearly for this." The leader called two fighters to his side and directed them to bind the wounded prisoner in chains. "These men will take him straight to the School of Fighters. I promise you, he will be fairly tried and executed!"

Jan left the leader with his men and went in search of Lyndsy. As he walked away, he felt the man staring at his back. *I wonder where he stole that sword?*

Jan rolled his eyes at the thought and kept walking. He turned the corner around a supply wagon and stopped. Lyndsy was on one knee. Benjamin stood before her.

"He Who Sees All, I greet you in the name of my people."

Jan watched Benjamin nod in acknowledgment. *Does he know what she is?* Jan walked to her side and felt her discomfort. She hid it well, but he could see she was in awe of Benjamin. He reached for her hand, and she gladly clung to him. He felt some of her tension release, but she was anxious. Still, he was happy she found comfort in his presence.

Benjamin noticed it also. "January, you look like you've been rolling in the dirt on Blood Plain."

The comment surprised him. However, Lyndsy laughed delightfully, and Jan realized his words had been directed at her. *So,* Jan thought, *he does know.*

Benjamin smiled at Lyndsy's laughter. He raised an eyebrow at Jan and said, "I think we can get two horses and ride ahead. First, though, I think you would rather wash."

"Let's go ahead and go. I have an idea."

They found two horses and walked them away from the wagons. When no one was looking, Jan cloaked Lyndsy in a spell. She changed shape and ran ahead.

When they started away from the initiate caravan, Benjamin spoke. "I have some interesting news. The woman I sought is the high cleric. January, she can't be over twenty-five seasons old. I do not know what Sunder has taught you concerning the School of Prayer, but to be that young and already the high cleric is, at the least, uncommon. We have talked much. What I say now is under strict restraint. Samantha, the high cleric, is a Vainian."

January reined in. *Vainian? No way! Nobody trusts a Vainian! High cleric? Why? What is she trying to do?*

"January?"

He turned; he hadn't realized he'd stopped.

As Benjamin started forward, he continued, "I know exactly what you're thinking. Remember, I have the sight. Sunder and I have spoken of this too. She is the high cleric of the School of Prayer. Only the king in Wizards Veil holds as much power and sway. Maybe. Yet, I see—she sits in council and serves Lyre faithfully.

"She spoke to me about the veil around Mirshol. She said that, sometime during the day when we first met, an unusual power shimmered through the school. She said it came from the direction of Mirshol. She didn't say it in so many words because something in her life has taught her caution. Nevertheless, I see that she knows what happened.

"Sunder got there the very next day and told me you'd accomplished your task. Sunder wanted to see her. We went together to talk to her. He went hidden; I suppose he wanted to study her before he made himself known. As he walked through the door, she turned directly toward him and smiled. She said, 'Hello, I am called Samantha. Will you not show yourself?'

"January, she is wise. She knows nothing about the cave or your staff, but she knows about you. She knows that we wait for you. She asked me to go with the fighters and tell you my thoughts before she meets you. She desires greatly that you trust her."

They rode on in silence as January absorbed Benjamin's words. After a long time, Jan looked back and saw that they had left the party far behind. Motioning for Benjamin to stop, he dismounted.

Jan uncapped a canteen and reached for his staff. Tendrils of feeling spread outward. He touched the green-yellow flat grass of the hill country. Allowing his senses to burrow in the rocky soil, he was told a tale of rodents, lizards, and snakes. Then the music of a fresh spring beneath his feet brought a slight smile to his lips. With one foot, he knocked over the canteen and let it soak into the soil. The bubbling mirth of the underground spring answered his call with a clarity that amazed him.

"January!"

Jan let his mind return. He allowed himself the pleasure of once again feeling the vitality of the grass before he opened his eyes.

A gushing fountain created a pool beneath his feet. Benjamin was watching the glowing staff in awe. Lyndsy's presence let him know she had been there too. With a sigh, Jan set aside the staff and stripped. Standing in the middle of the spring, he washed the dried blood and sweat from his body.

Lyndsy jumped into the water and drenched herself. Benjamin and January laughed to see wet paw prints appear on the ground. She paused and shook her shaggy coat. They watched drops of water fly.

"Come here, Lyndsy." He heard her pad toward them. He smiled when she jumped up, setting her paws on his chest, and licked his face. "Lyndsy," he whispered, "I want you to remain unseen until I'm sure of this high cleric. If no one knows you're with me, no one will know it when you're not. Understand?"

She licked his face again.

The School of Prayer consisted of three houses. The House of Prayer, the House of Thought, and the House of Song. The major house, The House of Prayer, was in all respects twice the size of the two minor houses, each of which appeared to have been carved from a perfect crystalline cube.

The House of Thought faced the House of Song. Both minor houses touched corners with the House of Prayer. Fifty yards from the ground, a walkway spanned the two hundred-yard distance between the two minor houses. At the center of the walkway, a huge spiral staircase reached to the ground.

A wall fifty feet high and ten feet thick surrounded the area of the school. The inside area of that wall was a half league square. In the southern face of the wall, the only entrance to the school, stood a single arch, thirty feet high and twenty feet wide.

As they rode through the arch, Jan was momentarily struck blind by a brilliant, white flash. After his vision cleared, he glanced around and realized Benjamin had experienced the same thing. However, the effect of *the light* to the seer's mind was far less. Gazing back up to the school, he saw it appeared to have a personality of its own. *It seems alive, the same way Light Lake is alive*!

The ride to the courtyard took them straight up the main road through the school's open market. Jan was awed by the hundreds of shops that lined the main road. The market square in Window had been a rough ring of portable tents and wagons. Only a few shops sat by the wealthier part of Window, and they were nowhere near the market square. These were all permanent structures, wood and brick stores with glass panes almost ten feet high. He wondered if everyone in the school was rich. Did they allow common people in their brightly painted, expensive-looking stores? Finally, they reached the courtyard and delivered their horses to the stables.

A seemingly endless walk through the House of Prayer brought them to a large foyer. Jan gazed around the hall in wonder. Beautiful tapestries and paintings adorned the walls. One tapestry caught his eye, and he moved toward it.

Nine female initiates to the House of Prayer stood on the edge of a battlefield. Dressed in white silks, each girl wore her top wrap pinned at the shoulder with a golden broach. Unlike any other cleric, these initiates wore long silver daggers strapped to their hips. Jan recognized them, although he didn't know how. They were the Golden Leaves—Virgin Healers. Blessed in ancient times to use great healing powers during the time of war, they had come to be at the same time that the School of Hope, or the One School, split in bitter feud. It was said that, one day, the Golden Leaves would rise again. January shivered as he considered Lyre once again at war.

He turned his head and forgot all about the Golden Leaves. A statue of a man, carved into the finest white marble, seemed to reach out and draw him forward. Jan stopped at the foot of the statue and gazed up at the flowing beard and deep-set eyes. "Myril," the inscription read, "First High Cleric of the School of Hope."

"I don't understand. He looks so familiar."

Benjamin stepped up behind him and set one hand on Jan's shoulder. Thoughts flashed through his mind. Once again, Jan beheld the White Wizard on Blood Plain. He turned to Benjamin in surprise.

"Don't say it. Just know and accept it."

Jan took a breath and nodded. He should have known. Maybe he did already know; it just hadn't registered yet. It seemed so right that the White Wizard would be a cleric. He wondered why he hadn't thought about it before.

"Come. You will have as much time as you wish to explore the school. I grow weary. Let me show you our rooms."

Benjamin led them down a long hall and out into the night air. They were standing on a balcony thirty feet from the ground. The middle of the House of Prayer held a large square garden. It was awesome. Pools and fountains ran from a central spring. Oak and elm stood side by side.

"It's so ... I don't know, quiet and peaceful. But I feel power."

Benjamin nodded in understanding. "Yes, this is a place of great power."

The old seer led them back into another hallway and into his room. Jan saw a yellow and orange flash as Flower jumped into his arms. "Flower, what are you doing here?"

"Oh, I wanted to see the House of Song. So, when I overheard Sunder say he was going to the School of Prayer, I *convinced* him to take me too."

"Convince Sunder?" Jan asked dubiously. "How?"

"Easy! I told him, if he didn't bring me, I'd go by myself!"

Jan grinned. "Yep, that would do it."

Lyndsy growled. Flower turned her head and looked around. She squinted and gasped as the white wolf registered in her mind.

"Lyndsy, this is Flower."

Flower dropped to the ground. As Flower approached, Lyndsy growled again.

"Lyndsy," Jan asked, "what are you so angry about?"

She's jealous. Can't you see that?

No, Jan thought, *I can't even see her.*

Flower glanced back. *You can't see her?*

Jan thought about it. *Why can't I see her?*

Flower took another step forward. "You are the mostest exquisitely lovely creature I have ever seen in my life!"

Lyndsy cocked her head, not at all sure she wanted to like this Mythit Jan seemed so fond of.

"Don't be angry, please. January is like my brother, and I love him!"

Lyndsy took one look into glowing Mythit eyes and felt instantly foolish. She didn't really know why she had been so angry. January had given her the right to kiss him. She knew good and well that Jan didn't truly understand what he had done. She just wanted it so badly!

The anger drained right out of her. She padded to Flower and looked her over. Flower had bright orange and yellow stripes that ran from top left to bottom right. The more she looked, the more she decided to like her. Just looking at the little Mythit made her want to giggle.

"Lyndsy, come with me. There is a joining room." He walked through the door and Lyndsy followed. As Jan shut the door, he lifted her spell. This time, he watched closely as she changed shape.

If she could do if faster, it wouldn't hurt so bad.

When she was finished, she tried to stand and Jan had to catch her. "Lyndsy, you must be dead on your feet!" He considered the distance they had traveled. As he added it up, his eyes grew wide. "One hundred leagues in three days. Damn! Lyndsy, are you all right?"

She looked up into his ice-blue eyes and pulled him down for a kiss.

Jan caught her behind the knees and carried her to the bed. She kept her arms around his neck and pulled him down with her.

"Stay with me."

Jan looked at her. She was a figure from a dream. "Lyndsy, you are the most beautiful woman I have ever seen."

She smiled against his chest, and mumbled, "I'll fight for you."

Jan wasn't sure how she meant that. He pulled the cover over both of them and rolled Lyndsy onto her side. She rolled halfway back, draped one leg across his thighs, and planted her head in the middle of his chest. Before Jan could push her unruly hair away from his nose, she was fast asleep.

Jan woke at dawn. Two robes were draped over a chair. He slipped out of bed and dressed. The sunlight drew him to a window, where he spied Sunder, Jasmine, and Flower sitting by the central pool. Flower felt his gaze and turned. She jumped up and whirled as she danced across the grass. Without a second thought, she scaled the vine-covered lattice to get to the window.

"Flower! This is a temple," Jan admonished. "You don't go around dancing and climbing the walls!"

"Yeah," Flower exclaimed, refusing to understand, "they never even walk on the grass. I'll bet they don't even know what a picnic is!"

Jan sighed and rolled his eyes.

"Go," Flower said. "Sunder wants to talk to you."

Jan walked out the door and down the hall. A tall woman in white robes stood waiting at the bottom of the steps. She was waiting for him, and he knew it. As he walked toward her, he asked, "Who are you?"

"I am the first servant of the house. I am to bring a young man to the office of the high cleric. You are he."

Jan walked down the steps and tried to look into the hood that hid the woman's face. "How do you know I am the one?"

"The description fits you."

Jan touched her mind and was momentarily taken aback to see an image of himself. Puzzled, he said, "OK, let's go."

He followed her through hallways that led to the lower levels of the House. With swift words, Jan used the Voice of Command. "Tell me about the high cleric!"

"I want you ..." She turned and recovered her composure. Jan was about to speak when she interrupted him. "Please, wait."

Jan could now read her. *I am the first servant of the house.* Those words were spoken in truth. He spread his hands and motioned her forward. "After you."

She led him down a flight of stairs that led to a wall. The high cleric touched it and spoke a word. The wall moved silently inward.

Jan stepped into the high cleric's office. As he gazed around the room, he was too moved to speak. Aesthetic value? What an amazing office! The crystalline ceiling was the bottom of the pond in the center of the garden. Exotically colored fish swam in lazy patterns over the top of his head. He turned with great effort and focused on the high cleric.

Sudden anger filled him. "Why didn't you just say you were the high cleric? Would you have me distrust you from the first moment we met?"

She threw back the hood and dropped her cloak over the arm of a chair. If January had been looking at her features, he would have seen a very tall young woman with long blond hair. He would have surely noticed blue eyes that were so pale one would think the color unreal, a kind of blue that one might see reflected through ice.

Samantha should have seen the mirrored image of straight nose and brow. She should have realized the startling ice-blue of his eyes. She did not. The greatest fear of her life stood before her. He was the only person on the face of Lyre that had to accept her on trust. To her, nothing else mattered. This day had been coming, and she knew it well. For the sake of her soul, she was required to measure up. "I wanted to see you and speak to you before I revealed myself."

"Why?"

Samantha sat down and steepled her fingers under her chin. "Please, be patient with me. I have my own reasons to watch my back, look twice at shadows, and make sure all they are, are shades of gray."

She was wide open. Jan realized she was purposely allowing him to see the truth in her.

"I want you to know, you are the only *man* I ever met who knows about the Voice of Command. They teach the principals of the mind work within the House of Thought, but they know not what it is that they teach." Samantha drew a quick breath. "What is your name!"

She used the Voice well. Jan let the force of her words wash through him. He waited a moment and then answered calmly, "My name is January."

As though she expected him to resist her strength, she nodded acknowledgment of his evasion. "January. I know a prophesy that concerns a young man named January."

"Oh?" January felt doom creep up behind him. Time seemed to stand still. His senses spread protectively around the room. He became aware of the high cleric's personality. She was so full of white light he wondered how she contained it. *What?*

Jan closed his eyes and breathed. *There's that aura again!* He thought about the spell around Mirshol, the beautiful personality of Light Lake, and the brilliant flash as he entered the school's main gate. *What is it?*

January opened his eyes. "Tell me this prophesy."

The high cleric bowed her head for a moment as if gathering strength. When she looked back up, there was a fierce determination in her ice-blue eyes. "First, you must know this. I *am* the high cleric. My word concerning the School of Prayer is law. I swear to you on my life that, if I can be of service to you, I will.

> He will be strong,
> but in need of faith.
> He will be wrong,

taught of the Wraith.
Strength of a dragon,
weak as a fawn,
nothing but rags on,
color of dawn.
Surely he'll fail,
lonely his trail.
Too soon to battle,
uncaring of harm,
bare bones rattle,
cut off his right arm.

Jan watched again as a man in black leather walked toward him. *It is said of the one who will come that he will come to battle too soon and cut off his right arm. I will test this prophesy of My Lovely Lady.*

Jan sat down. He wondered where she had heard this so-called prophesy. It had the stench of an evil curse. He hoped he could trust this woman. From the way she held herself wide open to his mental inspection, he knew she could not lie to him. "High Cleric, where did you hear this prophesy?"

She hesitated only for an instant. "In a cavern in the Black Mountains on the outskirts of Vanity. It was part of a sacrificial rite."

"What?" Jan leapt to his feet. "How in the name of Song did you get there?"

She looked down at her reflection in the polished oak tabletop. "I grew up there."

Jan fairly shouted, "What were you doing at a sacrificial rite?"

Samantha looked straight into Jan's eyes. "Performing a sacrifice. I was the one holding a young virgin's arms. It was her blood that wrote the runes of the prophesy on the surface of the black marble altar."

"You have a lot of—"

"*Silence!*" Samantha commanded. "You can judge me when you have spent ten seasons in fear of sleep for nightmares' sake. I have looked in the mirror every single day and have slowly learned not to loath and despise myself. I do good work here! You, alone, know this about me.

"I have told Benjamin little, but he understands more than my simple *spoken* words. Please, January," Samantha said in a softer tone, "at the least, take me at face value. If I were trying to deceive the school, would I be answering your questions?"

Jan calmed himself. She was certainly sincere, but there was one thing.

"Now," she said, reading his train of thought, "you are Mythit trained." At his incredulous look, she explained, "It is written in your heart."

Jan gazed at her. *No one could know that.*

"You have heard me speak plainly. If I were evil, would you not know it?"

Jan remembered the personalities of the black Mythits. No, her aura was pure. A thought occurred to him. He created a mental image and projected it into her mind. Her eyes opened wide in recognition, and then she looked away.

"High Cleric," Jan said, walking around the table to stand at her side, "I'm sorry. You should have told me that."

Samantha set her hands flat on her desk and bowed her head. After a moment, she whispered, "When you leave here, I would like to go with you." She looked up again into ice-blue eyes and, for a moment, felt a sense of déjà vu. "Please, call me Samantha."

January simply nodded. What more could he say to the only other human who had walked into Mirshol, bathed in Light Lake, and left the forest sane?

16

The Bow of Myril

Jan returned to Benjamin's room at noon. Sunder and Jasmine sat in the window. Benjamin was sitting at the table reading from a large pile of scrolls.

Sunder turned to gaze at a pot of flowers. *I saw you walk by the garden entrance with Samantha.*

Jan curled his fingers, seemingly inspecting the dirt under his nails. *What do you think of her?*

Sunder glanced at Jasmine and blinked. Jasmine thought, *January, that woman is a marvel. Trust her. Her worth is far greater than you realize.*

"January!" Benjamin exclaimed as he looked up from the scrolls. "I didn't hear you walk in. Hungry?"

Jan felt suddenly weak in the knees. "Hungry? I don't remember the last time I ate. I'm starved!"

You're always hungry!

Benjamin walked to the door and pulled a cord. After a few moments, a servant appeared.

"How may I serve you?"

The old seer said quickly, "This is a special occasion. Roast, I think, should suit us well. Ah, you may serve me further still by bringing a raw steak."

"Raw steak?"

Benjamin nodded. "My young friend is in need of relief from a few painful bruises."

"The house doctor would be happy to see to you."

"Doctor!" Benjamin exclaimed in mock indignation. "I'll have no fancy city doctor working his leeches on my young friend!"

The servant smiled and said in a conspiratorial whisper, "I know how you feel. I don't trust city doctors either!"

After the servant left, Jan eyed Benjamin. "What was that all about?"

Benjamin actually grinned. "Would you have me tell him that there is a hungry werewoman present and in need of sustenance?"

Jan blinked. "I see." He turned to the joining room door and started to walk in.

Don't you dare!

Jan took a hasty step back and looked toward Jasmine. She smiled and shook her head. *Stay out until I'm ready!*

Flower?

Yes. Go away!

Jan shrugged and went to the table. He picked up a scroll and started to read. After a few moments, a feeling of great delight rushed through his senses. He glanced up and saw Benjamin's eyes grow wide. Sunder stood up. A slow, secret smile crossed Jasmine's face, and her red eyes brightened in intensity. He turned his head.

Lyndsy stood in the doorway. She was staring shyly at the floor. She was wearing a white knee-length dress. A wide, soft pink velvet sash encircled her slight waist. Pink silk slippers and gloves shimmered as sunlight reached through the window to embrace her. A large pink rose sat upon her right ear. Her thick, snow-white hair tumbled loose over her shoulders and down her back.

Jan went to her and held out his hand. She reached out and very slowly met his gaze. Jan whispered, "You are the moonlight on the smooth surface of a quiet pond."

She looked startled for a moment, and then she looked away, too embarrassed to speak. Jan saw her glance toward Flower. The Mythit's huge grin spoke volumes. Raising one pink-gloved hand, Jan kissed her open palm.

Lyndsy's personality turned bright red. Jan watched as she gathered courage. She set her shoulders, and with a deliberately defiant look at Jasmine, she wrapped her arms around his neck and pulled him down. She gave him a sound kissing that momentarily took his breath. As she leaned back, she glanced at Flower. Then they both looked toward Sunder and Jasmine.

Jan knew he was missing something. He knew something had just happened that he didn't understand. Even Benjamin stared down at Lyndsy and offered her an approving nod.

Sunder gazed at Jan and was about to say something. Jasmine held up her hand for silence. The tiny pink, red, and white Mythit leapt down from the windowsill and walked to their side. Lyndsy released his hand and faced her squarely.

Jasmine set her hands on her hips and narrowed her glowing red eyes. "You will fight by his side. You will guard his back with your last breath. There will be little time for peace in his life. I see that you understand something of the nature of my foster son and know there is a rough trail ahead of you. Still, this needs to be said. In all things, you will guard and protect him."

Jasmine paused for effect and then shouted, "I will accept nothing less of One Who Walks Alone!" Then she gave Lyndsy a heartwarming smile. "Moonlight! It suits you well."

Jan watched Lyndsy melt beneath Jasmine's forceful personality. He realized she was shaking and almost in tears. Yet she was filled with wonder and gratitude. *What, in the name of Song, is going on here!?*

Lyndsy's eyes opened wide at Jasmine's last words. She held out her hand to Jasmine, and the Mythit took it. "It is as you say," Lyndsy whispered. "By the Vow, it will be as you say."

Jan looked to Sunder, hoping for some kind of explanation. He didn't get it. Then in one fluid motion, Lyndsy whirled and stared at the door.

"What is it?"

Lyndsy ran to the door and threw it open. "Meat!"

Jan laughed as he saw the servant pushing a cart down the hall. Once again, his knees felt weak. "Oh, that smells good!"

Jan grabbed the platter and brought it in. Lyndsy followed with a jug of water and a bowl of fruit. Closing the door, she fairly leapt at the table. Jan watched her glance at the silver lids on the platter. "That one's mine!"

If anyone noticed her devouring her food, no one mentioned it. Jan was just as bad, and this the Mythits were quite used to. From time to time, he would look up from his plate and smile.

Flower gave Jasmine a knowing smile. *Smitten!*

No, thought Jasmine, in mild humor. *Bitten!*

After lunch, they sat and talked about what they had been through in the last twelve days. Benjamin had arrived with little adventure. When he talked about his path around the mountains, Jan asked him about Terror Trail.

Sunder realized January's discomfort and said that it wasn't something to talk about within the walls of the School of Prayer. He cautioned Jan, with a short story about the Red Wizard's temper and the blessing around the school and told him to wait until they were out of *her* presence.

There was a knock at the door. The Mythits faded as Benjamin went to answer it. The high cleric entered. Samantha now wore her robes of office. They were white, trimmed in gold at the sleeves, neck, and feet. A wide gold band circled her waist.

Jan and Lyndsy both noticed the holy symbol embroidered on the waistband and were shocked beyond words. Lyndsy jumped up and ran to the other room. Jan stood still as he gave Sunder and Benjamin questioning looks. Neither one seemed to recognize the congruence.

Samantha had been stunned to silence as she noticed the white skin and red eyes of the slender young woman. She missed all of the attention on her until she snapped back to the present. Turning to Jan, she was about to say, "We should talk," when Lyndsy came back into the room. She held the bow and quiver reverently as she went to stand before the high cleric.

Samantha looked down on this strange girl with white hair and magenta eyes. Her senses were overwhelmed at the suppressed emotion the young woman was feeling.

Lyndsy gazed up at the high cleric filled with hope, longing, and awe. A tear rolled down her cheek. "This is a gift. Please accept it."

Only then did the others in the room realize that the bow was the same as the holy symbol embroidered on the high cleric's waistband. Lyndsy placed the bow and quiver in Samantha's hands. Immediately, it flared to life. Runes, invisible until now, burned white hot.

Benjamin spoke in awe. "The Bane of Death, the Black Dragon!"

The Mythits came within the realm of human vision and approached. Samantha stood holding the bow in a tight grip. She saw, in her mind's eye, an aged cleric in white standing guard behind a blue-robed wizard. A huge, black dragon spit sickening, dark red flames. Blue negated the evil fire with a flick of his wrist. White held the bow, arrow nocked. He pointed it skyward and let the arrow fly. The golden tip sparkled in the sunlight. With a tremendous blast, the dragon trembled in fear. A shower of white sparks fell on the black dragon and caused it obvious pain.

The white-robed man nocked another arrow. The black dragon, cowering, spoke a single word. The wizard in blue nodded once and then pointed to the sky. Only then did Samantha see that the dragon was perched on the edge of the school's roof. With a broken look of defeat, the black dragon took a long look around and then flew away.

Samantha came to herself to see Sunder and Jasmine watching her closely. She looked at Benjamin, January, the girl with red eyes, and a Mythit she had not felt before. They were all gazing at the bow in wonder. Only the two elder Mythits seemed to realize she had experienced something different.

"Why did you pick the bow as your symbol?"

Samantha answered the seer's question. "It is the holy symbol I am most familiar with."

Jan turned and walked into the other room. He felt his staff calling him. He returned a moment later. All three gems were blazing with life. The look on his face commanded silence. He spoke softly. "The bow receives power from the blue gem."

Jasmine shook her head. "You're mistaken."

"No, I'm not wrong. Can't you see the power flowing from the staff to the bow?"

"Yes," Samantha answered.

"No," Sunder said.

Jan looked incredulously at the Mythit. "You can't see that?"

Sunder grinned, nodded in the affirmative, and then said, "Nope."

Samantha said, "I see a web of light flowing between us."

Jan stared at the orange Mythit. "*You* can't see that?"

"Nope."

Jan looked back at Samantha. He caught his breath. "What is that stamp of personality?"

"Personality?" Benjamin asked.

Jan glanced at him. "You!" It was an accusation. "You have it too!"

Flower asked the question almost all of them were thinking. "Which personality are you talking about? We have nine auras going at the same time."

Jan set down the staff. He turned to the high cleric. "Samantha, put down the bow."

She obeyed.

"Lyndsy, come stand by me." Jan pulled her with him away from everyone else. "Sunder, you all have this mark except Lyndsy and me."

Sunder looked closely. *What in the name of Song is he talking about?* After he couldn't find anything, he said, "I don't see anything different. Lyndsy's personality is stronger than everyone else, but I think that's just the way she is."

"I can't explain it," Jan said in defeat. "It's like a white halo out of the corner of my eye. But when I pay direct attention to it, it blends in with everything else."

Jasmine shook her head. "We don't see it."

"It's still there."

Samantha said, "I don't see it anymore."

"I'm losing my mind!"

It was such a heartfelt statement it sent Flower bursting with laughter. "You have the strongest mind I've ever seen."

Sunder laughed. "You mean the hardest head."

Jan threw back his arms, looked up at the ceiling, and yelled, "Ahhh!"

Jasmine raised one white eyebrow. "You'll find an answer. You always have."

Samantha felt a touch of unease in the warmth of the room and turned her attention to the petite young woman. "Sister, what troubles you?"

"High cleric," Lyndsy stammered, "I didn't mean any harm or to be disrespectful. Please don't be angry."

Jan felt waves of guilt coming from her. He reached for her hand, and as they touched, he saw the same scene play over and over in her mind. "Lyndsy," he said reassuringly, "she won't be mad at you."

Samantha tilted her head, curious, and offered a smile.

"I, I was the, uh, I was the one who walked up to you in the temple and told you to send a search party."

"Sister," Samantha said quietly, "you did well. Actually"—she turned to Jasmine—"I thought it was you."

Jasmine acknowledged her words with a slight nod as though she might have been expecting it.

Samantha reached back down and picked up the bow. "What has just happened here makes the reason for my visit all the more important. January, are you familiar with the name Melody, sometimes known as the Black?"

"Always known as the Black!" Sunder said in disgust.

Jan picked up the staff. With a glance at Sunder, he answered, "Yes, I know the name."

Samantha steeled herself for a barrage of questions and continued, "I have seen the inner chambers of the stronghold of Lince Posh. She has in her possession a great number of magical artifacts. She seemed to think the day was near when they would come alive with power."

To Samantha's surprise, no one asked. She finished quietly, "Because of what we have just seen, I think that day has come."

Jasmine turned to Jan. "She is right."

"What can we do about it?"

"I don't know," Samantha said. "But if I understand the significance of your staff, I think you could do something about it."

"I don't even know its capabilities."

Sunder wrinkled his nose and gazed from Lyndsy to Jan. "Now is as good a time as any to start learning."

Jan also glanced at Lyndsy. "Well, there is something I wanted to try."

Sunder, tilting his head toward Lyndsy, repeated, "Now is as good a time as any."

Jan scowled at Sunder. *How does he always seem to know what I've been thinking?* He pulled out his little pouch of gold coins and jewels. With two fingers, he plucked out a slim gold chain. The staff came alive in his hand. Jan thought the process through. A small amount of force, triggered by suggestion, flowed from the staff to the gold. Even before he opened his eyes, he knew he had *spelled* it correctly. Turning to Lyndsy, he fastened the chain around her neck.

"Change."

"Jan, no!" Lyndsy protested with a sidelong look in Samantha's direction. Jan raised his hands. "Sooner or later …"

Lyndsy hesitated and then, realizing the nature of each individual in the room, sighed. "All right." She started the change … and was finished. With a bark of surprise, she jumped out of her clothes.

Samantha looked down, astonished. A white wolf stood at her feet.

In the blink of an eye, Lyndsy changed back. "Jan!" She threw her arms around his neck and smothered him with kisses.

Jan circled her bare waist with one arm as she slid back to the ground. "The necklace only works once—change and then change back. If you were to try it now, you would change normally."

Samantha looked around the room and realized she was the only one who seemed to notice Lyndsy's state of nakedness. She was so caught up in her own thoughts she almost missed Jan's words. Almost. *Change normally?* Without thinking, she blurted out, "You're a werewolf!"   .

"I'm sorry," Lyndsy stammered, "I didn't—"

Samantha held up her hand and stared directly into Lyndsy's eyes. "Never," she said fiercely, "be ashamed of who and what you are!"

A flood of suppressed emotion fell away from Lyndsy with a single breath. She stood tall and proud as her magenta eyes filled with appreciation for Samantha's understanding.

Samantha stooped and picked up the dress. Lyndsy, realizing she was breaking human custom, looked quickly at Jan. He gazed around the room as though he didn't realize her problem. Then he looked straight down at her and grinned. To Lyndsy's total discomfiture, she blushed crimson. "It's not fair! After the time we've spent alone, how can you still make me fill this way?"

Flower grinned mischievously. "Does it feel good or bad?"

Lyndsy blushed again and reached for the dress, but as she slipped it on over her head, they saw that she was grinning.

Sunder!

Jasmine looked up, Flower looked down, and Jan looked out of the window. Sunder became instantly intent on the back of his hand. *Yes, I'm here.*

A group of fighters will ride toward you at dawn. They seek January and his sword. They think he stole it from somewhere.

Sunder gazed up at Jan. Still gazing out of the window, Jan thought, *This was sure to come.*

They will not find you if you don't want them to.

Flower and January looked in astonishment toward Samantha. Samantha ran one finger down the string of the bow. *There are many places in the house where you may hide. However, I must offer them hospitality.*

Jan took only a moment to think and then said, "I think it's time to pay the School of Fighters a visit."

Benjamin looked surprised at the sudden change of subject but nodded obvious approval. Lyndsy folded her arms beneath her breasts and angled her head. With complete confidence and just a hint of sarcasm, she said, "Yes, I would like to see the so-called fiercest fighters in all of Lyre."

Jan smiled in anticipation. "Well then, tomorrow we ride."

Samantha walked to her chambers. She felt the special contact formed by the Mythit Jasmine. As the high cleric stepped into her room and shut the door, Jasmine appeared. "You will soon tell January all that you know of the Vainian Mythit Kingdom. He now knows you are Mythit trained, but he doesn't know anything about you, not really."

Samantha looked at the tiny red, pink, and white figure before her. She thought again of how the black Mythits should have been. This ancient figure in front of her was a child in the presence of the Mythit Poison. Only Sunder seemed to reach beyond Poison in seasons. To behold the integrity and bright, clear personality of these Mythits of Light gave her a deep sense of hope. "I will try."

Sunder waited for a moment alone with January. When the time came, he drew out a little silk pouch and placed it ceremoniously in Jan's hands. Jan opened the drawstring and looked inside. He smiled as he saw the embroidered silver stars on the violet armbands.

"You have been tried. It is your right."

17

POSSESSED

They rode at dawn. Lyndsy ran scout. Around her neck was a slim gold chain. Sunder sat before Benjamin, and Jasmine rode with Samantha.

January looked down at the top of Flower's head. "Out with it."

Flower giggled. "Jan, when did you tell Lyndsy she could kiss you any time that she would?"

"What?"

"January."

Oh no! She only calls me January when she wants to play all-knowing big sister!

"When you gave her the right—"

Right?

"By were custom she became your first."

First?

"The first is the title of the mother of the pack. Remember when she kissed you in Benjamin's room?"

"Of course!"

"She was making a statement," Flower continued. She was thoroughly enjoying Jan's discomfiture. "Even a challenge!"

It was a revelation Jan wondered at. He well knew he had missed something.

"Remember what Jasmine said?"

"Uh."

"Jan! I'm surprised at you! Don't you realize what these things mean to women? Jasmine said, 'You'll watch his back. You will guard and protect him. I will accept nothing less!'"

"Jasmine gave her permission!" Jan accused.

Flower tilted her head and looked up at him. "I call it a mother's blessing."

Jan smiled.

"January!"

He glanced back down at the top of her head. "What?"

"What do you mean, what?!" she snapped. Oh, she was enjoying this. "You seem to have missed the best part!"

Jan gave the top of her head a sour look.

"Don't look at me like that! Don't you remember the last of Jasmine's words?"

Jan shrugged. "'Moonlight, it suits you well.' That's just because I said she was the moonlight on a lake or something like that."

"Or something like that!?" Flower said sarcastically, "Jan, every were has a name they would never tell a human. It's just were superstition, but they think a human who knows their name can somehow keep them from the change."

Jan's jaw dropped open. "Moonlight is her real name? Moonlight," Jan repeated. "That's a beautiful name."

"Ah," Flower said smugly, "that's better."

They had traveled barely a league when Lyndsy returned. She changed shape and reported twelve riders in fighting gear. She went to Jan's side and grabbed two wraps from his saddlebags.

Jan dismounted and drew out the little silk pouch. With a glance at Sunder, who considered his actions with amusement, he pulled out an armband and tied it around Lyndsy's biceps. Offering her his arm, he held out the other band.

Lyndsy gazed at the silver star. Then, following Jan's lead, she tied it to his arm.

January set his hands on her shoulders. "This is a warrior's symbol. It represents my name. Maybe I presume too much. Lyndsy, will you wear my symbol?"

Lyndsy caught her breath and swallowed a sob that came out of nowhere. She nodded, unable to speak. She blinked back tears as Jan cupped her cheeks and gazed into her soft magenta eyes.

The thunder of hooves broke their spell. Jan returned to his mount and tossed Lyndsy her staff. As he strapped on the Sword of Corillion, he paced ahead of the horses. Lyndsy walked to his side and stopped. She looked up into his eyes. With a slow smile, she paced five steps ahead of him and then turned to face the riders.

The twelve riders reined in ten paces from the small party. One of the fighters Jan recognized turned and whispered to the leader.

January, Samantha thought, *the leader is named Captain Slith.*

January folded his arms across his chest. "Captain Slith, it has come to my attention that you ride to invite me to your school. I would like to know why?"

The captain, clearly startled, regained his composure and demanded, "What is your name?"

"In a moment. First, I would like to know why."

Jan could see the man's mind working. "You are needed for the trial of the prisoner you sent to us."

False.

"I'm only going to say this one time," Jan stated flatly. "Do not attempt to deceive me."

"Are you calling me a liar?"

"Captain," Samantha said calmly, "state your business."

"I ride on the order of the war general."

Jan gave a long, weary sigh. "Why?"

"It will be explained to you when we get there."

"Never mind, I'm not going after all." Jan turned and took a step toward his mount. "Let's go back to the School of Prayer."

"Now see here, boy," the captain said as he dismounted, "you're coming with us to answer for the sword you carry!" He advanced, hand on hilt.

Jan turned. When he took one step too many, Lyndsy brought her staff around in a blur. It stopped a finger's breadth from the Captain's chin. He tried to draw his sword. Lyndsy reversed, rapt his knuckles away from his side, and then brought the staff back up to the captain's chin. He looked down at the small figure with the staff. She was smiling, sweetly.

Jan raised one hand to his chin as though deep in thought. He scowled as he looked the captain over in great distaste. "Tell this general," he said quietly, "that it would please me to visit his school. I give him this warning, however—the Sword of Corillion is mine. If the subject is broached one time, just one time, I will leave. My lady, you may dismiss the captain."

Captain Slith looked down into the strange magenta eyes of the girl standing before him. Her smile had vanished. Her entire demeanor was that of a weapon. Those strange red-pink eyes held the steel chips of a veteran—a tried and seasoned veteran. Her poise spoke clearly to his battle trained senses.

"Captain," Lyndsy whispered quietly, "if my lord's wishes are not strictly obeyed, I *will* be offended. You do not wish to offend me. My lord places his honor in my hands. If his honor is abused, I will take it out on you. Captain, you are dismissed."

With a strange lightening of heart, he gave her a hand-on-hilt salute. Turning smartly on one heel, he walked to his horse and mounted. As he rode away, he heard whispers from his men. He let it go. He had a great deal of respect for the kind of courage he had just witnessed. *If they were my children, I would be proud!*

Lyndsy walked to Jan and looked up into his ice-blue eyes. That so much emotion could be contained in such a small body amazed him. She said very seriously, "You do me honor."

Jan returned just as seriously, "It is your right."

Turning, he went to his horse. As he set foot in the stirrup, he saw the look Flower was exchanging with Lyndsy. He had said the right thing.

They reached the School of Fighters and found an honor guard waiting for them. The guard led the three riders through the streets and markets of the school. Jan realized both schools had been built exactly the same.

Lyndsy walked last in line. She noted, after careful scrutiny, that no one followed. As they reached the single gate that led to the inner courtyard, Jan halted and allowed Lyndsy to come forward. Jan watched her aura flash as she realized his intent. He was well pleased to see astonished looks as Lyndsy walked through the gates, inspected the courtyard, and then turned and motioned the riders through. Flower, in particular, was amazed at the closeness she sensed between the two.

Captain Slith stood on the steps to the House of Fighters. He waited as the party dismounted and approached. Dismissing the fighter at his side, he faced Jan. "I am instructed to bring you straightaway to the council chamber. I swear I will do my best to help you in any way I can. I don't like their attitudes, but who am I to judge my betters? The bandit you captured is there. He has a serious accusation against the girl," he said, nodding to Lyndsy. "High Cleric, it is good that you are here. He claims the child is a demon."

"What?"

"First," Lyndsy said, "I am not a child, and you will not call me that again. Second, the only demon here is that man who was going to rape a group of initiates from the School of Prayer!"

Captain Slith looked surprised. "Nothing was said of this."

Samantha and Lyndsy's outraged exclamations caused silence in the courtyard. Captain Slith held Jan's gaze and said. "Come, we will deal with this." He turned to lead them in.

Jan glanced at Benjamin. "We?"

"It would seem you have made a friend."

They followed.

When they walked through the council room door, the fighters at the table turned to watch them. Jan felt a hot flush of intensely conscious dread and slammed down mental walls. Eight men sat around the central table. Eight men, paired, stood guard in the room's four corners. When Benjamin led the high cleric through the door, the eight men at the table quickly rose to their feet.

Jan and Lyndsy were both watching the prisoner in the far corner. Neither one realized the fighters rose in respect to the high cleric. They saw the men rise and were instantly back to back. The Sword of Corillion was in Jan's hand before Lyndsy's silk wraps settled into place.

Jan had felt a foreboding presence all the way down the hall. Sunder and Jasmine had wondered at it but couldn't figure it.

"January," Benjamin said, "you have nothing to fear in this school."

Lyndsy smelled Jan's reaction to dread. She didn't understand that particular emotion, but her own senses were reeling in danger. "January?"

"I know, I—"

The Mythits appeared between the fighters and the party.

"What in the name of Song is that!"

"They're Mythits! By the sword! They're Mythits!"

Sunder paid them no heed as Jasmine surveyed the room. Neither he nor Flower knew why Jasmine had chosen to appear, but they had come with her.

"Samantha! Look!" Jasmine exclaimed, pointing at the prisoner.

Samantha turned. She too had felt the wild emotion running through the room. Now she saw it clearly. "He is possessed!"

"You accuse me, daughter of demons?" In one fluid motion the bandit jumped up and broke the heavy chains that bound him to the wall. Surprising the two guards at his side, both went down under the flailing chains. With a harsh laugh, he picked up both swords and turned.

Of all the warriors in the room, only Jan and Lyndsy reacted. The closest man to the bandit watched dumbly as both swords arched down at his head.

Jan blocked the blows from connecting. One blade bit deep into the table. Jan's sword hilt slammed the man backward. "Lyndsy, stand guard!"

She stepped back even as she reached his side. An older fighter drew his sword and paced forward. Lyndsy's staff barred his path. "Don't get in his way. He needs room to swing."

"You will die, fool! I will drink your blood in front of your little were slut. Then I will show her the meaning of lust!"

Jan felt Lyndsy's sudden rage. "Lyndsy, no!"

The demon attacked. Jan blocked a two-handed sword stroke that dropped him to one knee. He lashed out from his crouched position, and the demon was forced to jump back. Jan pushed up and forward with a backhanded slash from the hip. The demon leapt smoothly to one side. Even as Jan got to his feet, the demon rocked his world with another two-handed blow. With his right hand on the flat of his blade, he took the force into his arms and shoulders. The Sword of Corillion rang like a bell.

I can't take too many of those!

Jan lunged. As the demon sidestepped, Jan turned and brought his sword around. Another two-handed blow. This time, Jan was prepared. He stepped in, turned his sword point up, and held. It was too fast for the demon to compensate. The force of its own swing ran both wrists across the razor edge of Jan's blade. As the tendons were sliced, the hilt floundered in unfeeling fingers.

Jan turned and knocked the sword from the demon's grasp. With a quick reversal, he hammered his hilt into the demon's chest. Stepping out with a half turn, he spread his feet and raised the sword level across his eyes. The body crumpled and fell to the ground.

Samantha walked forward. "The demon is gone." She knelt down by the body. "He is still alive. Somebody help me." With both hands, she grasped the man's wrists and looked back up. "Please! He'll die!"

Jasmine went to her side. "January, put the man on the table."

"He tried to kill him!" Lyndsy said in great anger.

Jasmine turned and gave Lyndsy a long look. "Werewoman, he wasn't the one who did this. The demon is gone."

Once again, Jan got the feeling that he didn't understand the words spoken. It was as though Jasmine had said something entirely different. Picking up the man, he walked with Samantha and set him on the table.

"Strips of cloth, quickly!"

Jan went to Lyndsy. "She's right."

Lyndsy looked up, and for all the world, Jan could have sworn that Lyndsy looked guilty. "I know she's right." She turned and went to the closest fighter, pulled his dagger, and hurried back. Cutting strips of cloth, she handed them to Samantha.

Jan, Jasmine thought, *help us. He's dying. Use the staff!*

Jan unwrapped the crown of the staff and called the gems to life. Tendrils of thought probed the body as he touched it. He could feel the heart laboring too hard and pumping too little. *I don't know what to do!*

Calm down, Jasmine thought.

Look! It was Samantha.

Jasmine and January both felt Samantha's personality insinuating into the man's aura. The high cleric's senses became her hands. The veins in the arms constricted; the heartbeat slowed.

Jan saw what she was doing. As the blood flow stopped, he was able to discern the sliced layers of skin. With two fingers, he pressed the cut closed and found himself tuned to the white gem. Instructions of cell structure unfolded within his mind. In awe at his own senses, he began the process of mending cells.

Jasmine stood between them, one small, furred hand on either shoulder. With one mind, they both realized it was the Mythit's mind allowing Samantha's contact to the white gem. Samantha and January were able to work independently. She kept the heartbeat under control. January worked the cells to rebuild and grow. After what seemed an eternity, they finished. The wound was healed. Two fine lines of healthy pink skin were all that remained.

Samantha took one deep breath and passed out. Lyndsy caught her as she fell and slowly let her slump to the floor. Holding her head in the crook of one arm, she sat. Jan tried to help, but he felt so weak he was barely able to find a place to sit before he too fell to the ground.

"He's a wizard!"

Sunder climbed up on the table and went to Jan's side. He gazed down at Lyndsy and Samantha and then turned back to Jan. "You have learned control."

Jan looked up. Even sitting on the edge of the table, Sunder was barely taller. Jan also looked down at Lyndsy. "You have taught me many things. But when I was alone in Mirshol with the most desirable woman on the face of Lyre, that is when I started to learn control."

"In the name of Song! Samantha!"

Everyone turned to Jasmine. "What is it?" Jan asked, suddenly worried.

"It? I … I …" Jasmine looked up. She made a quick decision. For now, it would be her secret. Surely Samantha didn't already know! Jasmine watched Samantha and January standing side by side in her mind's eye. Samantha had walked through Mirshol and bathed in Light Lake. She wondered why Sunder hadn't yet made the connection. Sunder had an annoying way of knowing everything before she did. It was all so obvious! "January," Jasmine said evasively, "Samantha should be dead for attempting to use the power of your staff."

Jan grimaced. "I thought about that, but she seemed to know what she was doing. Will she be all right?"

"Ridiculous!" Jasmine stated. "She's as healthy as a horse. She needs sleep, but she'll be fine in the morning."

"Good," Lyndsy said, relieved.

Jan turned to look at the fighters. They were just standing there, watching. He was about to speak when Sunder turned on them. The little orange Mythit walked to the center of the table and set his hands on his hips. "The Sword of Corillion belongs to him! You try my patience at your own peril. The only human living who has any kind of vague claim on it would be the weapons master of the Knights Alliance. Corillion gave that blade to me. It was mine to give away as I saw fit! Only because of who you are do I make any explanation at all. If one word is spoken out of line, if one doubt is put into words, I will bring my family to this house and make your human lives miserable!"

He smiled thoughtfully. "Oh, what a wonderful idea! Such a grand playground for fifty Mythits! Just think of the mischief we could make! Maybe I should go get them anyway—"

"No, no, that's not necessary!" one of the fighters blurted out.

Captain Slith said, "After what has happened in this room, I see no reason to continue this."

"Yes, exactly!" the fighter said quickly. "Captain, show our guests to their quarters at their convenience." He then turned to Jan. "Please, accept our apologies. We did not know."

Samantha lay listening. January picked her up and carried her through the corridors to their rooms. She knew Jasmine had probed her for just an instant and wanted, terribly, to know what the Mythit had found. Jasmine's excitement had been so intense it had awakened her from unconsciousness. What did she find? What did she know?

The Mythit Sunder seemed oblivious to the strictures of the Clerical Vows. Jasmine was the first person she had ever met who consciously understood the nature of a holy vow. Benjamin was, in all respects, hallowed, but the old Seer was unaware of the implications of holiness. Why did Jasmine have this understanding? What had she found? Yet, what really caused the high cleric to wonder, was one little thing. Why couldn't *she* discern it?

January had wanted to visit the School of Fighters ever since he knew of its existence. When Sunder gave him the Sword of Corillion and started his training, Jan had serious doubts about Sunder's knowledge of fighting. After one season, he knew better. After two seasons, he wanted to visit the school and show off his skill. As any good teacher will, Sunder perceived his desire. With arduous training, both mental and physical, along with strict tales of the past, Jan learned restraint.

As Jan lay in Lyndsy's arms that night, he considered this. He thought about his time alone with her. He had been very sincere about not knowing what control was until he and Lyndsy were alone. From the beginning, he realized her powerful sexuality. Flaunting and full knowing, she had tried again and again to fire his passion. Until this werewoman came into his life, he hadn't really known the meaning of the word!

The first three days were like that. Lyndsy seemed to be on a sliding scale between outrageous flirtation and angry misunderstanding. It had all changed at Light Lake. Something had changed her outlook, and January still hadn't been able to figure it out. She was still calculating with her presentation of herself, but there was a difference.

Lyndsy's senses were keen to say the least. She was a wolf, a warrior, and a woman—and in that order. Since Jan had pounced into her life, she was now woman, warrior, and wolf. She had always known she was not pleasing to the males of her pack. Even worse, she was too ugly to touch! The morning after he changed shape, she had again smelled his desire as they woke in each other's arms. Such a glorious scent had never been directed toward her in her entire life! A sudden wash of shame had come from him as he'd jumped to his feet. Angry? No, she had just wanted to roast him over a slow fire, that's all. She was obviously to revolting to be in contact with. Her hopes were crushed. There was no way he would ever want to do *that* with her!

But she just couldn't leave. She had been compelled to stay. Then he'd been so kind and understanding, so caring and openly impressed with her, that she had become honestly and thoroughly confused.

He had said, "Lyndsy, you are so beautiful it's hard to believe you're real." She'd looked at him crookedly, smelling for the lie. He was serious. Oh, but it felt good to be alive!

As she snuggled up close and breathed his wonderful scent, she considered Sapphire's words. Lyndsy had learned a lot in those few moments.

Sapphire had said much, but her last words had been, "He is in need of a companion, someone willing to fight by his side. He needs your courage and help. A willing body to warm his furs is not what he needs!" Ouch! Sapphire's words had supplied her rage with fuel, but it had been done in such a way that she could only be angry with herself. The blue wraith had seen this and said very sincerely, "Moonlight, he watches you and likes what he sees. You need not worry over who is on his mind."

After they'd left Light Lake, Jan had seen the change in her. The insecure, angry, hurt, resentful, shy, awed girl had changed her shape to a fiery young woman. Her strength of character was absolutely irresistible. That was when Jan had learned control.

18

SLIM CHANCE

Trumpets sounded the beginning of a new day. Lyndsy and Jan were both eager to watch the fighters in practice. They ate hurriedly, checked on Benjamin and Samantha, and then went to find the training grounds. They didn't have to look very hard. News of the day before was all over the school. People were all eyes as they stepped into the corridor and stopped.

Jan spoke to the fighter nearest to them. "Where are the practice grounds?"

"End of the hall, left, and straight out the door."

They started walking and noticed that everyone in the hallway followed at a respectable distance. The open yard was similar to the garden within the School of Prayer—except that this garden was a training ground. And not at all peaceful. Swords clashed on shields. Officers and trainers walked about shouting orders. Fighters, marching, chanted in rhythm.

They walked out into the yard to watch. In moments, all practice had ceased. Fighters turned to look at the pair. Jan felt Lyndsy tense as all eyes swung in their direction. He knew she didn't like to be around too many people at once, and all of the attention was making her feel caged.

Jan saw a row of quarter staffs and led them toward it. He drew out the two silver-starred armbands and handed one to her. As he wrapped her arm, he whispered, "There may be fighters here who understand the meaning of this symbol. Wear it proudly."

Ah, he thought, as he watched her relax into a reserved position, *that was the right thing to say.* He stood still as Lyndsy tied his armband to his biceps. Then he motioned to the row of staffs. "Show me how to use a staff."

Her eyes opened wide in surprise. "Are you sure?"

"Absolutely."

As they walked to the rack, all eyes followed. Lyndsy inspected them with a critical eye. "That one," she said, pointing. "It's your size."

He plucked it from the rack and turned to look at her.

Lyndsy watched a ring of fighters circle behind Jan. She felt nervous and didn't want to show it. Then her eyes fell on the silver star, and her breast swelled with pride. "The staff is an extension of your reach. It has no edge." She started pacing, keeping eye contact with him. "Not only is there no single place to put your hands, no matter how you place them, the staff has two ends. You must forget the sword. It has a hilt. When a staff swings, one end goes out, the other comes in. The return of a staff is more important than the end that strikes. You must always be aware of both ends. Watch." She turned to a practice dummy and demonstrated how she allowed the end to come in along her side while the other end struck. "When you reverse, elbows go up, and the staff comes in. Always try to keep your elbows in. Try to keep your motions up and down. If your elbows point out, you are in danger from a quick sword stroke."

Jan was quickly wrapped up in her instructions. She was doing far better than he thought she would. He was vaguely aware of a few other fighters drawing staffs from the rack.

"I want you to place one foot forward, one to the side. Feel your body. Feel your balance. Watch your feet. The power of a staff is different than a sword. A staff depends on force from your shoulders, forearm, and the swivel of your hips. A staff is much lighter than steel—"

"Ha! Any fool knows that!"

Lyndsy turned to a tall young fighter who was twirling a staff with three fingers. She eyed him narrowly. "I have no time for your nonsense. If you do not wish to learn, then remain silent."

"What is this? Make-believe?" the youth taunted. "Learning to fight from a girl?" The young man looked around, sneering at his peers.

Jan noticed that a few appeared to be intimidated and one or two moved to put back their staffs. Jan saw Captain Slith standing to one side, arms folded, eyeing the situation with a slight smile. He turned back to the fighter. "I suggest you be quiet or leave. She looks in no mood to play games with a little boy."

"Ha! I'd teach her the meaning of the word!"

Jan glanced back at Captain Slith. The now grinning Captain nodded approval. They both looked to Lyndsy.

Lyndsy saw the look in the captain's eyes. Her expression became deadpan serious. She walked up to Jan and said clearly, "Don't worry. This *little boy* won't take long."

Lyndsy walked forward. As the youth twirled his staff, she said, "Watch your feet!" and attacked. Left, right, left, whip up, jab. She went down to one knee and swept both of his feet out from under him. "I said watch your feet! Get up!"

This time he was wary.

"Elbows in!" She attacked.

He blocked the first strokes well but was forced back by the sheer fury of her blows. She dropped to one knee. He jumped back and out of her way. As she rose to her feet, she nodded. "Very good."

Standing poised, she grinned up at him. "Now, you attack me."

He did. Instead of blocking or backing away, she stepped in. One end of her staff ran down her side and stopped his swing. She pushed up and barely tapped the bottom of his chin.

"You cannot turn. If you place one foot in front of the other, you can swivel your hips and simply turn your head."

She stepped back. "Again!" This time Lyndsy backed up. Block, block, right, and then in one fluid motion she sidestepped and worked her staff up and down, hard. Her motion knocked the staff out of the young man's hands. She spun on the ball of one foot and stopped her staff as it kissed up to the back of his neck.

He stood still, looking down at her.

"Your final lesson is never, and I mean never, underestimate your opponent!"

He bowed, and stammered. "I'm sorry, I didn't—"

She cut him off. "No need. Is this a lesson in manners or training for war?"

Jan watched the faces of the fighters. At first, they looked worried. The youth was apparently a troublemaker and a fair hand with a staff. When Lyndsy landed him flat on his back, their expressions changed to wonder. Her continuous instructions brought nods of approval from the trainers. This was combined with no small amount of respect for her skill. Captain Slith, Jan noticed, came to his side and was hard-pressed not to burst into laughter.

With Lyndsy's final instructions, Jan went to her side. A few of the trainers went with him. A barrage of questions concerning her skill and her teachers made her blush in delight.

"*Clear the yard!*"

The call stopped all conversation. The first general of the School of Fighters was standing on a podium in the middle of the court. Jan recognized him as the same fighter who had asked his pardon the night before. It was one of Sunder's lessons that made him realize that any office of rank was null in council so that each person present could speak his or her minds among equals.

"Captain," the general said, "see the fighters out and then return." As the initiate fighters cleared the yard, the general approached Jan and Lyndsy.

"A delegation has arrived from the Knights Alliance. They seek the sword you carry. I did not tell them you are here, but surely gossip has made the fact known." The general paused for a moment as if gathering courage and then said, "I want you to know we wished you no ill will. It seemed to us at the time that it was our place to find out how that sword came into the possession of a boy. You must realize, of course, the value of the sword."

"I understand."

The general gave an audible sigh. "Good. Now, do you wish to change your style of dress? It would be easy for you to appear as one of us. You could watch and judge them before you made yourself known."

Jan glanced at Lyndsy. If they knew about her, then they could hardly conceal their identity. He knew there was no way she would leave his side. "No, bring them in as they will."

They waited in silence. Jan saw the shimmers of three figures as they walked through the door. Lyndsy smelled Flower's scent and scanned the yard. Jan watched her, intrigued, as she pinpointed the Mythit's presence by smell. She glanced up at him to see if *he* knew. Without saying a word, he gave her an almost imperceptible nod and smiled. Lyndsy smiled in return.

Four men walked through the entrance and approached. Lyndsy moved to one side and held her staff in the crook of one arm. Jan saw that the first two men were sizing her up with cautious care, while the other two seemed amused.

"Stop there and speak!" Her tone of voice held enough authority to make the other two lose their sauce.

Jan and Lyndsy both recognized one of the first two men at the same time.

"You!" Jan exclaimed.

Lyndsy stepped sideways, held her staff ready, and raged. "Snake! I let you live once! You tempt fate! This time you will pay in blood for the deaths of my *children*!"

The man stepped out from the other three and put his hands together. It was a gesture of peace. "I don't know what you're talking about."

Lyndsy fumed. She smelled his truth. He would stink of lies if he knew. "You don't even recognize me! Softtail and Laughing Eyes will never—"

"Lyndsy," Jan said gently.

"I swear," the man said, "I have done many wrongs in my life, but I have never killed children."

The other man who had first scrutinized Lyndsy stepped between her and the man he had vowed to protect. Hands open and outstretched, he said, "I, too, know where this man is from. You have a need to listen to his words." With careful motion, he reached one hand into the pocket of his cloak and then withdrew it. Setting his hands behind his back for a brief moment, he then brought them out. Lyndsy nodded to his right hand with a puzzled expression on her face. The man watched her actions and gave her a curt nod. With his left hand, he reached out and grabbed air. Opening his hand as if holding something fragile, he lowered his head.

Lyndsy was astonished. She repeated the gesture and said, with a conspiratorial smile, "As you wish. I will listen to his words. Then I will kill him."

Jan gazed at the lean, cloaked figure. *What was that all about?*

The man Lyndsy wanted to kill turned to Jan. "You gave me my life. How you did that, I don't know. I was cut from shoulder to hip. Yet, when I came back to myself on the border of Mirshol, I was alive. I found that I could move and looked myself over. I tell you, you gave me my life. I now give it back. Unless"—he looked at Lyndsy—"she decides to take it.

"I have much to say to you. But first you need to be told that you are in grave danger. You are known to the Dark Lady I once served."

Truth.

"She summons a demon to kill you. I don't know what has happened, but when I went back, the little black ones were all over the place. They never were completely visible before. Now I know that the day she has awaited is here. She holds magic that Lyre has not seen in a thousand seasons.

"The demon may already be summoned. I know it was to be difficult this early in the land's reawakening. But the creature, Poison, is more powerful than her daughter, and they stand together. Believe me, their combined strength is undefeatable. They have a greater purpose, but of that I hesitate to speak."

Jan looked at the first general and the captain. Now seemed like a good time for a reality check. "Speak it, I want the leaders of Lyre's defense to hear it."

"You already know what I would say?"

"Yes."

The man turned to the general. "They will break the bonds that hold the Dark Lord from Lyre."

"That's not possible!" the first general exclaimed.

Jan turned to the general and said very seriously, "Not only is it possible, it *will* happen. We're lucky; we are forewarned."

"But the magic"—the general stopped and then finished—"has returned."

Jan turned back to the stranger. "What's your name?"

The man answered with a shadowed, distant frown. "I have no name. I am nameless."

Jan saw Samantha and Benjamin enter the yard. Whatever he might have expected, he was surely surprised. As the stranger with no name looked upon the high cleric, he took a deep breath and yelled, "Bitch! What are *you* doing here?"

Lyndsy was fast. Jan was faster. Lyndsy's swing was calculated to smash his skull. Jan caught the butt end of her staff from behind and snatched it out of her hands. She didn't even hesitate. Lyndsy reached for the first general's dagger. Jan caught her around the waist and held her arms. Shaking in rage, she quit struggling. She was surprised, but she didn't know if she could break Jan's grip.

Jan glared at the man and spoke through clenched teeth. "You have a slim chance of leaving here alive. Slim Chance, explain yourself!"

"*No!*" Samantha yelled. She gazed at Jan with pleading eyes. "Please, this is a private matter."

"I want an explanation," Jan said tightly.

Samantha turned to the first general. "Leave us. I beg you."

The first general scowled at the stranger with cold eyes. "If by some chance they let you live, I swear, if you enter my school, once gone, you will die." Calling his men to his side, they left the yard.

Jan waited until they stepped through the arch. He turned to the man who companioned Slim Chance and gave him a hard look. They held each other's gaze for a moment and Jan suddenly *knew* everything would be all right. Both of these men were firmly woven into his future. He took a deep breath, and said, "Slim Chance, explain yourself."

Slim Chance gave Samantha a withering glare and said, "Don't you know what you have masquerading in a high cleric's robe? This bitch," he said clearly, "is the daughter of Melody the Black!"

Silence.

Jan felt Lyndsy fighting the change. She was almost past the point of caring. Jan wrapped her within his thought and forced her senses to calm.

Samantha stood still. Jasmine appeared in front of her. Samantha set her hands on the Mythit's shoulders for support.

Tell them.

Samantha nodded. "What he says is true. I am the daughter of Melody."

"No!" Lyndsy shouted.

Flower appeared in front of Lyndsy and smiled up at her. Lyndsy blinked as Flower turned around and leaned back against her thighs.

Samantha took a deep breath and faced January. To her, no other opinion mattered. "I was taught by Melody the Black to worship the Dark Lord. She wished that I become her second." Samantha swallowed. "I worked very hard to please my mistress. I cannot say I did not want it. Whether you accept me or not makes no difference. I can only say, in the presence of you who know truth"—she glanced at Jasmine and Benjamin—"that I am Melody's deadliest enemy."

Samantha turned to Slim Chance. He held her gaze and offered no quarter. Samantha knew this man was changed. Would he be able to believe the same of her? He was an imposing figure to the human population of the Lince Posh stronghold. She suddenly realized she wanted his approval. "I have decided to go with this unlikely group where they will. In Lyndsy, January, and Benjamin the Seer of Lake Town resides a power far greater than *hers*." She turned once again to Jan. "That is, if you will still have me."

Lyndsy blurted out, "Of course!"

Samantha looked in Jan's eyes. "January?"

Lyndsy whirled on him.

Jan frowned down at her. "Woman, control yourself."

It had the desired effect. Lyndsy snapped to attention.

"High Cleric," January said, "I wouldn't have it any other way." He watched as a flood of doubt and fear fell from Samantha's aura. All that was left was that stamp of personality that he didn't understand. A thought dawned on him. *That's why Jasmine is so sure of her.*

Jasmine watched him. She heard his thought and smiled. *'You are correct. That is the reason.'*

Jan blinked and looked down at the top of Lyndsy's head. She was fit to burst. "At ease."

Lyndsy shouted, turned, and fairly leapt into Samantha's embrace.

Tears came suddenly to Samantha's eyes. A part of the truth was known, and she was still accepted. Would she find the courage to speak the rest?

"Slim Chance?"

The man turned.

"Can you believe her?" Jan asked. He could see the Vainian was unafraid. He realized Lyndsy as a threat but didn't fear. The man either had courage or a secret or both. Either way, Jan had already decided to like this Slim Chance.

Slim Chance said casually, "I don't know why I do, but I do. Do you realize that I have known her since she was a child? I held her on my knee and offered comfort as she cut her first teeth. Well," he said, with a suddenly distant look, "I *want* to believe her."

The passion in his quiet voice made Jan look twice. Since he hadn't really had a chance to look the man over, he took a moment to assess him.

He was a big man—broad, powerful shoulders—not too tall, not even as tall as Samantha; black hair, a short beard, and piercing black eyes. They held an intensity that vaguely reminded him of Sunder, although he couldn't say why. He carried a broadsword strapped across his back, hilt standing up from his left shoulder.

Eyes touched his back. He turned to see the other man watching him. This man could be dangerous! His tall whipcord frame had the look of a weapon. Long gray hair hung loose off his shoulders. A proud, straight nose separated wide hazel-green eyes. A thin, drooping mustache moved in the slight breeze. They held each other's gaze for a moment, and then Jan noticed the glimmer of gold on the sword hilt at his side.

A beautiful, gold-crafted scabbard contained a work of art. The inlay on the hilt and pommel flickered in the sunlight. Swirling gold thread covered an ivory hilt that was so yellowed with age and use Jan knew it was at least half as old as the Sword of Corillion.

Jan turned his attention back to Slim Chance. "It's good you think you can trust the high cleric. I have a mind to take you with me."

Slim Chance glanced at Lyndsy, and asked, "You want me to travel with someone who wants nothing more than to pound me into dog meat?"

Lyndsy didn't know why, but the situation seemed suddenly hilarious. She burst into laughter. It was so heartfelt and contagious that soon everyone was laughing.

Jan watched Jasmine and Flower. They were *playing* irresistible humor. Samantha saw it too. Still holding Lyndsy in her embrace, she allowed herself to get caught up in their flow. Flower turned and wrapped her personality around him. Hands working, she touched his aura and tickled his humor. Giving in, he picked her up and joined them.

19

A Piece of Past: 3

After they bathed and ate, Samantha asked January and Lyndsy to bring Benjamin to her guest room. Jan knew her reason. Before she had a chance to speak, he said, "I don't know why I decided to have him with me. It's just a feeling, like I *know* I can trust him."

Samantha's return was silenced by the old seer's gaze. The fire in his eyes stunned her to stillness. Benjamin took a deep breath, looked into Samantha's soul, and said, "I see this man standing over your body. He holds a bloody sword and weeps. He is protecting you from a sea of warped creatures that chills my blood!"

Benjamin's green, fire-flecked eyes turned back to their normal dark blue. Samantha bowed her head. "I have no right to judge him. I have no right to judge any. January, this man holds great power! He is *well* trained in the black arts." Samantha gazed up at the ceiling. Her mind played over a memory. *I have often prayed for his soul.*

A knock at the door stilled any other speech. Samantha opened the door, paused, and then let the two men in. Slim Chance stood by the door while the other man entered and sat down. Jan took another good look at this obvious warrior. He had dressed himself in what appeared to be a ceremonial half suit of armor. The breastplate was polished steel, no insignia or emblem at all. Arm and leg plates were hard leather, tooled, and studded in silver.

For the third time, Jan was amazed when the Mythits decided to show themselves. Sunder went straight to the stranger.

The man looked at Sunder with a smile. "Do I know you?"

Sunder laughed. "Of course you do! I haunted your keep better than any ghost. Speak what's on your mind, humble child of a great father." Once again Sunder burst into laughter, as though he had just said something ridiculously funny.

The man turned to January. "I am the weapons master of the Knights Alliance. The Sword of Corillion brought me here. May I see it?"

Jan held his staff with one hand. Truth be told, he did not want this man to touch the sword. Something told him that a fate was going to be established right here and right now. There was nothing he could do about it if that was the case, but he would have liked to have had some say in the matter.

Sunder stepped into Jan's lap and reached out to the weapons master. He laid his palm flat against the man's forehead. Then he grinned like a fool and turned to Lyndsy and Benjamin. "Young man, werechild, behold! Jan, let the son hold the blade of his father!"

Jan reached for the scabbard and held it forward. The weapons master grasped the hilt and drew the sword. With great interest, he turned the hilt.

Whitefire flared on the edge of the blade. It ran in a stream down to the tip, circled underneath, and returned up the back. Runes, carved into the cross guard, flared to life. The weapons master gazed in awe and spoke a string of lilting words unfamiliar to most of the humans in the room.

Lyndsy leaned forward and stared into the weapons master's eyes. She repeated the words with their proper inflections. Those who listened heard a bittersweet song of burning passion.

The weapons master turned to her in wonder. "Those words are recorded in the *Histories of Corillion*. They are not translated. Do you know their meaning?"

Lyndsy turned to He Who Sees All. Benjamin held Jan's gaze for a moment and then nodded to Lyndsy. Lyndsy faced the group and said, "In midwinter, during the first night of the new moon, these words are always spoken":

> I will go
> I will fight
> I will die
>
> With this blade
> With this staff
> With this bow

On battlefield
In the mountains
On the Plain

I will go
I will fight
I will die

You shall live
Child of peace
Free of fear

In a city
On a farm
In the forests

Learn to sing
Learn to grow
Learn of life

I Swear,

I will go
I will fight
I will die!

As Lyndsy finished reciting the Vow of Blood Plain, Jan saw a beam of white light spring from the seer's forehead. The light split into branches and twined with the personalities of everyone in the room. A scene appeared in their minds.

Corillion, stripped of armor, three seasons before the final battle, fought a weremale sword to sword. A ring of were circled the two warriors. The White Wizard sat on a horse just out of the ring. Corillion bled from many wounds; the were was covered in his own blood.

They fought as the moon rose. From time to time, one or two of the were would look up to watch the Lady's path as it scorched the night sky.

The White Wizard rang a silver bell. With a final effort, the were renewed his assault.

Corillion stood firm block after block, attack after attack. He demonstrated to the greatest fighter of the were that he was better. Corillion attacked with a final flurry of blows that staggered the were to his knees. As the moon passed behind the Vile Mountains, Corillion struck the blade from his opponent's grasp. It flew skyward, caught the last rays of the moonlight, and sparkled like fire. The sword fell, point downward, and buried itself halfway to the hilt in the dust of Blood Plain.

On that night, the were swore fealty to the White Wizard. The leader placed his hands on the Bow of Myril and repeated the words the wizard spoke. White took Corillion's sword and burned runes into the hilt with his fingertips.

The high cleric of Lyre then raised the Scepter of Light over his head and shouted. The Black Mountains shook. A brilliant white light sprang from the scepter and burned like the morning sun.

The White Wizard invoked the name of the Creator and altered the curse of the were.

Jan came to himself. He stood, blinking, from the aftermath of vision. His staff blazed rainbows in his grasp.

Lyndsy knelt at his feet weeping tears of pride and joy. Jan reached down and pulled her to her feet. Tear-filled magenta eyes held him in awe. "I saw! I saw! The first swearing of the Vow of Blood Plain!"

Jan looked to the weapons master. The man was shaking, the Sword of Corillion held tenderly in his arms. With one finger, he caressed the length of the blade as though it were the most precious thing in all of Lyre.

Exalted in power, Jan reached out and touched the blade. He looked deep into the steel and saw the structure of the finely wrought metal. For the first time, he noticed a spell that bound the metal almost to the point of making it indestructible. With the power of his staff, Jan recreated the same alloy of steel.

Those gathered watched in awe as the staff appeared to flow like liquid in his hands. A sword formed in his grasp. A long, thin blade came into existence as the oaken staff shrank. The white gem came to rest in the pommel; the red and blue gems set themselves just above the oaken cross guard.

Jan felt the tightly packed cells of the wooden hilt and knew that they were stronger than steel. The long blade sparkled with glimmering hues as the torchlight played gentle games. He himself looked in awe at what he had done.

The weapons master blinked like an owl. "That is the loveliest weapon I have ever seen."

"Lyndsy, I …"

She caught him as he fell. Leaning to one side, she sat down hard, still holding Jan in her embrace.

Jan swallowed. "That took a lot out of me. Weapons Master, the Sword of Corillion is yours. You will need it."

"I don't think—"

Sunder interrupted him. "It will serve you well, and yes, you will need it."

Benjamin said, to no one in particular, "These days are filled with wonders."

Jan smiled at Benjamin with great affection. Looking back to the weapons master, he asked, "One more thing?"

"Name it."

"What did you have in your hand, out in the yard, to keep my lady from killing Slim Chance?"

Even faced away, Jan felt Lyndsy blush, but she answered for him. "He had a lump of sugar."

"A what?"

The weapons master grinned. "I thought that she might be were. We at the Knights Alliance are familiar with the were. I wanted to test her sense of smell."

They all burst into laughter.

"Slim Chance," Jan said weakly, "how does it feel to have your life saved by a lump of sugar?"

Slim Chance couldn't answer. He was laughing the hardest.

Jan woke from a dream in the middle of the night. The dream became real as he found Lyndsy's almost naked body wrapped in his arms. A rush of desire filled him, causing blood to hum in his veins.

Oh, how I want her! What do I have to give? Is she really happy at my side? He plucked her shaggy white hair from across his face and tried to move away from her warmth.

She opened her eyes. A soft smile brought a surge of loving, fiery passion.

The scent of his desire slammed into her senses and caused her to moan. She raised up on one elbow and kissed him soundly.

"Lyndsy, I can't—"

Lyndsy touched his lips and frowned. The hardest thing she had ever done in her entire life was get out of bed and put on a robe.

He watched her move. With great effort, he stilled his pounding heart. "Woman, I'm glad you did that. I don't think I could have."

She glanced back at him and thought of their travel through Mirshol. Confused and hurt, she thought, *Does he* really *want me?*

"Lyndsy, I'm eighteen seasons old. You are?"

"Sixteen seasons. January, I don't understand why you—"

"I don't know," he said quickly.

Don't know what? Did he know what I was going to say?

Jan's mind was in turmoil. He didn't hear her thought.

20

YOU DO ME HONOR

The weapons master of the Knights Alliance, the best swordsman Lyre had to offer, was hard-pressed to hold his own.

The Mythit taught him? Give me an army of Mythits, and I'll fight anything!

The yard was full, every eye on the pair. Try as they might, the sword masters could not read Jan's style. Style was everything. A student always imitated the master. If he was capable of increasing his own skill, he would add to that style. Jan's fighting had no place in their frame of reference. They were constantly amazed as Jan demonstrated one new motion after another. His fighting was flawless.

Jan had started the spar with moves Sunder had dubbed the Baby Colt Walk. The weapons master had played right into his hands. Slight stumble, off balance, apparent bad footing. The trained fighter had quickly learned not to underestimate this youth. For the fifth time in half an hour, the blade the weapons master used flew from his grasp.

The older veteran looked from his sword on the ground to the youth before him. "You are a sword dancer."

Higher praise could not be given. January offered him a formal bow. He turned and saw Lyndsy standing next to Samantha. Tapping the flat of his blade in his open palm, he raised one eyebrow. Everyone turned to the lithe, white-haired figure. A slow smile split her wide, full lips.

Jan walked to the center of the yard and stood poised. Lyndsy paced closer, the look in her eyes pure challenge. "Do not mistake me," she stated seriously. "I am She Who Walks Alone." Twirling her staff with three fingers, she charged.

Jan danced backward as he blocked a flurry of blows. He sidestepped, turned, and brought the flat of his blade around, fast.

She leaned into the block and stopped the steel, hard. Down on one knee, she swept empty air as Jan jumped. Without losing momentum, she rose and stepped gracefully away as the blade whistled though the air. But even as she twirled, Jan reached in and gave her a solid swat across her backside with the flat of his blade.

The fighters roared with laughter at the surprised look on her face.

Oh! How dare you!

A fast series of blows made Jan step away. She calculated his moves to the quick. When he stepped out, she brought the butt end of her staff around. She leapt forward and rolled. Jan moved forward as she came up behind him. He tried to bring his sword around to block, but he was too late. He felt the sting of her staff across his rump.

The fighters went wild.

With a rhythmical series of quick strokes, Lyndsy was forced to retreat. Jan slipped. Lyndsy countered so fast her staff became a blur. Jan's misstep was a fake. Lyndsy received a second swat as her own momentum played against her.

Samantha and Benjamin went to the weapons master's side. The master said in awe, "I'm glad I didn't fight her. I don't think *my* masters would approve if I were beaten by a girl child."

"Indeed," Benjamin agreed.

Captain Slith grinned. "She taught my finest quarter staff fighter the meaning of the word!"

Lyndsy held up her hand, rose up, and gave Jan a kiss. It was such a surprise he stood blinking as she dropped, reached back, and brought her staff in.

The roar of the fighters was deafening.

Jan let his senses spread. The strength of the wild aura was awesome. His personality settled on Lyndsy. With a twist of thought, he could control her and dull her senses. He let her go.

Sidestepping, he spread his feet, and held his sword in both hands. The blade slanted up and came to rest horizontally across his chest.

Lyndsy rocked back, front foot set on ball. With her right arm extended, she twirled the staff.

Quiet.

Lyndsy's high-pitched scream and Jan's roar filled the courtyard.

They came together and clashed. Jan darted in and was blocked. Lyndsy hammered her staff right and left but could not get through Jan's guard. Circling, they came together again and beat at each other's defenses. Then, with the elegance of dancers, they moved apart.

One last time they came together. With the speed and training of the Mythit illusions, Jan simply beat Lyndsy's lightning reflexes. In rapid succession, he gave her three quick swats.

Lyndsy stopped and stood still. She gazed at him with a strange expression on her beautiful, flushed face. Deliberately, she went to one knee and laid her staff on the ground. "You give me respect. You let me keep my pride. Your kindness has won my heart. You now show me there is no shame in defeat. I say this truthfully; since I earned my name, I have never been beaten. Man of Mirshol, what will you give me next?"

Mirshol? The word spread through the fighters like wildfire.

Jan sheathed his sword. He took two steps and held out his hand. Lyndsy reached, and Jan pulled her to her feet. Wrapping his arms around her lithe form, he kissed her. She reached up and wrapped her arms around his neck. Jan gazed into her eyes, oblivious of the crowd.

Lyndsy smiled and whispered, "You do me honor."

Samantha watched the intercourse of their personalities. The glory of the intimate expression almost took her breath. Blinking back a flood of tears, she said, "They will teach fear to the hearts of the damned!"

"They are both dancers," the weapons master said. "I would have wondered who taught him if I hadn't seen the Mythits with my own eyes. As for the were, they have always been renowned for their skill with weapons."

"High Cleric, is it permissible for a human to join with a were?"

Samantha turned to Benjamin. "No, it is not. Yet, by the Creator, if they ask it, I will perform the service myself." She felt sudden goose bumps cover her skin as Benjamin's eyes flared yellow-orange. Slowly, they faded back to normal. "What is it?"

The Seer of Lake Town looked quickly back toward January. "It is nothing."

She gazed at him curiously; he was telling an untruth. Nevertheless, his personality did not fog in response. To his mind, the untruth was acceptable. She shrugged, *who knows what a man with his eyes sees?*

The black raven circled the School of Fighters training yard. It waited until the proper moment. As the old seer's aura settled back to normal, so did the cursed figure in clerical whites. Much blood had been spilled to achieve the strength necessary to daunt the high cleric. Melody the Black had performed the sacrifice herself. Now, it was time. The black raven uttered the curse.

Samantha felt a shadow pierce her soul. Slim Chance yelled, "No!" and caught her as she fell.

Jan and Lyndsy rushed to their side. Jan stared down at the shadow inside of Samantha's aura, and asked, "What happened?"

Slim glared at the sky. "Melody the Black has tried to murder her own daughter." He shook his fist at the sky. "You will die slowly for this!"

Jasmine appeared in the folds of Benjamin's robes. "Captain, clear the yard. Jan, feel her mind."

Jan drew his sword and laid it across Samantha's breast. He set both hands on her forehead and felt for her thoughts. The breath he had been holding hissed between his teeth as he saw her dreams. Fire! Leaping sprays of choking fire. "What is this?"

Jasmine shivered. "It's a *curse*."

Jan tried to find something to grasp but could not. "What can I do?"

Jasmine stepped away from Benjamin and knelt by Samantha's side. With her left hand, she grasped the white gem in Jan's sword. Jan felt suddenly full of the Mythit's thought. Jasmine reached down and placed one hand on the high cleric's forehead. Jan felt the pulse of the curse and was amazed as Jasmine began to tap her fingers in time to the pulse. *Jasmine, what are you doing?* Jan asked.

Hush. It's all right. Be careful not to break my contact.

Jan felt her begin to insinuate herself into Samantha's thought. In the next instant, just as Jasmine found a handhold on the high cleric's mind, Jan pushed a small force of power through the white gem. "Samantha! *Wake!*"

Samantha opened her eyes and jumped up into Jan's arms. "Oh, Mother!" she wailed. "Why? Mother! Please?"

"It's OK," Jan soothed. "It was only a dream."

"January! Melody is not my mother! She murdered our parents. They tracked them down and killed them by the northern tip of Mirshol!"

Jan looked into her eyes. *She's delirious*, he thought. "Samantha, it was only a dream. It's OK now. You're back."

"No." Samantha gasped. "You don't *see*!"

Lyndsy looked at them and gasped. "January, the high cleric is your sister!"

With a sigh, Jan said, "The high cleric is *everybody's* sister."

"January," Benjamin said carefully, "it's true. Samantha is your natural-born sister."

Jan looked at Jasmine.

"It's true."

He looked back at Samantha's face—same nose, mouth, hair, sparkling ice blue eyes. Jan wrapped her in his arms and held her tight. *Why was I the last one to see it? She walked through Mirshol. She used the power of my staff that should have killed her. Killed her?* He glanced back down at Jasmine. "You should be dead!"

Jasmine shook her head. "Over ten thousand seasons ago, I fashioned that gem myself."

"In the name of Song!" Jan exclaimed in awe. "You were the Mythit of Myril, the White Wizard!"

Binban and his brother Myril sat beneath an ancient oak in the Forest of Life. "I caught a Mythit and *bound* it." Binban grinned. "It was very angry. It bit me! He told me he had allowed me to catch him. I think he just didn't want to admit that I'm smarter than he is."

Binban reached up and caressed the lowest branch of the oak. A green fire came to life and danced on the edges of the leaves. Myril watched in awe.

"The Mythit taught me this. He said it's called tree fire. It doesn't even harm the tree! It can be done with any leafy plant, but the emanation from a tree's soul is stronger. Come here."

Myril pushed himself to his knees and came closer.

"Touch it. It's not hot."

Myril reached out with his hand. No heat! He felt the flames tickling his fingertips and smiled.

That same night, Myril walked through the trees. He sang a song of love and life, filled by the beauty that surrounded him. Such was his passion that he imagined the trees joining his tune.

A blur danced by in a whirl of leaves. He reached out and grasped the Mythit. In the darkness, he couldn't really see the creature's features, only two florescent red eyes. The eyes blinked, and the high-pitched voice of the

Mythit sang the last verse of the song he had been singing. "And the stars fly free across the sky."

A tear came to his eye. He let the Mythit go.

At dawn, he sat alone huddled by a small fire. Myril looked up. The Mythit was there, watching him. Female. She was splotched with red, pink, and white, as though paints had been randomly spilled on her. Her bright red eyes gazed at him, curious.

Myril smiled and thought about all of the jasmine his mother had painstakingly tried to grow on one the edge of the mighty forest. "Jasmine."

She wrinkled her nose and tilted her mushroomed, spiked head. "Jasmine," she repeated in her singsong voice.

On that morning, the Mythit Jasmine *chose* to be there. No other Mythit before or since chose to be *bound*. It allowed the one thing that could defeat the Dark Lord. Laws of Lyre's nature allowed two free minds sanctification.

It hadn't happened before. Nor had it happened since. Nevertheless, it would happen again.

Twice.

21

HE WOULDN'T TAKE IT!

January and Slim Chance walked alone. Slim made the request. Jan agreed. Lyndsy had stated bluntly and to Slim's face, "I don't trust you!" Jan went anyway. He alone, or so he thought, knew Sunder followed.

"One of Melody's favored was here. We must leave this place. I tell you, Poison is putting all of her effort into this summons. She is one with them. This early in Lyre's reawakening, it should be hard for her to do. I feel her ease in this. It makes me wonder at the nature of the thing she calls."

Jan stopped him. "You seem to know a lot about this. How?"

"I am one of Melody's many grandchildren."

"You're her what?"

Slim looked hard at him. "You accepted Samantha as such. I tell you true, I do not believe her dream."

Jan didn't *realize* Slim's last words. "I'm sorry. I've had so many revelations lately. I'm surprised I didn't expect it."

Slim saw that his words concerning Melody went unheard. Didn't the Mythits of Light already know the background of these children? He decided to let it go. "Listen, I have much to say. You do not realize what power you have contained within your staff-sword."

They spoke long into the night. Slim told January tales of power, all kinds of spells and uses. Jan was constantly amazed at the insight and wisdom this man held.

Jan stopped him with a curiosity. "Slim Chance, do you mind that nickname?"

He laughed. "It would seem the name fits."

"OK, Slim Chance, how old are you?"

Slim looked up at the night sky. "That star," he said, pointing, "is called, in the Vainian tongue, Tirnolin. I have watched that star spin in a circle for over three hundred seasons."

Jan could hardly believe what he was hearing. "You're over three hundred seasons old? You don't look a day over thirty."

Slim thought for a moment and then explained. "Any of Melody's children can be taught the mind work. It makes the body age slower."

"I see."

They walked back into the school and went to their separate rooms. Lyndsy waited anxiously. Sunder appeared as Jan shut the door. Instead of addressing Jan, he went straight to Lyndsy. "Slim Chance is true to January. I also don't understand why, but it's true."

Lyndsy nodded in satisfaction. Jan saw that the matter was settled. *Why couldn't I convince her?*

Lyndsy woke up at dawn. Flower sat in the window. As Lyndsy blinked and yawned, Flower thought, *Lyndsy must not be herself this morning.*

As if on cue, Lyndsy's head snapped up. She rushed to her clean wraps and snatched them from the line. Holding them bunched in her face, she breathed in the scent of wildflowers.

Flower watched her radiant smile and was well paid for the flowers Jan had asked her to go find. Lyndsy stretched, twirled, and danced around the room. She was still naked, and her white hair flew around her like pale smoke.

She is beautiful! I wonder if she knows how sincere Jan is when he calls her the most beautiful woman in Lyre?

Lyndsy stopped dancing and went to the side of the bed. She whispered, "I love you, my January. Please want me the way I want you! I couldn't bear it if you didn't. I know you don't know were customs, but by your actions you have made me your woman. I like to pretend you know what you've done."

Flower heard, although the words were barely audible. *She really doesn't know!*

Jan woke with a start. Lyndsy frowned as he sat up fast.

"What is it?" she asked. "A bad dream?"

"Yes! No! Lyndsy, Slim was right. The Mythit, Poison, has summoned a demon. The reason it's even taken her this long is because it's the same demon that haunts Terror Trail. It was in that man's body, and she couldn't find it. Lyndsy, this time it comes in its own body! I saw it in my dream."

Running feet came to a stop outside the door. "January!" Samantha shouted as she threw open the door. "Oh," she turned away, surprised.

Jan and Lyndsy looked at her and then each other. Lyndsy plucked her wrap from the end of the bed and pointed at it. All of the sudden tension in the room fled as Jan laughed.

"You can turn around now," Lyndsy said with a grin.

Samantha turned. "Jan, I saw the demon in my dream."

"I know," Jan said quickly. "What can I do about it?"

Samantha looked sharply at Lyndsy and then looked suddenly blank. "Nothing."

"You mean I can't avoid it."

Samantha's expression was strange.

Jan stared at her, and then he used the Voice of Command. "High Cleric, I need your knowledge. *How do I fight it*?!"

The Voice had the desired effect. Samantha brushed off his attempt to control her, and she began to think clearly. "No, it can't be avoided. If I were to—"

The Mythits appeared. Jasmine said firmly, "High Cleric, don't say it."

Samantha looked down. "Jasmine, it must be done. *You* know what a demon can do. It's too late; what's done is done. Jan and Lyndsy don't—"

"Quiet!" Jasmine commanded.

Samantha shook her head. "Jasmine, since first I met January, I have respected him. I quickly realized that I love him. Now that I know he is my brother, that love is tenfold! I *must* do everything that I can for him. You have played the role of his mother. He even thinks of himself as your son. How can you hold this back from him?"

Sunder burst into laughter. His purple eyes glowed with mischief. "You don't want him *lost*?"

"No."

"Then let's put that aside for a moment," Sunder said, trying to hold back laughter. "Why don't you ask the werewoman if she's lost what you think she lost?"

Samantha's first thought was, *How do I ask, tactfully, if Lyndsy's lost her virginity?*

Jan heard her and wondered. *What, in the name of Song, does that have to do with anything?*

Flower leaned over and whispered in Lyndsy's ear. Lyndsy dropped her head in shame. Now they would know she wasn't a woman. Sixteen seasons old and *still* a lowly maiden. But, if it was important, she should say something. "No," she said ruefully. "I have offered it to him many times. He won't take it."

Sunder choked on his laughter. Flower slapped both hands over her mouth and started to turn purple. Samantha sat down heavily and sighed in relief. "I'm sorry, I just assumed … Well, that changes everything."

Why? Jan wondered.

"The demon will have no power over your mind. He will only be able to use physical strength and magic. I think I've heard its name, if it's the same one."

"Wait!" Jan said quickly. "What does Lyndsy's virginity have to do with this?"

"Yes," Lyndsy asked, "I want to know too."

Samantha's mouth closed so fast her teeth clicked.

Sunder, now under control, said, "It's really very simple, although it's not Lyndsy she's really referring to. You didn't give in to lust, even though I would hesitate to call your feelings toward each other by that name. Lust is the Black Mythits' greatest weapon against humans. Demons also use it. It could use lust to enter your mind."

"I don't understand."

"Let me try to explain it to you," Jasmine said. "You have seen the personalities of the Black Mythits. Did you see their color as dark and thick, smoke like and choking?"

Jan nodded. "It almost choked me."

"Demons live in a realm of a kind of personality. They, like Mythits, are physically aware of aura. A demon can grasp and strangle, squeeze and bind anything but a clear, bright personality. If there was a sour note echoing in your aura, the demon could grasp it."

This explanation Jan understood all too well. He swallowed hard. "I can't say I haven't desired her."

Lyndsy looked at him. "Jan, what you say is true, but"—she turned to Jasmine—"I have smelled lust in men. He *never* smelled like that. I don't understand about personality, but I can tell you lust also smells thick and choking."

Samantha sighed. "It's too bad most people can't see the way that they stain their souls. The smell of the stain attracts evil like bees are attracted to honey. It is in this way that Melody finds those humans most useful to her."

Jan asked curiously, "Why couldn't you tell by just looking at me?"

Samantha smiled. "It's not that easy. As Sunder said, he would hesitate to call your feelings by that name. Besides, an evil person can clear his or her aura by thinking of sweet things. You have to be around someone for a while. Their true colors will eventually come out. Glances indicate nothing, but momentary thoughts. The truth is, I'm sorry for presuming. I have already witnessed the clarity of your personality."

Jan eyed Jasmine. "What were you stopping Samantha from saying?"

Jasmine thought carefully. "You have been told many times by Sunder that an ability given isn't appreciated as much as an ability earned."

Jan's gaze was that of someone not willing to accept an alternate answer. His gaze moved from Jasmine to Samantha.

Samantha knew what Jasmine wanted to hide and why. Still, she could give a half-truth. "January, there are clerical abilities that *should not* be given to anyone no matter *who* that person is. I will say this: A man and a woman married by a cleric before the Creator share a special union. Many people have different degrees of clarity in their personalities. Some people, unfortunately, are not very spiritual. Their auras are then subject to the whim of those able to touch them. However, the *blessing* of a cleric changes that. It is like a shield. So long as the man and woman are faithful to each other, their feelings, no matter how strong, are protected by their vow. Inasmuch as lust is concerned, between husband and wife, they are safe."

January heard the subtle way Samantha spoke. He decided a partial answer for now was better than none. He shrugged it off. At least it now made sense. He thought of the way the Mythits in Mirshol used personality. Many times they had shown him how they touch or caress an aura to get a response. Mythits played with personality on a tangible level. If a demon could do what they did—and do it with malice—it could have a devastating effect on the victim.

Samantha thought for a moment. She had something she had wanted to ask, but she knew January wouldn't like it. *Well, here it goes.* "January, you helped Lyndsy change shape by setting a spell in that necklace. Could you change me into a bird?"

"No."

"January, you haven't even tried."

"I can't," he said reasonably. "I knew when I did it for her that I couldn't do it for just anybody. The first reason is obvious; she already knows how to change shape. The second reason is more important. I don't really know you. Lyndsy and I became very close, very quickly. We can read each other well. If I were to change you, I couldn't, as it is now, be sure of your mind. You may not remember who you are. If you flew away and we couldn't catch you, you would spend the rest of your life in a bird's body!"

"We could join in thought."

"Samantha," Jasmine said, "there are places in your mind where a man does not belong."

"He is my brother."

Jasmine frowned and thought only to Samantha, *High Cleric, there are places in your mind that a* wizard *should not see!*

Samantha gazed out of the window. *Jasmine, this is not incorrect. If he asks about the Light, I can honestly say I don't know. You should know*—that *power must be realized.'*

Jasmine's face filled with wonder. Only Samantha really understood. "You two are unique," she said. "I have lived for over ten thousand spring-times. Until January came into our lives, I thought I had nothing left to learn."

Samantha turned to January. "We should be alone."

"*Hold it!*" Jan exclaimed. "First, you're going to tell me why you want to be a bird."

Samantha smiled. "To spy in Vain."

"In vain is right. You're not going to Vain! Forget it!"

"January, I could learn much."

"Learn how to get yourself killed? Forget it. You're my sister!"

Ah, catchphrase! Samantha stared straight into his eyes. "I am the high cleric of Lyre. It is my sworn duty to place myself and my life in danger, if there is need, to protect the people in my land. Every single life is in my care. Would you prevent me from doing my duty? I know the land of Vain better than anyone. In this I am needed. War is never far from Melody's mind. I can tell you in which direction she can strike. She may be preparing for battle right now. January, you know you must help me. Too much is at risk!"

Her speech was flawless, Jan thought. No wonder she had taken the place of the old high cleric!

Benjamin looked at January. "She is correct."

Lyndsy narrowed her eyes at him. "It is her right to choose. You must help her!"

Even Flower didn't realize Samantha's use of the Voice. "She is free to do what she must, *little* brother. Her courage is great!"

Sunder grinned, acting the part of a scolding mother. "Yes, Jan, you must help her! You really must!"

January and Jasmine burst into laughter. "All right, all right already!"

They sat on the edge of the bed, hand in hand, minds linked. With great care and great interest, they read bits and pieces of each other's lives. January was surprised at the studies Samantha had been put through. She could read the most ancient of Lyre's languages. Her herb lore was greater than his own, although her knowledge of plants was mostly for the mixing of hallucinogens, poisons, and narcotics.

She fed him memories that defined her, memories that would allow him to keep her mind aware of itself. Even though she was very careful, she still let private scenes slip.

There were teachings of black clerical power that January was revolted to see. At one point, he almost pulled away. Then he realized her body was convulsed with racking sobs. Terrible shame filled her. He began to understand just how much she had truly overcome and was instead filled with pride for this woman who was his sister.

He felt her calm as his love for her filled her. January wanted to give her something back, so he allowed her to see pieces of his own life. She watched him grow up in Window—the street urchin, the beggar. *How could he have become what he is now?* She watched as he met Sunder. He let her see bits of his training and a few glimpses of the Mythits of Mirshol. She felt a touch of jealousy at the closeness of Sunder, Jasmine, and Flower, but it left as soon as it came.

Not wanting to miss anything, she slowed him down as he met Lyndsy. She smiled at the many inadvertent misunderstandings. Every bit of attention January gave to Lyndsy was dear to her. *Oh, what a man my brother has become!*

They smiled at each other as they broke the bond. Samantha turned to the balcony and called, "Lyndsy!"

Lyndsy came into the room. Samantha held out her arms. Lyndsy approached her, shyly bowing her head as Samantha drew her into a warm embrace.

"Sister, you are a figure of beauty!"

Lyndsy looked up, startled. "Me?"

22

DEMON!

"It will come after dark. No matter where you are, that is where It will appear," Slim Chance had said.

They traveled a league east of the School of Fighters. The Weapons Master and Captain Slith had been adamant about coming with them. January had conceded. He wanted Benjamin and Samantha well protected.

Slim Chance pulled January and the high cleric aside. As Jan studied the ground, Slim spoke. "It will probably use fire spells. It will continually try to enter your mind. The demon can speak words that will stun your senses. Above all, do not become angry. That would give It a handhold on your, uh—"

"Personality?"

"Personality." Slim repeated. "That is an appropriate word—*personality*."

"Take this." Samantha offered him a silver necklace that held a symbol of the Bow of Myril. "It is blessed. It will only keep It from physical contact, but that may help."

Jan accepted it gladly. He felt the hair on the back of his neck rise as he put it on.

Slim Chance scowled. "It comes!"

Jan walked away from the others as he drew his sword. Tendrils of thought spread from his mind as he wrapped himself in calm.

A wisp of black smoke appeared and started to grow. A filthy black aura seeped into the air as the demon started to form. One clawed hand, holding a huge broadsword, came into existence. The sword was bloodred and wet.

As it dripped, each drop hit the ground and sent up little puffs of hissing, blue-black smoke.

Illusion! Jan realized.

The other hand came through. It ripped at the air as the whole demon leapt out of the magic window. Fat ivory tusks were turned up from its fang-filled mouth. Thick black horns curled from the back of its head and circled around to the front of its face. Wide-set, dark red eyes blazed hatred for all that walked under sun and stars. Its bloated, naked body looked amphibious, sleek, and covered in slime. Growths of scales bound all of its joints, elbows, knees, shoulders, knuckles, and hips. Eight feet tall, it took two steps and peered balefully at the humans in front of it.

A slow, wicked smile crossed its fat black lips as it smelled fear from all but one. Looking down at the werewoman, it snarled. "Slut! I'm still ready to show you the meaning of lust!"

With courage January could not at all comprehend, Lyndsy stepped away from the group, folded her arms beneath her breasts, and glared at the demon. Then she smiled. The demon took a step back, and January could have sworn the demon was daunted. Lyndsy stamped the end of her staff to the ground. "Hear me, lesser fool, I swear by my fathers, if you kill my man, there will be no place in Lyre you can hide. I am She Who Walks Alone and I am a steward of the Curse. You will cower in fear to think what I might do to you where no humans may see. Don't mistake *my* words!"

The demon raged and then looked to the high cleric. His rage turned to hideous laughter. "Twenty-eight times in one night, with a different man each time, she satiated her lust! Look," it raged, as it turned back to January. "Behold, your precious sister, the whore!"

The demon tried to set an illusion of rot and sickness around Samantha, but the high cleric stood her ground and shrugged it off.

Jan reached out with thought, called the sword to life, and twisted the air. The demon turned on him in fury. It spat a harsh *word*. Jan watched a filthy, black rune take form in the air and fly toward him. He brought up his sword and deflected it to one side. That surprised the demon. It took a quick assessment of the blade and emanated a twinge of fear.

Fear? Jan thought as he watched the demon's personality thicken.

"I fear nothing!" it charged.

Jan easily avoided the slow but powerful strokes. "You fight as badly as you did before!"

"Fight this!" The demon pointed his sword. Jan sensed the power building and felt his own sword respond. He knew, with a twist of thought, that he could negate the demon's magic. He was so surprised to see it change and burst into flames, he barely had time to knock it aside as it spun off of the tip of the demon's blade. It fired three more in quick succession. This time Jan negated two but couldn't stop the third. As he leapt to his right, the fire struck with a detonation that rocked the ground beneath his feet.

Immediately, the demon tried to force its way into Jan's mind. His revulsion at the touch made it easier. Jan felt the demon step inside his body. Desperately grasping his sword, he focused on the gems. A bright, searing pain burned along his nerves. It felt strange, as though he were disassociated from it. The demon scrambled to leave Jan's personality, and it was then that he realized it wasn't his own pain that he was feeling. The demon howled, furious. Jan charged, swung, connected. The demon's arm flew off, severed just below the shoulder. To the dismay of all, it laughed. Jan watched in horror as a new arm began to grow.

Hysterical laughter filled the air. Glowing, dark red eyes filled with evil glee. "Fool!" it screamed and leapt full upon him.

Jan couldn't move swiftly enough. The demon picked him up—and dropped him in rage. Narrowing its eyes on the silver necklace, it turned to face Samantha. "Whore! This is your doing!"

Jan watched the demon spit a long string of curses. Glowing, black runes shot like missiles at his sister. Jan thought his reality must be slipping because Samantha's personality turned into glorious white fire. The evil black runes splattered against the high cleric's aura and simply dropped to the ground. Jan blinked at the puddle of black evil at her feet and watched in relief as it faded away.

Of a sudden, he realized the demon was building power in its huge broadsword. With all his might, he pushed off with both feet and ran the demon through.

Flailing in burning agony, the demon swatted January with one great swing of its massive arm. Jan, still grasping his sword, flew twenty feet through the air. He landed flat on his back. All the air in his lungs whooshed out. The demon charged. Jan rolled to one side and felt the blade rush by his face. The impact of the broadsword connecting with the ground brought him back to his senses. With a great gasp, air rushed back into his lungs.

Jan pushed himself to his knees and looked up. The demon held the broadsword with both hands. It was drawing back for a swing that would cut him in two. Gathering strength, Jan pushed up with both hands firmly on his sword hilt. He felt the blade slide into the fat belly of the demon's slime-covered body. He thought a silent thought, and all three gems came to life. White fire shot from the white gem and ran up the blade. As the fire touched the demon, a pastel rainbow of sparks engulfed them both. Then, in one blinding flash, the demon was gone.

Jan hit the ground, and everything went black.

⁂

Ice-blue eyes opened with a start. January realized he was in a bed within the walls of the school. His whole body relaxed as he slowly lay back down.

Lyndsy and Flower sat in a chair. The Mythit was singing a song about Light Lake. Lyndsy watched Jan sit up. She set Flower on the ground and quickly went to his side. Jan turned his head and saw Samantha standing on the balcony. Her back was to him. She was tense and seemed very frightened. Flower's upturned, pale pink eyes gazed at him in concern. Lyndsy leaned forward and asked, "How do you feel?"

"Sore, hungry, starved!"

Flower's glowing eyes brightened. "You're always hungry!"

Jan looked back toward Samantha. *Flower, what's wrong with Samantha?*

Flower said, out loud, "The high cleric has grown fond of Lyndsy. She fears what Lyndsy now thinks of her. The demon's words about her were true. Strange," Flower said, watching Lyndsy's head snap up. "I tried to tell her she should be more concerned with what the weapons master and Captain Slith may say about her. She laughed and put that aside as though it meant nothing to her."

Jan watched Lyndsy's face as it filled with sudden comprehension. Then her wide-set magenta eyes filled with anger.

"*Samantha!*"

Samantha whirled.

"Lyndsy," Jan began.

A five-foot, pale-skinned, white-haired flame of righteous fury turned on him. Lyndsy pushed him back down as he tried to sit up again. She glared into his eyes and said in complete control, "Lay down, remain still, and be silent!"

Samantha walked in from the balcony.

Lyndsy pointed at the chair. "You, sit!"

"Lyndsy, I—"

"Shut up!" Lyndsy fumed. She stood, hands on hips, feet spread, glaring as Samantha scurried to the chair.

Jan knew how that felt.

"How dare you judge me! How dare you presume to know my mind!

By the Vow, High Cleric, perhaps you do not know what it is to be spurned. I would *never* give you my love and then snatch it away! Do you think me fey? Look at you!"

Lyndsy's face softened. She leaned forward and cupped Samantha's cheeks in her pale, fair hands. Gazing deep into Samantha's ice-blue eyes, she whispered, "My sister, *you* are a figure of beauty!"

Samantha blinked, startled. "Me?"

Flower's laughter filled the room. Lyndsy straddled Samantha's thighs and sat in the big woman's lap. As she laid her head on Samantha's shoulder, she said, fiercely, "You are my sister, Samantha. How could I do anything but love you?"

Jan watched as Flower's personality beamed in the warmth flowing from Samantha and Lyndsy. He saw silent tears run down the high cleric's cheeks as she softly stroked Lyndsy's shaggy, white hair.

23

HEAT

"**I**t's not the same with me."

"I know."

"She shouldn't go alone."

"I know."

"She may need help."

"I know."

"Look—"

"Slim Chance," Jan said with a grin, "maybe you should go with her."

Slim Chance blinked. "Ah, I knew you'd see it my way."

Two hawks flew west as the sun set. The larger bird of prey carried a little silk bag. Lyndsy watched Samantha and Slim Chance as they faded into the horizon. "Oh, how I wish I could fly."

"Do you really?"

"What?" Lyndsy asked, still intent on the horizon.

"Do you really want to fly?"

Lyndsy turned. After she realized he was serious, she grinned like a wolf. "Yes!"

"Good," Jan said, pleased. "There is something I want to do."

Sunder and Benjamin sat and talked. Jan and Lyndsy knocked on the door and walked in. "I'm taking Lyndsy to the cave."

Benjamin nodded.

Flower popped in. "Do you need a chaperone?"

Jan picked her up and set her on his shoulders. "Somehow, I just don't think being a chaperone is your calling in life."

Sunder laughed. "I think you're the one who needs a chaperone!"

"No," Jan said in mock seriousness, "what she needs is a nursemaid!"

"Men!" Flower exclaimed in disgust. "You're all alike. Come on, pleee-ase. I *want* to go with you!"

Lyndsy frowned. "Jan, I think she should come with us."

Jan saw the note of seriousness in her expression. "OK," he said, giving in, "and the Flower will grow on the mountain."

"Radical!"

No one saw a huge eagle, carrying a Mythit, which carried a wrapped sword, fly from the balcony. The night guard on the west tower wasn't asleep. He was just facing the wrong direction. He was staring wide-eyed, open mouthed as a white falcon ate his meal. It had landed right in front of him, pulled the slab of meat from his bread, and then jumped on the wall. Lyndsy waited until Jan and Flower were out of sight and then screeched and flew away.

They landed next to the crystal pool at sunrise and changed shape. Lyndsy pounced on Jan and fairly kissed him senseless. Walking on air, she danced out of his arms and threw back her head. "Oh! That was awesome!"

"Look!"

Jan caught his breath and turned to Flower. The striped Mythit was tracing designs on the surface of the crystal pool with her furry little fingers. Jan had to grin at her excitement. "Walk on it."

Flower took a hesitant step out onto the surface. Setting one foot, she burst into laughter and jumped out as far as she could. Soon, she was running and sliding, watching the tracers catch up to her as she came to a stop. "Come on, Lyndsy. This is great!"

Lyndsy twirled by January and slapped his rump. Laughing at his expression, she blew him a kiss and went to play with Flower.

Jan watched her sway toward Flower and quickly turned his head. The personalities of Flower and Lyndsy were beginning to overwhelm him. He turned back and saw that Lyndsy's personality was positively hot. That was the best way to describe what he saw. Even as he watched, her aura shimmered with a faint rainbow. Jan shook his head. *I must be tired. It just doesn't work that way!*

"Lyndsy."

She turned and beamed at him. He felt her heat slam into his senses. He quickly cleared his throat and pointed to the far edge. "There are stairs straight ahead. It's the way to the front door. Just go down the steps and wait."

Flower tilted her head. "Well, where are you going?"

"I'm already there."

Lyndsy and Flower watched in awe as Jan stepped out into the crystal and sank out of sight. The light of the crystal trailed behind him. Finally, all that remained was a dim glow coming from the depths of the pool.

"Wow!" Flower exclaimed. "I want to do that!"

Jan slid through the inner door of the crystal pool and paced across the outer chamber. When he opened the front door, he looked past Lyndsy and once again gazed through a faint rainbow of personality. Taking a step back, he paused to take a better look. When he met her eyes, he almost gasped. She was dripping in passion, lips red and full.

She eyed him through thick, white lashes and stepped into his embrace. Throwing her arms around his neck, she pulled him down for a kiss. Jan felt his knees go weak as her warmth fired his blood.

Lyndsy jumped back in sudden fright. "Oh no! Jan, I have to get out of here!"

"Lyndsy, what's wrong?" Jan saw the rainbow of her aura grow stronger. He reached out. Lyndsy stepped back into his embrace and once again fired his blood with her kisses. With a great deal of effort, she pushed herself away again. Squeezing her fists, she turned. "I'm going to the top of the mountain. Don't follow!" With that, she scrambled away.

Flower jumped in front of him as he took a step. "Don't!"

"Flower," Jan asked, suddenly worried, "what's wrong?"

"Did you see her personality?"

Jan smiled. "Yes, I've never seen anything more beautiful in my life!"

Flower shook her head. "I guess I am the chaperone." She turned and looked at the stairs. "Jan, Lyndsy's in heat."

Flower told Jan about were customs. When a werewoman came into her time, she would leave her pack's territory and go into the mountains. Only the first of the pack leader was allowed fulfillment in her heat.

"That's cruel," Jan stated.

Flower shrugged. "That is just the way they are. They emulate the wolves. Jan, they don't go without sex. Only when a werewoman is in her time can she become pregnant. The truth is, as you should have noticed by now, werewomen are very promiscuous. It is their nature."

Jan said seriously. "They should have the choice of whether they want children or not."

"They do!"

"You just said—"

"Jan, they are free to leave and form a new pack any time a male and female choose to. However, their right to do it might be challenged."

"Still—"

"Jan," Flower said in exasperation, "there is no gainsaying a people's customs. They've been doing it for time out of mind. I'm worried, though. Her nose is so keen, even in human form, your presence even this close is probably driving her crazy!"

Jan sighed. Only one thing to do. He turned and walked back to the crystal door.

Lyndsy sat on the edge of the mountain. "I should jump! Oh, he smells *sooo* good! No! If another demon came, it could kill him or worse." She quickly rationalized the situation. "I would fight the demon! Demons can't touch me!" Lyndsy jumped up and started for the stairs.

"Wait! What am I doing?" She went back to the edge of the mountain and sat back down. She sniffed the air. Jan's scent filled her mind. "Ohhhhhhh … MMmmm … *Stop!*" she commanded herself.

It didn't do any good. "I should jump! I just couldn't bear it if anything happened to him!" A huge, fat tear rolled down her cheek. She breathed in. "Oh! *What a man!* He smells so good I could just … Damn! Fight it, girl!" She tried to physically shake his scent out of her head. "I'd jump, but then I couldn't *have* him. Oh, he smells so, so, so—*delicious!*"

Lyndsy leapt to her feet and started for the stairs again. "What am I doing!" Pressing her hands to her face, she screamed.

Flower heard Lyndsy's scream and hurried up the steps.

"Flower," Lyndsy wailed as the Mythit came into view, "help me! I have to leave here. I'm too close! I …" She blinked as the madness diminished. She sniffed the air. "Where is he?"

"In the crystal pool."

Lyndsy gulped air in an effort to calm her nerves. "Good, but this still isn't going to work. Flower, I'm trying, but … I guess if he stays in there and I can't smell … Oh! That smell!" Lyndsy smiled dreamily.

"That bad, huh?"

"Bad?" Lyndsy blinked. "Yes," she said ruefully. "Don't let him out of there. I'll ravish him!"

Flower laughed. She looked at Lyndsy, five feet tall, ninety pounds soaking wet. "I don't think," she started and then she thought about Lyndsy's fighting skill. "I don't think he would be unwilling," she finished.

"Really?"

Flower gazed at her. "Lyndsy, I don't think you realize the way that January feels about you."

Lyndsy turned away. "I know he likes me now, but he'll find a normal woman and …"

Flower felt all of Lyndsy's insecurities as the werewoman burst into tears. She didn't know what to say. She knew Jan very well. How could she convince Lyndsy that there wasn't a woman alive who could have taken his heart the way she had?

Jan sat on the edge of a bed reading from a pile of scrolls. The Red Wizard had documented the were in elaborate detail. Red's praise for their fighting was impressive, to say the least. Jan ran across a story about an albino werewoman named Moonlight. She had also used a staff. *I wonder if Lyndsy knows this story?*

Her whole life had been a tragedy. The last female of a pack, even unloved and terribly abused, she had still sworn vengeance against the Vainians that destroyed her people. She had valiantly hunted them one by one. When she'd completed the compulsion of her vow, she'd jumped from the highest precipice in the Vile Mountains.

He continued his reading and found many examples of the were's dislike for things not normal, such as white or black fur. The degradation these individuals were put through made Jan marvel that Lyndsy had survived so seemingly unscathed.

He finished the last sentence of the paragraph. "They usually die never knowing the comfort and love of a mate."

Jan looked up and saw a picture in a tapestry he hadn't noticed before.

"Lyndsy."

Flower watched the werewoman sniff the air. A hot flame lit within her magenta eyes; her personality became a prism. Flower thought to tell Jan to leave, but as all Mythits must, she was sharing in the flood of emotion. All she could say was, "*Wow!*"

Lyndsy turned and saw Jan, head and shoulders above the surface of the pool. The strangeness of the sight made her snap. "Jan, leave now, please!"

Jan shook his head. "Come here. Trust me."

Lyndsy gladly gave in. She walked to the pool and eagerly caught hold of his upraised hand. With a gasp of surprise, she took one great breath as her head sank below the surface. Blinking, she saw they were drifting to the bottom.

She was holding her breath. Jan tried to speak and realized speech wouldn't work here. For the first time, Lyndsy heard Jan speak in her mind. *Don't hold your breath.*

Lyndsy gasped in surprise, involuntarily breathing in. Jan watched her face as she said something, calmed, and looked around. Jan grinned and pointed down.

Lyndsy saw the floor coming up. They landed gently on its smooth surface.

Are you feeling OK?

Lyndsy instinctively tried to pull away as she realized they were still holding hands. Jan's grip caused her tug to pull them together. Jan wrapped an arm around her shoulder and held her close. He knew that, if he let go, she would become inanimate. Hesitantly, she looked up at him. Jan saw that the fire was gone.

"Yes," Lyndsy tried to say.

Speak with your mind.

"How?"

Jan read her lips. *Try counting to ten in your head.*

One, two, three, four—

See? It's easy.

Her whole body seemed to tense. *You can hear me?*

Perfectly. Are you sure you're OK?

Lyndsy looked away, embarrassed. *Jan, I still want you, but I'm not out of control like I was up there.*

Is this why you wanted Flower to come with us?

She turned and gazed back into his ice-blue eyes, *'Yes. Are you mad at me?*

Jan frowned. *Why would I be mad at you?*

He didn't get an answer to that question. Flower's thought burst into the crystal chamber. *Jan! She'll ravish you! Jan!*

What?

Lyndsy burst into laughter as she pointed. Flower was pressed up against the crystal door, fingers splayed, nose and forehead scrunched against the surface. Her pale pink eyes, darting from side to side, glowed with worry as she tried to penetrate the crystal with her senses.

Jan! Where are you? I can't see anything! Look out, January! Lyndsy's going to ravish you! She said so!

He had to bend as Lyndsy fell to the floor. She couldn't stand. She was laughing too hard.

Did you say that? Jan asked, incredulous.

Yes! Lyndsy convulsed into a fresh fit of giggles.

Jan couldn't help but laugh. After they caught their breaths, they went to Flower. The Mythit's pale pink eyes were almost crossed as she tried to see in. Lyndsy reached down and out and grabbed the Mythit by one heel. She pulled the Mythit into the pool upside down. *Look what I caught!* Lyndsy thought in mock surprise.

Too small. Throw it back!

Throw it back?'

No! Lyndsy ran her fingers along Flower's ribs. *I want to ravish it!*

Stop! No! Stop. Cut it out. Please, stop!

When Lyndsy was finished "ravishing" Flower, they went to the bed and looked through the chest of treasure. Flower shook her head in wonder, and then she looked suddenly at Lyndsy, *Will she be able to* speak *when we leave?*

Lyndsy looked blank. Then it dawned on her. *You can always talk like this!* She realized, with a flood of memories, that Jan and the Mythits did indeed share thought. She pictured Jan in a hundred different poses apparently lost in thought. Gazing out of a window, looking at his fingernails, scratching his chin. She looked up. *Will I?*

Jan shook his head. *I don't know.*

Give her a magic charm, Flower suggested.

Lyndsy looked up hopefully. Jan nodded as he thought about it. *I think I can do that.*

Lyndsy wrapped her arms around Jan's waist and squeezed him tight.

Look! Flower pointed at a partial mannequin that had appeared in a corner. It wore the whites of a high cleric. The robe was embroidered with pale blue bows all along its luxurious collar. Each bow was a representation of the Bow of Myril. A gold and oak scepter stood next to the mannequin. A ring of twelve diamonds surrounded a huge pearl that was set in the scepter's crown. Thin silver bars, also representing the Bow of Myril, were set into the wood. At the end of its two-foot length was a gold etched cap. *The Scepter of Light!* Jan thought in awe.

Lyndsy turned her head and jumped to her feet. Jan saw her expression and gazed along her line of sight. A long ivory staff hung on the wall over the entrance. Wolves, dancing in all positions, were carved in fine detail over its entire length.

How did her *staff get here?*

Jan lost his grip as Lyndsy started forward. She froze in place with one foot raised. *Yep, she knows the story.* Jan stood up, still holding Flower's hand. They walked around Lyndsy and faced her. She was suspended in midstride, a strange mixture of envy and awe on her pale angled face.

Is she all right?

Yes, Jan responded, *she's fine. Flower, do you know how beautiful she is? Do you see her the same way I do?*

How can I not? Flower teased. *You paw all over her like a sick puppy in love!*

Jan exclaimed, *I do not!* as he looked down at the Mythit. He laughed as he saw the expression on Flower's face, tongue hanging out, paws up, big sad eyes. *Flower, I love you!*

I know, she said, wrinkling her nose and panting. Then she straightened and pointed up at him. *That's the problem! You need to tell her you love her. Before you came up there and got her, she said, "He loves me now, but he'll find someone normal, and—"*

And what?

And she started crying, that's what! Jan, Flower said seriously, *I am six hundred seasons old, and I have never felt such heartache from anything!*

I know.

You don't know. You weren't there.

Jan set Flower on his shoulders. He picked up the scrolls and opened them. *Can you read, six hundred-season-old little girl?'*

She slapped him upside the head. *Gimme that!*

Read this. Start here.

Jan walked to the staff and plucked it from the hooks. The wolves on the staff were carved so perfectly they almost seemed alive. As he touched it, he felt a shimmer of magic and saw a protective spell that ensured its strength. The red gem in his sword came to life and acknowledged the spell.

I understand.

What?

I guess you do know a little bit of the way that she feels. Jan, that's terrible.

Jan thought wryly, *There's no gainsaying a people's customs; they've been doing it for time out of mind.*

She slapped him upside the head again, *Don't get uppity with me,* little brother!

Jan felt the crystal around him and concentrated on a few things he would like to have. He felt goose flesh rise on the nape of his neck as he realized everything he wanted was within the room. Walking over to a finely sewn sable cape, he eyed a pair of white kid boots. *Excellent!*

Flower pushed Jan's long ponytail out of her face and looked over her shoulder. 'Wow! *Are you gonna make a fairy princess?*

In a moment, he answered as he drew his sword. Moving back to Lyndsy, he scanned her body, *Flower, I'm going to do a little magic. I need to put you down for a moment.*

Flower frowned. *Am I gonna take a nap too?*

Yep.

Well, OK, but you better bring me back first!

I will, little sister.

Jan set her down and let go. Flower's eyes quit their glow. Jan grinned to himself and turned back to Lyndsy. He had been thinking of how to bring her out of heat and thought he might know a way. Holding the sword over Lyndsy's head, he called the gems to life, *Here we go …*

Hurry up.

I'm finished.

Flower narrowed her eyes. *Lean down here so I can slap you upside yo head.*

I'm serious. You just don't realize the passing of time.

Flower shrugged. *OK, whatever you say.* She clearly didn't believe him.

Flower, take these and put them on her. Whatever you do, don't touch her skin. Jan waved the sword and levitated Lyndsy up off of the floor. When Flower was finished dressing her, they stood back to take a good look.

The Mythit's pale pink eyes sparkled in delight. *She looks like a figure from a dream.*

Jan smiled and set the staff in her hands. *One more thing.* Jan went to a full-length mirror and pushed it in front of her. Then he moved behind her and rested one hand on her bare shoulder.

She looked startled for a moment, and then a slow smile added life to the image in the mirror. A full-length sable cape covered one shoulder. Pristine gloves and snow-white, knee-high boots contrasted exquisitely with the blue-black fur. Her bright red wraps and a hot pink headband made the overall picture purely feminine. Yet, the way she grasped the ivory staff left no room for doubt.

Jan smiled shyly. *It seems to me that the werewoman Moonlight has returned.'*

She looked at his reflection in surprise. *Do you really know whose staff this is?*

Yes, my Moonlight. I know.

Lyndsy's eyes widened at the use of her name. She turned in his arms and gazed up into his eyes. *I was nothing before you came into my life. If you leave me, I will be less than nothing. I will have known what love is and know that I have it not.*

Flower was going crazy, poking him. *Tell her! Tell her!*

Lyndsy looked down at Flower. *Tell me what?*

Flower had the look of mischief incarnate. She lied, *Oh, I forgot you could hear my thought.*

Come. Jan led them to the door.

No! Lyndsy tried to pull away, but Jan picked her up and carried her through. She tensed, waiting for the insanity that was sure to come. After one breath, she relaxed and realized her heat had passed. "What happened? How?" Lyndsy leaned back and looked suspiciously down into his ice-blue eyes. "Did you do something?"

"Not yet," Jan answered.

"What do you mean, not yet?" she asked, pretending not to notice the shy look he was giving her.

"In a moment." Jan set her down and turned away. He had gone deep into her form as he had scanned her. Not even physically touching, he had, nevertheless, been overcome by the powerful sexual need that had rushed through her veins. "First, I have to go get something from the crystal chamber."

"Not so fast!" Lyndsy said firmly. With a sweep of her cape, she stepped around him to block his entrance. "Tell me," Lyndsy demanded, "what you haven't done yet."

Jan dropped to one knee. "I love you. I want you to always be by my side. If you say no, I'll understand, but at least think about it. Please?"

Lyndsy's eyes grew round. She could not believe what she was hearing.

"Lyndsy, will you be my first?"

Lyndsy shook her head in disbelief. She thought of the smells of love-making coming from the tents in the land of the were. She remembered the scents of couples as they gazed into each other's eyes. The terrible memories of Sha's first vanished in an instant. The fury and jealousy she had fought so hard to deny faded away. January wanted her! All the bubbling, bursting joy of life that she thought she would never feel found its way straight into her heart. Lyndsy threw back her head and shouted, "*Yes!*"

January watched her shaggy white hair settle over her eyes. The hot pink headband seemed to change them to liquid fire. *How can anyone not find her beautiful?*

Lyndsy stepped forward and cradled his head between her small breasts. She rubbed her cheek in his hair and kissed the top of his head the same way she liked him to do to her. Even kneeling, his head was just below her chin.

They landed on the balcony and changed shape. Giggling and stumbling around in the dark room got them washed and bedded. Lyndsy curled up next to Jan and was instantly asleep. In that moment before dreams, Jan heard voices.

We need to get back now!

This is terrible! I can't believe such single-minded hatred was once the one I considered Mother. I know now that she isn't … but I loved her!

An overwhelming feeling of loss and pain flooded Jan's senses; he was startled to wakefulness. *Samantha? Are you back?*

Hello?

Samantha!

January?

Yes, where are you?

In Vain!

Fear!

Samantha, what's happening?

Jan suddenly found himself wading through a mental sea of emotions. He was being pulled headlong through darkness. Hate, fear, loathing, anger! *Samantha!* Jan opened his mind's eye and saw a fat black widow spider spinning a filthy, glowing red web. He fought to pull away and realized he was bound to Samantha's senses. *No!*

Jan hurled himself away and wrenched Samantha from the webs. A cool wash of relief flooded his mind.

January! That is you!

Yes!

Still bound in mind, they realized at the same time that Melody had noticed Samantha's presence and had reached out to bind her. *How is it you are here?* Samantha asked.

You called me.

I didn't call you.

Never mind that now, Jan thought. *Melody knows you're there. Come back!*

Jan felt Samantha's agreement. *We're coming.*

Jan opened his eyes. Lyndsy had arms and legs wrapped around his waist and thighs. Sunder was sitting on his chest, hands pressed against his forehead. Jasmine stood on the bed looking down at him. She watched his personality burst back into the room. "He's clear!"

Jan sat up. "What happened?"

Lyndsy sat up with him, arms still wrapped around his waist. "You were floating off the bed."

"I was what?"

"Floating off the bed."

"How?"

"Don't ask me," Lyndsy snapped. "You're the wizard!"

"*I* don't know!"

Sunder inspected his personality with a critical eye. Jasmine waited while Sunder looked. When the orange Mythit nodded, Jasmine said, "Call your sword."

Jan looked blank for a moment and then, "Oh." His senses spread to the sword lying on the table. He watched the violet tint of his aura touch the hilt. With a thought, the blue gem came to life. He reached out with one hand as the sword levitated to him.

"That's what I thought," Sunder said. "You called the power of your sword in your dream. That can be dangerous."

"It wasn't a dream. Samantha was in my mind. Somehow, we formed a link in our meld."

"That doesn't surprise me," Jasmine mused. "After all, she is your sister."

Sunder's purple eyes sparkled in humor. "Fate!"

Jasmine burst into laughter. Sunder gave Flower a quick grin. Then they too laughed.

Jan just gazed at them as though they were crazy. They wouldn't explain. He refused to ask.

24

The Scepter of Light

"Sooner or later, I will have to go to Wizards Veil. When I go, I might not want the king to pay particular attention to me."

Benjamin nodded. "I understand. And you are right. Yet, I believe, very soon, the king will see you and know what you are."

January glanced at Sunder but spoke to Benjamin. "I want you to play the part of a traveling magician."

The old seer gave Jan a rare smile. "Oh? I am almost afraid to ask."

Jan laughed. "It won't be hard." He reached under the bed and picked up a little oak box.

When Jan opened the lid, Sunder took in a swift breath. "I had no idea those were in there! Blue and I spent ten seasons making those. Do you realize what you're holding?"

"Yes," Jan answered, grinning at Sunder's reaction. He reached into the box and pulled out two strings of rings. "Benjamin, with these rings, you will seem to be the greatest wizard since the passing of the Three." With deft fingers he worked a gold ring loose and passed his sword over it. The blue gem came to life for an instant and then went out. "Here," he said, handing Benjamin the ring. "Put it on."

Jan paced to the washbasin and filled a glass with water. He set it on the counter and returned to Lyndsy's side. "Benjamin, point your finger at the glass of water and say, as quietly as you can, *crack!*"

Benjamin pointed at the glass and whispered. The glass broke into tiny pieces; the water splashed on the table and dripped down to the floor.

"Hey," Flower exclaimed, "that could be useful."

"Indeed," Benjamin agreed, eyeing the ring.

"Try this one." Jan handed him another. "Say the phrase *as light as air.*"
Benjamin repeated it.

"Now try to lift the bed."

"There's no way—" Lyndsy started to say.

But Benjamin reached down with one hand and lifted the brass bed both Jan and Lyndsy were sitting on.

Flower clapped her hands in delight. "Turn it over!"

Lyndsy eyed Flower mischievously. "Wouldn't you just love to spend the night upside down, out of the window, hanging by one furry ankle?"

"You wouldn't dare!" Flower said, shocked. That produced a round of laughter.

Jan pulled out another ring and spent a long time holding the sword over it. After a while, they began to wonder what he was doing. Finally, he gave it to Benjamin and told him to point it at Lyndsy and say *guise.*

Benjamin did. Everyone but Lyndsy gasped in awe. Jan nodded approval. "Lyndsy, you will need a good disguise to make you less noticeable. Go look in the mirror."

Lyndsy went to the mirror. She recoiled at the figure and then reached up to touch her face. Her eyes were blue—the rich, dark blue of a deep pond at sunset. Her skin was tanned, with a sprinkle of freckles scattered across her nose. She ran her fingers through shaggy, light brown hair. "It's, I, I always wanted to be like this!" She tilted her head and smiled a dreamy smile.

Flower frowned. "I like you better the other way."

Lyndsy's eyes opened wide. "Why?"

"Because you're different. Now, you're the same as everyone else."

"But I *want* to be like everyone else!"

Sunder frowned too. "Do you really? Tell me, werewoman, is there a better female in your pack?" Sunder watched her brow knit. "Tell me the name of the best warrior you lived with. Tell me the name of the best hunter. The best tracker. What is the name of the best Guardian of Blood Plain?"

Lyndsy looked down at her feet, then back up at her reflection.

Sunder continued. "*You* are the best. Moonlight, why are you the best?"

Lyndsy answered so softly they almost couldn't hear her. "I *had* to be."

Jasmine saw the pain in Lyndsy's eyes. "Moonlight, if you were always as you appear right now, would you have tried so hard to show your people that you have worth? I've never seen a better werewoman with a staff, and I was alive when the were first appeared in Lyre. How many fighters, men or women, have ever beaten you in a real challenge?"

Lyndsy glanced at Jan and whispered, "One."

"Child, you are the only woman I would willingly give my son to."

Lyndsy gazed back into dark blue eyes and saw, really saw, just how much being albino had shaped her life. At the age of fourteen seasons, she had earned the honor of single sentry duty on Blood Plain. Only fourteen men held that title with her. To gain that right, she had challenged Sha, her foster father, the pack leader. On that day, Moonlight of the were had become She Who Walks Alone. Very few werewomen had ever been trained that well. In this day and age, none.

Lyndsy smiled at her reflection. She had never thought of herself as anything but cursed. She had never thought a man would ever have her. There wasn't a male in her pack who would ever desire her. Their revulsion at the sight of her had constantly filled her nose with disgust, her magenta eyes with tears.

She watched January's reflection as he stood and walked up behind her. With a wave of his hand, he negated the illusion. He pulled her back against his chest and ran his fingers through her long, shaggy hair. She watched the way he touched her. She had to blink as he kissed her crown and settled his chin on the top of her head. Then he met her eyes in the mirror.

"I guess I could learn to like you the other way, but *you* should know what I prefer." Wrapping his arms across her breasts, he hugged her tightly and closed his eyes with a sigh.

Lyndsy did some growing up in those few moments. Long ago, she had accepted being different. That was when she'd vowed to be the best at everything she tried. For the first time in her life, she realized she was grateful for it.

Benjamin watched the Mythits weave a mood. He realized Jan was set apart. The young man knew of the Mythit's compulsion. All together, they were in a closer kind of contact than he had previously known.

He grasped the idea that Mythits could draw picture memories from a mind. That was the only way they could have known of Lyndsy's past. He remembered well, four seasons ago, in midwinter, on Blood Plain, feeling a strange déjà vu as he accepted the Vow from this small albino weremaiden. He would never forget the moment of *sight* that showed his death. That feeling came back to him now. He blinked, trying to will a scene of sight to come to him. Nothing happened.

After a time, he gazed down at the rings on his fingers. "I think being a wizard might have its merits." Smiling, he looked up and realized Sunder was studying him.

Samantha and Slim Chance flew through Jan's window the next morning. They washed and dressed as Lyndsy went to find Benjamin. When the party was all together, they sat down to talk.

Samantha spoke first. "The land of Vain is preparing for war. I have no doubt at all. The signs are everywhere. Even as we speak, Vainian fighters are training in the ancient ruins of Saduj. There are thousands of men in the ruins. From our vantage point, they looked like a black mass of ants on a hill.

"We traveled the main roads leading to and from Vanity. When we reached Condescension, I had a terrible feeling of foreboding come upon me. My misgivings led us to the River of Dreams that follows the main road to Wanton."

Samantha paused and stared at her shaking hands. She took a trembling breath and continued. "To make a long story short, we reached Wanton and found the city in turmoil. Her ports were filled with ships that sailed to the north—not south, north. Do you know what that means? Melody must be thinking of bringing Kringe back to life! Her power is awesome. I know that, for many seasons, she has inspired the lusts of Vain's kings to covet the entire land. I never really thought she could do it. I'm beginning to wonder. I am the high cleric; I keep the school's books. Vain's population is as great as the rest of Lyre. Melody *has* the resources to win if she strikes quickly. I fear for my land! Slim, you understand the weapons we watched them practicing with. You tell them."

Slim sat back and paused to think. He was mildly amazed that January had accepted him so easily. He had Mythit blood; he knew about truth sense and understood that was the reason January and the Mythits trusted him. The werewoman was another matter entirely. He didn't know if he could do it, but he had to manipulate Lyndsy. Persuasion would result in hot, angry answers. That wasn't what was needed here. The were had guarded Blood Plain's Black Mountain border for ten centuries. The girl's insight was critical. He had to win her trust. How?

"Well, the troops use plain weapons. It is in my mind that they are simply the wall between the real strike force and us.

"We watched a line of catapults in practice. They hurled stones at the remnant walls of Saduj. Their aim, I first thought, was downright terrible.

I was wrong. Off to one side, a single catapult threw crystal boulders that exploded on impact like nothing I've ever heard of before. The detonation blew a hole in a wall was no less than twenty feet thick!

"This implies two things. First, it says clearly that Melody's magic users are quickly coming into their power. They have been taught the magics and only needed Lyre's reawakening to make their studies real. Melody will not be on the battlefield. From the power of the spells I saw written in those crystals, it will take more than a few magic users to tend them. So, I would guess there will be at least five or six wizards that follow those catapults. Do any of you realize the other implication?"

They sat quietly. Jan and the Mythits glanced at each other with questions in their eyes. Slim turned to watch Lyndsy think. To him, the turning of her wheels was obvious. He hid his smile as she looked up.

"Walls twenty feet thick?"

Slim nodded.

"They will attack the Knights Alliance," Lyndsy said in amazement. "That is the only place in Vain's range that a weapon like that would be useful."

Ah! "Lyndsy," Slim asked, "if you were in charge of their wagons and train, where would you approach from?"

"There's three ways, but ..."

Slim studied her inner reasoning. He listened to her train of thought. As the light came on, he knew he was right even before she spoke.

"I would go through the gap at Vanity and cross Blood Plain." She shook her head in sudden fright and continued. "But first, I would sail with troops from Wanton and take them around the back of the Vile Mountains." She turned to Jan. "They're going to try and ambush the *were*. That's the only way to clear Blood Plain. Jan, it's the only way! They will try to kill my people. We must warn them!"

Slim spoke. "She is correct. I have already thought it over. I just wanted her opinion. The were will play a major role in this battle. I have thought also, no matter the target, Melody must attempt to destroy the were. They simply guard the Vainian border too well. Melody could not move in secret any other way.

"Now, we need to know how to contact all of the separate packs and warn them."

Lyndsy's whole body tensed in an instant. She realized in a flash that Slim had been leading her. Her magenta eyes spat flames as she turned to face him. "There is a *slim chance* that you will die a clean death if my people are betrayed. How can I be sure of you?"

Slim stood up, twined his fingers behind his back, and bowed his head. It was a gesture of were status that held great meaning. Lyndsy was surprised only for a moment. The group watched as Lyndsy drew a dagger from Benjamin's belt. She then walked to Slim Chance and set the tip against his throat. "I accept this choice in the name of January's integrity. Speak you well, Slim Chance."

Slim watched the fire burning in those hard, pale eyes. Never before had he feared death. This small woman held his life in her hands, and her seeming lack of care made him wonder if he weren't the greatest of fools. "I will not," he stated hesitantly, "now or ever, make any action or speak any word to put a were in danger. I say to you now that, should the need arise, I will lay down my own life for the sake of your people."

Lyndsy's eyes narrowed. She wanted to kill him. She wanted to drive the dagger through his throat and smell the salt of his blood. He had been a part of the Mythit band that had killed two of her children, but this act of faith was sacred. If she let him live, she would be bound to ever after consider him brother—as though he were of her own pack. She breathed in deep, letting his scent tell the sincerity of his words. Very slowly, Lyndsy let her hand fall away. "Slim Chance, you may yet live a long and healthy life." Stepping away from him, she gave him a crooked smile. "You dare much."

Slim raised both eyebrows. "Far be it from me to argue with that!"

Lyndsy threw back her head and burst into laughter.

"We'll put off any visits to Veil," Jan said. "We should go to the Vile Mountains straightaway—tonight, if possible. Lyndsy, Slim, and I will do this." At Samantha's protest, he held up his hand. "Yes, I know, you are the high cleric." Jan grinned. "You need to warn the school. I'm not saying don't come. Slim, can you be rested by tonight?"

Slim looked questioningly at Lyndsy. "Yes, but I think we should make haste."

Lyndsy grinned like a wolf. "I can fly farther and faster than you, any day of this seven day, in this moon, in this season!"

Slim smiled down at the fiery figure standing before him. "Oh, I don't doubt that."

"Lyndsy?"

Lyndsy turned and saw Flower making elaborate hand signs. Turning back to Jan, she rolled her eyes toward the pack they had brought back from the cave.

Jan narrowed his eyes at Flower but said, "I don't know. I suppose Flower could do the honors."

Flower jumped to her feet and rushed to the mirror. "High Cleric, come over here." As Samantha walked to Flower's side, the little orange-and-yellow striped Mythit climbed up on the bed. Twirling her finger, she motioned for Samantha to turn around. Flower produced a silk Mythit wrap and tied it around Samantha's head for a blindfold. Then she started unhooking the high cleric's robes.

"Flower," Jasmine said in weary tones, "I think the high cleric has the right not to be stripped in public."

"Oh! Jan, Slim, Benjamin, turn your heads! Sorry, High Cleric."

Samantha's gown puddled at her feet. She felt another silk gown go over her head. Flower's small fingers buttoned up the back and tied the sash. A light shoulder circlet came next and settled in place. "Now, everybody can look. Lyndsy, give me the box." Samantha heard the tinkling of jewelry and noticed the slight weight as Flower fastened it around her neck. "Good," Flower said in delight. "High Cleric, you can take off the blindfold."

Samantha stood in front of the mirror and gazed at the full-length gown. Shimmering, white Mythit silk clung loosely to her tall frame. Tiny pale blue symbols of the Bow of Myril ran the full length of the collar. A white-gold necklace set with fire opals shed gentle rainbows. "It's beautiful!" She turned and saw that Flower was holding a long oak box inlaid with white gold and ivory.

"Open the lid."

Samantha pulled the pin from the catch and caught her breath as the diamonds in the scepter's crown caught and rejoiced in the light. She reached in and reverently withdrew the scepter.

Jasmine caught Jan's eye. "Do you *know* what that is?"

Jan nodded.

"*My children*, you take much upon yourselves."

"It is their destiny," Sunder said gently.

Samantha touched the oak with her thought; the Scepter of Light gleamed to life. Neither she nor Jan was surprised to see the white gem in his sword answer the call.

Samantha glanced at Jasmine and saw her shaking her head. "Jasmine, do you have such little faith in me?"

Jasmine looked away.

Samantha, the high cleric, the Creator's gift of love to Lyre, walked to the Mythit and offered her the scepter.

As she neared, Sunder's head snapped up. A look of great surprise caused white sparks to flash in his purple, glowing eyes. The giant pearl in the scepter's crown shimmered with luminous opalescence. He never knew it was possible for that particular equation to be stored within a power tool. Sunder, the Blue Wizard's Mythit, did not know until this moment. Instinctively, he reached out.

Jasmine stopped his hand. She gazed into Samantha's ice-blue eyes, and asked, "High Cleric, do you truly understand?"

"Yes."

"What is it?" Jan asked.

Sunder looked away. Jasmine bowed her head. Samantha ran her fingers around the diamonds in the scepter's crown. "I will need this; I feel it in my bones. I swear—"

"Don't!" Jasmine commanded. "Do not say you won't."

Samantha turned to Jan. "Trust me in this."

"OK," Jan said simply.

He watched Sunder and thought to his innermost self, *I didn't think I would ever see him truly scared. What is the power in that scepter?*

Jan and Lyndsy went to see the weapons master and Captain Slith. The two warriors had become fast friends. The animosity between the School of Fighters and the Knights Alliance was great. The captain had overcome much to show friendship openly within the House of Fighters.

Jan repeated all that Slim had said. Lyndsy described the gap in the Black Mountains. The weapons master, intimately familiar with the area, nodded agreement and amazement at her assessment.

"How will you travel to the Vile Mountains?" the master asked.

"We will fly."

"Can you take me with you? I should be at the alliance as soon as possible."

Jan nodded. "Yes, I think I can get you there."

"Will you take me too?" Captain Slith asked.

"No."

"Why?"

Jan gazed at the fighter and saw his yearning to go. He almost changed his mind. Almost. A feeling came upon him that Samantha would need him, but how could he explain that? "Captain, I need you here. I must admit, I don't like your generals. A pompous show of ritual will not win a war. War is coming. I want a confidant in this school."

"I see."

"Captain," Lyndsy said shyly, "I wish I could take back my words when first we met."

Lyndsy was shocked when the captain reached out to embrace her. As he stroked her hair with one calloused hand, he whispered, "Since first we met, I've thought many times that, if I had a daughter, I wish she would be just like you."

Lyndsy swallowed a sob as she returned the embrace. She thought about the ready acceptance from the humans and the Mythits. It sure was nice to be liked!

Of all the were, only her father gave her any affection, but Lindon's status as One Who Walks Alone would not allow him to see his own daughter raised. Lyndsy smiled. A silent tear rolled down her cheek and soaked into the captain's leather shift.

25

kiss?

Jan had decided on a show of power. The Knights of the Alliance would soon be relied upon for most of the northern defense. He thought to let them know that magic was on their side also.

In the hour before sunset, the day after they left the School of Fighters, a Pegasus carrying the weapons master landed in the alliance courtyard. They were escorted by a falcon and a huge black hawk. The weapons master dismounted and unwrapped a bundle of clothes. Lastly, he carefully uncovered the hilt of a glowing sword.

The alarm that had first sounded brought knights to the courtyard by the scores. The Pegasus waited patiently for the yard to fill. When the men stopped moving and the yard was filled with silent awe, the glowing sword drew itself from its scabbard and hung suspended in the air.

The pile of clothes spread apart, revealing an ivory staff and a huge broadsword. The staff settled at the feet of the white falcon; the broadsword lay at the feet of the hawk.

The falcon changed shape. A slender young woman appeared, standing proud and unclothed. Red eyes watched the knights with an air of secret delight. She lifted one arm, and a violet, silver-starred armband leapt from the pile and tied itself to her biceps. Another long fold of violet silk leapt from the pile and wrapped itself around her lithe form. The staff jumped up and into her hands. The proud bearing and authority, combined with her exotic beauty, left not one warrior's heart untouched.

The hawk shrieked. In a flash of light, a man appeared. Neither young nor old, he too stood naked. With a shout, the clothes unraveled an elaborate set of leather armor. The man stood still as the armor buckled and fastened onto his powerful body. Long black hair and deep dark eyes bowed down to the sword at his feet. He shouted again, and the sword jumped up into his hand.

The Pegasus whinnied. In another flash, a tall young man stood in its place. Long blond hair fell straight off of his shoulders and hung in a tail down to his rump. He extended one arm and a violet silver-starred armband wrapped itself around his biceps. A long strip of violet silk jumped out of the pile and wound itself around the youth's hips.

The weapons master bowed low. He grinned, noticing Slim's disguise hid him well from the few of his men who might recognize him. He then turned and drew the Sword of Corillion. He smiled again, seeing their expressions as the hilt blazed with fire.

Jan calculated this display to the quick. He stepped forward and pointed his sword at the ground. White fire ran down the blade and burned the runes on the hilt of the Sword of Corillion into the hard-packed earth. Then the sword tip came up and shot a bolt of blue fire into the sky. "Hail! Long live the Knights of the Alliance!"

In a flash, all three figures vanished.

The weapons master turned from side to side, brandishing the Sword of Corillion. "Long live the Knights of the Alliance!" As he gazed at the faces of his men, the high cleric's words came back to him. *They will teach fear to the hearts of the damned!*

Jan levitated their invisible forms over the wall and well away from the eyes of the sentries. Touching down, they became visible. Slim was laughing so hard he fell to the ground. Lyndsy almost joined him until she saw the look in Jan's eyes. She sobered instantly. "What's wrong?"

Jan shook his head. "It's too easy. I could have done all that without the extra rings, or the power of the three gems, but I would be exhausted."

Lyndsy smiled. "What's wrong with that?"

"Melody has more magical objects with uncounted spells stored in them. I fear the damage she can do without any effort at all."

Lyndsy nodded in understanding. This time she did not smile.

They reached the Loom River well after dark. Lyndsy was adamant about going into the swamp on foot. Since nothing traveled the swamp at night, they made a camp.

Jan stood last watch. Near sunrise, as the stars faded, he saw a wolf watching him from across the river. It kept watching for a moment and then started to pace back and forth on the river's edge. On a wild impulse, he drew his sword and called the gems to life. The wolf turned to the tall grass behind it and then turned back to watch. Jan held the wolf's gaze for a long moment. The wolf stopped pacing and stared right at him. With a sudden brilliant flash, he let the power of the gems go. The wolf stared at him for another long moment and then faded into the grass.

Lyndsy woke and saw Jan gazing across the river. The scent of were was faint in the air. He turned and saw her sitting up. She returned his quick smile and blew him a kiss.

"Well, you look bright-eyed and bushy-tailed this morning."

She shook her long shaggy hair and laughed. Jan saw the smudge of dirt on her nose, the mud on her feet, and the dust in her hair. He remembered their first travel through Mirshol, sleeping on the ground and always at least a little dirty. She was once again the wild creature he had first met. He smiled, realizing he liked the difference. Still smiling, he went to her and kissed her good morning. And as always, she returned it with fire.

Lyndsy, in wolf shape, led the way as they entered Virile Swamp. They followed a meandering trail, trying to keep to fairly solid ground. Their travel was very slow, less than half a league by midday.

Lyndsy caught a large eel when they stopped to eat. Jan changed her shape with the power of his sword. She offered them some of the long, slimy serpent. But neither Jan nor Slim would eat it. Biting into the raw flesh, she watched them watch her. Wiping at the juice running down her chin, she licked her lips. "Delicious!" Receiving the grimaces she was waiting for, she burst into laughter. She looked up at Jan through her bangs, her magenta eyes filled with mischief. "Kiss?"

Near sunset, the gnats and the mosquitoes became unbearable. Lyndsy stopped and changed shape by herself. Slim, seeing the change for the first time, wondered how anyone could endure such pain so often. He commented on it, and Lyndsy shrugged. "Pain is part of life." Slapping a biter, she looked at both men. "You're not going to sleep in the swamp without fur.

The insects are far worse than this after dark. When we get where we're going the smudge pots will keep them away, but out here we'll be eaten alive!"

"Worse than this? January, turn me into a wolf!"

"You're right," Jan said seriously. "I'm not sleeping in this." They wrapped the packs. Jan left the hilt of his sword sticking out of a bundle.

"Hurry," Slim said, standing naked and waving his arms. "This is ridiculous!"

Lyndsy brought another eel just after dark. She grinned like a wolf, remembering having to fight the instincts of a bird in falcon form.

Slim sniffed the air and saw the eel. His mind said *no*, but his mouth said *yes*. Jan padded to her side and bit into the eel. They played tug-of-war until the eel ripped in half. Slim came closer, hesitated, and then bit off a mouthful and ate it.

It tasted wonderful, warm, and sweet.

When they had eaten it all, Lyndsy licked Jan's nose. With a laugh that sounded like, "Yip, yip," he returned the kiss.

The next morning, they traveled in wolf form. Jan and Slim carried their supplies with a makeshift set of harnesses. Lyndsy traveled unencumbered so she could scout the trail.

They stopped in the afternoon, and once again, Lyndsy changed shape on her own. In wolf shape, Jan and Slim felt her pain more keenly. Slim was stressed to share so much pain. She finished her changing and stretched as though nothing had happened. Slim let his muscles relax; he hadn't realized until then that he had been so tense.

Jan watched Lyndsy frown at Slim. In wolf form, he was suddenly filled with the scent coming from Slim Chance. It wasn't exactly fear that he smelled, but he could plainly see Lyndsy's disapproval of the emotional display. By were standards, he was exhibiting unacceptable behavior. What other things did they need to know?

She waited until they had changed shape and then went to stand before Slim. "You need to hold yourself steady. My people are fierce. They despise displays of certain emotions. It's too late now for much explanation. There is a large group of were just ahead of us. Slim Chance, just act as though you're facing people for the first time that you might have to fight with. Fear in battle is understood. Everyone but the insane fears before a fight. They will just think you are wary and ready to face danger. Hold their gaze." Lyndsy paused for a moment. She looked at Slim, and said reassuringly, "I saw you spar with the weapons master. You *are* a good fighter."

He had lived a long life. To have a sixteen-season girl give him reassurance was new to him. He laughed a loud booming laugh that echoed over the marshland.

Jan smiled at Lyndsy as she nodded approval. "Well, if they didn't know before, they know we're here now."

26

PACK LEADERS AND THOSE WHO WALK ALONE

They slogged through a three hundred-foot mire of soggy mush and were pleasantly surprised to stumble up onto dry ground. As they passed through a group of trees, they found a clearing containing some twenty odd clay and straw huts. Two wolves stood sentry at the foot of the path. Lyndsy motioned to them, and they stayed in place; nevertheless, they both growled as Jan and Slim passed.

The huts formed a circle. As they walked between them, they saw a group of close to fifty were standing around a firepit. Many of them were completely unclothed and seemingly unaware of it. Jan thought about Lyndsy's dislike for clothing and realized it wasn't just her. Modesty did not seem to be something the were concerned themselves with.

Lyndsy had told January he must be in charge of this first meeting. He should speak plainly, even harshly, so they could smell the truths of his words. As a female, Lyndsy was not allowed to be here, but as One Who Walks Alone, she had the right. He had read more in her words than she'd realized.

A big, barrel-chested man approached them. He wore a large two-handed broadsword strapped across his back. His demeanor showed anger, yet Jan got the impression the anger was not directed at them.

Jan said, "I am here bearing evil news that concerns the were. Your people may be in danger wherever they are."

The big were scowled and motioned them forward. "Come." He turned and walked back to the circle of were. Jan watched his back and then warily led Slim and Lyndsy into the ring around the firepit.

The first thing Jan noticed was a small group of were standing to one side. While whispers were passed around the gathering, these few men said not a word. To Jan's surprise, Lyndsy went to them and held out her hand. It changed shape to a paw. Jan felt her concentration. One man held up his hand and answered the gesture. Jan felt intense pain screaming along his nerves as they both stopped in mid change. Then the male's hand changed slowly back to normal. Not until his hand was whole did Lyndsy allow her paw to change. Her face was blank.

Jan's senses, keener than even those of the were, found very little expression of emotion. One of the group stood and, to Jan's amazement, slapped Lyndsy on the rump and gave her a fond embrace. The old were gazed over the top of Lyndsy's head and met his eyes. Jan got a sudden and overwhelming impression that he was looking at a man who was on the edge of insanity. There was no sign, nothing strange, no particular difference in personality. It was just an impression. Then he realized he was looking into the same set of eyes whose gaze he'd held at the edge of the Loom River.

Jan turned his attention back to the rest of the were. Many of them were now looking from him to Lyndsy in wonder. He gathered his thoughts, not knowing what to make of the depth of their personalities, and turned back to study the were with the broadsword.

The big man spoke. "Human, it would seem your news isn't fit to hear. I warn you, your lives are in our care." It was a strange statement. The words spoken sounded like a threat, but the intent was an obvious attempt to put him at ease. Jan did notice how the statement was taken by the rest of the were. He also realized most of the were present deferred to him.

OK, here we go. "There is a force of arms training in Vain. I believe they plan to attack the Knights Alliance." He paused, waiting for a response. None came. "If this is their plan, they will have to go through you to do it. I don't believe for a moment that they would challenge you openly. I think they would try to fall on you from behind in as great a number as they can muster. Or they might try to spy your movements and set a trap."

He paused again. Very little reaction. He gave Lyndsy a quick glance and saw her slight smile. *OK.* "I think you are their main concern. If they wish to attack the Knights Alliance, then it would be necessary to wipe you from the face of Lyre."

A small whisper spread through the people. Still no real reaction.

What are they thinking? Don't they care? Then it dawned on him. They were too intent on his scent and their own type of truth sense. They must already know of the Vainian movements.

The big man asked. "Who are you? Where are you from?"

January narrowed his eyes. "My name is January. I come from my home in Mirshol."

"Liar!"

The were broke out in curses. Those not holding weapons picked them up or drew them. Lyndsy was suddenly standing in front of Jan. She drew the cover from her staff and threw it on the ground at the big were's feet. She then stripped and threw her wraps down also. With a quick glance at Jan, she held out her left arm. The violet, silver-starred armband flew up and tied itself to her biceps. All of the were were quieted seeing Lyndsy's actions.

The big man drew his broadsword and snarled. "Bitch, it is not your place to fight for this human!"

Lyndsy raised an eyebrow at her stepfather in pure insolence. She yawned. "I don't really know why, but I care that you do not die this day. Believe me, Sha, you would rather fight me. And you are wrong. This *is* my place. I have sworn my staff at his side." She raised her chin toward the old were in the little group. Then she turned back to Sha and said in a suddenly cold voice, "I am his first. This is my place." She stamped her staff down hard and started circling.

The big man stepped back. "She is bewitched!"

The old man from the group came forward. He looked at Jan as though he had just witnessed something terribly funny and *needed* to share it with someone. As he stopped before January, he grinned like a wolf. "Do you know my daughter's true name?"

Daughter? Jan blinked. "Yes."

"Did she tell it to you?"

Jan thought about Flower sitting in front of him on the horse on the way to the School of Fighters. "No, as a matter of fact, she didn't."

The old were's eyes sparkled in humor. "Man from Mirshol, who told you my daughter's name?"

Jan tilted his head to one side. The old were was playing a game. Leaning forward, as if to give meaning to a special secret, Jan confided, "A Mythit told me."

Lyndsy's father roared with laughter. He was laughing so hard he had to bend over and hold his knees for support. The rest of the were were shouting and yelling, trying to get the big man's attention. Lyndsy was shouting and screaming to drown out the rest.

Jan grinned at Lyndsy's father. Then he drew his sword and shot a bolt of power straight up into the sky. A ground shaking *boom* silenced everyone. Well, almost. Lyndsy's father was laughing so hard tears streamed down his face.

Lyndsy faced Sha and said coldly, "I walked with this man for eight days in Mirshol. I have seen Mythits! He Who Sees All has blessed this human. If you doubt him, then hear this, my man has fought and killed a demon! You think me bewitched? You are a fool! Smell the truth for yourselves and quit acting like a pack of bitches!"

Jan stepped forward. "We are here to help. I want to fight at your side. This land is in great need of the were. I can help you fight the magic they set against you. The were are renowned as the fiercest fighters in Lyre. Yet, I say to you, you cannot fight them with weapons alone."

Lyndsy snarled. "He speaks truth for all to know."

The big man nodded thoughtfully as he gazed at Jan's sword. "The were dislike magic, but we see that it lives again. Man of Mirshol, we too have seen the Vainians preparing for war. We caught two spies foolish enough to venture out onto the Plain of Blood. You seem to know we will fight them no matter where they choose to strike. That is well and good. We keep the Vow. But who of us will fight by *your* side?"

Lyndsy's father stood up and rubbed his hands together. He turned to the group set apart and made a few simple hand signals. After a silent moment, one were from the group signaled back. Jan watched a burning light kindle in Lyndsy's eyes.

Lyndsy's father turned to Sha and said, "Those Who Walk Alone will fight with the man from Mirshol."

"No! I forbid it!"

Another older were from the small circle laughed out loud. "Sha, you are not the leader for We Who Walk Alone. We gave our clan status back even as our pack leaders gave up the right."

Jan raised his hand. "Sha—"

The big man jumped back as if burned. "Fool! You have spoken my name to a wizard!"

"Sha," Jan continued, "this fear you have about names is what is foolish. Even if it were true, *I* would not do that to you. Why would I wish to control you? You are of value as you are. Nevertheless, I swear by my name that I would do that to no one."

Although they didn't want to, the were smelled his truth. Many gazed at him in wonder, for all legends said wizards were to be shunned and feared. Yet, this young human came to them without fear and spoke his mind without any shadows on his words. The *were* had great respect for a man well spoken.

The circle of Those Who Walk Alone gave him the hand sign of friendship. Jan crossed his arms and returned a slight nod.

Lyndsy smiled in satisfaction but quickly returned to the present. "The Mountains of Kringe are being inhabited. I think we should look in that direction for an attack. We should send a spy straightaway."

Sha narrowed his eyes. "How do we spy over dead, cracked earth?"

Jan shrugged. "We fly."

"I will go," Lyndsy said. "You should stay. There is much you should know if you are to help as well as you are able." The last part was directed at her father.

Lindon nodded. "What he asks will be answered."

Lyndsy stepped up to Jan. She gazed over her shoulder and then at the gathering of pack leaders. Reaching up, she wrapped her arms around Jan's neck and pulled him down for a kiss. Leaning back, she licked her lips and raked his face with passion-filled eyes. She pressed herself against his thighs and pulled him back down for another kiss. He was overwhelmed, heart pounding. Desire rose in him like a flood. Giving in, he gathered her up and returned the kiss.

After a long moment, Lyndsy slid back to the ground and turned around. Setting hands on hips, she glared at the men. "Tell your bitches that I, Moonlight, She Who Walks Alone, will deal harshly with any who dare trespass on what belongs to me!"

Sha breathed in the scent of January's desire. "Strange."

Lyndsy's father smelled their scents and grinned from ear to ear. "Moonlight, I never thought I would see you play the role of woman." He smiled at January. "I am pleased to see it happen. Why don't I smell his musk on your body. Do you *know* him?"

Jan blinked, not really sure he was understanding the question.

Lyndsy sighed. "No. Not yet."

"Why not? He obviously wants you."

Lyndsy grinned impishly. "It's a long story."

"Is something wrong with him? Is it because he's a wizard?"

Now Jan understood and was flustered by such casual talk of sex. "There's nothing wrong with me."

Lyndsy bit her lip to keep from laughing. "I think I should go."

Thank you! Jan thought. "Are you rested enough to go now?"

Lyndsy's face was turning red. She was still trying not to laugh. She barely squeaked out a, "Yes."

Jan drew his sword. With a flash of light for effect, Lyndsy changed shape to a snow-white falcon. All of the were gasped in mingled fear and delight. She jumped up on Jan's arm and stilled so he could place a gold chain around her neck. Once again gasps were heard as she disappeared. Jan threw up his arm, and they heard the flapping of wings.

Slim thought, *I would like to look to the mountains of Vain. Will you be all right here alone?*

Jan looked around at the were as they watched him. *Yes.*

Slim stepped out of his leathers, and Jan changed his shape. With another gold chain, the black hawk flew away.

Sha studied him intently. "You don't fear to be alone with us?"

Jan shrugged. "No, I don't fear you."

Sha grinned. "You must be very good with a sword to feel so secure."

"Sha," Lyndsy's father said, "you are out of line."

Sha ignored him. "Come, let's spar."

Jan looked at the swords the *were* carried. Those who used swords used mostly long swords. Lyndsy's father carried one. "Sir, lend me your weapon. I will not have it said I used magic."

He studied Jan for a moment and then grinned like a wolf. Offering the hilt, he said, "My name is Lindon."

Jan drew the sword and saw the runes of the Vow etched into the blade. Silence reigned over the clearing as he quietly repeated the words of the Vow. Sha gazed at him in wonder. "Do you know the meaning of what you have just spoken?"

"Yes."

Sha smiled in kindness for the first time. "Then we will spar as brothers."

January followed Sha's lead and stripped to fight unclothed. He studied the big were's body language as the rest of the pack leaders made a circle for them to fight in. Raising Lindon's sword, he signaled that he was ready.

Jan used the Baby Colt Walk and immediately lured Sha into attacking. Before the were even realized what had happened, the tip of Jan's sword stood poised a fingerbreadth from the big were's throat.

"Hi!" someone shouted.

This time, Sha was infinitely more cautious. A fast, tight circle of swings from the broadsword made January dance backward. As soon as Sha gained a rhythm, Jan switched hands. Setting one foot forward, he blocked with a bone-jarring swing and reached in to lay the flat of Lindon's blade against his opponent's side.

"Ho!"

Sha grinned like a wolf. The big were came straight in, way off balance. Jan recognized the attempted lure. Instead of taking the opening offered, he switched back to his left hand and attacked from the other side.

Sha stepped back, barely keeping pace with lightning strokes from the young human's blade. He had one trick that might give him the advantage. When the right downstroke came, Sha reversed his hold and stopped the blade on the edge of his hilt. It surprised Jan completely. But as Sha once again took the initiative, Jan danced back and out of the way.

Jan stood back and took stock. He had almost lost a point. The score was two to nothing. One more score for him, and it would be finished. Twirling the sword by the hilt, Jan leapt forward to attack. Sha took the bait and tried to knock the weapon from Jan's grasp. The broadsword flew past his face as he stopped and snatched it back. Turning on the ball of one foot, he stepped in. The tip of his blade spun around and stopped at Sha's heart.

Lindon clapped his hands once, "Ha! Enough. Three to nothing!"

Sha stood back and sighed. "Aye, human, you fight well indeed."

Jan was thinking about all of the different moves Sunder had drilled into his head. With childlike enthusiasm, he smiled. "Show me how you blocked that downstroke!"

Sha blinked. He expected jeers or condescension; Jan's praise at his skill even in losing rendered him momentarily speechless. He raised an eyebrow at Lindon. Lindon just grinned and nodded.

Sha, Lindon, and January walked through the swamp. Jan spoke freely, answering any questions they could ask. Lindon noticed that Sha was quickly taken by the young human's easy manner and sharp intelligence.

At one point Sha walked ahead to scout the trail. Jan stopped Lindon. "Does it matter to you that I love your daughter?"

Lindon was seemingly startled at the question. He gazed at Jan curiously. "I don't understand."

"I am not were," Jan said carefully. "Does that put me beneath her?"

Now Lindon looked truly shocked. "You are human. How could you be beneath a were?"

Jan learned much from that simple statement.

Sha found Jan's tracking skills to be adequate, but his hunting skills were less than that of a were child half his age. Lindon smiled to himself as Jan listened carefully to Sha's instructions in stalking.

A little later, Jan saw a jay perched in the limbs of a shrub. He let his mind caress the small personality. Raising one hand, the jay came and landed lightly on his finger.

"You don't need to hunt!" Sha exclaimed.

Jan looked over the bird's head. "I could not kill a creature I have shared thoughts with. In Mirshol, the predators don't even eat meat. If I wanted to eat meat, I would have to hunt it."

Lindon looked at him in wonder and nodded as though he had just grasped an unfamiliar concept.

Sha merely stated, "That seems foolish. If I could call animals to camp, I wouldn't hesitate to eat them."

The next morning Jan was taken to a clearing to speak privately with Those Who Walk Alone. The talk turned quickly to battle strategies, and Jan was impressed by their knowledge of tactics. They discussed the best places to join battle with the *stupid* Vainians.

Jan listened and put in his own thoughts from time to time. From the first, he noticed their way of thinking as a group. When a thought was spoken, they would consider it and accept it or reject it as a whole. Leading the Vainians into the mountains by any means was wholly approved of.

Jan asked them about leading them into the swamp and received a seemingly incomprehensible answer. The youngest of Those Who Walk Alone, a huge bear of a were, said, "Fighting in the swamps is for pups."

Pups? Did they think it childish to fight in the swamp?

He asked them how many were Walked Alone. One of the older were told him the number was currently fifteen, Moonlight being the youngest and newest. They told him messengers had been assigned in the night to warn the pairs of were out on the plain. Only one of Those Who Walk Alone was on Blood Plain at this time. Two were sent from a pack leader named Snarl had been sent to take his place. Nevertheless, Blood Plain was a huge area to cover, and there just wasn't any way to contact every pair.

"I don't like it," Jan said. "We can't lose any were."

Sensing Lyndsy's return, he held up his arm and looked around. She settled on his wrist so he could remove the gold chain. Then he set her down and changed her shape.

Lyndsy quickly shook the falcon instincts from her head and took a moment to breathe. When she was sure of her senses, she crouched down to her heels and told them the news. "This is bad. Right now, an army of Vainians is marching on the passes leading to Lychantorrid."

"How far?" Lindon asked.

"Halfway across the flats. At their current rate of speed, they will reach the mountains in two days."

"Moonlight, that is not a problem. No one can attack us from there."

"That *is* the problem," Lyndsy insisted. "They should know that. Unless they forget their history, we have slaughtered them every time they try."

Jan frowned. "They will use magic. What are your defenses for the passes?"

The huge young were who had spoken of pups said, "We have preset rockslides everywhere. When our children misbehave, their punishment is to create and map a rockslide. There are no passes safe for the Vainians. The mountains are also lined with caves holding an endless supply of spears and arrows. Ten thousand humans trying those passes could not walk into Lychantorrid a hundred strong." As he spoke, he listened to his own words and realized that what Moonlight said was true. "They *should* know better. I don't really think they'll try the passes."

"We need more birds," Lyndsy said absently.

Jan nodded. "But who?"

Lyndsy wrinkled her nose as excitement filled her senses. She blinked as she met the eyes of Those Who Walk Alone. Then she burst into laughter. "How many do you want?"

In five hours January sat with all thirteen of Those Who Walk Alone. There were many things about the were that he didn't understand. Their mindset, internal train of thought, and reasoning were extraordinary. He quickly learned that their primary sense was smell. It was necessary to think in terms of scent rather than sight to penetrate and access their deeper thought patterns. As he first reached the center of their personalities, he was overwhelmed at their great joy in emotion. From the way they appeared, he had noticed they seemed not to show emotion at all. He couldn't have been more wrong; their love and joy in life was great.

He gave as much as he took. They saw flashes of the mighty Forest of Mirshol. Individual scenes of the Mythits were received with a knowing, quiet respect. As Guardians of Blood Plain, each were to walk had traveled the length of Mirshol's western border. Every were felt a secret desire to see and know what was hidden in the enchanted forest. Their feelings for this gift that he gave burned his senses with the fire of awe. They seemed to think the glimpses of the animals and the forest—to behold that which no others had seen—a gift beyond price. Perhaps it was, but Jan's intent had only been to give back and share for that which he had taken.

When he got to the huge young were, he stopped the meld early. "I don't think you need my help. You can already take a bird shape."

"I don't understand."

Jan touched his mind again and looked closer. This young were had the natural ability to take any shape that he wished. The ability was a dormant trait, and Jan was intrigued that he had even noticed it.

Jan thought about a big, lumbering bear that he had made friends with when he'd first entered Mirshol. He coaxed the were's mind to feel the bear. Touching the *instructions* of a bear within the blue gem, he gave the were a mental push.

"January!"

Jan opened his eyes and burst into laughter. The were sat before him, maw agape, staring at his paws in wonder.

"Change yourself back," Jan said.

The were started the change and Jan immediately stopped him. "No, you remember what it is to be yourself. Move through the change in an instant." Jan reached out and set his hands on the bear's head. With another mental push, he helped the change happen in the blink of an eye. When the huge were sat before him again, Jan smiled. "You can take any shape you like. Practice this; it is a rare gift. Tell me, what is your name?"

The were looked at him warily. "Now look," Jan said, "I don't understand this taboo about names. It really makes no sense to me. Besides, if you hesitate to tell me your name, why would you let me in your mind?"

At that reasoning, the were grinned in embarrassment. "I am Swiftfoot."

Jan pondered the name. "Swiftfoot, you need to think of ways to use this gift."

Even as he spoke, the sight came on him. He saw a huge bear throwing black-clad Vainians right and left as though they were leaves in a storm. A tall, beautiful forest-born woman fought with a long sword at his back. Her eyes were green, her hair was a curly, honey-red. She did not have sandy brown hair. She did not have the light gray eyes of the were. This tall forest-cloaked woman was human. Jan knew instinctively that they were lovers.

Swiftfoot said, "I will try."

Jan blinked away from the vision. "I know you will."

Sha was a pack leader. Those Who Walk Alone were set apart from all of the packs. Any were who chose to challenge a pack leader, beat him in combat, and didn't choose to take the place at the head of the pack could enter the exalted group. That were was ever after named One Who Walks Alone.

Sha gazed through the brambles at the edge of the clearing and saw Moonlight standing next to the human. A smile lit in his eyes as he remembered the day she had challenged him in the circle.

Lindon had been a member of the elite for as long as Sha could remember. Those Who Walked Alone were allowed to have children, but they had to be fostered in a pack. There was no birthright to Those Who Walk Alone. Lindon and he, himself, had taught Moonlight how to fight. At the age of six, she had walked away from camp and clan. She had quickly become a solitary child, and Sha thought she was having problems reconciling her albinism. Not knowing what to do, he'd left her alone.

At the age of fourteen, she had come to his hut. Nobody had seen her for two seasons. The whole pack gathered and laughed and jeered as she silently drew the Circle of Challenge. The thought had struck him that he could let her win. She could not take his pack; only a male could be Pack Leader.

Two extra seasons of solitary training had left Moonlight introverted and quiet. He had no idea of the tempered intelligence that sat behind those strange magenta eyes. She didn't even stand up to his chin!

Sha nodded to her and began to prepare himself for the fight. Sudden silence swept over the clearing as Those Who Walked Alone stalked out of the brush.

Sha would never forget the look she gave him when she realized he was letting her win. Oh! What a beating he had taken from that brown blur of a staff! Bruised and bleeding, his collarbone broken, Sha had found himself pinned on his knees.

As Sha walked into the clearing of Those Who Walk Alone, he watched January pull her into his embrace and kiss her. Their affection amazed him. He knew no were would ever have her. As her foster father, Sha was truly happy for her. *They suit each other.*

Jan heard the thought and turned. He waited for Sha to walk up the incline and nodded a greeting. "Sha, we need your advice." He quickly explained about the group of Vainians approaching the mountains.

Sha's grin broadened as he listened. He obviously thought the Vainians to be great fools. "How many?"

Lyndsy answered, "Three hundred fifty, including the pack train. Two hundred are on foot; the rest ride."

Sha said immediately, "It's a trick. They try to lead us from the place they really want to attack."

Jan nodded. "That's what we've been discussing, but where do they really want to be?"

Sha thought for a moment. "Maybe," he said slowly, "they plan to take Lychantorrid from the front."

"That's impossible," Lyndsy stated. "There are simply too many of us there. We always watch. If this is their plan, then they are such fools they have no business playing at war."

Sha studied Moonlight silently. In three days, he had heard more speech from her than ever before. He wondered if her external boldness was calculated to impress the human. He shrugged the thought aside. "Vainians have always fought foolishly. Why should we think that they have suddenly grown brains?"

After it was said and done, Sha decided to keep Lychantorrid empty. It wasn't exactly a camp. It was really just a central meeting place for were festivals. He sent runners to various camps, charging them to appoint runners wherever they arrived. In two days, the Vile Mountains would have eyes in all directions.

"I feel this a waste of time," Sha said. "Fighting in the mountains should be for the pups."

Lyndsy grinned like a wolf. "I wish I could be there if the stupid Vainians decide to attack the swamp!"

Jan saw Sha grin at the thought and wondered again if he understood them correctly. Did the werelings really fight?

27
That's My Little Girl

She stood on the flat surface of the black marble altar. Colors swirled like fog around her sensual, black-skinned body. They were thick, harsh colors, reeking of greed and lust. She drank deeply from the *lust pool*. It was enriched by the personalities of the ring of black Mythits that surrounded her. Eyes closed. She felt them as a wall of power.

Poison, Melody's mother, worked the personality of the ring of Mythits to a fevered frenzy. Rich, vile waves of oily liquid lust pulsed in chanted rhythm. The golden veins in the altar began to glow.

Melody had waited for over nine centuries to have her lusts quenched with such exquisite ecstasy. Every nerve in her half-Mythit body was laid bare to soak in the sweet syrups of heat. Hot sparkling fingers of condensed personality twined around her ankles, working their way up to penetrate the core of her being.

Poison watched in evil delight as her daughter screamed in the fulfill-ment of the fusion-binding of the black Mythit's circle. Now the time was right. Now the first works of black clerical power could be brought to bear. With the inherent power of Mythit empathy, Poison searched the fabric of Lyre for the ethereal doorway leading to the Forest of Dreams.

Melody felt the essence of the binding come near. Tendrils of feeling reached out with cruel fingers and grasped the soul of the demon that had failed to bind the Young One on the outskirts of the School of Fighters. The demon screamed in agony as Melody the Black, the last evil cleric of the Dark Lord, touched him with the flow of Lyre's Clerical River.

Poison watched Melody render the demon to its component colors, and, thus, into flames. Anger kindled in Melody's glowing, bloodred eyes. She held the flames in both fists and ripped tendrils of fire from the demon's soul. All of the minds present heard the demon scream at the sure hands of Melody's skillful torture.

The veil of the Forest of Dreams sprang up like a sheet of white gossamer. The reaction to this action was the momentary freeing of the black ethereal hell gate. Demons on the border of the hell gate wailed in greedy hunger as Melody ripped pieces of flaming personality and pushed them through.

Poison smiled in pride as she witnessed her lovely daughter feeding the demon to the bound souls beyond. When the demon was stripped of its inherent light, all that remained was a smudge of shadow. Poison whispered to no one, "You are, indeed, my daughter."

When Melody was ready, Poison searched the gossamer veil for the mind that her lover, Dagdor the Black, had once cursed. With quiet teasings of power, she lured it forward.

Melody felt the two opposite veils on either side. The personality of whom she searched came closer and stood at the edge of the white veil. Holding the smudge of shadow that was a demon, she reached out. With one hand, she pushed the demon through the hell gate. With her other hand, she grasped the personality bound to the Forest of Dreams. The exchange was made—one for the other. A naked man fell forward, gasping, and lay huddled at her feet. Melody whispered words, the first part of an evil prophesy she, herself, had created:

> Comes the Black Dancer,
> Slayer, the Wise.
> Born of the Mancer,
> with hate in his eyes.

> Comes the Dream Seeker,
> man lost in time.
> Silver-Tongued Speaker,
> ware, verses and rhyme.

> Comes the Swords Maker,
> Lover of Dead.
> He is life's taker,
> evil, his breath.

Comes the Betrayer,
hopeless despite.
Gembol, the Slayer,
the wrong is the right!

Comes the Black Dancer!

Melody knelt at the side of the human and produced a platinum disk inscribed with her own black widow symbol. "Touch the amulet."

The man looked up. Bright green eyes lay hooded beneath thick, brown hair. "No."

Melody twined her fingers in the clear flow of his personality. Her slender, black-skinned hand balled into a fist and squeezed. The man writhed in pain. "Touch the amulet."

The man refused.

Melody stood up and smiled. Gathering strength, she reached for Lyre's Clerical River. Black-hot light shaped a sword that mingled with the Mythit nature of her being. With another soft, almost tender smile, she ran him through.

Horrible pain rushed his nerves in blinding, pulsing torment. A scream echoed off of the walls.

"Touch the amulet."

This time the human quickly obeyed.

"Very good. Now, speak your name."

White-lipped, jaw clenched, the man again refused.

Melody laughed. With a twisting wrench, the blade burst into clerical fire. "Speak your name, now!"

"Slayer!"

Melody allowed the sword to fade away. The man cowered in fear at her feet. "Stand!" She watched his sweat-soaked, naked form slowly rise. Grinning, she gazed at his lean, strong body. Every inch of his six-foot frame caused her eyes to burn in lust-filled delight. "You belong to me. Obey me without question, and I will let you loose in this land of men." She reached up and caressed his cheek as she gazed into his bright green eyes. "All I want you to do is kill one man. Can you do that?" Before he could answer, she reached out and grasped air. A beautiful, golden-bladed, platinum-edged long sword appeared in her hand. "Take it."

The man grasped the hilt. Gembol Slayer, Dragon Seducer, Evil Cleric, Sword Dancer, and Sword Maker, gazed once more on one of the many blades that he himself had made. In a dreamy bass voice, he asked, "One little man?"

"Yes."

Gembol Slayer turned the blade and swung it through the air. Hearing the whistle, he began to laugh. Melody the Black laughed with him.

Poison grinned. "That's my little girl!"

28

PROPHESY

Slim Chance returned to Virile Swamp at dusk. He found January speaking with Sha and Lindon. "I don't know what's happening, but I know I don't like it. Nothing is moving. The land of Vain sleeps."

Jan told him about the small force of Vainians marching on the Vile Mountains.

"It just doesn't make sense," Slim said, brooding. "They know they can't make it through those passes. I've heard them talk often enough about it."

That statement made Jan pause. Slim's background could give them a lot of insight into Melody's plans. Jan gazed at Slim and asked, "What would *you* do if you had access to the magical stores Melody may control?"

Slim grinned. "With their magic, I would either blast my way through the mountains or set an invisible shield around an army and march it right up to the alliance gates. While you were busy with the pitiful force to the north, I would blast the Knights Alliance to rubble."

Slim blinked at his own words. Jan nodded; a slow smile spread across his face. "That's what they're going to do. We need to get to the alliance."

Slim shared his smile. "If they think we're occupied in the mountains, they won't expect us there at all. They will expect the knights to stay within their walls. If we could get a force of *were* behind them, have the knights ready with a charge, then we could surprise them as they lift their shields to set up the catapults. It will surely take a small amount of time for them to set up their machines. During that time, we will cause them considerable damage."

Lindon smiled at the thought. "The were will make a hole in their army that they will find hard to repair."

Jan sighed. "I will take Those Who Walk Alone, and we will make it our business to destroy their supply lines. The quicker we take their spirit, the quicker it will be over."

That night, Those Who Walk Alone flew with January and Slim Chance to the Black Mountains. He explained to them that invisibility couldn't hide tracks or scent. All they had to do was find the path the Vainian army had taken.

Toward dawn, Jan began to worry their assumption had been wrong. Perhaps an invisible army marched on the heels of the force behind the Vile Mountains. Perhaps the plan was something else entirely.

At sunrise, they gathered and were prepared to scour the last area when Lyndsy came running into the group. "Swiftfoot found them!"

After a quick discussion on the proper line of attack, Jan turned to Slim Chance and handed him two gold chains. "Go to the Knights Alliance and find the weapons master. Tell him our plan. As soon as the army becomes visible, look for the signal. Take care, Slim Chance, you're my right arm!"

As one, they snapped to in recognition of what Jan had said. "Your right arm," Slim repeated in awe. Then his face flushed with anger. "That whore sent me to die. She knew!"

Jan played the prophecy over in his mind:

> Too soon to battle,
> uncaring of harm,
> bare bones rattle,
> cut off his right arm.

Jan gazed at Slim. "So, does that change anything?"

"Yes."

Jan's eyes flashed a question.

Slim Chance grinned. "It means I'll find more satisfaction in proving her wrong! January, there is another prophecy that goes hand in hand with that one. I think you need to hear it."

Jan took a deep breath. "It's better to be forewarned. Speak it."

"Walk with me a moment. You should hear this alone." Slim led Jan out of earshot and spoke the verses:

Comes the Black Dancer,
Slayer, the Wise.
Born of the Mancer,
with hate in his eyes.

Comes the Dream Seeker,
man lost in time.
Sliver-Tongued Speaker,
ware verses and rhyme.

Comes the Sword Maker,
Lover of Dead.
He is life's taker,
evil his breath.

Comes the Betrayer,
hopeless despite.
Gembol, the Slayer,
the wrong is the right!

Comes the Black Dancer!

Comes the Red Dancer,
Lita, the Fool.
Born of the Chancer,
with love in her eyes.

Comes the Dream Changer,
woman lost in time.
Spoken, the Ranger,
with songs of the mind.

Comes the Sword Teacher,
lover of life.
She is the Reacher,
Slayer's red wife.

Comes the Faith Holder,
hope is her might.
She is the Molder,
the wrong is the right!

Comes the Red Dancer!

Comes the Young Dancer,
Seally, the Proud.
Born of the Rangers,
with fire in her eyes.

Comes the Dream Breaker,
mind grown from rape.
Harsh-spoken Saker,
no songs she sings.

Comes the Vow Taker,
Beloved of the Were.
Blood Plains' Vow Breaker,
All songs are hers!

Comes new School's Leader,
The Sword is her might.
Seally, the Student,
the wrong is the right!

Comes the Young Dancer!

Slim watched Jan's face as he spoke, hoping for some insight he himself did not possess. Melody had spoken those verses with relish, a seemingly bittersweet taste. "Do you understand any of it?"

Jan shook his head. "I thought you would know. All I can see is three sword dancers. I don't know."

"I don't like it," Sha said quickly. "We should have a larger Pack!"

"You don't think two hundred were enough?" Lyndsy asked.

"Two hundred were can beat a thousand Vainians without casualties," Sha boasted. "But how do we know the Knights of the Alliance will hold up their end?"

Lyndsy lowered her head and gazed up through her bangs. A sly look sparkled in her bright magenta eyes. "Their weapons master is a man of honor. He will welcome a fight. Sha, he is a warrior. I think they will try to fight harder against the stupid Vainians to prove they are the better fighters."

"Never!" Sha exclaimed with great conviction. "*We* are the better fighters!"

As Sha stalked away shouting orders, Lindon gazed at Moonlight and January. His daughter had never been good with words. Even he was used to her single, clipped syllable questions and responses. Yet, she had said the one thing he would have never thought of to put Sha from his worries.

Lindon saw that they shared an unspoken closeness that allowed January's faint nod to show his approval of her words. Even more, she who did not care at all for any other's praise glowed with warmth from her man's approval. He wondered at the affection of this young human that must have been required to bring Moonlight out of her shell.

Yesterday morning, he had come upon January and Moonlight sitting among a group of whelps. Jan was telling the tale of Moonlight, his daughter's namesake. He told the children in secrecy that Moonlight was now holding the very same staff the legend spoke of. Lindon had taken a closer look and realized it was true! It *was* the same staff. Not for the first time, he marveled at the quiet dignity of his daughter. She hadn't said a word. Any other were would brag and boast unceasingly about an ancient weapon of legend.

Moonlight handed the staff to the whelps and smiled with her man as they passed it around, exclaiming in delight at the perfect carvings of little dancing wolves. She admonished them to keep it a secret. Nevertheless, the secret had gotten out. Lindon had noticed an older were, now and then, stealing glances at the staff when they thought no one knew.

Lindon reached out on impulse and drew his daughter into his embrace. Jan saw the misty look in the old were's light gray eyes. Lindon said softly, "My Moonlight has turned into a fine, strong woman!"

"What was that all about?" Lyndsy asked as Lindon turned and walked away.

Jan smiled after him. "I don't know."

Those Who Walk Alone flew over Blood Plain. Jan homed in on the magical device tuned to Swiftfoot's mind. The young were had been following the Vainian army under a spell of invisibility. As they touched down, Swiftfoot approached. Jan set up a screening sight barrier. After the mental film became opaque, he changed the rest of the group.

Lindon asked, "What news?"

Swiftfoot spoke quickly. "They travel at a steady but slow pace. I think we are three leagues from the gates of the alliance. At their present rate of speed, they should reach their goal by tomorrow morning."

"Good," Jan said. "That will give Sha plenty of time to set up his force."

"Sha?" Swiftfoot asked.

Jan explained the plan. "That's good," Swiftfoot remarked. "I know the wagons are trailing the main army. We'll finish their supply train, and then we can fight too!"

Jan smiled at his enthusiasm but said, "We will all get our fill of fighting before the sun sets tomorrow."

Jan looked over Blood Plain toward the army he knew was there. Lindon set a hand on his shoulder. "January, they will wish they had never come."

"I hope so. I sure hope so."

29

FLOWER WANTS TO KNOW!

Samantha played the dream over and over. *Please don't let me be too late!* Flower and Jasmine stood at the edge of Mirshol watching the high cleric pace back and forth. The moonlight glimmered off her golden hair. Her personality was bright. Jasmine saw the stamp of the vow that the high cleric had taken four seasons ago.

"Jasmine, do you think January is in danger?"

It was a question without a reply. Samantha was asking Jasmine to reach across space and find Jan's personality. They both knew the Mythit could not do that. "I don't know."

The two Mythits glanced over the group of fighters. Captain Slith and twenty fighters had volunteered to be her honor guard. Samantha had used the Scepter of Light to set their minds in a deep sleep. Benjamin had ridden into Mirshol with Sunder. They returned an hour later with a small herd of horses. Benjamin had dismounted and given them an elaborate explanation of what he wanted from them.

Samantha had stood motionless, thinking the old seer insane. Apparently, Samantha had not witnessed the special qualities of the Mirshol animals as she walked through the forest. Flower remembered again, bursting into laughter at Samantha's shocked look as the horses backed up to the carts and waited for Benjamin to strap on the harnesses. They now stood on the west edge of Mirshol. Samantha wanted to continue immediately, but Benjamin and the horses needed sleep. With great reluctance, the high cleric said she would let them rest until dawn. Sunder assured her he could get some fresh horses while she and Benjamin rested.

Samantha turned and walked back to Flower and Jasmine. She looked down on the pink, red, and white Mythit. "Jasmine, I'm scared. A summons has been made, and I don't understand the strangeness of the weaving. Something very unusual has happened to the fabric of Lyre."

"What?" Flower asked, compelled by curiosity. The brightly striped, orange and yellow Mythit looked from Jasmine to Samantha and then back to Jasmine. "Well, say something. You know something I don't!" she accused.

Samantha turned away. Jasmine's eyes intensified their glow.

"Mother!"

Jasmine let out a sigh. "Flower, when you were made you didn't know about the *equation* that holds Mirshol. You didn't know about the equation that kept us hidden from the personality blind eyes of men. Do you remember when you first discovered them?"

Flower gave Jasmine a rueful grin. "Yes. I was furious that you never told me."

Jasmine nodded. "Do you remember why it was so important that you learn these things for yourself without being told?"

Flower answered with a sinking feeling. She wasn't going to get a straight answer this time either. "Yes. The lesson was that power given isn't appreciated as much as power learned."

"That's part of it," Jasmine said carefully, "but even more important, power, without understanding that power, is too easily abused."

"Yes," Samantha said, "and abused power always corrupts the one who uses it."

"That's not fair!" Flower protested. "January is the kindest, mostest wonderfulest human alive! How can you say he would abuse it if he knew about it?"

"Flower," Samantha said gently, "you are right about January, but even he must learn of this power on his own. If it is meant to be, the question will occur to him. When he finds the question in his mind, he will soon find the answer."

"OK," Flower said slyly, "just tell me."

Jasmine watched Samantha's nose wrinkle in a strikingly Mythit-like fashion and was so stunned by the sight she almost missed the high cleric's silent question. She looked to the morning sky and placed a white binding on her thought so only the high cleric could hear. *No. No other Mythit will ever learn of this. For time out of mind, I am the only one who has ever known.'*

The high cleric followed Jasmine's gaze up to the stars. *Jasmine, what is your role in this play for power?*

Flower scowled at the lack of an answer. "Well, when is Sunder going to get back?"

Jasmine turned her gaze on Samantha. "I wish I knew."

30

BATTLE OF THE KNIGHTS ALLIANCE

January watched the blue flag flutter in the breeze at the top of the gate tower. The knights were ready. Swiftfoot touched down and changed shape. Jan quickly brought him into the shield.

"Sha is ready."

"January," Lindon hissed, "someone is coming!"

Lyndsy sniffed the air. "There's more than a few."

January raised his sword. A mass of aura came into stark view all around him.

"We're surrounded!" someone yelled.

Jan called the gems to life and disrupted all invisibility in the area. Those Who Walk Alone found themselves in the center of a ring of Vainians. A black-furred Mythit shouted in glee, "I told you someone followed. I told you!"

Lindon counted fifty Vainians, including the black-robed wizard next to the evil Mythit. As Lindon walked to Jan's side, he offered the courtesy that many were offered a Vainian caught on Blood Plain. "You have one chance. Go back to Vain and live or stay here and die."

The evil wizard looked at the filthy, ragtag bunch of were and laughed. With a hand motion the Vainians attacked.

Jan stepped back and watched as the elite were formed a spinning circle. Half of them fell in, giving the outer ring room to swing. Even as the Vainians tried to break the ring, Lindon shouted an order. The inside ring charged full strength into the Vainians as the outside ring fell back. Vainians dropped around the outside of their perimeter. Blood sprayed onto the hard-packed earth.

January heard Lindon shout and jumped into the formation. The deadly tip of his long sword flicked out and sliced a man from shoulder to elbow. With a fast reversal, the Vainian behind him watched in stunned horror as the tip of Jan's blade came out of his companion's back. Jan looked for his next opponent as the body fell to the ground.

Lindon shouted.

January back stepped and saw that over twenty Vainians were already down. Lyndsy flew through the air and smashed a leather, iron-studded helm with the butt end of her staff. Her reversal caught the man behind the first and knocked a long sword fifteen feet through the air.

A sudden buzz of power caught hold of his mind. Jan turned and watched the aura of the evil wizard's staff as he gathered force. Stepping to the center of the were's ring, he concentrated on the magic. A burst of liquid flame shot from the end of the wizard's crystal-crowned staff. Jan slammed a wall of thought directly in its path and absorbed the heat. It splashed against his senses and simply fell to the ground.

The Vainians leapt from the flames. Making a quick decision, he got a running start and jumped across the open ground.

A spell was instantly bound to his senses. Jan hesitated, not knowing what it was. A tingling sensation spread around his feet. Webs of black spider silk wrapped around his ankles and started to climb. He tried to step out of it and fell to the ground.

Two Vainians charged him. Lyndsy came out of nowhere. Screaming her rage, she ended their threat for all time.

Jan reached down and tried to cut the webs with his sword. To his great surprise, it worked.

The evil wizard was gathering force. He wanted to blast this young wizard into tiny, bloody rags.

The Mythit beside him screamed, "Hurry, hurry, he's getting up!"

The wizard brought both hands together and grasped the crystal in his staff's crown.

Jan didn't know what else to do. He wasn't close enough to attack, and the force the evil wizard was gathering was great. So, he did something completely unexpected. With a thought, he grasped the personalities of Those Who Walk Alone and flung them into bird shape. Taking three steps forward, he spread his senses. A strange sensation tingled the bottoms of his feet. Eyes wide, he stopped and *squared*.

Squaring was one of the two ways a Mythit fades. Pulling his senses in, he blocked out everything and remained silent.

The Vainian wizard saw the young man step into the thick of the Vainian fighters. Without a second thought, he cast the power ball at his own men.

The twenty-five remaining Vainians didn't stand a chance. They died instantly in a thick, dark ball of flames.

Jan sat still, contained in the shielding of his own personality. As the dust settled, he opened his eyes, *unsquared*, and stepped lightly away.

The black-robed wizard was gone.

Those Who Walk Alone touched down in a circle around him. With the power of his sword, he changed them back.

"Anyone hurt?"

Lindon's eyes were wild with excitement. His quiet voice seemed almost tranquil. "No, not yet."

"Look!"

Everyone turned to see Lyndsy pointing at the field before the keep of the Knights Alliance. A huge army came slowly into the realm of normal seeing. Catapults, already assembled, were being hauled to the forefront of the Vainian lines.

"There must be five thousand Vainians out there," Lindon commented. "That should make Sha happy."

Jan set his gaze on Lindon. The old were's grey eyes were wild with excitement. January just shook his head.

A flurry of trumpets sounded over the field. They watched as the alliance gates were slowly opened. "Come!" Swiftfoot shouted impatiently. "Hurry, or we'll miss the fighting!"

Sha saw the army appear. His eyes widened in surprise as he beheld the size of the Vainian horde. He now had 280 were waiting for his signal. Two score males and one score females would be fighting in wolf shape. Sha watched the gates of the keep come open. As the Vainian force became aware of the knights, the were in wolf form scurried to the front lines.

"*Now!*" Sha shouted.

Those Who Walk Alone ran to the supply train under a spell of invisibility. They found the water wagons first. With so many Vainians, the supply train was huge. They simply hadn't pictured how many wagons it would take to haul the army's supplies.

Jan strung a line of destructive spells around the slats of five wagons and called the were away. The wagons were blown to pieces, and the whole area was drenched in the sudden downpour.

"This isn't going to work," Jan muttered to himself.

A force of Vainians rushed to the wagons when they heard the explosion. The last thing they ever saw was a group of soaking wet were appear before their eyes.

The Knights of the Alliance had not confronted an enemy comparable to this Vainian assault in over nine hundred seasons. They were used to patrolling the Black Mountain borders and fighting an occasional battle during their search for raiding parties. That was a chore suitable for a dozen riders wearing the lighter attire of half armor. Now, the weapons master, dressed in full armor, set his ponytailed helm on his head as he suppressed a fierce grin that raised the ends of his drooping mustache. Five hundred mounted and fully armored knights waited for his signal.

The Sword of Corillion rang free of its sheath as the watchtower shouted the were's attack. Freedom, the master's warhorse, reared and slashed air with hooves as his rider's excitement flared his proud nostrils. With a shout, the Knights of the Alliance drew steel and followed their master as Freedom leapt at the gate.

The thunder of two thousand hooves caused the Vainians to quake. A wall of polished steel charged the first ranks of pikemen. They smashed the unprepared barrier like so much rubble in the face of a ram. The untried, poorly trained Vainians cowered in fear as they watched the knights hammer the pike line to the ground.

The weapons master wheeled and shouted his triumph as he saw that no knights had been downed. Yet no one heard his shout. An earthshaking explosion seemed to split the air asunder. Fighting the reins, he turned to see two catapults throw large black crystals at the wall of his keep. The next explosion threw their mounts into a panic.

Bouncing in his saddle, he glimpsed the breach in the walls of his fortress. The Vainians swarming the first catapult created a shield barrier and stormed the hole.

"Knights! Knights! To me!" Sword raised, he chased the black-clad fighters who dared to invade his keep.

The sound of thunder rocked the earth. Jan gazed at the smoke clearing the walls and saw the breach in the thick stone.

"January!"

He turned to see Lyndsy standing on the seat of a wagon. Leaping to her side, he looked down and caught his breath. The wagon was full of sparkling black crystals.

A *building of power* registered in his mind. Catching Lyndsy around the waist, he whirled and pushed her aside. Even as he moved, a bolt of black power crisped the air above his head.

"In the name of Song!" Standing back up, he leveled his sword.

Two black-robed wizards stood together about ten feet apart. One was again building force. The other fired.

Jan let the power come. In the air, he took control of the force with a twisting slap of thought. A crackling display of power seared the air, balanced on the tip of his sword. Jan slashed left and released the power at the other wizard. The wizard tried to deflect the force, but the control of his own building drew the crackling ball like a magnet. Lyndsy shouted as the charges exploded together. Bloody scraps of fried flesh fell like evil rain.

Jan thought out a solid cube. The power of his sword made it real. As the first wizard staggered and got back to his feet, the cube caught him on the head, lifted him off of his feet, and slammed him into a group of charging Vainians.

Those Who Walk Alone formed a circle around the wagon. Jan saw the Vainians take in the appearance of the were and slow in indecision. Kneeling down to examine the stones revealed the incomprehensible force bound within each crystal. Both of these wizards had been tending the seals. Even now, the facets were beginning to decay. Soon, the entire wagon would be blown into infinity. Jan took a calming breath and counted. Thirty stones. He couldn't even begin to imagine the hole that would be left in the ground if they all detonated in one place. "Swiftfoot!"

The young were jumped out of the fight. Lyndsy leapt from the wagon to take his place.

"Swiftfoot, I need a big horse, and I need it now!"

Swiftfoot jumped up on the edge of the wagon and looked down. His eyes opened wide as he glanced at the catapults and then back to the wagon. "You want me to pull this wagon? By the Vow! I think we need to get out of here!"

Jan grinned. "You don't understand."

Sha led the were on. The pack leaders followed his hand signals perfectly. Taking control of the western flank, he proceeded to drive east. Sha saw that the effect on the Vainians was a renewed attempt to regroup. More and more Vainians were turning their attention to Sha's small force. Two more explosions sounded, and with shouts from the Vainian leaders, all of the black clad fighters in his area turned to attack him.

The were held their ground and fought fiercely. Sha noticed, with grim satisfaction, the mass of dead Vainians covering the field. However, more were coming. He waited until he was almost completely flanked and then called a retreat.

The Vainians chased after them. Sha grinned like a wolf and sent a quick set of hand signals to the other pack leaders. All at once the were turned and charged. Surprised Vainians stopped dead in their tracks. Most of them were falling over each other trying to back up and prepare for assault. The were smashed into the black-clad fighters and cut bloody paths deep into their ranks. Before the Vainians could regroup, Sha called another retreat.

He was hard-pressed not to laugh. Those stupid Vainians were still following! "I wonder how many times I can do that to 'em ?"

The weapons master rode down the group of Vainians that had charged his wall. Calling for his knights to rally, he gathered his men and compelled the Vainians backward. He knew that, at this moment, the men inside the alliance were stringing the spike nets Slim Chance had contrived.

Vainians on the ground were no match for mounted, fully armored knights. Nevertheless, before long, they would simply be outnumbered and dragged from their horses. All he needed was to give the men inside enough time to string the nets. Rallying his men for a second time, he stood in his stirrups, and shouted, "Charge!"

"Charge!"

An impossibly huge, sandy brown horse leapt into motion as January yelled. He rode on Swiftfoot's back. Those Who Walk Alone stood or knelt on the sides on the wagon. January leveled his sword and fired blasts of power. Vainians dove for cover as the mad wagon followed the smoking line of the young blond wizard's power balls.

As they plowed through the scattering men, January gave Lyndsy hand-down signals. She, in turn, directed the were to throw crystals, two at a time, from the wagon. Jan had bound each crystal with a spell. As soon as the wagon was out of range, Jan would turn and detonate the black crystal explosives.

Turning on Swiftfoot's back, he watched as the first catapult exploded in a fury of flames. In the course of their mad dash, three of the ten catapults were destroyed before the Vainian leaders even realized what was happening. Swiftfoot had approached the fourth catapult when Jan saw the other six rear back to fire.

Those Who Walk Alone fought the fighters who chased the wagon. Lindon hung over the edge, one leg hooked inside the wooden frame. His long sword swung like an axe felling Vainians right and left. A sudden sharp pain flared in his thigh. He glanced sideways to see an arrow through his leg. The small iron tip had passed through and lodged snugly into the wooden slats of the wagon. Lindon rolled his eyes and stifled his laughter. "I ain't gonna fall off now!"

As the fourth catapult went up in a ball of flames, Jan saw the other six discharge their crystals. The sound from that explosion was deafening. A breach in the alliance wall appeared as the dust cleared.

Once again, the weapons master was forced to turn and defend the walls. This time, he knew, there weren't enough men to repair the gaping hole in his fortress.

Heeding the call of the weapons master, the Knights of the alliance raced to the enormous breach in the wall and turned to fight.

Swiftfoot rode on. The fifth catapult blew to pieces as they flew by. January's sword cleared their path as power bucked and kicked from the tip of his blade.

Bloodred Mythit eyes watched the approaching wagon. The wizard at its side stood poised, waiting for the right moment to strike.

Jan saw the clearing ahead and directed Swiftfoot's path toward it. Too late. The wizard threw a black bolt of power at the horse's feet. Swiftfoot swerved, and the wagon spilled. Black crystals rolled everywhere.

Those Who Walk Alone jumped from the wagon and came up fighting. No one noticed Lindon trapped beneath the ruined transport.

Jan saw the wizard at the last moment and jumped. His sword came up as he rolled, but the black-robed figure darted to one side. Without a second thought, Jan leapt to his feet and gave chase. A group of Vainians made way for the black robe and then closed in on the young blond dancer.

Surrounded!

Jan fought a battle all his own. This was the kind of fighting he had been trained for. He was a sword dancer. And he danced.

By ancient and now lost definition, a dancer was a whirlwind of muscle and weapon. Trained by the Mancer of Lispin Shark, the dancers had become legends that had lasted through eight thousand seasons. Dancers were trained beyond the seeming ability of humankind. During the terrible wars between Shark and Dagdor the Black, the Lispin Shark Dancers cut their teeth in the Demon Wars. By the end of a dancer's training, they could walk separately onto the battlefield, destroy anything within reach, and walk out again unharmed.

The Vainians closed in. January raised his sword blade level across his chest. "I do not wish to kill. I don't seek your deaths."

A tall, whipcord Vainian sneered, thinking the youth had lost his mettle. "It's your bloody death we seek!"

Jan attacked. Three strokes, in the space of an eye blink, shattered the Vainian's blade, sliced his breastplate from neck to hip, and drew a fine line across his eyes. The Vainian dropped to his knees as Jan whirled on the ball of one foot. The edge of his blade sliced through weaponry like a hot knife through butter. Vainians dropped in a circle around him. The whistle of his sword and the calm, unwavering style of his dance caused the Vainians to fear. They stopped their attack and backed away. Fifteen men lay in a circle around his feet.

Given room, Jan took stock and saw the elite were trying to cut a path to his side. The Vainians followed his line of sight and quickly pressed another attack. Jan slashed at blades in front of him and whirled to fight the Vainians behind him. As he fought, he looked at the carnage around him and realized he wanted a different way out. It served no purpose to stand here and slay these men. They probably didn't even know why they were here.

Thinking quickly, he gathered force from the gems in his hilt. He created a wall of force and pushed. Concentric rings of power blasted through the Vainians, sending them sprawling in a circle around him.

Lyndsy dodged through the tumbled men and reached Jan's back. The rest of the elite were caught up to them, formed their spinning circle, and began a retreat. Jan knew their formation was precision in motion and didn't worry about the Vainians around them. What he did worry about was the wizard and the Mythit that had, once again, vanished. He was about to grasp personalities and fling them into bird shape. Then Lyndsy yelled, "Where's my father?"

Jan swept the area from side to side and found no sign of the older were. "Was he on the wagon?"

"Yes!"

"Let's go back!"

Those Who Walk Alone slowly worked their way backward.

Sha had thought to lead a group of Vainians into the hills that circled the northern point of the Black Mountains, destroy them, and come back for more. His small force of were could easily fight there unhindered. For the fifth time, he signaled an attack.

A loud explosion made everyone, were and Vainian alike, pause to look. Sha gazed in the distance and saw that a large portion of the alliance wall had been blown away. The Vainians, shouting their triumph, turned and ran back to the fields. Sha immediately sent those in wolf form to chase at their heels. Signaling his archers, he readied an advance.

Arrows rained down on the middle of the Vainian lines. The black-clad fighters at their backs stumbled over their fallen comrades. A were in wolf form follows the animal instincts. With the ancestry of the great timber and mountain wolves they emulated, piercing howls rent the air as the wolves charged.

Sha heard an answering call from the southern plains and turned to look.

Samantha stood on the Plain of Blood. Her small group of fighters stood behind her. Three tiny figures and a gray-robed old man stood at her side. When they first spotted the trail of dust, they thought it must be a large force of Vainians going to battle. Samantha had called upon the powers of the Scepter of Light and discovered, to her surprise, only five vaguely human minds. "In the name of Song! Those are wolves!"

Camlee stopped the wolves. Barking commands, he and the other were changed shape. When he stood naked on the plain, he walked alone to meet the group of humans. He Walked Alone because he had the right. Summons had reached him, but he had refused to return. His thoughts were that he should gather as large a pack as he could muster and lead them to Lychantorrid.

He walked closer. None of the humans held their weapons at the ready, but each one was armed. His attention kept returning to the tall woman in disconcerting white robes.

All of his anxieties flew far, far away as he drew near. The tall blond haired woman smiled at him, and a warm rush of love flowed into his heart. Catching her scent, in disbelief, he was amazed that she was sincerely pleased to see him.

Then it happened. The woman turned ever so slightly, and he caught sight of the bow strapped across the woman's back. His legs turned to water. Quaking in sudden fear, he fell to his knees. The bow!

Samantha started forward and quickened her pace when the were fell. Kneeling at his side, she caught him in her arms and embraced him. "My brother, you need have no fear of me."

Holding his hands, she helped him to his feet. The were shook so badly he almost fell back to the ground. Samantha called the scepter to life and twined with its power. Sweet peace flowed from the high cleric into the personality of the frightened were.

Camlee's aura cleared; an uninhibited smile lightened his rough, craggy face. Looking up into the ice-blue eyes of the high cleric, he felt awe in the presence of a legend come to life.

Samantha smiled into gray eyes. "I have need of your pack. A battle is being fought. Will you fight at my side?"

"Of course!"

Sha turned to look. He blinked, in no way believing what he was seeing. A woman on a white horse galloped into battle. Long blond hair streamed behind her in her wake. A star, come down from the sky, sparkled like a rainbow in her upraised hand. So great was her speed that she outpaced the fighters behind her. And on the tails of the fighters was a pack of children over two hundred strong.

Sha stared dumbly as the star-bearing woman leapt over the backs of the Vainians and plowed into the horde. The fighters and wolves, screaming and howling war cries, rushed into the backs of the black clad Vainians.

With a wrenching twist of his head, he forced himself back to awareness. Turning, he was glad to notice every other were standing dumbfounded by the sight. A huge smile spread across his face. From deep within him a bloodcurdling yell brought the rest of his force to their senses.

They would never forget the profound way in which a high cleric had, at last, come into their lives. In a frenzy of emotion, they charged to the aid of the children. Very few did not begin the change as bloodlust finally came to the were.

Those Who Walk Alone found themselves truly alone. The taxing chore of plowing through the enemy had brought them to a standstill. Jan felt his strength draining. He had used more magic today than he had since he'd first made the staff. He could, and probably should, use his remaining strength to cast the were into the air.

Swiftfoot, the youngest of Those Who Walk Alone next to Moonlight, was a calm thinker. He had control. He had been taught discipline to an infinite degree. Or so he thought. He felt the change coming on as rage took him over. *I'm not going to die like this!* With iron fists, Swiftfoot stilled his racing heart and changed shape.

In the blink of an eye, Jan watched the huge young were turn into a giant bear. Leaping from both feet, Swiftfoot pounded his way through the Vainian fighters. Jan shook his head as a premonition tingled his senses.

The Vainians scattered as the bear smashed his way back to the wagon. Lyndsy and Jan rushed at his back and slid to a halt next to the broken carrier. Lyndsy crawled underneath the carrier, saw the arrow, and spat a fluent curse. Swiftfoot reached down and easily lifted the ruined sidewall. Turning on her back, Lyndsy scooted beneath the boards and snapped the feathered end. Placing both feet against the wagon, she grasped Lindon's thigh and slid the leg off of the shaft. Her father gave a quick gasp, grinned like a wolf, and passed out.

Swiftfoot threw the wagon over like so much kindling. A fierce yet tender growl came from deep in his throat as he bent over and picked up Lindon with one powerful arm. Turning his massive form, he proceeded to pound his way out of the fight.

As January followed, he realized he was the only one who wasn't injured. A long, thin cut ran down the back of Lyndsy's arm. Her hand and staff were coated in dried blood. A few were limping. The eldest of Those Who Walk Alone was constantly swiping blood out of his eyes.

Swiftfoot ran on. Standing four feet above anything on the field, he scanned the area for the quickest way out. Then something caught his eye and made him wonder. A white-robed woman on the back of a white horse rode like fire through the Vainians. She was charging straight toward him. Black-clad bodies fled in terror before the purity of her might. Calm came over him; he growled in delight.

Samantha saw a huge bear carrying what had to be a wounded were-male. She turned toward them, trying to get a better look. When she spotted Lyndsy's snow-white hair, she knew she was headed in the right direction. Catching Jan's startled gaze over the heads of the fighters, she passed like a righteous wave through the black army.

A series of explosions sounded as Samantha reached Those Who Walk Alone. Gazing over the field, she watched as another portion of the alliance wall was blown to bits. A whole line of mounted knights went down as they were showered by the rubble of blasted stone.

The high cleric reached back for the Bow of Myril. She didn't see the were's awed looks of recognition, didn't hear the exclamations of disbelieving wonder. The high cleric nocked and loosed a gold-tipped arrow.

Swiftfoot gazed at the white figure in awed reverence. He watched her calm eyes scan the field and narrow. As Samantha fired, he turned his huge furry head to see the nearest catapult explode in a shower of splinters. The enchanted figure on the white horse nocked and loosed four more arrows. Swiftfoot stood amid the battle and looked on in wide-eyed wonder at the burning piles of smashed machinery that had dared to stand against her!

Gazing back at the figure, he saw a wild pack of children fighting to gain their position.

January came forward, and to the great surprise and consternation of the elite were, exclaimed, "Woman, what in the name of Song are you doing here!" She looked down on him and laughed. Ripples of delight passed through the minds of the were. Without missing a beat, Jan grinned. "Nice shootin'!"

"Come," Samantha said, holding out her hand. "We have to talk."

Jan hesitated as the wave of wolves swarmed around them, barking and growling greetings.

"*Now!*" Samantha commanded.

Jan reached out and jumped up behind her. Holding out his hand, he caught Lyndsy's staff. With a quick thought to his sword, he changed her to wolf shape. Samantha wheeled her mount, saw that Those Who Walk Alone had a clear path, and proceeded to leave the field.

Jan watched from his vantage point and saw that the Vainians were quitting the fight. A mass of black-clad troops turned to the Black Mountains and started to flee.

Jan decided to wait until Samantha stopped before he spoke. After a while, he wondered if she was even going to slow down. He let his senses wrap around her and felt a deep sense of fear—fear for him.

"Wait," she said quickly, "I'll tell you everything. First I want to get out of sight."

January gazed ahead and saw Benjamin, far in the distance, standing with the three Mythits. Lyndsy burst into an all-out run. As Samantha reached the group and dismounted, Lyndsy jumped up on his chest and licked his face. Smiling, he changed her back.

"Lyndsy!" Flower exclaimed in shock. "You're bleeding!"

Lyndsy twisted her arm and looked at the dried blood. "Oh, it's only a scratch."

"Scratch indeed," Samantha said impatiently. "Turn around and let me see it!"

"It's nothing, really."

Lyndsy stood still as the high cleric and Flower tended her wound. She smiled hugely as her two sisters fussed over her hurt. As Samantha drew out a pouch and salved her arm, Lyndsy wrinkled her nose. "Ouch! What is that awful stuff? It smells terrible!"

Flower stood up and set her furry hands on her small hips. Glaring at the werewoman, she scolded, "Serves you right! Just look at yourself!"

Lyndsy laughed and scooped Flower up into her arms. Pinning her wrists, Lyndsy tickled Flower ruthlessly until the furry little tyrant squirmed helplessly in her strong embrace. "Well," Lyndsy said, imitating Flower's scolding tone, "what kind of trouble have *you* been getting into?"

Flower pouted. "None!" Lyndsy watched the play of emotions in the Mythit. She smiled to herself, as Flower seemed to suddenly grow brighter. "Lyndsy! You should have seen all the wolves! I didn't think there were that many wolves in all of Lyre!"

Jasmine rolled her eyes. "There will be time for tales later. Right now, I think Samantha has something to say."

Samantha finished wrapping Lyndsy's arm and stood up. She thought of the dream and gave an involuntary shudder. "Yes, I have something to say." The high cleric related her dream—Melody, Poison, the summons, the seemingly demon figure, and the sword. When she finished speaking, she remained silent watching Jan think.

Jan realized she was waiting for him to speak. He didn't really know what to say. "From the way you charged into the battle looking for me, you seemed to think you might already be too late. If a creature like this was under Melody's control, wouldn't she have used it in this battle?"

Samantha crossed one arm beneath her breasts and rested her other elbow on her wrist. Rubbing her chin, she spoke slowly. "I don't know, but I do know she would love to see us suffer. It wouldn't, however, be like her to send something like this and not be there to enjoy it."

"One thing still bothers me," Benjamin put in. "What if it's someone else and not either of you this thing is after?"

"Who else could it be?" Samantha asked.

"January," Sunder asked, "where is Slim Chance?"

31

Who Understands What Children Sing?

Slim Chance had done his duty. The weapons master was prepared for the attack. At sunrise, Slim saw a blue-black crow sitting on the wall of the keep. It watched as the knights prepared for battle. Slim Chance felt wrath kindled in those glittering, round eyes.

He turned from his stance at the wall and entered the stables. Finding an ash bow, he nocked an arrow, and walked back to the huge double doors. As he gazed outside, a familiar, cold tendril of fear was thrust into his personality. Slim almost laughed at the foolish attempt to control him. He looked up and found the eyes of the crow glaring at him. Slim recognized that look. It was Darron, one of Melody's new twisted favorites. With a harsh cackle, it flew away.

Slim ran to the wall and climbed the closest ladder. Scanning the horizon, he spotted the crow flying north. "Sentry," Slim yelled, "tell the weapons master that I have an important errand to run."

The sentry watched, mouth agape, as Slim Chance stripped, changed shape, and flew away.

He caught the crow at the edge of the Loom River. Strong talons wrapped around neck and wing as they hit the ground and rolled. They both changed shape, Slim's hands now around the smaller man's throat. With his other hand he grasped the black widow clerical device and threw it into the water.

"Darron, you are about to die. Tell me your errand, and I will make it quick and painless."

The thin lips of the young evil cleric widened in a sneer. Sucking in breath, he spit in Slim's face.

Slim's fist broke Darron's nose. "I ask again," Slim Chance said in feigned irritation, "who are you to report to and why?"

"I'm to report the whereabouts of the slut, Samantha."

Slim's fist pounded the man again. "That was for lying to me. I'm no fool. Samantha isn't trained well enough to keep Melody from scrying her. This time you will tell me the truth. Who are you looking for and why?"

No answer.

Slim squeezed.

"OK, OK, she's after you!"

Slim's deep voice was full of danger. "What does she want to know?"

"Just where you are."

Slim slid one thumb over Darron's eye and pushed down.

"I swear!" the evil cleric screamed in pain. "That's all she asked! Just find him and tell me where he is!"

Slim raised an eyebrow. "Why?"

"I don't know!"

"Do you know how Melody probes a mind?" Slim asked. "Have you seen the soulless body that remains?"

The man squirmed in his grasp. "*You* can't do that! Why threaten me with it?"

"I know the Mythits of Mirshol."

"Please," Darron begged, not knowing that the Mythits of Light would never do any such thing. "I don't know. I swear!"

"Your oath means nothing to me."

The initiate, evil clerical mind, looked into Slim's wise eyes, trying to think of something to say. What would buy him time? This man had been one of Melody's favored for over a hundred seasons. There were too many things he might know that would surely cost him his life.

Slim watched the darting eyes in the weasel-thin face. *He doesn't know anything.*

The little man's eyes opened wide as he was allowed to take a deep breath.

Slim Chance let the man live. Darron's last words before he left him naked and weaponless were true but irrelevant. His death, Slim thought, would not hurt Samantha as much as Melody might think. However, to the black bitch's way of thinking, one never knew. What was the overriding reason Melody would want him dead? True, he knew many things that could prove useful to anyone fighting her. Somehow, he knew, there was more to it than that.

He flew over Virile Swamp out of curiosity. There was a clashing note that gave the major harmonics of nature a twist. He reached the meeting place of pack leaders and was surprised to see over a hundred werechildren romping in the area. After a closer look, he was sure there were only four adults present. He realized this must be one of the places that the were left their children so they could go and fight without worrying for the whelp's safety.

Slim circled the camp a second time and then flew north. The foreboding sensation of his hawk instincts took him faster. He realized of a sudden that everything was too quiet. Then he stumbled across a large force of Vainians. They were making their way slowly into the marshland. Equipped with nets and clubs, Slim realized, with a sinking heart, that they were after werechildren.

Slim Chance knew better than anyone what Poison could do with them. The changes she could make to any creature were beyond reason, but she could do far worse with children that could already change shape. Poison could conceivably call back the curse that had been lifted by the White Wizard. That would be the most dreadful, devastating change imaginable!

Slim saw, finally, that this had been Melody's plan from the beginning. Why hadn't he realized it before? This entire scenario—the Vainians advancing on the Vile Mountains, the battle at the alliance, was only a diversion so these men could capture werechildren.

He circled, undecided. Should he go for help or should he stay with the children? *Those are children!* he thought in sudden fury. With another long look at the Vainians, he turned and flew away.

As he reached the clearing, his hawk senses felt the first, faint explosions that rocked the alliance keep. Not wanting to alarm the kids, he landed and changed shape on the skirt of the swamp. He went to the closest sentry and told him about the Vainians. The sentry listened to his words and then turned and walked into the clearing shouting orders.

Slim watched, amazed, as the children scampered to a hut and withdrew dozens of tightly woven baskets. Each basket was inserted with long, fiber-filled intestine tubes. The older children set the infants in these baskets and strapped them shut. Without a word, the baskets were carried into the swamp.

Slim paced the area watching the young were. Some of them were setting traps, carefully pinning them, and making sure they were razor sharp.

After a short amount of time, the older children came back into the clearing. Slim saw that the infants had been left behind. Very few had been left to watch over them, wherever they were.

When they were all gathered together, the sentry called them to attention. The werechildren came and stood before him nearly one hundred strong. He asked Slim to describe the Vainians in great detail. Slim started speaking, and the sentry directed him to speak to the children. Feeling rather foolish, he turned and told them all that he had seen. Their numbers were about five hundred. They would be outnumbered five to one.

Slim watched them as he spoke. They stood quietly, the soft rasp of blades on whetstone the only other noise. He told them of the nets and clubs. This caused some laughter. One child, a male of about nine seasons, whispered fiercely, "Those stupid Vainians!"

When he was finished speaking, the sentry asked, "Who will *rope* the fire lines?" Every single hand was raised. The elder laughed at this show of enthusiasm. "Now, now, this is a task best left to the smaller pups." He then looked them over and picked out six young children.

Slim was no judge of age, but he estimated the six to be about five seasons old. He also noticed that the sentry had picked three males and three females.

The females in the group who were in or near puberty wore a string and strap around their slender, maidenly hips. Slim got the impression that the strap between their thighs was only to keep dirt and dust from private places. The single string skins were surely not designed for the sake of modesty. The males who were becoming men also wore simple loincloths. None of the younger children wore anything at all. The six, unclad, were of themselves very similar in size. Slim Chance was, therefore, very much surprised when they separated into boys and girls to prepare them for whatever it was they were going to do.

He followed the boys and watched with guarded curiosity as they were smeared with a thick, rank substance from head to foot. The sentry also watched, directing more here, a little there. When they were done, the boys and girls regrouped. "Now," the sentry said gravely, "get the snares and eel bait. Remember, be careful. This is no drill."

Slim watched the majority of the children go to a hut and drag out bundles of wicked-looking spikes. After passing out the bundles, they quickly dispersed into the swamp and vanished from sight. All at once, the severity of the situation struck him. His eyes widened, incredulous. "These are children!"

He walked back to the six youngsters. Their hands were being bound within thin waterproof bags. All four adults stood around watching this critical work. Slim walked to them, shaking his head. "These are children. How can they fight so many Vainians?"

The older sentry looked at him with a secret smile. "What would you have us do?"

"Hide them," Slim answered promptly.

"Hide them? There are only four of us. How could we watch them in the swamp?"

"Don't watch. Just hide them."

All four of the sentries burst into laughter. "They would only sneak back here and prepare to fight!"

"What?"

"Slim Chance, you saw me direct them. Don't you realize they already know what to do?"

Slim quieted. He saw one of the six holding flint and steel. Two of the older children wrapped her hands in the waterproofing. One of the boys was being tied around the chest with a long, insulated rope.

"What are they doing?"

The youngest sentry, a were kept from the battle because of a splint on his leg, answered, "The pups will bury fat skins of eel oil beneath the surface of the swamp. The six will be taken into the muck and buried to their chins. They will sit at six points of a circle and await the older whelps as they draw the Vainians into the trap. When the Vainians are in the circle, the oil skins will be emptied, the six will raise their arms, rip open the waterproofing, and strike the flints."

"Are you all crazy? They'll die! Do you sacrifice your children so easily?"

The sentries and the children laughed. "Do you really think we would leave them there? Look, the ropes they are bound with will be strung around a second, larger circle. The older pups will wait for the first flames and then pull them from the muck. The six know very well to roll in the slime-covered surface in case they do start to burn."

Slim gazed at them, obviously unconvinced. "Well, where are the infants?"

The oldest sentry grinned slyly. "We're roasting them for dinner in case we get hungry."

"What?!"

The four sentries began to laugh. The were children present were all snickering and whispering among themselves. The oldest sentry gasped and asked, between breaths, "Don't all humans think we eat our children?"

Slim felt the worry drain right out of him. They were just too confident.

"Slim Chance, it is the custom of our people that the pups defend the swamp. In the long history of our people, Virile Swamp has never been taken. The only reason we are even here is because, in other things, pups need looking after. This is different. Look at them. Do you not see that they are taking this seriously?"

"But they're only children. How can they fight?"

The oldest sentry looked at him for a moment and then spoke quietly. "Slim Chance, our children grow up fighting. Do you know that She Who Walks Alone killed a full-grown ram at the age of six seasons? She went into the mountains alone. Probably, knowing her, climbed the highest peak in the Vile Mountain Range. She was gone for almost one full moon. She returned with her ram, half dead, and covered with so many cuts and bruises that only her white hair named who she was. On that day, she became her own person. Usually our children wait until they are between nine and twelve seasons. Still, they must, each and every one, perform in such a manner to be considered adult. One third of the *children* here have done so. A few of them have been training with weapons for three or four seasons.

"They grow up fighting each other. They all know that they will have to fight their fathers for the right to take the pack. No male submits to a life as a follower without a fight. Females fight each other for the right to become first. Understand, these are not human children."

The youngest sentry smiled at Slim's blank look. "Do you wish to help?"

Slim gave in. "Yes."

"Come."

Jan and Lyndsy flew to the alliance wall. They found the weapons master directing placement of the wounded. Knights backed away from the two naked figures, remembering the first time they had seen them.

Jan gazed into the master's grim eyes. "Where is Slim Chance?"

The weapons master frowned down at a wounded knight. "He changed his shape and flew away."

"Did he say why?"

"Not to me."

January gathered Those Who Walk Alone and flew north. Billowing black smoke filled their horizon long before they reached the pack leader's meeting place. Jan knew it came from the swamp and worried for the werechildren. What was happening?

The thought that Melody might try and capture were had occurred to him too. Visions of the past made him understand the fear in this thought. When were had first appeared in Lyre, a four hundred-season war had been waged. The bloodiest histories of Lyre were written in the last days of the Three. It was during that time that the Red Wizard had reawakened the strictures and arts of sword dancing after more than six thousand seasons of disuse. Jan's anger and fear kindled as he flew.

His fears proved groundless. They reached the clearing in the swamp and saw hundreds of dead Vainians littering the marsh. A few survivors were in the far distance, trying to outrun the arrows of the pups.

Wheeling in the air, they flew back to the clearing. Werechildren were everywhere. Vainian captives were tied or staked to the ground. Those Who Walk Alone touched down, changing shape as they landed.

Slim's voice boomed over the excitement of the horde of children. They came upon him as he seemed to rage over five young whelps. As they drew near, they realized he was telling them over and over about how brave he thought they were. They seemed to be taking it with weary patience. Jan couldn't figure it.

"Slim?"

The big man turned, a huge grin smeared across his face. "January!" He quickly rushed to Jan's side, bragging and talking about the werechildren. "You should have seen it! Never, never, never seen nor heard of anything like it in my whole boring life! Ha! Those stupid Vainians thought they were just going to march in here and steal them some children!"

The five small ones came closer as they listened to Slim talk. He reached down and picked up a young female. Tossing her in the air, he laughed as he caught her. "See these kids? Any mother would be proud! Covered in muck from head to foot, fire blazing all around." Slim paused and gazed at Jan and Lyndsy as if for the first time. "What are you doing here?"

Lyndsy burst into laughter. "He *looks* OK to me. What do you think?"

Jan just shook his head. "Well, he's all in one piece, but I don't know if he's all right."

Slim looked at them dumbly.

"January?"

Jan turned and saw Swiftfoot approaching. "Three children are wounded. One, very badly. Is there any magic you can do?"

"Perhaps."

Jan followed the huge *were* to a hut. Three children lay on cots. He looked them over and scowled. Two were not seriously hurt, but one young female had been shot by an arrow. It still protruded from the center of her chest. Jan touched her mind and felt the presence drift. *She can't be more than six seasons old!* The arrow was very near to her heart. If it were removed, it would bleed faster than he could possibly mend it. "Lyndsy, I need Samantha. I need her now!"

Lyndsy bent over the girl and gently brushed the sweat from the small brow. Jan saw tears run down Lyndsy's cheeks. Lyndsy swallowed hard. "How can we bring her here fast enough?"

Jan turned away and sat down on the ground. Holding the sword before him, he let his senses spread.

Samantha!

January?

Samantha, I need you!

Where are you?

Samantha stood still, cloaked in gray. She heard and felt January come into her mind. Jasmine was standing before her. The Mythit looked up into the high cleric's face, questions whirling in her glowing, red eyes. Samantha watched Jasmine fade from her sight. She felt January's mind wrap her in tendrils of thought. *What are you doing?*

I need you. Children are dying!

Samantha suddenly saw January sitting in front of her. Instinctively, she stepped forward. Her surroundings changed. She found herself in a small hut. "Where am I?"

January opened his eyes. Weariness washed over him in waves. Samantha turned and gasped as she saw the young weregirl lying on a cot with a bloody arrow sticking out of her small chest. Jan tried to stand but found that his legs would not support him. The power he had used to create a *window*, which he did not even realize he could do, had almost drained him of strength.

Lyndsy rushed to his side and helped him to stand. Once again, he called the sword to life and felt power stream up his arm from the depths of the blue gem.

Samantha turned to Swiftfoot, who stood at the door. Sensing the fear-within-awe, she smiled and offered a friendly nod. "Please, stand outside the door. We must have peace to perform our healing."

Swiftfoot looked at the bright yet darkened eyes within the gray-hooded cloak. He would never forget those eyes. Dropping to one knee, he bowed. Rising back to his feet, he stepped outside and drew the skin door cover.

Samantha turned back to the girl on the cot. "January, I can feel that you are dead on your feet, but I need your strength." Reaching into her cloak, she grasped the Scepter of Light and nodded approval as the blue gem in Jan's sword fed her strength.

The children of the were gathered around the hut, waiting quietly, watching curiously as the blue and white lights from within sparkled in their young gray eyes. The few who had been sent to dig up the buried baskets of the infants trickled back into the clearing and joined the group. Soon, all of the werechildren were there. Swiftfoot watched, from his post at the door, as Sheela, his half-sister, picked up her harp and started to play.

Long after sunset, the bright blue and white lights flared brilliant and went out. The children watched as the rough skin cover was thrown aside. Samantha, robed in gray, who in the future all would call *Mother*, walked through the doorway holding hands with two of the werechildren. One young whelp walked up to Samantha and wiped at the tears streaming down his face. Samantha set her hand on his head and smiled. "Your sibling sleeps. When she wakes, she will be hungry and thirsty. Will you go inside and watch her for me?"

The child nodded with a flood of sweet tears and went inside.

Samantha gazed over the children and found the player of the harp, the soul that had given her strength. She walked through them, aware of the eyes on her. Stopping in front of the female, she unclasped her cloak and let it fall to the ground.

The high cleric reached out and ran her fingers lightly across the forehead of the young woman. She found the thing she'd known was there since the soul first started to sing. The high cleric unstrapped the Bow of Myril and handed it to the young woman. "Hold this for me. May I play your harp?"

The high cleric of all of Lyre accepted the harp as she handed the Bow of Myril to the first cleric of the were.

The sentries and Those Who Walk Alone listened to the inspiring music as the tall woman started to play. When she started to sing, they exchanged looks of great surprise. The children of the were joined her song as they watched. The music was like no other music they had ever heard. It was light and sometimes fast, gentle and strong. The very essence of life seemed to be in that song. They did not understand a single word.

The high cleric and the children of the were sang a song of love and life in a language only children could understand. Lyndsy stroked Jan's forehead as he lay with his head in her lap. A flicker of light came into the blue gem on his sword. She felt it tingle up her arm and starburst in her breast. She started as she met Samantha's eyes in sudden understanding. She watched the high cleric smile as her ice-blue eyes passed over the children. Every time her gaze settled on a child, a glimmer came to life like a halo around the child's head. A tear, a hope, a deep feeling that she couldn't name filled her and spilled from her as she smiled. With a look to the stars, she thought of the Creator and of the probation of the were and gave thanks for her sister.

32

DEMONS BE DAMNED!

January slept all of the next day. As the sun set, he woke up next to a small fire with Lyndsy in his arms. She was smiling, gently caressing his cheek with her fingertips. The waning moon was on the horizon. Lyndsy's white hair and pale face were crowned in the Lady's light. "My Moonlight."

Lyndsy gave him her profile as blood rushed to her scalp. Hesitantly, almost shyly, she turned back and kissed him. Jan wrapped his arms around her and pulled her as close as he could. Lyndsy parted her lips and breathed into his mouth. Jan gazed at her as she raised her head. Her lips were full, hair ruffled, eyes a deep violet. Lyndsy's personality was fairly dripping in desire.

"Lyndsy."

Lyndsy gave him a quick kiss to silence him, and then she pouted, and laid her head against his chest. "It's not fair, you know." Jan felt her jaw clench as she continued. "I don't want to be like the rest—"

"What do you mean?" Jan asked softly.

Lyndsy tossed her head, pushed up, and straddled his hips. Placing both palms on his shoulders as though she were holding him down, she asked fiercely, "Do you really love me? Do you really desire me? Can I truly please you?"

"Yes, yes, and yes."

She gazed deeply into his eyes and said very seriously, "Demons be damned! I can't wait anymore! We can fight them together!"

Jan watched her breath catch. Tears welled in her eyes.

"Oh Jan! I don't want to die not knowing what it is to be a woman! All my life I knew I would never *know* a man. That's why I tried so hard to do and be everything else!"

Hot tears ran down her cheeks and dripped on his chest. He reached for her shoulders and pulled her down. Lyndsy's mind was almost frantic. He watched pictures go through her thoughts.

Children in a pack were cared for and raised by all. Who can resist a small child or a puppy? Love was poured on them. They were constantly held and cuddled. A scolding or a growl was always followed by a hug or a lick. Loving approval was the reward for proper behavior.

Lyndsy had been shunned all of her life. Wolves do not care for that which is different. Even more, Sha's first had slain Sha's chosen and taken control of his pack. It was the way of the were. When Lindon Who Walks Alone brought Moonlight to be fostered, Sambra resented it. Sambra's anger only grew as she realized she could never win Sha's heart. Lyndsy became the target of Sambra's fury. January watched Lyndsy sitting alone, hurt and rejected, as the other pups romped and played together.

She had been tolerated for her father's status. Those Who Walk Alone were allowed children, but the young had to be raised as fosterlings in a pack. Jan saw Lyndsy, in another scene, somewhere in the dark, huddled under a bush in the rain, whimpering.

"January, please, I beg of you, don't ever leave me! I couldn't bear it. I swear, if you decide to take another woman, a normal woman, I won't ever …" She couldn't finish. Her body convulsed into sobs.

Jan rolled them over, pulling Lyndsy beneath him. Only when he felt her shake did he realize just how small she really was. She looked up at him, eyes brimmed in tears.

"Lyndsy, don't you remember what I asked of you at the cave? You will be mine, my only love. There isn't a woman living who can stand beside you. My Moonlight, I will never leave you."

Lyndsy's tears stopped. She raised her head and listened, almost hungrily, as he spoke. He kissed her head back to the ground and smiled into one magenta eye. When he leaned up to rest on his elbows, she wrapped her arms around his waist in fear he would try to move away.

"I love you, Lyndsy."

She smiled. Jan watched as a hot fire lit in her eyes. Pulling him down, she kissed him greedily. Running her fingers through his hair, she found the strip of silk that bound his ponytail and loosed it. Jan caught his breath as her hands began a caressing dance along his shoulders and back.

"Lyndsy."

"No."

January fought for control. *We can't do this, not yet.* Spreading tendrils of feeling through their personalities, he almost gave himself up to the shared passion that seared their desire.

Lyndsy watched Samantha come into her mind's eye. She heard again the high cleric's conviction that this act could be turned into lust. With a tremendous effort of will that no werewoman had ever wished to use, she stilled her racing heart and breathed to clear her senses. "January, get up!"

"No."

"January, please!"

He smiled to himself and whispered in her ear. "I don't want to."

"Stop that!" Slapping his shoulders, she pushed him up.

Jan sighed as he rolled over. He could not, in all honesty, tell himself that he had done the right thing.

A gray-robed figure stood silently, watching.

Five children entered the ring of light shed by their fire. Jan and Lyndsy sat apart as if they were afraid to touch each other. Lyndsy looked up and saw mischief in their eyes. Jan blinked as their personalities danced with secrets. Sheela pointed at Jan. The two young females grabbed his hands and pulled him to his feet. Sheela walked around him and made an elaborate show of looking him over. After a while, she nodded, seemingly satisfied, and spoke to the females. "Take him."

The older girl turned her attention to Lyndsy and pointed at her. The two males went to her side and pulled her to her feet.

"Sheela?"

"Silence!"

Lyndsy's mouth clicked closed. She watched Jan being led away. The two males smiled impishly as Sheela walked into the night. Lyndsy looked down at them. "Where are we going?"

"You'll see!"

They led her to a secluded place in the marsh and stopped. One pup set a cloth over her eyes and tied it. Lyndsy stood still as they ruffled her hair. The ever-present scent of wildflowers suddenly filled her nose to brimming. Then each boy took a hand and once again led her away.

They walked for quite a while. The boys were careful to tell her where to step and when to stoop. The sounds of nature were suddenly cut off, and she knew she had been led inside of a hut.

She was turned sideways. The blindfold was removed. She blinked and laughed in delight. Jan stood before her, his hair, crowned and braided with wildflowers.

"It has come to my attention that you two are in need of a chaperone."

They turned together to see Samantha sitting on a wooden stool with Sheela in attendance at her side. The high cleric's ice-blue eyes sparkled. "Either you two get married, or you get a permanent escort."

Jan looked at her in disbelief. "Samantha, I think—"

"Silence!" Sheela demanded. "Do not interrupt the high cleric while she speaks!"

"You have a problem," Samantha continued, "and I intend to solve it for you. You don't want to be a bad example for the children, do you?" She waved her hand. Jan and Lyndsy turned to see all of the children in the marsh standing behind them.

Lyndsy said to no one. "This is a conspiracy."

"Do you wish to be mated or will you live in frustration? I will offer this only once. I am prepared to perform the service myself. I tell you, moonlit meetings will soon become more than either of you can bare."

"You were spying on us!" Lyndsy accused.

Gray eyes sparkled with laughter. Sheela said quietly, "No. *She* wasn't."

Jan looked at the young were. "I see."

"Will you accept my offer?"

Jan looked down at Lyndsy. She was fit to burst but waited for him to speak. "Well, I don't know—"

"What?!" Lyndsy shouted.

Jan caught her fist before it could connect. Pulling her close, he set his mouth over hers, and swallowed a long string of curses. She stilled, slowly wrapping her arms around his neck.

Sheela cleared her throat.

"Well?" Samantha asked.

"Yes," Jan answered. He looked down into Lyndsy's magenta eyes and smiled. "Any other answer would probably get me flayed."

Lyndsy smiled sweetly and said nothing.

33

Insecurities

The were returned from battle the next day. Benjamin, Captain Slith, and the weapons master were with them. January did a double take as every grown were went down to one knee as He Who Sees All walked by. Lyndsy distracted him by shouting as a group of travois came into view. As he followed after her, he saw Lindon strapped to one of them. Lyndsy did not even ask about the leg. Instead, she went into an excited explanation of the day before.

Lindon smiled at her excitement but obviously did not understand. "Why?"

"Father, humans get married. It's like taking a vow."

Again. "Why?"

"To pledge that they will be true to each other."

Lindon raised an eyebrow. "Moonlight, no bitch would dare challenge you as a first. You will be his mate until the day you die."

"Father," Lyndsy said in exasperation, "it's a human custom."

"Oh."

The were had watched the high cleric lead a seemingly numberless pack of children to battle. They watched her white light outdistance her force as she charged, alone, through the Vainian fighters. Swiftfoot had elaborated in great and glorious detail about her exploits with the Bow of Myril against the Vainian catapults.

Samantha stood within the buzzing personality of their awe. She had tried to speak to them, but every time she approached, they would fall to their knees, stare at the ground, and answer her with single syllables. She was beginning to feel alone here among so many people.

She heard Slim's voice. He was telling a crowd of were about the bravery of the children. She had heard parts of the story before, but not all of it. She listened in wonder as Slim told the story from his point of view as he flew over the battle.

The female who had almost died of the arrow wound had been one of six in the greatest danger. The same female, healthy and hale, stood before them now. Slim told them how she had been shot as she raised her hands. Even in the face of death, she had found the strength to rip open the waterproofing and ignite the oil. As the other children pulled her from the flames, they had seen the arrow wound and had taken her to the hut to die.

The little werebitch blushed at Slim's boasting and turned her head. Seeing Samantha, she smiled up at the big woman and went to her side. The other children had been watching for her, and now that she was here, they all went to her. She didn't hear Slim tell them how she had come to heal the child. She didn't see the renewed looks of wonder and awe. Samantha was letting the warmth of the werechildren wash away her insecurities.

One of the were listening to Slim Chance came before her and knelt at her feet. Samantha looked down, almost angry at the worship they gave her. "Stand! I am mortal, like you. I am not worthy of your worship. The Creator alone deserves such humility. I am a woman, his servant. I only do his work."

The were stood but still wouldn't meet her eyes. Wringing his hands, he tried to speak. Samantha watched him for a moment and then set one hand on his shoulder and lifted his chin with the other. She said quietly, "If there is anything I can do for you, I will do it."

"No," he said hesitantly, "I would thank you for the life of my sister's child." The weremale blinked and looked down at the child.

"I see." Samantha said with a smile. "It is for you to thank the Creator. By his will alone, she still lives."

"Can I do anything to repay you?"

"Repay? What price would you put on your niece? No, you owe me nothing. I do have some questions. Would you answer them?"

"Yes."

"Good. Let's start with your name."

The were looked momentarily surprised. Then he gave her a slow, toothy smile. "Snarl."

❦

"I need some help. Will you two help me?"

Fluffy and Sharptongue looked up. It was the tall man that Moonlight was in love with. They looked into his startling blue eyes and sighed. "Yes."

"I need some wildflowers. A lot of them."

"Sure."

With a small sun-browned hand in each of his, they walked into the swamp. The fragrant little blossoms of different flowers grew few and far between, but with the help of the two females, Jan soon had as many as he would need. As soon as he found a dry patch of ground, he called them to his side.

"Whatcha gonna do?"

"Weave a basket?"

"No silly, too many flowers!"

Jan sat down and drew out a little glass jar. Motioning to the ground next to him, he said, "Sit down and watch."

One sat on either side of him. He noticed they sat as close as they could without actually touching him. With a smile, he laid the sword across his lap. "You have to promise me you won't tell anyone how I do this."

"Whatcha gonna do?"

"First promise." He looked at Fluffy.

She shrugged her small shoulders. "OK, I promise."

Jan turned the other way. This one looked doubtful. "Come on, you don't want her to see this all by herself, do you?"

Sharptongue rolled her gray eyes and sighed again. "OK, I promise too."

Jan turned back to his sword and brought the gems to life. He smiled at their exclamations as he unstopped a gourd.

The werelings watched the water pour up out of the container and float in the air. Flames shot up from the tip of the sword to heat the water. Wide gray eyes watched the tall blond man cut the blossoms from the stems and toss them into the globe. Soon, flowers floated and danced within the suspended sphere. It took quite a while for the man to cut away all the stems, but they didn't care. Fluffy wondered for a moment why she couldn't smell them anymore. The thought quickly left as she gazed, fascinated, at the rainbow mix.

Jan finished cutting the stems and glanced at the two. He smiled to himself and added the illusion of sparks and bright flashes. He felt well rewarded as they gasped and sighed in wonder.

Slowly, he allowed the mixture to cool. The water evaporated until he thought the mix perfect. Setting the glass beneath the now discolored blossoms, he squeezed the remaining moisture into the jar. After he plugged it, he shook it and popped the top back off. "Finished."

"What is it?"

"It's called perfume."

"What's perfume?"

"Something that smells good." With one finger, he smeared some on the end of Fluffy's nose.

Fluffy clapped her hands in delight. "Oh! That smells wonderful!"

Sharptongue pouted. "I want some too!"

Jan laughed and spread a drop on her nose as well.

Lyndsy walked through the swamp, alone. Doubts and fears had once again surfaced from the depths of her childhood. She hated feeling this way! "What if he grows tired of me? What if he really doesn't love me? He'll find some kind, soft, normal woman and leave me." Leaning back against a moss-covered rock, she slid to the ground and wept. "What's happening to me?"

"You are about to be thrashed worse than you've ever been thrashed in your whole, short life!"

Lyndsy looked up, startled. Flower stood before her, bristling in wrath. She pointed a big stick at the werewoman and scolded, "How dare you say January has no honor—that he is a liar and a vow breaker!"

"I would never say that!"

"You just did! If he grows tired of you, he has no honor. If he doesn't really love you, then he is a liar. If he left you, he would be an oath breaker!" Flower gazed at Lyndsy sternly. She didn't know just how deep the werewoman's insecurities were buried. When Lyndsy set her face in her hands and sobbed, Flower's bright heart began to melt.

Lyndsy drew in a choking breath. "Flower, I'm just no good for him!"

Flower's skin started to twitch. "Lyndsy, stop crying."

Mythits and emotion are one. It was their greatest tool, but Lyndsy's sadness was so intense, Flower was quickly falling into the depths of sorrow. For the first time in her long life, she was being forced to endure an emotion she could not control. She couldn't move; she lost the ability to square. She could not deny the gloomy empathy from overwhelming her. Flower's bright, soft pink eyes grew cloudy. Her bright, yellow and orange fur started to fade. *This must be how it happens to the Black Mythits. I guess I never really understood.*

Lyndsy blinked away a big, fat tear. All her fears vanished as sudden concern for her little friend took over. *Flower looks terrible! Drooping and wilted like a plant too long without sunlight.* Leaning forward, she gathered the Mythit in her strong arms. "What's wrong, Flower? Are you sick?"

"No, it's nothing. I'll be all right in a moment."

"You look awful!" Lyndsy frowned as Flower started to *look* normal again. "I love you, Flower."

Flower smiled, feeling the very truth of Lyndsy's words as love and concern filled her personality. "I love you too, little sister."

"I didn't mean it, you know. I didn't realize what I was saying. I'm just *so* afraid! I never felt this way before."

Neither have I, Flower thought, *neither have I.*

34

GEMBOL SLAYER

Jan stood by a hut watching the children. He had seen something from the corner of his eye and turned to look. Letting his senses spread, he watched the personalities of the werechildren.

There's that aura again. Every child has it! He studied that clear, bright light residing in each of them. *What is it? It taunts me, always coming to the edge of my mind to reveal itself and then fading away. I almost recognize it, and then it's gone.* "I will find an answer!" he said out loud.

Even as he set his gaze on Samantha, she jumped to her feet. Her eyes met his and he was stunned by her sudden fear. As quickly as he could, he rushed to her side. "What is it?"

"Slim!" Samantha exclaimed. "Where's Slim?"

Slim Chance sat at a fire with Benjamin and all of the war leaders. Sha was telling the story of the first weapons master of the Knights Alliance. In great detail, he gave them the were version of the fight that lasted all night. When Sha started to speak the verses written on the hilt of the Sword of Corillion, Slim Chance saw a wisp of black smoke appear out of nowhere. He tapped the weapons master's shoulder and pointed.

The shocked look on the master's face told Slim he well remembered the last time this had happened. Slim tapped Sha on the knee and whispered, "Clear the area quickly. Get every werechild that has not spoken the Vow away from here right now!"

Something in Slim's voice set Sha into immediate action.

Within a minute, the smoke turned into flames and grew. Samantha rushed into the clearing and almost passed out. She called the Scepter of

Light to life and was instantly aware of thick fingers of evil thought. Passing one hand before herself in a gesture of denial, she watched her own wall of personality spring into place. Fresh, clean air rushed back in.

Slim walked calmly to the black fire and drew his sword. Jan ran to Slim's side and was assaulted by the evil that seemed to twist nature itself. Surrounding his personality with the power of his sword, he calmed and breathed to keep the air clean. *How is Slim Chance remaining so calm?* Standing back, watching, Samantha thought the same thing.

The flames grew, and a shape began to form. The leaders of Lyre's defense watched as a man appeared. A perfect face was sat within thick, light brown hair. Bright green eyes were wide set beneath arching, full brows. The gaze they held spoke nothing of evil, even though his aura was midnight black. His arms were folded across his chest. His straight, lean body outlined fine muscles that rippled as he breathed. A black silken skirt hung from his narrow hips to his knees. Jan gazed in recognition at the red, ruby-studded armband that wrapped his left biceps. It was an ancient symbol—signature of a sword dancer. Everyone in the clearing stopped. They seemed to be in awe of the sheer pride and elegant perfection of the figure.

With blinding speed, he reached and drew a golden-bladed, platinum-edged long sword from thin air. Before anyone could move, he pointed its tip at Slim Chance. Too close! Jan tried to catch the spell as it flew through the air. He caught sight of Samantha turning to wave her hand. The silent spell hit Slim full in the chest. Jan waited for Slim to fall, waited for the reaction to the evil curse. Jan thanked the Creator that Samantha had somehow caught that spell, for Slim's only response was a slight widening of his eyes.

The man stepped forward and lunged. He was fast! The golden blade ran Slim through. Then the figure cursed in rage as the illusion of Slim Chance faded away. To everyone's surprise, Slim appeared ten paces behind him, arms folded. The man-figure didn't even blink; he attacked January.

Jan sidestepped, swinging as the man passed him. Pouncing, Jan forced him backward with a fast flurry of strokes that should have ended the fight.

The black-clad dancer blocked Jan's swings and stopped his retreat. A sudden, completely incongruous smile showed white teeth as they stood toe-to-toe swinging and blocking. The entire group stood spellbound as the two dancers danced. The lightning, steady beat of gold on steel caused every trained warrior to distrust the sight before them.

Then the black dancer stepped back and leveled his sword. Black-hot flames erupted down the blade. Even outside of Samantha's clerical shield, they felt the heat.

"January!" Samantha shouted.

He didn't hear her. He saw the flames, and with a graceful sweep, his own sword turned to frost. Jan shared a smile with the man before him as they both compensated for the opposing magnetic forces.

The man attacked. Jan stepped in and blocked, hard. Steam enveloped the two dancers. Jan closed his eyes and felt for his opponent's personality. Swing, block, swing. Sidestepping, Jan blocked along his left thigh. As fast as lightning, he blocked down his right. Attacking with quick, tight upstrokes, he forced the man back and out of the fog. Dropping to one knee, he back-armed his sword in an arc before him.

Jan opened his eyes and watched the man land catlike and stop. A grin of great satisfaction spread across the figure's face. January got the impression that a great teacher had just paid him the highest of compliments.

Sha watched January come out of the steam, fighting with his eyes closed. He looked quickly to the other fighter and saw the same thing. Awe took the fiercest pack leader the were had to offer. January, he thought, had only toyed with him when they had sparred seven days ago. He looked around the ring of watchers and felt an incomprehensible pride in the young human.

Sha turned all of his attention back on the figures as the red-banded man attacked. The golden blade came straight down. He gasped as Jan seemed to stumble and fall. January set his point down and bowed his head. The golden blade came to a jarring stop as it was blocked by the fingerbreadth space on the pommel's tip. Rolling backward, Jan planted both feet in the man's stomach and pushed.

"Yea!" shouted Sha, pounding the weapons master on the back. "I taught him that move!"

The figure flew through the air.

"Samantha!" Slim shouted. "Look!"

Samantha turned, looking to see what Slim could be pointing at. She saw Melody's face as though through a window. Without knowing why, she raised the Scepter of Light. Melody looked down at her in surprise, and then she was suddenly furious. Samantha felt the presence. The scepter in the hand of the high cleric flared white-hot. Melody screamed in rage and blanked out.

The black dancer gazed at the high cleric in obvious distaste. As he looked back to January, the scowl left and he smiled. To the utter amazement of all present, he quickly looked back at Samantha and then back to January and burst into laughter. Extending his sword, the black fire went out. Still laughing, he sheathed his sword and scratched his chin. Bright green eyes settled on the violet armband marked with the silver star. Nodding in what Jan took to be approval, he bowed and then disappeared.

Jan stood still, watching the place the man had last been.

Lyndsy went to his side and wrapped her arms around his waist. Jan set his arms around her shoulders and looked down into her eyes. She was glowing, full of pride. Slim moved toward them as Jan looked back up. "In the name of Song, Slim Chance, I thought you were a dead man. Samantha, how did you stop that curse? It was too fast for me, and I was right next to him!"

"It wasn't me," Samantha said quietly.

Jan turned back to Slim. Slim unclasped the gold necklace that enabled him to change shape. With a uniquely sad smile, he handed it back to January.

"You don't need it."

"No."

"You can change shape without it."

"Yes."

"I see."

"We have much to talk about."

Jan nodded.

"Later," Lyndsy said. "First, you have to marry me!"

35

The Dance of the First

They came and woke Lyndsy before moonset. She blinked once, tapped the hand covering her mouth, and nodded.

Those Who Walk Alone were hunched down in the swamp. They watched Moonlight walk as Swiftfoot led her into the area. Moonlight was She Who Walks Alone. The first bitch to enter the elite since anyone could remember. A vague story of another She Who Walked Alone was set at least three hundred seasons in the past.

Lyndsy stopped as her nose picked up the scent of Those Who Walk Alone. A slight smile touched her lips as she remembered the first time this had happened to her.

"Moonlight, Daughter of Lindon, is it your intention to become the first of the human named January?"

Lyndsy's brow knitted at the question. She answered slowly, "No. I will be his wife."

"Unacceptable. You will be his first."

Lyndsy folded her arms beneath her small, bare breasts and lifted her chin. "He doesn't understand our customs. Besides, I Walk Alone. I need no one's approval."

"Moonlight, this is for your own good. Your pups must be raised correctly."

"Daughter," Lindon said kindly, "I would not have your whelps fostered by another. I could not bear it, again."

"Our children will be strong. They will survive."

Swiftfoot laughed quietly. "No doubt, your whelps will be strong, but we will not be changed from our purpose. You must be his first."

Lyndsy sighed. "Swiftfoot, how do you think the pack leaders will react to this? Most of them resent We Who Walk Alone enough as it is."

"Sha has been told. He thinks it a wise idea. January will be a pack leader, at least in name. We have seen him take the wolf shape."

Sha had been told? That stunned her. *He thinks it a wise idea?* She couldn't believe it. *Only one time has he ever shown me favor.* Anyone but him!

"Moonlight, after the fight that we all witnessed yesterday, I tell you plainly, there isn't a pack leader living who would challenge him. None of us would challenge him! He *is* what the weapons master calls a *sword dancer.*"

"Yes, a very fitting name."

Lyndsy's heart swelled with pride at the ready agreements that statement had caused. "I understand how being a pack leader would influence him. I even admit I can already see the value of my status as a first. But, how do we convince the rest of the were?"

"We leave that to you."

"Oh?"

"The Dance of the First."

Lyndsy groaned. "No. I can't do it."

Lindon smiled to himself. "You can do it. You don't see the way he looks at you when he thinks no one watches. Believe me, he won't last halfway through! All the more reason, if he is to be pack leader, the other bitches must know his heart belongs to you."

Lyndsy brightened, thinking of an out. "I will beat any bitch who even thinks about seducing him!"

"Moonlight, the bitches will ask for the dance."

Lyndsy remained silent. She knew he was right. January was by and far the most beautiful figure of virility she had ever seen. Why wouldn't the other bitches think so too? *What if I can't do it? What if he doesn't respond?*

She bowed her head. Cold chills covered her body as she thought about her past attempts to appear desirable. Her open willingness had caused were-males to stink of disgust. She remembered the young were she had tried to seduce when she first came into womanhood. His face had contorted into such a grimace of loathing she'd had nightmares for a moon. Even January had not yet bedded her. Maybe he didn't really want her either. She would be shamed if he didn't respond. How could she dance the Dance of the First? "I can't do it!"

"Moonlight," Lindon said softly, "you will dance just like you do everything else. The Dance of Moonlight will become a matter of song."

"Oh, no." Lyndsy groaned. "I can't. I just can't!"

☙

Lyndsy rolled onto her back and squinted as the late morning sun glimmered through the opening of the hut. Frowning at Jan's absence, she sat up and rubbed her eyes. Her motion stopped as the fresh scent of wildflowers brought back memories. Reaching out, she snatched her wraps from the hanging string, bunched them up in her face, and breathed. The wonderful scent filled her nostrils and caused her to moan in pleasure.

Laughter startled her. She blinked and saw Fluffy and Sharptongue standing just outside of the doorway. Playfully, she jumped up to chase them. As they laughed and scampered off, Lyndsy saw Flower surrounded by weremaidens.

Flower stood nose to nose with a female barely four seasons old. Lyndsy frowned as she noticed that all of the young females were there and watching. Flower disappeared, and they all gasped. She reappeared behind the little were and shouted, "*Boo!*"

The female jumped a foot in the air, arms waving. The other maidens shouted and clapped. "Do it again!"

"Yes, do it again!"

Flower turned her head and saw Lyndsy. With a cry of joy, she ran and jumped into Lyndsy's arms. Although she didn't know it, the weremaidens' esteem for the ugly albino immediately grew a hundredfold. Lyndsy caught Flower up and kissed her.

Flower wrapped her legs around Lyndsy's waist and leaned back to look in her eyes. "All the men came and took Jan away. We were waiting for you to wake up, sleepyhead! Gotta getcha ready for y'r weddin'!" Flower wrinkled her nose and grinned. "You's gonna be real purty!"

Wiggling loose and sliding to the ground, Flower caught Lyndsy's wrist and led her to a little wooden stool. Apparently, the Mythit had been talking to the females for some time because they all set to work washing and dressing her. A bright red blush flushed her face as the Mythit pointed and directed the maidens. She hadn't expected this treatment. She didn't have any real female friends. She was touched more deeply than she was willing to admit.

Flower stood back, watching and giving imperial direction when and where she saw fit. At one point, she asked casually, "Sha asked Jan if he was willing to be a pack leader, at least in name. Kind of an honorary title."

Lyndsy was suddenly tense. "What did Jan say?"

Flower had thought she was going to surprise the werewoman with that comment. Because it didn't work, she gazed at Lyndsy suspiciously. "Jan asked if it would take away your status as One Who Walks Alone. He was worried you would somehow be thought less of. Sha said you would have an increased status as a first. Then Jan asked if there would be any problems with the other were."

"What did Sha say?"

"Sha said he wouldn't let anything stop January from being a Pack Leader. He said he would personally take any challenge that came up."

"Sha said that?" Lyndsy asked incredulously.

"Yes."

All Lyndsy could think was, *Well, maybe I won't have to dance.*

Flower watched her closely. *Dance? What does that have to do with anything?*

With Flower's critical guidance, the maidens performed a seeming miracle with the too slim, too short, too pale, magenta-eyed young woman. Sharptongue stood back looking at the exotic effects of the Mythit's inspiration. "I don't believe it. Moonlight, you look gorgeous!" Her gray eyes opened wide as she realized what she had said. "I'm sorry. I didn't mean—"

"It's OK," Lyndsy said ruefully. "I'm used to it."

Fluffy frowned at Sharptongue. "Foster sister, you look ravishing!"

Flower grinned.

The were knew the high cleric was going to perform a strange ceremony, so they gathered to see what she might have to say. Their fear of her had been slightly reduced as they watched her, from time to time, talking closely with Snarl and Silvertail, his first. Still, she was the high cleric. Long ago, the high cleric—Myril the White, Lyre's first high cleric—had lifted the horrible curse of the Dark Lord..

Because of Myril, the bow was their only holy symbol. All were esteemed the Bow of Myril above all others. For almost a thousand seasons, the bow had not been seen or heard of. Then *she* had come from Blood Plain followed by hundreds of wolves. She charged alone through battle carrying her white light like her war banner. In moments, she had destroyed five catapults, something it had taken the young wizard and their own elite half the morning to accomplish. Then she had turned, her work seemingly finished, and made a path so that Those Who Walk Alone might live.

Yet, her work had only started. The were returned to Virile Swamp to learn that she had come and worked healing to save the lives of three insignificant werechildren. She now belonged to them.

Samantha fell instantly in love with the rich but simple culture of the were. Never had she met a group of people all in one place that revered the Creator down to every last mother and child. She did not know it, but her love for the were would require a price. That price, she would soon think too much to bear, but in the end, she would know that price to be nothing compared to that which she received.

Samantha walked out of the hut the children had built for her. Silence immediately followed her appearance. Gazing over the gathering, she raised the Scepter of Light. "In the name of the Creator, I greet the faithful. He Who Sees All has spoken to me and bears witness that each of you has taken the Vow and kept it. The Alliance of Knights came under attack, and you rushed to their aid. You have reason to be proud!

"I speak of the Vow because it has meaning here today. It is not the custom of the were to vow faithfulness to a mate. It *is* a custom among humans. I will perform a ceremony today and accept a vow—not from the werewoman, Moonlight, but from the man. Before this day, it has been forbidden that a human should join with werekind. Today I say this. I am Samantha, the high cleric of Lyre. I hold the keys to the laws of the Creator in stewardship. This key I now return to the land, on this day that law ends."

The Scepter of Light flared brilliant. January came out of a hut. He wore a headband of bright blue. A golden, silk cord was braided into his long ponytail. Layered violet and deep purple skirts hugged his hips and fell in folds to his knees. His sword was strapped across his chest, the hilt standing over his right shoulder. Piercing ice-blue eyes held the enchanted gaze of the were gathered. Not a werewoman remained unmoved by the sight before them.

Flower stood within a hut across the clearing. She was well pleased by the female's reactions. She had dressed him herself, knowing how well the bright colors complimented his form. She snickered to herself and grinned. "They ain't seen nothin' yet!"

"Flower, I'm scared."

"Don't worry about it."

"Flower, I can't go out there!"

Flower's eyes narrowed. "Lyndsy, do you see that woman over there? Do you see the way she's trying to get Jan's attention?"

As Flower expected, Lyndsy's eyes burned bright. "That worthless bitch! This time Shawnsa has gone too far!"

Samantha raised the scepter.

Lyndsy stalked out of the hut and came to a dead stop. Eyes blazing, she had thought to go and stomp the bitch who was so shamelessly flaunting herself for Jan's attention. All eyes turned to her, and she caught herself.

Lyndsy watched their faces. She blinked. When they didn't laugh at her, she was surprised. Her magenta eyes widened in amazement as she saw some of the younger males pushing each other out of the way to get a better look.

She stood still, a hundred soft violet and rich purple streamers drifted from her throat, arms, and legs. A dark red wrap wound tightly around her small waist, hugged her maidenly hips, and then hung loose in folds to her knees. Another red wrap cupped her small breasts within soft folds, embraced her shoulders, and tied at the neck. A crown of bright pink wildflowers that caused her eyes to appear as liquid fire bound her shaggy white hair. Many males wondered that they had never found Moonlight so devastating in her beauty.

Suddenly shy, she walked forward, eyes downcast. A quick breeze caught the long streamers and seemed to wreath her in glorious violet and purple smoke. She stopped before Samantha, spread her arms, and bowed low. Standing slowly, she turned to face January. Lyndsy was overwhelmed by the look of awe he gave her. Impulsively, she reached out with one slim white finger and pushed his mouth shut. Turning on one heel, she gazed out at the people she had known all of her life. After a silent pause she turned back to January; reached up; and pulled him down for a long, deep kiss. Her passion was so great that January lost his breath. All witnessed his scent and saw that he had eyes only for her.

Samantha said sharply, "You witness the intent of a pack leader and his first to create a clan. Do I hear challenge?"

Swiftfoot and Lindon stalked to either side of the trio. All of Those Who Walk Alone approached and formed a half circle behind them. Sha pushed his way through the crowd and stepped in front of January. Turning to face the were, Sha planted both feet, and rested his hand on the hilt of his broadsword.

Snarl threw down a gourd and stomped on it. Cursing a blue streak, he walked up the path. Gazing angrily right and left, he yelled, "It is said the sharp tongues and swift anger of the were is legendary. Is there no one to challenge?" He stopped and faced Samantha. With a guarded expression, he asked, "High Cleric, do we represent ourselves poorly?"

Samantha gazed over the crowd. "Nay, I have witnessed my were brothers and sisters in battle. You are fierce!"

Approving murmurs ran through the people. Snarl turned and asked again, "Well, are there none here to call challenge?"

No answer.

Sha burst into laughter. "What of you, Snarl?"

Snarl turned back and glared at Sha. "What? Fight all of you for the insult?" Of a sudden, he barked a laugh and grinned like a wolf. "Do you think I'm crazy?"

Samantha held up the Scepter of Light. White fire burned from the diamonds in the crown. "It is done! We will witness the vow tonight before the maiden becomes a woman!"

To the lasting delight of the were, Lyndsy blushed crimson.

The joining of a pack leader and first was cause for celebration that almost equaled the festival held in Lychantorrid every spring in the name of the midwinter ritual of the Vow of Blood Plain. A true joining happened for only two reasons. Either a pack leader or first had been challenged and beaten or a pair sought to form their own pack and had won any challenge. No one had challenged the new couple's right. No one dared. This time, no dead or maimed pack leader or youth was to be grieved over. The celebration would be joyful.

Lyndsy thought the vow would be spoken with her kiss. Someone had been telling Samantha were custom, and she damn well wanted to know who it was! The vow was not yet taken; there was still time for the dreaded dance.

Walking out of the hut had been hard. If Flower hadn't provoked her anger, she may very well have still been in there refusing to come out. Now, the Dance of the First came to her mind. She felt her skin crawl. *I can't do it!*

A small invisible figure stood by her side. *That's what you think!*

Samantha sat with Silvertail and Sheela. She listened to the inspiring intricate music of the were. As a second-season initiate in the House of Song, she was well versed in the complexities of written music. This particular ballad had been created hundreds of seasons ago, and Samantha felt regret that she couldn't speak with the one who had created it. As far as she knew, there were no songs from the were in the archives of the House of Song. She told herself firmly that it wouldn't be the case for much longer.

A group of children came and sat before her. "Samantha, sing us a song!" "Yes, please!"

One of the young whelps gave the first speaker a glare. "She said call her high cleric in front of grown-ups!"

Sheela laughed at the look of shock on Silvertail's face when the pup called *her* Samantha. When the other whelp made the scathing comment about grown-ups, Silvertail also burst into laughter.

"Yes," Sheela asked, "sing for us, High Cleric."

Samantha reached for Sheela's harp and ran her fingers across the strings. After she plucked a few chords, she began a sad, old myth set to music that she dearly loved:

> In the age before time, in the land of Lyre,
> no creatures yet walked, only groves of green trees.
> The mountains of Seas, spied a dry realm;
> they left their deep oceans and stood in the sun.
> The Leaders of rock gazed to and fro;
> they loved the tall trees and went to find places.
> Five different ranges, Families of Mountains,
> where now is Mirshol, roamed the grandest.
>
> Oldest and largest, named Father Mountain,
> had three lovely daughters, called The Three Sisters—
> wanting to grow, to outdo each other,
> Father Mountain watching, grew swiftly angry.
> "Quit thy growing. I am your Master!"
>
> Three Sister Mountains ceased their growing
> but ever desired to always be better.
> Watching the waters, letting them trickle,
> they found in delight, caverns within them.
> A new game they played, unseen by the Father,
> to grow glorious caves and passage to others.
> Glistening fountains, shimmering spikes,
> silky smooth walls, golden deep pools.

One day, the Father, shifting his burden,
broke through a tunnel, found a stream flowing.
Following water, saw Daughter's doing.
In wrath Father spoke, his gift of seeing.
"Fish in the ocean, soon to grow feet,
walking on land, live under trees.
Find your deep caverns, open within you,
living defiled, evil in womb.
Go away Sisters, no longer Daughters!"

Three Sisters fled, moving together;
no other mountains, let them stand still.
Walking in sight of beloved mountains,
stopped to stand, the Three Sisters together.

Time brought the creatures, sight of The Father,
"Oh where, Father Mountain, where are your Daughters?
Standing alone, abode of Black Dragons!"

Benjamin listened to the strong, rich voice of the high cleric. He remembered the dream he had that had led him to Father Mountain and then to the School of Prayer. Without warning, the sight disfocused his eyes and drew his gaze inward. He watched as a huge black dragon touched down at the mouth of the Three Sister's caverns. He gasped as January walked from a grove of trees and faced the baleful creature. Jan stood alone. The black dragon crouched down and snaked his head a bare few feet from the tiny human figure before it. The Black Dragon spoke. January shook his head and held forward a strange staff that bore but one violet gem.

Benjamin watched January speak. In dismay, he found that this was not one of the rare times that words came with the sight. The huge, platinum horned head snaked back. It raised its fanged maw to the sky and laughed. A terrible feeling came over Benjamin. he found himself fearing for January's soul.

He is going to make a deal with the Black Dragon!

Sunder stood next to the Seer of Lake Town. Invisible to mortal eyes, he placed his small, furred palm on Benjamin's head. He saw, as Benjamin had seen, the sly look of the dragon as it answered Jan's question.

I wish Jasmine had never consented to show Myril the series of equations that explain the gift of sight. It makes life hard on good people. He just doesn't understand about January. The boy is no longer mortal, not subject so easily to the course of the future. We shall see.

Evening drew on. Lyndsy's apprehension grew way out of proportion. So far, the werewomen had only made teasing attempts to gain Jan's attention. She was secretly pleased to notice that Jan was oblivious and that he had eyes only for her. But the night wasn't over yet.

Samantha walked into the ring of dancers. The Scepter of Light flared brilliant. Music and talk quieted to silence. "It is time for the human, January, to take a vow. I ask again, is there any challenge?"

Shawnsa stepped forward. "The man we don't question." She turned to January, gazing seductively over one bare shoulder. "We know Moonlight is a warrior, but is she a woman? She looks like a boy in skirts!" Shawnsa offered Lyndsy a syrupy smile. "Maybe I could be his first."

Lyndsy's heart turned to stone. She heard someone shout, "Dance! It's time for the Dance of the First!" She was pushed into the ring. A few young bitches jumped up, laughing, and entered the circle. Someone pulled Jan to the center and sat him down. Cold fear smote Lyndsy's soul as she gazed at the other females. *He won't pick me. I'm ugly; they're beautiful.*

Fighting sudden tears, She Who Walks Alone turned and walked away.

Jan stood up to follow, but Sha pushed him back down. "Wait! January, you must stay. It is custom!" Sha saw the young wizard's frown and favored him with a wicked grin. "If you truly love Moonlight, nothing else matters. If this hardheaded bitch dances herself to the ground without turning your head, she will be shamed! Far worse than she thought to do to Moonlight. If you fail to respond to her charms, then Moonlight will be avenged. Think on that!"

Lyndsy walked out to the marsh. She held herself rigid, still fighting the flood of tears. Flower appeared in front of her. The bright, striped Mythit had to fight to keep the wash of anguish from *drenching* her. Lyndsy looked at Flower as two fat tears filled her eyes and rolled down her cheeks.

"Give up just like that, huh?"

"Flower, I—"

"I know," Flower mocked, "you can't!"

Lyndsy watched Flower stomp angrily away and fade from sight. "Flower, come back! Flower, please!" Despair came swiftly to take her. She shook as huge sobs wracked her small body. The will to live faded to naught.

She couldn't understand how it could hurt so badly! Never in her life had she felt anything toward another, but then she had found love. Now, her love had been cruelly ripped from her grasp. Thrown on the ground! Stomped underfoot!

Wham!

"Ouch!"

Wham!

"Ouch!"

Lyndsy jumped up and ducked the next blow.

Flower followed through and hit Lyndsy, hard.

"Flower! Stop! Flower!"

Lyndsy was ready this time. Flower swung, and Lyndsy caught the butt end of her own ivory staff. Holding firm in the middle, she pushed down with her back hand and lifted Flower up off of the ground.

Hand over hand, Flower swung from the staff and kicked. Lyndsy caught her by one ankle and pulled the staff away. She held Flower upside down, at arm's length, and was amazed to see the Mythit sputtering curses and swinging her fists.

"Flower, would you quit?"

"*No!*"

Lyndsy couldn't help it. She burst into laughter. "Flower, you look ridiculous!"

"How dare you!" Flower shouted. "After all my plans and long hours of work, you just turn your back and walk away! I planned for days how to make you a figure from men's dreams, and you …you …" With another curse, involving Lyndsy's obvious female canine ancestry, she started swinging her fists again.

"Flower! I'm sorry. I can't dance! Never even tried. Who would dance with me?"

Flower went suddenly limp. "Put me down."

"Will you quit?"

"For the moment."

Lyndsy flipped Flower up in the air and caught her by her wrists. Flower looked up into Lyndsy's eyes as the werewoman set her on her feet. Lyndsy watched those unique pale pink orbs glow brighter. Little white specs appeared within the growing pink field.

"Lyndsy," Flower asked, smiling, "how do you twirl your staff with just one hand?"

Lyndsy let the weight of the unbalanced staff carry itself around. With a slight wrist motion, it started to spin.

"Faster."

Lyndsy used her fingers and let the momentum build.

"I thought you used your whole arm, but you just use your wrist and fingers. Change hands behind your back."

She did.

"Wow, faster! Change hands behind your back and then over your head."

Lyndsy gracefully executed the motions, her style and ease creating a picture of overwhelming beauty.

"Now this is the kind of dancing *I* want to see!"

Lyndsy saw the weapons master watching her and then turned on Flower. "You're trying to trick me again!"

Flower clasped her hands behind her back, rocked back and forth on her heels, and grinned.

"It won't work."

The weapons master glanced at Flower and then looked back to Lyndsy. "I think you misjudge him. He loves you dearly. He tried to run after you, but Sha held him back."

Lyndsy blinked up at the master. "Really?"

"Yes. He is a sword dancer. I tell you true, I would rather watch you dance with your staff then watch that shameless, wanton, half-naked woman flaunt her body at me."

A touch of fire flickered within magenta eyes.

Flower smiled and used the Voice. "You gonna let that shameless hussy take *your* man?" As she watched, Flower could almost see the steam start to rise. Lyndsy's personality turned bright red.

"Yes," the weapons master said slyly, "it's really awful, the way she wiggles and bounces her body at him."

Flower watched wisps of personality begin to blaze.

"Child, go show your man the meaning of the dance."

As Lyndsy turned up the incline and stalked away, they heard her say fiercely, "I'm not a child! I'm a woman!"

Lyndsy walked through the ring of watchers and into the dance circle. She stalked up to Shawnsa and stopped. In scathing tones, she glanced at January and mocked. "It seems you've lost your charm. He looks bored to tears."

Spinning away, she twirled her staff. At first, she danced with single-minded attention to her stave. She wasn't aware of the eyes watching her. For the first time in her life, she realized what it meant to move in time to the music.

The Dance of the First was accompanied by an enchanting tune, slowing one moment and building the next—soft piping of reeds and flutes, loud clashes of drums and steel. Everything flowed together to give a dancer a wide variety of slow sways that built to wild abandon. Lyndsy caught up to the music, kicking and stomping. Breaking away, she skipped in a circle until she was in front of January. Giving him her profile, she gazed over one shoulder and lowered her eyes. Looking back up, she licked her lower lip and blew him a kiss.

Shawnsa had been failing. Miserably! As she danced, she watched horrified as Jan's frown turned into a scowl. Knowing full well what men really liked, she had moved to seduce him. Swishing her flaring hips and bouncing herself had only made the gorgeous man scowl worse. The weremales were laughing at her!

When Moonlight lowered demure eyes and blew him a kiss, he had obviously been charmed. Shawnsa stopped and watched him watch her. With a final attempt, she walked in front of him, and let her string wrap fall away. She moved slowly, alluringly, trying to keep herself between the man and the ugly albino woman. Suddenly furious, she watched January lean from side to side, looking around her.

She had lost, and she knew it. Not caring that she was breaking the rules of the dance, she plopped down in his lap and kissed him.

She felt a tap on one shoulder. Turning, she felt a hand grab her hair and pull her to her feet. Lyndsy tossed her staff in the air. A small, white fist came out of nowhere and connected with Shawnsa's jaw. Lyndsy reached out and caught the staff as Shawnsa hit the ground.

Smiling sweetly, she danced away. She didn't see Shawnsa jump up and run from the circle. The music was building. Leaping high in the air, she landed in a flurry of violet and purple smoke. Arms stretched wide, she arched her back and spun on the ball of her left foot. Her staff became a blur, cutting the air with a hum.

Jan watched her spin. Streamers followed her motion in a wreath of rich colors. She was beautiful.

Lyndsy stopped and struck air forward, backward, up, down. Changing hands behind her back, she brought the staff across her breast as she went down to one knee.

As the music began to slow, she circled Jan and tossed him the staff. Moving slower and slower, she smiled as she truly began to enjoy herself.

Gazing over her shoulder, she blew him another kiss. With small steps, she sashayed from side to side until she was standing in front of him. Lifting one slender white leg, she swished up her skirts. Tossing her head, she drew a line from her knee to midthigh and started making tiny circles.

Jan reached out, and she danced away. Coming back at him she swayed her hips and gave him an impudently saucy smile. She saw the way he was looking at her and said so only he could hear, "What are we having for dinner tonight?"

Lyndsy moved closer until she was almost touching him. She rolled her shoulders, and her top wrap slid halfway down her arms. He reached out. She put both arms down between his and pushed out. Backing away, her nose in the air, she silently shook her finger at him.

This time, she thoroughly enjoyed the cheering of the crowd. Lyndsy smiled as the weapons master shouted, "Aye, that's the way. Show him who's the boss!"

The music started to build. Legs pumping, arms swinging, she danced.

Jan was having a hard time breathing. Lyndsy almost always prowled like an animal on the hunt. He always liked that about her. She was very strong for her size. She always used strength and poise when she flirted with him. Not tonight. Tonight, she was all woman—sensual grace, single-minded in her attempt to make his blood boil.

As the tempo increased, she stood in one place and waved her arms. Following one hand with her gaze, she wove figure eights in the air. Changing hands, she followed her own body's motion and swayed with the music. When the steel and drums began to pound a thrashing beat, she jumped and started running in place. Head down, arms swinging back and forth, she started to circle and danced back toward him.

She was in a state of euphoria. As the music again slowed, she broke away from the music, spinning in fast, tight circles. Slowly, she ceased into perfect time with the music. The drums finally stopped, and the soft reed flutes took over. Dropping to her hands and knees, prowling forward, she tossed her hair and crawled up to Jan. Moaning in pleasure, she opened her mouth and shivered. Leaning forward, she pursed her lips and feigned a kiss.

Jan closed his eyes and leaned forward. He felt Lyndsy's hot breath just in front of him, so he kept leaning. Quickly opening his eyes, he reached out and caught himself.

She was right in front of him. Jan breathed in the scent of wildflower perfume. Her magenta eyes flashed as her gaze burned his personality. She was so full of desire he thought he would surely go mad.

Lyndsy dropped her head and slowly looked back up. Gazing at him through her thick bangs, she licked her lips and growled.

That was too much. Jan stood up and pulled her into his embrace. The wild cheers from the were were deafening.

"Enough!" Samantha shouted. The high cleric walked into the circle with Sheela at her side.

Jan stood still and let his mind clear. Lyndsy was panting, her breath heating his chest.

Samantha handed Sheela a silver chain set with a large star sapphire. Sheela pressed it against Jan's forehead and smiled as it glowed to life. Jan heard Samantha say, "Yes, that is what I meant."

Sheela nodded.

"January," Samantha said loudly, "will you swear that so long as Moonlight lives you will not know another woman?"

The were whispered around the circle.

"I swear it."

Jan felt Samantha and Sheela's attention on the sapphire. Nothing happened.

"It is done."

"No," Lyndsy said. "It isn't."

Lyndsy turned and picked up her staff. Facing the were, her eyes lost all emotion. She gazed long at the werewomen and leveled her staff. "Be warned, the dance is finished. I swear by the Vow that I will show *no* mercy to any bitch who dares trespass on my territory!"

She turned and wrapped her arms around January's neck. With a quick look over her shoulder, she kissed him thoroughly, long, and well.

They reached the clearing and stopped in front of a small mud hut. Lyndsy, riding on Jan's back, slid to the ground and peeked into the opening. She gasped as a fat gourd of water was poured over her head. Blinking drops from her lashes, she turned to him and offered him a pout. "Trying to put out a fire?"

Jan grinned as he picked up another gourd. "Yeah. Did it work?"

Lyndsy wrapped her arms around his waist and gazed up into his eyes. "Nope."

Jan leaned down to kiss her, but Lyndsy laughed and snatched the water gourd from his hands as she pushed away. "Kisses only make the flames bigger!"

Jan caught her around the waist and lifted her in his arms. Lyndsy wrapped her legs around Jan's waist and poured the gourd over his head. Jan raised an eyebrow. "Nope. It doesn't work."

Lyndsy reached behind Jan's neck and started working on the tie that bound his ponytail. She pursed her lips and smiled as Jan's gaze settled on her mouth "Whatcha thinkin'?"

"About putting out that fire."

Lyndsy let the braid fall as she worked his hair loose. She looked back up into his eyes and felt herself blush. "Could we try to smother it?"

January burst into laughter. Ducking his head, he carried Lyndsy into the hut and laid her on the marsh straw mattress.

Somewhere in the night, an owl called; a wolf howled; and a white-haired, red-eyed maiden became a woman.

36

MOONLIGHT AND JANUARY

Lyndsy woke late in the morning. January's arm was draped across her throat. His right thigh was settled over her hips. His shoulder pinned her hair to the ground. She was pressed against a rock that dug into the small of her back. Every inch of her body was sore. She thought she had surely died and gone to heaven.

She turned her head as far as she could and grinned at Jan's face. Never in her life had she felt so utterly cherished. A tear of joy ran down her cheek as she replayed last night. He was so strong! So handsome, so kind, and oh, so gentle. *I am your First. And last! Moonlight, the first of January. January and his first. Moonlight and January. January and Moonlight. The wizard and the white wolf!* She burst into a fit of giggles. *Oh! Life is good!*

She smelled fresh meat and rolled her head the other way to try and look outside. She could barely see a small silver tray. Heat waves wisped off of the top of the lid. She gave a small pout. *They cooked it!*

Her smile quickly returned as Jan stretched and smashed her against the rock. He blinked and looked into her eyes. "If you keep smiling like that, your face will crack."

Lyndsy laughed, a deep, throaty laugh that set Jan back on fire. Rolling onto his back, he pulled her on top of him.

Lyndsy crossed her arms over his chest and looked down into his eyes. Feigning innocence of his desire, she asked, "Sir, are you hungry?"

"You know I'm always hungry!"

They finished both meals and went out to wash. January couldn't get enough of touching her. Lyndsy beamed in delight as they constantly stumbled over each other, too entwined to even walk straight. When they weren't touching, all she had to do was look at him, and he instantly pulled her close.

Jan caught a fistful of her hair and ran his fingers through the soft, shaggy mass. He glanced down and saw two new bruises high on her back. With gentle hands, he turned her around and lifted her hair. "What happened to you?"

Lyndsy looked down at her toes, embarrassed. "Flower beat me."

"What?"

"You heard me!" Then she grinned. "You should have seen her. I never thought a Mythit could be so fierce. She's just so small!" Lyndsy giggled, remembering Flower, upside down, swinging wildly and cursing the thick skulls of young women.

Jan looked at her wryly. "Does it really surprise you that something so small can be so fierce?"

Lyndsy blushed and looked away.

Jan gazed at her profile and pulled her back into his arms. *In the name of Song, you are so beautiful!*

Lyndsy's color deepened. Shaking her head, she looked up, exasperated. "How can you make me feel this way when no one else can?"

Jan grinned to himself, remembering Flower's words. *Does it feel good or bad?*

Lyndsy threw up her hands and pushed away, laughing. Jan started as he realized she was hearing his thought. He watched her pick up a cup and a water gourd. Jan thought, *Don't drop that cup!*

Lyndsy looked down at the cup, puzzled. Then she did drop it. "You're in my mind! I almost forgot what that's like! How?"

Jan shook his head. He gazed at her personality and blinked. A fine web of light seemed to reach between them. He stilled his mind and tried to analyze *the light*. Even as he paid attention to it, it started to fade from his mind. *That wasn't there last night.*

Lyndsy looked up at him, waiting for an answer. "Hmm?"

Jan shook his head. "I don't know how. Try to think to me."

Lyndsy's heart started to pound in her chest. She tried to think words but couldn't seem to do it.

"Wait," Jan said. He led her back to the hut. "Sit. Give me your hands." Lyndsy sat down across from him. "Now, try again."

Lyndsy started thinking, but Jan could only make out stray syllables. He realized she was too excited. "Breath deep; calm yourself. If you're feeling emotions, use it to your advantage. Let your feelings set power to your thoughts. Think individual words, slowly, crisply."

I love you so very much. No one has ever given me such warm affection and kindness like you do every minute of every hour of every day!

Jan nodded. "Much better. Try again."

Lyndsy's eyes narrowed. *If you do not tell me that you love me too, I will go get my staff and give you a sound thrashing!*

Jan laughed. "I love you too."

Lyndsy smiled impishly. "Much better. Try again!"

"Don't sass me. Now, let all emotion go. Sit perfectly still. Tell me something. I know, tell me how to make fire with a spindle and bow. Feel nothing, no emotional content at all; it is much harder to do."

You take ... frayed ends ... in a pile. Grind them ... fire board.

"Wait." Jan thought for a moment. He reached for his pouch and drew out a thin gold necklace that held a small opal. He put it on. "Look at the stone. Focus on the little specks. Pierce it with your eyes. Think clearly, pronounce each word."

Lyndsy breathed. She wanted this so badly it was hard for her to remain calm. Finally, she settled her racing heart and did what Jan asked. *You take crushed, frayed ends of wood. Put them in a pile. Grind them well and put them on a fire board.*

"Much better."

"I'm not finished."

"For now, you're finished. Believe me, it is enough." He smiled.

She was beaming with the pure wonder of a child who had just discovered some new and wonderful secret. He remembered the headaches he'd had when Sunder first started teaching him the controls and various techniques of mind speech.

He stood up, still holding her hand, and lifted her up off of her feet. She wrapped her arms around his neck and laid her head on his shoulder. As he carried her toward the edge of the marsh, she wondered if people actually lived through feeling this glorious.

Jan set his chin on the top of her head and gazed over the plant life. Walking to a stunted hackberry, he dug his toe into the soil and bent over. "Pick that plant with the small, red, fuzzy buds. Pull it up carefully. Try to get all of the roots."

Lyndsy reached down and slowly pulled the plant out of the dry soil. Jan found another red-budded plant and told her to pick it also. After they collected four of the plants, Jan carried her back to the hut and bent over so she could pick up the water gourd and cup.

"Pour some water in the cup and wash the dirt off the roots. OK, now pinch the buds and put it all in the cup. Good. Set the cup by the sword. Carefully. Don't let the cup touch the steel. How's your head?"

She was surprised he'd asked because she was starting to get a headache. It seemed to get worse as she realized it. "It hurts."

Jan called the gems to life and caused fire to heat the cup. Soon, it began to steam. He set his palm on the top of Lyndsy's head and kissed her ear. She looked up and smiled, wincing slightly from a sharp pain.

Jan let the fire die and watched as the cup cooled. Lyndsy tensed now and then, and Jan knew it was from the cramped veins in her head that screamed as blood was forced through them. "Hurts purty bad, huh?"

Almost imperceptibly, she nodded. Jan reached out, careful to make no sudden movement. With one finger, he squeezed the buds against the edge of the cup so they would release their potent painkiller. "It's ready. Drink this." He held her head in the crook of his arm and pressed the cup to her lips. Slowly, she started to relax. "Tastes purty bad, don't it?"

She wrinkled her nose and stuck out her tongue.

Jan cupped her cheek and kissed her forehead. He gazed down at her small, straight nose and frowned. "You look pale."

Lyndsy gave him a slight, sarcastic smile. "I always look pale."

Jan laughed softly. He pushed the hair from her face and gently brushed her cheek with his fingertips. "Woman, you are the meaning of loveliness."

She looked up into his blue eyes and thought that a very hot flame was their best description. He was holding her close and looking at her in a way she knew he had never looked at anybody else. His heartbeat was a soothing balm against her face. She smiled a huge smile that seemed to run from her hair to the tips of her toes. As she fell asleep in his arms, she wondered again if being in love and feeling such bliss wasn't, somehow, fatal.

She woke, smiling from a dream she couldn't remember. Realizing that she was alone, she rolled over and looked around. Jan was outside dancing with his sword, naked. The sunlight gleaming on his sweaty body caused delicious knots to form in her stomach. She curled her fingers in the straw mattress, stuffed her face in the grass, and giggled. She had known from the scents of other couples that making love must be something very wonderful. She'd even imagined what it must be like to smell that happy. By the Vow! Her silly little head couldn't have imagined this if her life had depended on it!

Still bursting with giggles, she gazed back out of the entrance. She watched him swing, block, slash, and feint. He was dancing a dance she had never seen before. It was obviously practiced and practiced well. Lyndsy shook her head gently and then more vigorously. No pain at all. Jumping up, she grabbed her staff and went out to join him.

Jasmine told Flower, *"Leave them alone!"* Flower had determined, through an absolutely remarkable line of rationalities, that leaving them alone meant not letting them know you were there. She watched them dance, sword and staff creating a duo of motion that filled her snooping breast with awe.

She was amazed at the changes that Sunder had wrought in January. He used to be *so* clumsy! With a mind all his own, he had made fun of himself and created a sword dance that Sunder had promptly named the Baby Colt Walk.

The first time she had seen him perform this dance she had been terrified. For him! She was, at first, so tricked from just watching him act, she thought he would surely cut himself.

Lyndsy stopped to watch him perform this particular dance. Her nostrils flared as she tilted her head and glanced toward the brush. Shrugging her shoulders, she gazed back at Jan. She had seen him use this defense several times. As a fighter, she was very jealous of his ability to draw an opponent and so quickly make use of their sudden overconfidence. Now, she merrily watched his antics, laughing at the ridiculous expressions on his face.

Jan stopped and swiped sweat from his brow. His eyes settled on Lyndsy and blazed hot trails up and down her body. Lyndsy dropped her staff and walked into his arms as flaming wisps of personality swirled around her head and womb. They dropped to the ground and Flower gasped in awe as their personalities mingled to mate. She thought, as she watched the pastel colors—and not for the first time—that perhaps she should leave.

"Are you ready to teach me some more?"

"Are you? The pain won't bother you?"

Lyndsy looked at him sideways. "I am were. My life is pain. It is a part of my life."

Jan blushed. She was right. "Go get two of those plants, wash away the dirt, and put them in a cup."

"What?" Lyndsy exclaimed with a sassy pout. "You're not going to carry me?"

She laughed and leapt lightly out of the way as Jan tried to swat her. He smiled at her bare bottom as she walked into the swamp with a very over-exaggerated sway of hips.

"Let's start where we left off. Very calmly and precisely, tell me something."

Lyndsy thought for a moment and then gave him a detailed explanation on the proper way to tan a hide.

Good. Now stand up and walk to the edge of the clearing.

Lyndsy smiled as she stood up and walked away. She liked the feel of his voice in her mind. She reached the edge of the marsh and turned around.

Tell me something with feeling.

I love you.

Try something angry. Anger is harder to think through.

I'm not angry.

Tell me about that sexy creature who danced for me.

"What?!" Lyndsy shouted. She started toward him, fists clenched.

Angry now, aren't you?

She stopped.

Breathe. Say something.

If I had that little, stinking, worthless, shameless, good-for-nothing tramp right here, right now, I'd stomp her ugly face smooth into the ground!

Very good, but she's not that little.

Lyndsy's eyes flared. Her personality blazed a rich red.

Drop your emotion right now!

Lyndsy tried to calm herself, but she had worked herself into a rage and just couldn't let it go. She saw Jan, all of a sudden, jump up and draw his sword. He picked up her staff and threw it to her.

"Behind you!"

Her anger vanished. Lyndsy whirled, all senses alert. Nothing was there.

Jan walked toward her and stopped. "You must drop all emotion at a moment's notice. Right now your mind is clear, all emotion gone. Use whatever thoughts you need, but you *must* learn to drop emotion immediately."

Lyndsy realized the way he had manipulated her anger. She promised herself she wouldn't let him do it again. Nevertheless, she had learned a very important lesson in a very vivid way and knew she wouldn't soon forget it.

As she thought about it, she realized just how many times January had used emotion, and the lack of it, to change her train of thought. Especially in Mirshol, she had been angry, offended, self-conscious, and a full array of other emotions. She watched again as Jan always seemed to sway her thoughts quickly and precisely.

Lyndsy walked away and turned to look at him.

Jan followed her train of thought and nodded silent approval as her gaze turned inward. He watched her personality clear as she came to an inner understanding. When she walked away and looked back, he smiled. *Speak of something that you know well.*

There is a scar on the inside of your right thigh. It looks like a knife wound, short and straight. It is old, perhaps six seasons.

You walk tall and straight, toes pointed slightly inward. You don't have rough hands, although you use a sword constantly. I like the way you look covered in sweat and breathing hard! There isn't a man alive who would ever touch me, but if one tried, he could never do to me what you do with just a smile. I love everything about you, your strength and your kindness. What will you show me next? What wonders are in store for this young, skinny girl who has fallen in love with a dream?

Her thought was quiet and calm yet filled with a sincerity that touched him deeply. Her next lesson would have been just that—thought, which held intense emotion, while showing nothing to anyone who might be watching her.

He had indeed perceived her previous thoughts. A flowing of understanding had passed through the enlightening of her personality. Now he understood why Jasmine had taken him into the woods and terrorized him. As Lyndsy thought she understood, he hadn't really understood either. He recognized the openness in Lyndsy that had allowed Jasmine's entrance into himself. His fight was against fear. Lyndsy's fight, according to the nature of her being, would be against desire.

Jan squared, building passion as he moved. He came to a stop before her and set one palm flat between her breasts. She gasped as *vapors* of passion soaked into her personality. She looked up into his eyes, dumbfounded. She had gotten used to the filling of desire in his eyes and wondered that they were so clear. She breathed. He smelled of strict intent.

"Lyndsy, do you *smell* what I'm feeling?"

She swallowed hard. "No."

"But can you feel it?"

"How can I not? You are on fire!"

She couldn't resist. She moved his hand and reached out. As she pressed herself against him, she felt him let go. The sensation was simply too much. White-hot fire poured in, her knees turned to water, and he caught her as she fell. She gasped and moaned as his skin burned her nerves. Her mind was barely clear enough to realize he was carrying her toward the sword and the cup.

"Hurry!"

"No. Right now, while we're touching, clear your mind. Let all of the emotion go."

Lyndsy looked at him as though he were crazy.

"Do it!"

"No! I won't!"

Jan smiled. "You must. You wish to learn; I am teaching you. If you don't do it, I will leave you here to *cool off* by yourself."

"That's cruel!"

Jan's lips curved down into a frown. He said very quietly, "I know how you feel. I went through this too."

"What? And just who was it that filled you so full of desire you couldn't see straight?"

"For me the lesson was fear, not desire. At the time, it was what I was most vulnerable to. Please, Lyndsy, you must do this."

Lyndsy felt the echoes of heat flowing through her. Her pulse sent a constant ripple of need blazing through her body. She did not want to let it go. As she realized that she was, in a way, being selfish, a great sense of wrongness came over her. She tried to rationalize the thought away, but she knew what it was. It was lust.

Setting one hand over her heart, she breathed, slowly, fighting for peace. It took all of her strength to steady her breathing, and soon she was covered in sweat. She felt weak, very weak.

"Drink this. Good. Now go to sleep."

As the emotion left her, she became frightened. Irrational thoughts ran through her mind. *I failed. He really doesn't love me. How could he do this to me? How cruel and heartless to do this to me!* A part of her mind knew it was ridiculous, but she just couldn't turn her internal dialogue off. She was about to speak when Jan stopped her.

"Don't worry, I won't let you go. You will wake up in my arms. I love you, my little Lyndsy."

Slowly the fear went away too. She gave Jan a small smile and then a tiny pout. "I'm not that little."

Jan sighed as Lyndsy passed into sleep. He breathed in clean air as he let his shields drop. *Oh, that was hard! I almost couldn't bear it. I wonder if I gave her too much? Did Jasmine feel this rotten?*

Flower sat outside the clearing, listening. She said very quietly, out loud so Jan couldn't pick up her thoughts. "No, little brother, your test was harder, much harder!"

Lyndsy woke up in Jan's arms. She felt peaceful, happy. The memory of the day before was sharp and clear. It was, at the same time, distant. But she knew, as long as she lived, she would never forget it. Neither Jan nor Lyndsy knew it, but her experience would soon save both of their lives. She had sacrificed much in her very short life. She had worked and trained beyond reason to be the best fighter she could be. The tests and training of Those Who Walk Alone were strenuous and demanding. One of their tests seemed to be the most sinful feat she had ever performed—that she thought she could possibly imagine. What had happened yesterday was different, but it was surely the hardest thing she had ever done.

She smiled up at him. "Kiss me."

"No."

She opened her mouth to protest, and he dropped a fat bumble berry in it. She chewed it up and then another and another. Finally, she pursed her lips and gave him a mock scowl. "Bad breath?"

"Uh, no." Jan grinned. "Dog breath."

"Dog breath!"

Jan laughed as she pounded him with her fists. Exasperated, she exclaimed, "Men!"

"Men or man?"

"Oh yes, men." She grinned wickedly. "I leave them exhausted on the ground wherever I go!"

"Now, I want you to close your eyes. I'm going to hide. First, we will get a rapport going. Go ahead, tell me how you made that stuff that you put on your staff when we were in Mirshol."

The first thing that needs to be done is find sap from any plant that's thin enough to soak the wood.

Good, now close your eyes.

The sap ... plant ... wood ...

Wait. I'm losing you. Speak directly at me and then close your eyes and keep speaking directly at me. You have to know *I'm right there.*

OK, the sap from the plant is to soak the wood for weight. Water will only dry away.

All right, now quit pointing your nose at me. I forgot your sense of smell. Remember, anyone watching you should think that whatever you're doing is where all of your attention is.

Lyndsy turned her head as though suddenly intent on the tie of her wrap. *Now take the sap and rub it in. Get it as soaked as it will get. Work your way from one end to the other and then start over.*

All right. Now open your eyes and look for me.

Lyndsy opened her eyes and was surprised that he wasn't right in front of her. He had seemed to be while they were in rapport. Now, his presence in her mind was quickly fading.

You don't see me, do you?

Nothing.

Answer me.

Nothing.

It's too easy. You're making it hard.

Lyndsy threw up her hands. "I can't talk to you if I can't see you!"

You were doing it a moment ago. Speak directly to me.

Nothing.

Jan watched Lyndsy sniff the air. *That's cheating. Besides, I'm downwind.*

Lyndsy whirled, looking carefully over the area. *I'll find him. My eyes are better than he thinks!*

Very good! A little determination goes a long way.

Lyndsy stiffened as though caught in the act. Then she realized she *had* been making it too hard. Her gaze found a leaf, and she felt her rapport with Jan's mind come clearly into focus. *When the staff is finished, you find your insolent mate and beat him over the head with it!*

Jan burst into laughter, and Lyndsy pointed. "Yes!" She ran to him and jumped up into his embrace. Wrapping her legs around his waist, she hugged him tight and kissed him soundly.

Jan carried her back to the hut and heated the cup.

Flower watched in sheer delight. She had almost shouted in triumph with Lyndsy but had caught herself just in time. This time Lyndsy drank only two swallows from the cup. "Good. She's getting used to it." She watched for another long moment and then shook her head, amazed. How many times could they do that!?! Once again, she turned away, thinking perhaps it was time for her to leave.

For the next four days, they simply relaxed and honed their silent rapport. On the morning of the seventh day since their joining, January noticed Flower's presence. One moment, she was there, and the next moment, she was gone. His perception of this special place shifted. A piece of the overall personality of the small clearing was suddenly missing. When he realized it, he laughed out loud. "I think Flower has been spying on us."

Lyndsy frowned as they went in search of Mythit signs. She went directly to the place where she'd first smelled Flower's presence and showed him the prints of two little feet. Still frowning, she followed him as he circled the area and ran across another set of prints. There were five prints, toes pointed at the shelter and then three that turned and faded into the marsh.

Lyndsy bit her lip and giggled. Jan watched her curiously. Every time he glanced at her, she started to giggle. Finally, he asked, "OK, what's so funny?"

Lyndsy went to the stunted hackberry and made an elaborate show of peeking through and around the branches. Then she stood up, eyes wide, and clapped her hands over her mouth. Flushing, she turned quickly away. Walking into the marsh, she shook her head but then took another long look back at the hut and grinned like a wolf.

"She was watching us, wasn't she?" He looked over the prints again and realized each set was in a place where a Mythit could get a bird's-eye view of the hut. "That little varmint!" He turned to Lyndsy. "You think this is funny!"

Lyndsy burst into such a fit of laughter she fell to the ground. Jan set hands on hips and stared down at her. She was laughing at him! He suddenly felt as though he was the brunt of a joke, and he couldn't figure out why. "Woman, what in the name of Song are you laughing at!"

Lyndsy just laughed harder. Jan rolled his eyes and sat down.

Finally, Lyndsy calmed enough so she could speak. "You didn't know she was here?"

"What? You did?"

"Of course. I thought you knew!"

"No. And if I did, I would have ... I," Jan mumbled something incoherent.

That sent Lyndsy off into another fit of giggles. She tried to stop, but it was useless. After another long wait, she finally caught her breath. "Why are you so angry? She's just a child."

"Child? She's a six hundred-season-old sneak; that's what she is!"

"Tell me why you're so angry."

"Why I'm angry? Why shouldn't I be?"

Lyndsy looked at him seriously. She sat up and put one hand on his shoulder. When they first met, he had done this to her many times. She felt a certain satisfaction as she said, "I think this is one of those times. Explain to me why you're so upset. I really don't understand."

"Well," Jan scowled, "it's just that she shouldn't watch us, that's all." Jan looked quickly away.

Lyndsy asked very quietly. "You mean she shouldn't watch us make love to each other?"

"Yes," Jan exclaimed in exasperation. Then he caught the ever-present amused look on her face and realized what she wasn't saying. "You're enjoying this! You don't mind that she ..." He just couldn't finish.

"No. I don't mind. Why do you think I should? I'm surprised there haven't been other pups trying to spy on us."

Jan almost choked. *Other children?* "Well, among humans—"

"Oh!" she exclaimed, suddenly understanding. "This is a thing of custom. Tell me this human custom."

Flower's voice ran through his mind. *It is a matter of custom. They've been doing it for time out of mind.* "People just don't watch each other have sex. It's a private thing. If I knew anyone was watching, I would, at the very least, draw the skin over the front of the hut."

"I see." Lyndsy said, "For the were, it is not acceptable behavior for *grown-ups* to watch, but it's not the same for pups. Don't you know by now that the scent of lovemaking cannot be hidden. Every single male, female, and whelp knows every time it happens. How else do they learn?"

Jan just shook his head. He didn't know what to say to that. He thought about it for a good while, trying to rationalize why a people would see it that way. With a start, he realized what she was saying about Flower. "You think Flower is a child, and that's why it's OK for her to, uh ..."

"Yes."

Jan frowned. "She's not a child."

"Yes, she is."

Jan looked at her. She spoke with such conviction that it made him wonder what made her so sure. Curiosity just couldn't be held in check today. "Tell me why you think Flower is a child."

Lyndsy wondered what to tell him. What did she need to explain? If he didn't already know, he surely wouldn't understand the different scents between children and adults, maidens and women. He obviously was unaware of the way children shared a basic, common ignorance that seemed like curiosity but was really very different. Finally, she just said, "Jan, would you trust me on this? This is a thing that women know. Men try very hard to understand it, but they just can't."

Jan's look was unfathomable. This conversation had long ago become uncomfortable. He knew Lyndsy was enjoying it, seemed to know what she was talking about, and he would surely lose any argument about it. This suddenly seemed like a good place to drop it. "Women's business, huh?"

"Uh-huh."

Jan and Lyndsy walked into the clearing late on the eighth day since their joining. They watched, curiously, as a flurry of little robed figures saw them and ran in their direction. Jan saw Flower's face beneath a cowl and watched as she flew into Lyndsy's arms.

"Are you really my sister now?"

"Tell me you don't already know!"

"I don't, I swear! Well, I only watched for a minute!"

Lyndsy burst into laughter and tumbled Flower to the ground. Fingers in place, she tickled the orange and yellow Mythit mercilessly.

"No! Stooo op. Cut it out! If I laugh any more, I'll pop! Pleeeeease!" Flower trailed off into a fit of compelled laughter. Gathering breath, she gave it another shot. "Oh! I forgot! I have to tell you something."

Lyndsy stopped but kept her fingers in place. "It better be good," she said mischievously, giving Flower a few pokes for emphasis.

"It is! It is! Really, stooooop!"

"All right, what?"

"The weapons master, Sha, and Those Who Walk Alone bet all kinds of stuff on you and won! It was great. The females have been serving them meals for three days now. Sha even made Angryeyes and the other firsts wash everybody's clothes and hides six times! You shoulda seen it."

Jan watched Lyndsy turn three shades of red. When she got to purple, he asked her what Flower was talking about. Lyndsy was smiling fit to burst. Her personality was so full of pride, she was as red as her face, but every time he tried to get an answer from her, she would turn away.

One little weremale came up to Jan and said very seriously, "The bitches bet the men that Moonlight couldn't keep you in the furs for more than five days."

To hear this from one so young made it all the funnier. Jan burst into laughter, and Lyndsy just shook her head.

Jan caught his breath and asked, "You don't think that's funny?"

Lyndsy shook her head again, trying not to laugh. "Not really," she lied. She looked down at Flower. Flower saw *the look* come back into those magenta eyes and shuddered. Lyndsy set her fingers against Flower's ribs and grinned like a wolf. "But Flower thinks it's funny!"

And indeed, from the laughter that followed, Flower apparently thought something very, very funny.

37

A Piece of Past: 4

Jan found Slim Chance talking with Samantha. As soon as she saw him, the frown crossing the high cleric's brow lifted. Slim turned and rose to his feet. He stood still, watching Jan closely. Jan watched him turn and look at Samantha. They seemed to share a thought.

Samantha stood up and came to him. Silently, she wrapped her arms around his waist and laid her head on his shoulder. Jan blinked, mildly surprised, and hugged her back. After a few moments, she pushed back and gazed into his eyes. She seemed to be looking for something.

"January, I don't know how to say this. I have been told I could say anything to anybody and always use the right words. Well, thank you. Thank you for the land. Thank you for bringing me to the were. And thank you for being a part of my life." She smiled and fought back a tear.

Jan felt her emotions ripple across his senses. The one that seemed to override all others was pride—pride in him and herself. He smiled, seeing a look that Jasmine often gave, mother to son. Jan figured she didn't expect an answer, so he simply inclined his head.

Slim Chance stepped forward. "We must talk. There are a few things I want the other leaders to hear also. It concerns all of us, but most of what I want to say concerns you and your sister."

"Slim Chance," Samantha said seriously, "you are Melody's greatest threat."

"Anyway," Slim interrupted, "we must talk. Can we do this tonight?"

Jan watched both of them, wondering at Samantha's words. "Yes, tonight."

Slim stood still, gazing over the faces in front of him. The weapons master, Captain Slith, Sha, Swiftfoot, and Lindon sat to one side. January, Lyndsy, Samantha, and Benjamin sat on the other. He turned lastly to Benjamin. He knew from the personalities around the old seer that all three of the Mythits were present. His silent mind momentarily puzzled over their choice of location.

Benjamin gave him a slight nod, indicating acknowledgment of the attention. Slim snapped from his line of thinking and asked, "Seer of Lake Town, have you heard, or are you familiar with, the name Gembol Slayer?"

Jan started, remembering the prophesy Slim had spoken just before the battle. He saw Sunder stand up and walk to his side. Tendrils of thought sprang from the Mythit's aura and touched his mind.

Sunder and the Blue Wizard were four thousand seasons into their Wizard-Mythit binding when Blue changed shape to a stuttering lad and went to Lispin Shark for training. Through this change, Sunder learned, out of inherent curiosity, the arts of the dancers.

Memories from the Mythit's mind played before his mind's eye. A whirlwind of body and weapon made the fighting tool called *dancer*. Designed by the Black Mancer of Shark, dancers were first trained to repel the upstart Lords and little Kings that tried to invade his land. So well were they trained, it was soon taken for granted that, if a dancer was assigned an assassination, no castle or army or magic could stop it. The Dancers of Lispin Shark became a legend in their own time. And that was their doom.

The Dark Lord, at first, was well pleased with the Slayer Clan. Slayer devotion to his evil purpose made them perfect tools in his plans for Lyre's dragons. For this reason, he suffered the bloody feuding between Dagdor's demons and the Mancer of Shark. Yet, the dancers developed strict codes of honor that he secretly despised. Their efficiency and deadly ruthlessness against enemies soon caused him to fear. As humans flocked to the ever-growing Keep of Lispin Shark, the Dark Lord felt threatened in his own evil designs.

The plans for conquest of dragonkind fell apart with the sudden arrival of the Fangthane from *elsewhere*. His purposes were further inhibited by the defection of the Black Dragon, Death. Of a sudden, the Dark Lord was seemingly beset on all sides by forces he did not control. In fear of Death, who seemed to hold the younger black dragons in his mighty magic, and in fear of the son of Lispin Shark, he summoned Dagdor, his ever-faithful servant, and plotted the ruin of Shark.

As January watched, an entire Keep, an area larger than mountains, became surrounded by an inferno of evil magic. In the blink of an eye, it vanished. For as far as the eye could see, barren, lifeless plains stretched across his visionary horizon. The silence in the hut brought him back to reality.

Benjamin looked so blank and sat so quietly Slim wondered if the old seer had even heard his question. Slim was about to repeat it when Benjamin said, "I assume you refer to Gembol Slayer, the sword master of Lispin Shark."

"Lispin Shark?" the weapons master exclaimed. "I thought that was only a myth. Believe me, the Knights Alliance has records and, even more, artifacts of Lyre's history—especially weaponry. There was never any such place!"

Benjamin inclined his head. "There *was* such a place. Right now, it lies buried somewhere beneath a sea of blood. It stood on the southern point of Blood Plain when that area was the greatest of all forests, the Forest of Life. The fortress, Lispin Shark, was a keep to surpass any except Wizards Veil herself. Even the mountains of Kringe cannot compare."

"What happened to it?" Sha asked.

"I do not know."

Jan glanced at Benjamin, startled, but said nothing.

Slim Chance smiled grimly. "Well, it seems we have an incongruity in Gembol Slayer."

"What are you talking about?" Jan asked curiously.

"Gembol Slayer is, at this moment, bound under Melody's control. He wields a golden long sword of clerical nature. It is one of many swords that he, himself, made when he lived."

Jan's eyes grew round. He whispered, "The same man I danced with." Quickly he searched for Sunder's personality.

Slim gazed at Jan with a guarded expression. "Tell us how you felt about that dance."

Jan wanted, at that moment, to be alone with the yellow and orange Mythit. He knew if he didn't settle his thoughts, he might never get another chance. Unfortunately, Slim and the rest assembled were waiting for an answer. "Well, I don't know. He tested me, I guess. At least at first. I haven't really thought about it. We danced. He was trying to kill me; that I know. It was not a spar. It seems that he didn't want to." Jan frowned, looking toward Sunder's stamp of personality. "I have never been so tested. I don't understand—"

"Let me tell you what happened," Slim said carefully. "First, you must know this. He is no ally. He just plays a game with his current mistress, Melody. He is an evil cleric and a sword dancer. As Benjamin said, he was the sword master of Shark.

He is *summoned.* Bound by the same strictures that make binding demons possible. Demons dwell in a realm of thick, dark personality. They soak in their surroundings and learn to be aware. They have no corporeal bodies and soon learn to cloak themselves in any form they wish to take. You have seen the form of a demon. A demon, once summoned, comes in the form that it thinks itself to be. Unless there is something the high cleric and I have missed, this is extraordinary. I cannot stress this enough; it is cause for great fear that Gembol Slayer is genius enough to remember his true form after eight thousand seasons!

This is what happened. He built his personality into fear. As soon as the transition from Melody's side to Virile Swamp was complete, he cast the building aside. That made me pause. I saw Samantha put up her shields. However, you and I were within."

"I couldn't get January in my shield," Samantha explained. "His sword will not allow my protection."

"You did well, High Cleric. Yes, his sword will not allow your protection. Anyway, Melody was here. She watched the scene through a crystal." Slim gazed sidelong at Samantha and smiled. "Her access to us has now been permanently blocked. As I say, Melody was here. Gembol Slayer has played a great game, and for the moment, he has won. The death spell he fired at me was really a simple spell of message sending. I tell you, I almost blew it I was so surprised. He surely would have killed me.

"I disappeared, leaving an illusion of myself behind. I immediately let it fall and reappeared so Melody would think I had been prepared. Gembol then turned and made it swiftly known to Melody that both you and Samantha were using power. He showed her that January was the closest and most immediate threat.

"The message was swift to unravel, so I remained still to hear it. He said

Melody wanted me killed in front of Samantha. She wanted you to fear that she could strike anytime, anywhere. Your feelings of powerlessness would allow her scrying to become easier. Gembol also told me he was faithful to his Lord only. No one, especially no offshoot of Dagdor the Fool would ever rule him. He claimed you could do her much harm by destroying her home of Lince Posh. I have to agree with him.

"I came from the spell as your swords revealed their opposite powers. He did something then, speaking well of his training as a sword dancer and as an evil cleric. He opened his mind to me. He spoke well of you. He wanted to know how the art of dancing had survived such a long period of disuse. I told him I didn't know. He said he wished to know your line. I told him I didn't understand. He asked whose family the violet field and the silver star symbolized. I realized he meant the arm sash that you and Lyndsy trade every morning when you wake.

"January, I didn't know it had any particular meaning. I only knew you did this with great feeling. So, I told him it was yours alone—that I've never seen it before. As you ended your dance, he said to me, 'The right to wear the symbol is well earned. I acknowledge it.'

"As you fought, Melody's rage grew. She became careless, and I saw her. I yelled to Samantha, and the high cleric shot power through her scepter. I'm sure the crystal exploded in her hands." Slim laughed softly. "I would give anything to have been there and seen the look on her face."

"I wonder how long it will take the servant to be free of its master," Benjamin said, speculating. "The treachery of the Seven among themselves was even greater than the wars between Dagdor and the Three. I also wonder if Gembol would be greater in clerical ability than Melody. Perhaps we should act as the demon suggests and destroy Lince Posh. It could give us many advantages." Benjamin paused for a moment and then continued, "First, though, what is Slayer's reason for telling us this? Do we do his work for him?"

"No," Samantha said, "the amulet holding his name is what binds him to Melody. There is no way *I* know of to break that binding. Maybe he wants Melody frustrated and out of sorts for a while. But that won't last long. I tell you, she is strong! I think she will strike swiftly and in a way that reflects what has been done to her. It is a good idea, but we must first be prepared for what she might do afterward."

"We need more trained men," Captain Slith commented. "The weapons master and I intend to go to Wizards Veil and ask the king for more gold so we can fill the school and the alliance with fighters. Even now, both centers of the art of warfare are less than half full. It will take time. I wish I knew how much we have. Spies are few, at least in the school. We need more men."

"I have spies in Vain right now," the weapons master said. "As soon as the Vainians fled the field, I sent them, thinking they could wander in as failed fighters." Sudden anger took him. "They will pay for their treatment of my home!"

"Weapons Master," Samantha said softly, "do not do anything foolish. I forbid it. At least for now, they will be prepared for a counterattack. Please, hold your hands."

"High Cleric," the master said angrily, "I am no student to be lectured." He calmed, realizing who he was talking to. "I'm sorry. I'm out of line. I just hate, as you say, holding my hands. I know the reasons the land of the king has never struck Vain down, but as the warriors I shadow, I want to do just that! Destroy the threat! They will never change. I have seen their communities, cities, and towns. They are a slothful, black-hearted people. I'm always amazed at how quickly they prepare for war. It is the only thing they do well! With one good campaign, they will never do it again!"

"What about magic?" Swiftfoot asked. "What do we fight it with? You two won't always be around. How many wizards do we have on our side?"

"None," Jan said flatly. "Given time, we could teach a few, but who?"

The high cleric laughed. "I know a whole house that would die for the chance!"

"Who's house?" Swiftfoot asked.

"The House of Thought!" Jan exclaimed in sudden realization. "If I understand the house teachings, then they are primed for the mind work, but ..." He sighed and shook his head. "It just won't work."

Samantha inspected her fingernails. Lyndsy realized the action. She heard Samantha think, *The Mythits. They would never do it.* Lyndsy turned her head and saw Jan's almost imperceptible nod.

"Well," Jan said, "I could teach them certain simple spells. The destructive ones used in war are so easily learned that Slim Chance helped me explore them into existence in a single night."

"Why don't we have any already?" Swiftfoot asked curiously, "And why do the Vainians have so many?"

Jan hesitated to answer. They would smell an untruth. He couldn't just tell them the importance of Mythits to magic.

Samantha answered for him. "Melody the Black has been training a few wizards for centuries. It wasn't hard for her to make the training a reality when the magic awoke in the land."

"But why—"

Lindon put a hand on Swiftfoot's shoulder. "They are reluctant to speak of this. Don't press. Leave the magic to them."

Benjamin nodded to Lindon. "You are wise."

Slim spoke. "This is the reason I have called you all together. You may now have a better understanding of who and what we face. Above all, understand that, from this moment, a state of war exists between Melody the Black and January and the high cleric. Nevertheless, the battleground is Lyre, and the prize is possession of her people from the east to the western shore. The great wars of the Dark Lord against the power of The Three started this war, and it is our place to help January and Samantha in any way we can."

The weapons master rose to his feet. "The captain and I have stayed far too long as it is. We must leave. Rest assured, the alliance is already sending messages throughout Lyre to recruit any who wish to learn weaponry."

"Yes," Jan said quietly, "that is all we can ask. When will you leave?"

"Now. I have only stayed to see you two happy"—he grinned at Lyndsy—"and to enjoy the winnings of a well-placed bet." To the fighter's immense pleasure, Lyndsy blushed to the tips of her ears. He turned to Sha. "If ever you need us, we will be ready to help you."

Sha nodded approval as he stood. "Yes. And don't forget, the Sword of the Vow has yet to be tested."

The weapons master grinned. "The time will come, my friend. And although we won't be the fighters, I believe we will both be there to see it."

Swiftfoot and Lindon also stood. Sha turned to Slim and said, "This human I am proud to call friend. I will go and watch them leave."

Lyndsy, January, Samantha, and Benjamin watched them leave. By unspoken agreement, the whole group seemed to know that Slim Chance wanted to speak in private with January and the high cleric. Of course, Moonlight and He Who Sees All was a part of that group.

"January, now that we are alone, I will speak of myself. Neither the were nor even the weapons master knows anything about me, except that I lived in Vain and knew much about Melody. I fear what they would think about me if they knew."

"Slim Chance," Lyndsy said, "I made a vow when I held your life in my hands. They don't have any choice. You are accepted."

Slim walked to Lyndsy and crouched down before her. He placed a hand on her head and smiled. "I don't believe you will ever know just how much I appreciate you." To Jan, he thought, *This very young woman is a marvel. Her strength, quite simply, amazes me. So much in such a small body! The weapons master calls her a dancer. His praise is rarely given. He smiles when he looks at her, and that man doesn't smile at anything!*

Lyndsy caught her breath. Blinking, she smiled gratefully at the words spoken and unspoken.

Slim stood back up and cleared his throat. "I am a grandson of Melody. When I was very young, she trained me in thought. I was able to see the black Mythits through personality. She was surprised at this and quickly told me the meaning of what it was that I saw. When I was fifteen seasons, I roamed the streets of Vanity, watching the auras of the black Mythits. I thought it great fun to participate in their mischief and cruelty. I won't pretend I didn't know what I was doing, but the abilities of the black Mythits was something I couldn't resist.

"One day, I walked alone. I felt Mythits at one of the places I, uh, usually went to. When I got there, I found them manipulating a fat, drunken slob. He was raping a prostitute I had thought myself in love with. I slit his throat. In my anger, I reached out, caught tendrils of what you have aptly named personality, and tore the Mythits' auras to shreds.

"Melody was greatly pleased with me. She didn't like my reasons, I knew, but she said nothing about it. I tell you, that creature delights in corruption. I was, up to that time, the only spawn of hers born during the last thousand seasons who'd ever been able to even perceive the black Mythits. She taught me to read. I had access to all of the scrolls she hordes. You would be amazed at the histories that lay in the libraries of Lince Posh. At the time, I had no liking for that sort of learning. I was very young. She taught me many, well, many other things.

"One day, she asked me to go to the School of Prayer and be initiated into the House of Thought. I knew by then all that Melody herself knows about the School of Prayer."

"So do I," Samantha said. "She knows very little."

"Yes," Slim continued, "I think her warped mind assumes things that have no true bearing on those who worship the Creator. Anyway, I went. After a week of terrible nightmares and a constant state of cold sweat, I fled."

"You must have been very young," Samantha said, almost to herself. "Anyone truly evil would melt at the door—I mean in spirit. The Clerical Blessing surrounding the whole school is awesome in its purity."

"It is. I was blinded by its brilliance even before I reached it. When I returned to Lince Posh, I was very angry and went straight to the library. I found and read everything that vaguely spoke of the two separated schools. Most of the scrolls deal with the time in the past when the schools were combined and called the One School or the School of Hope.

"I'm telling you all of this for two reasons. One is that, if you decide to destroy Lince Posh, you should consider a plan that could save some of that hoarded information. Much useful knowledge would otherwise be lost. The other thing is this; Samantha believes I may now pass the blessing that surrounds the School of Prayer. January, only one of Mythit blood can teach magic effectively. I intuitively know the proper spell components a human would need to mimic the use of a Mythit. Granted, magic users who use natural components can never think to achieve the powers of those bound by Mythitkind, but it should be enough if we can train even a handful quickly. I would like to do this for you. You have a path to walk in life that will not allow you the luxury of the time needed. Let me do this for you."

January grinned. "Slim Chance, you are welcome to it. I wonder, though, at the depths of Melody's wisdom in the meaning of *my right hand*?"

Samantha shuddered and said with feeling, "It is deep."

38

The Old Curse

Lyndsy tapped Jan awake. Motioning for him to remain silent, she led him out of the camp. She reached Samantha and Benjamin, already waiting, and led them into the swamp. A chill ran down her spine as she made her way into the marsh. Once again, old fears found niches in her mind. *Will he still love me after tonight? I'm the youngest!* After a long march, Lyndsy stopped them and sniffed the air. The three silent figures watched her pinpoint a direction. With a nod of self-confirmation, she led them through a bunch of brambles and into a small clearing.

Those Who Walk Alone drifted in from the darkness and motioned for the humans to find a place to sit. Lindon turned to his daughter. "Moonlight, you are the youngest. This burden is given to you."

Lyndsy took a deep breath as she gathered courage. She walked to the center of the clearing and stripped. She said quietly, sarcastically, "I finally got him in my bed, and now you want me to run him off!"

Soft chuckles sounded while He Who Sees All, the high cleric, and January wondered what she was talking about.

She turned to the guests and avoided Jan's eyes. Trying to calm her nerves, she set her gaze on Samantha. "The first high cleric, Myril the White, broke the curse the Dark Lord created us with. High Cleric, sister, we are the were; we do not forget."

Moonlight, the first female to be given the title of One Who Walks Alone in over three hundred seasons, stood tall. She silently raised her open palms to the New Lady and started to change. The snapping of bones and cramping of muscles was a hideous music in the silence of the swamp. All three humans realized very quickly that this was not the change that they had gotten used to during their time with the were.

They watched Lyndsy bite back gasps of pain as her form slowly changed. They began to wonder at what they saw. She was changing much too slowly. Her small breasts swelled huge, rippling with muscle. Her arms stretched, growing thick and long. She raised one hand, reaching forward. Instead of fingers shortening to paws, they grew longer and slender. Her nails turned to hooks and grew.

A thin, hairless tail appeared at the base of her spine and grew as she lashed it from side to side. She took a staggering step and then another as her feet began to change. Her toes grew together, displaying more wicked, hooked claws. The heels tortured her calves as they snapped. The ball of her foot grew away from her heel on a slender stalk.

Last, her face. It cracked and broke so suddenly Samantha gasped and panted in shared pain. Moonlight's snout grew impossibly long. Her ears rose high on her head, spiking to points. Her magenta eyes slanted up at the corners as her face slowly mended itself. Her white teeth stretched to jagged points until she could no longer keep her mouth closed.

The streams of pain ceased as this change came to an end. Turning in a slow circle, raising her arms, she showed the humans what she had become. White, short fur covered the grotesquely beautiful figure. Wispy thin, white hair hung lank from her head and shoulders. Throwing her arms wide, she gazed up at the new moon, and screamed. Then louder. And louder. And louder.

A half league away, the people of the were woke in their huts. A piercing scream of raw hatred echoed through their land. They knew this sound well. Every new moon it happened. A reminder. Huddled together, they gathered their children and remembered their vows.

Lindon stood and approached his daughter. "Look well, High Cleric. This was the natural end to our change before the high cleric, Myril, removed the curse. The form that Moonlight has taken was only a part of that curse. Every moon during the fullness of the Lady this happened to every adult *were* in the land. During this time, we roamed Lyre in mindless insanity. It always ended many lives, always brought us never ending grief.

"There was a time, before Myril laid the grace of the Creator upon us, that we considered genocide. An evil pack leader, named by humans, the Black Terror, almost achieved the destruction of humankind in the north. If it hadn't been for the Red Wizard, we would have slain his pack, killed our own children, and then ourselves. What you see here tonight we do so we might remember what we were and be honored by what we have become.

We are the were, created by evil, the children of demons. We were redeemed by the grace of the Creator. We do not forget." Turning to Lyndsy, he said, "Daughter, it is done."

Slowly, step-by-step, Lyndsy changed back. Jan wondered, as he had so many times, that she could be so strong. This was a forced change. It was taught. He suddenly realized why Swiftfoot could take any form he wanted. Any of the were who could take this shape could take any shape they wished. Since Swiftfoot had previously been the youngest, and since Lyndsy was rarely in the land of the were, Swiftfoot's mindset was not so strictly tuned to one shape. Their changing knew no limits. They just didn't realize it. This shape was as different as a bear or a bird.

He came away from his thoughts as Lyndsy stopped. She was a woman, but her head and shoulders were still in the form of the wicked-looking werewolf. Jan gazed into her eyes and saw that she was terrified. She feared that his feelings for her had changed. Gathering strength, she turned away and finished her upper body.

She dripped agony in blazing flashes. Still, to those without the means to see, she appeared calm and dispassionate. Her jaw muscles clenched, and she was Lyndsy once more.

Samantha held her stomach and broke into a sweat during this final change. Her skin crawled at the pain she bore—far worse than childbirth; they went through this all the time! In camp, some children changed three or four times a day. She shook her head in wonder. More than once, she had tried to pick up a child and comfort him or her. She was always amazed at how quickly the werelings shook it off. A few moments later, it was forgotten.

A surge of hard emotion shot through her. She looked up to see Jan walking to Lyndsy's side. He wrapped his arms around her small form, Samantha felt him push her fear and insecurities far away. He had built a very small amount of power. Samantha felt Jan drench Lyndsy in pride. She wondered briefly why he hadn't used a softer emotion. She barely finished the thought when a wash of love flowed through her.

A soft rainbow shimmered around the edges of Lyndsy's personality. Samantha watched Jan open her aura as the rainbow soaked in. The high cleric watched the soft white aura of Jan's vow circle Lyndsy's soul and wreath her in comfort.

Jan, she is so beautiful! So strong. I'm always stunned when she thinks herself ugly. I keep forgetting she is a sixteen-season girl. Sometimes I'm very angry at Sha's first for raising her the way she did. Lyndsy is so insecure. I wish I could take it away and never let her feel that way again! Samantha blinked and realized with a start that Lyndsy was gazing directly at her. *Lyndsy?*

Lyndsy smiled. *If you weren't the high cleric, I would stomp you into the dust for calling me an insecure little girl!*

A night bird was rudely awakened and startled into flight as a brother and sister burst into laughter.

Samantha stood before the were. The Scepter of Light sparkled in her upraised hand. Sheela knelt before her, head bowed.

"The weremaiden, Sheela, daughter of Laughing Feet and Angryeyes, has opened her heart to me and made known her wish to be instructed in the ways of the Creator. I will give this to her willingly. She will accompany me to the School of Prayer. In three seasons, when she is seventeen, I will take her first vow if she is still willing to give it. She will dwell among humans and learn their ways. If at any time she chooses to return home, she is free to do so. The cleric must search his or her soul and be willing to do his or her work.

"This is the first time, in the long history of Lyre, that a were will enter into the priesthood. It has never been recorded, but it is taken for granted that the were are forbidden clericship. Times are changing. I say the were are a more righteous people than many humans I have known. I am Samantha, the high cleric by the choice of the High Council. My word concerning the School of Prayer is law."

The high cleric bowed to the were and commanded Sheela to rise. Sheela rose to her feet, her single skin wrap flying in the breeze. Samantha embraced the weremaiden and kissed her brow.

Benjamin watched the two figures embrace. The light from the scepter reached down and touched Sheela's aura. The sight unraveled before his mind's eye...

Sheela hugged her naked breasts. Her lower lip was split, her body covered in sweat and dirt. She was tied to a group of young women who were naked and covered in filth. A group of ruffians herded them into a clearing at the edge of a forest and prepared to rape them.

Sheela gazed through watering eyes. A tear ran down her cheek. She spoke. Benjamin wondered what she said, for all eight of the young women with her turned away from her and bowed their heads. Sheela glanced at the ruffians and then back to her companions. She spoke again. The eight young women fell to the ground.

A thin, gold necklace clasping a single moonstone glimmered around the weremaiden's throat. The ruffians were prepared for their evil and started toward her. Sheela raised her head proudly and spoke again as tears ran down her cheeks. They laughed at her.

She touched the necklace and changed shape to a werewolf of the old curse, far larger than little Lyndsy. With a flurry of fangs and claws, Sheela tore the ruffians to pieces. She changed shape back to human form and fell to her knees. Drenched in blood and shredded flesh, she put her face in her hands and wept.

A pure white light settled around the naked figure. Sheela raised her head as if she heard a voice and turned to look...

The Seer of Lake Town snapped from the sight. The were were cheering something that the high cleric had just said. Benjamin turned quickly to January. "The little gold chain, the one with the moonstone, Sheela's going to need—"

January blinked away a tear. "I know."

"High Cleric?"

Samantha turned and saw January standing in the doorway of her hut. She wondered why he'd used her title. After all, they were alone.

"Lyndsy and I are going to Mirshol."

Samantha nodded. Now she had a good idea about why he'd used her title. "What do you want me to do?"

Jan snickered and grinned. "Well, I think you should stop by the Knights Alliance and give them your praise."

Samantha smiled evenly. "I had already planned to do just that. Any messages?"

"No, but I want you to give this to Sheela. Tell her very seriously that it will change her shape in an instant to whatever shape she may need and then change her back. It will work only once. It will also touch the minds of any she loves or is close to and send them into slumber."

"The sight?"

Jan nodded. "Yes."

Samantha went to him.

He gazed into her ice-blue eyes and smiled. "I love you, my sister."

She smiled gratefully. He hugged her and kept her close. She started to cry and tried to stop. Lyndsy peeked in and saw a tear roll down her cheek.

She went to them and wrapped her slim, white arms around both of them. Smiling, she set her head against Samantha's shoulder.

Are you feeling insecure, sister?

Samantha was filled with the strong sense of admiration emanating from the small woman. *Not anymore.*

Hey! I want some too!

Samantha felt little arms wrap around one thigh. Flower's head rested against her hip. Fresh tears brimmed and fell from her cheeks as the high cleric reached down and ran her fingers through the spiked topknot in the Mythit's crown.

39

WINDOW

"Take me too!"

"No way. Not a chance. No."

"Pleeeeeeease!"

"No, absolutely not. Don't even think about it!"

"I'll tell Lyndsy all the things you've said about Marshy!"

"That's blackmail."

"Yep."

"We're only going to be there for a few days."

"Sounds good to me!"

"Flower, you're not going with us!"

"What are you two talking about?"

"Hi, Lyndsy! Guess what? Do you know what Jan said about this little—"

"Flower, would you like to go with us to Window?"

"Gee, I thought you'd never ask."

I'll get you for this, you furry little weasel!

Flower jumped up into Lyndsy's arms. "Lyndsy! Lyndsy! January called me a furry little weasel!"

"You *are* a furry little weasel."

"Unfair! Two against one!"

Jan gave Lyndsy a mischievous grin. "Why don't you do the honors?"

Lyndsy grabbed Flower, pinned her to the ground, and set her fingers against Flower's ribs.

"No! *Nooooooo!*"

Lady Reefa of Window heard the silver bell announcing customers in her boutique and turned to the door with a singularly catching smile. She blinked in alarm. Standing in the doorway, an almost naked young man tossed long blond hair over his shoulder and grinned at her shocked expression. Piercing, ice-blue eyes deepened in some unfathomable good humor as she tried to regain a little composure. She knew he was not trying to intimidate her. He could be described as innocent if it weren't for his assessing gaze. It was just the way the youth set one hand on the hilt of his sword in complete nonchalance that rattled her.

The girl was an even stranger sight. While the young man seemed at ease, the girl looked positively terrified. She was, nevertheless, a stunning sight. Shaggy white hair billowed around her sharply angled face. Magenta eyes, not quite red but not really pink, were wide set in her smooth, pale face. Her appearance was startling, as though she were chipped from marble. She was dressed, like the young man, in two dirty, ragged, violet silk wraps. The poor dear was shaking nervously.

"Lady Reefa, I owe you this." Jan stepped forward and handed her a silver twenty piece.

Who refuses free coin? As she stepped forward to take it, she smelled the rich perfume and wrinkled her old nose in pleasure. "Wildflower!" Her gaze turned sharp as she reassessed the young woman. "Child, where did you get that wonderful perfume?" Reefa felt a sudden tension, an instinct that sharpens with age. She looked closely at the young woman and thought to herself that she somehow looked paler.

Lyndsy swallowed. "I'm not a child."

"Girl, if you're thirty seasons, by my count, you're still a child. Come, tell me where you got that perfume. You smell wonderful, really. I'd like to know."

Lyndsy blushed, shyly gazing at her feet. "My, uh, husband made it for me."

Reefa looked perplexed but didn't say anything.

Jan's grin broadened. "We would like to buy some clothes, Reefa. I believe my lady would look gorgeous in soft colors."

Lyndsy, hand me the perfume bottle.

Lyndsy drew out the perfume. Reefa's eyes brightened. Jan held the little bottle up to the light and then handed it to Reefa. "Tell me, how much is something like this worth? Just out of *curiosity*, of course."

Jan used the Voice. Reefa became very curious indeed. Popping the cork, she sniffed the rich perfume and tried to hide her delight. "Oh, I think it's worth three pence."

She's lying.

I know. "If I could bring you five bottles a month, would you pay forty silver pennies? You could sell them easily."

"Eight pence apiece?" Reefa said in feigned shock. "Not worth it."

She's thinks that's too much!

I know, but we're getting closer.

With a start, Lyndsy realized Jan was going to find out how much the perfume was worth whether Reefa wanted to tell him or not.

"The lady in the shop down the street said six pence apiece, but I've known you for a long time and—"

"I don't know you."

"But you're willing to pay six pence apiece?" He used the Voice.

"Yes. No! I mean—"

"Never mind, I'll take the six from her."

"Wait! I'll give you six."

She doesn't like it, but she still wants it.

Then six is a good price. "OK. And you do know me. About four seasons ago, I was carrying a crate and walked through your front window."

"You!"

"Yes. Now, my lady needs some clothes, and I want the best." Jan turned to a white summer dress embroidered at the shoulders with fat red strawberries. "Lyndsy, try this one on."

Lyndsy untied her bottom wrap and handed it to Jan.

"*No!* Wait!"

Jan looked through the shop. Thank *Song* no one else was in the store. *Humans don't undress in front of each other.*

Lyndsy blushed. *I know that! I forgot.*

As Reefa caught Lyndsy's wrist and hauled her into a change room, Jan caught up the dress and set it over Reefa's shoulder. Grinning to himself, he waited for a few moments and felt rewarded for his patience. Lyndsy stepped out of the change room and gave him an uncertain frown. He smiled in return and noticed the pleased look on Reefa's face. Pointing to a full-length gown trimmed in red and pink lace, he motioned for Reefa to take Lyndsy back into the change room.

Jan waited for a few more minutes and blinked as Reefa dashed out of the change room and giggled as she scooped up some ribbons and rushed back in.

Lyndsy stepped through the curtain and blushed. Jan's jaw dropped open. "In the name of Song!"

Lyndsy looked up through ribbons and bangs with a questioning gaze.

Her expression changed as she saw the shimmering pools in his beautiful eyes. She smiled hugely and paced up to stand before him. Turning, she saw the pleased look on Reefa's face. Lyndsy turned back to Jan, wrapped her arms around his neck, and pulled him down for a soul-shattering kiss.

"Child! That's no way to behave!"

Lyndsy jumped back so fast Jan almost fell to the floor.

No kissing in public?

Jan grinned ruefully. *No.*

Lyndsy shook her head. *Strange people.*

Jan fought the urge to pull Lyndsy back into his arms. "Reefa, we'll take them. I want this gown too." He pointed at a full-length violet gown trimmed in pale red and soft pink lace.

Reefa shook her head. "Look, I admit I've been having a little fun here, but these gowns are expensive. I really don't think ... Wait, I'll tell you what. You can have the white summer dress for five bottles of that perfume."

"Thirty pence, huh?"

"Yes, that's a fair price."

She smells like she's being very generous.

Jan nodded. "I really want them all. I can pay for it. How much?"

"Well, two gowns and a summer dress, one pair of slippers, and the ribbons. I would have to say two gold pieces." She frowned and looked at Jan doubtfully.

Lyndsy burst into laughter thinking about the huge chest of gold in the crystal chamber. Jan set his arm around her shoulder and nodded. "That is a fair price." He reached into a fold of his wrap and pulled out a little, fat pouch. Opening the drawstring, he plucked four gold coins and handed them to Lady Reefa. "My turn."

Market Square was alive with people. Jan led Lyndsy through the crowd of tents and wagons as he waited. Lyndsy held the crook of Jan's arm with one gloved hand, shyly aware of all the stares she was receiving.

They stopped at an open-bed wagon that sold some kind of wonderful smelling breads. Jan picked out a small, rounded piece that contained a bright red filling. He wrapped it in wax paper and handed it to her. Lyndsy blushed as she accepted it. The woman at the wagon called her a lady and kept saying how lovely she looked.

Lyndsy bit into the sweet roll. Her eyes grew wide in surprise. "This is delicious! What is it? Is it magic?"

The woman saw the innocence behind the question and smiled warmly. "They're called sweet rolls, my lady."

"Sweet rolls." Lyndsy laughed delightfully. "I've heard of them before. You must be the best sweet roll maker in the whole city!"

Jan turned his head and grinned at Lyndsy's expression. He caught sight of what he had been waiting for. The hand reached into his pocket. Jan snatched the boy by the collar and lifted him up off of the ground. "Don't I know you from somewhere?"

"Lemme go! I ain't done nothin'!"

"Dolen, it's me, January."

Dolen's glare turned to shocked amazement. "In the name of Song!"

Jan set the boy on his feet and asked, "Where's everybody at?"

"Swimmin' at Lake Side, most likely."

Jan grinned. "Think they're hungry?"

Dolen rolled his eyes. "You kiddin'. They's always hungry!"

"Well, then. Let's buy a feast. How many sweet rolls do we need?"

Dolen grinned back. "Fifty!"

Jan threw back his head and roared with laughter. "Fifty it is!"

Jan led them from stand to stand buying cheese, milk, and bread. As they walked, a few of the other street urchins found them and tagged along. They all came to a stop at an open grill and watched wide-eyed as a fat man in a greasy apron turned a pair of turkeys on a spit. Jan looked down at the faces of the children. They were still and silent, watching wistfully as the man turned the crank.

Dolen wiped his mouth with the back of his hand. "Think you could 'ford one a them suckers?"

The corner of Jan's mouth turned up in a half smile. "No."

"Oh," Dolen said, very nearly brokenhearted.

"I'm gonna buy 'em both."

"What!" Dolen exclaimed. "Naw!"

"Yep."

"Wow! You's rich!"

They carried the food on a cart January rented for the day. They pushed it all the way out of town to where the street children always spent their summers. Over twenty kids were either in the water or on the bank.

Lyndsy caught sight of one girl, perhaps a season younger than herself, as she stripped off a long, baggy, tattered dress. As she held it inside out, she drew pieces of bread and half rotten greens from hidden pockets. Two little girls and a boy caught the morsels of food in grubby fists and immediately stuffed their mouths. Hearing the wagon and exclamations of the other children, the girl turned and saw them. Lyndsy saw the sudden tension in her stance and knew she was frightened.

Just then, the boy, Dolen, ran ahead of the wagon and scurried down the hill. "Marshy! Marshy! Look, it's January!"

The girl dropped the ragged dress. Lyndsy noticed she wore wraps in the same manner Jan had first dressed her. All of the children stood and started toward them, sniffing the air. Marshy hesitated, and then she started walking. She stared in open-mouth wonder and quickened her pace. She jumped into Jan's arms at a dead run and smothered him with kisses.

"In the name of Song, Janny! We thought you's dead f'r sure! Look atcha, all dressed up like some kinda gentleman!"

She dropped back, still holding his hands, and looked him over. "A sword! You crazy? Gonna cut'cher damn fool head plumb off!"

"If you don't get your hands off my man, you'll lose them!"

"Lyndsy!"

Marshy jumped back wide-eyed and blinked at the exotic young woman. "I'm sorry, my lady. Jan's big brother nearly to ev'r one here."

Lyndsy swallowed her sudden jealousy and felt instantly foolish. She heard and smelled the sincerity in the girl's words and wished she hadn't said anything at all. "No, it's me who should be sorry. Would you do me a favor?"

Marshy did a double take. Any other lady would never ask, just demand. "Yeah, if'n I can."

"Help me out of this dress. I want to go swimming."

Marshy looked at Jan in surprise, and then a slow smile wrinkled her freckled, pert nose. "Jan, I think I likes y'r lady."

Jan grinned. "Hurry up." He pulled the tarp off of the cart and rubbed his hands together. "It's chow time!"

Marshy produced a knife from her wrap and cut a thick piece of turkey. Turning back to Lyndsy, she motioned her to the trees. "Come on, don't need no boys watchin' a lady *get out of 'em!*"

Lyndsy pulled a bundle from the cart, caught up her staff, and followed.

Marshy led Lyndsy into the trees. When they were out of sight, she stopped and turned Lyndsy around to get at the buttons. "You a princess or somethin'?"

Lyndsy smiled. "No. I'm a girl just like you."

"Awe, come on! Girls like me ain't dressed like you."

"Really, January bought this gown for me today."

"Jan *paid* f'r it?" Marshy asked, incredulous. Then she narrowed her eyes. "I figured it's probaly you at got it f'r him."

"Believe me, where I come from, your old dress is a luxury."

Marshy turned down the sleeves and caught the hem so Lyndsy could step out of the gown without letting it touch the ground. As she folded it over one arm, she gazed at Lyndsy's naked body and whistled. "In the name of Song! Ain't no wonder he fell f'r ya. Smokes, girl, you's a dream come to life!"

Lyndsy shook her head in amazement. *This* girl she could believe. She couldn't figure out why humans seemed to really like the way she looked. *Strange people!*

Lyndsy rummaged through the bundle and found a wrap to cover the gown. While Marshy tucked and folded, Lyndsy drew out two more wraps. She tied one around her hips and watched as Marshy picked up the silk. The girl gasped as she felt the fine Mythit silk. Caressing her cheek with the incredibly soft material, she closed her eyes and sighed. Lyndsy smiled knowingly. "There's another set of silks in there if you want to wear them."

Marshy's eyes popped open. "Really? Wouldja really let me?"

Lyndsy pulled the other two wraps from the bundle and handed them to her. Reaching back in, she found the perfume.

Marshy watched the exotic woman pop the cap and tease a drop onto her finger. She could hardly believe her eyes as the lady smiled and reached to spread the drop on her neck.

Marshy closed her eyes and breathed. Lyndsy felt her heart melting. To cause such feelings in another young woman pulled a cord in her personality that had never been touched. Not knowing why, she reached out and gave the girl a quick hug.

Marshy opened large brown eyes and asked, very softly, "What's y'r name, my lady?"

"Call me Lyndsy." Lyndsy laughed. "Call me anything. But quit calling me my lady!"

Marshy's freckled cheeks blossomed with a girlish blush. "Yeah, that's what Janny called ya."

"Janny?"

Marshy gave Lyndsy an impish grin. "Janny. But don't say it to 'is face 'less y'r mad at 'im." She winked. "'E hates it!"

As they walked back through the trees, Lyndsy studied the children surrounding January. She quickly realized that very few of them were close too Marshy in age—just one other girl and one boy. The rest were children. A few, the ones Marshy seemed to be in charge of, couldn't be more than two or three seasons old.

"Marsi!"

Lyndsy watched one of the youngest notice their presence and come rushing toward them. A skinny little girl with a sweet roll in each fist jumped up and exclaimed, "Look, Marsi! Sweet roll!"

"Yeah!" Marshy laughed as she reached down to tickle the little figure. "I thinks ya got more on y'r face than ya do in y'r tummy, ya fat little piggy."

The child bit off a huge mouthful and mumbled, "Ain't no piggy!"

Lyndsy stood back, still watching the children. She paid particular attention to the little ones surrounding January. She bit at her lip and sniffed as she noticed his attention on all of them without being partial. An overwhelming pride filled her breast as she understood that there was no favoritism being shown. How she wished she had been here to watch him grow up!

She turned her head, afraid she might cry, and saw all the girls gathered together on one side. They were laughing among themselves, and Lyndsy's sharp ears heard January's name being mentioned over and over. She watched Marshy go to the cart, cut another chunk of turkey, and stuff it into a split loaf of bread. She stuffed the makeshift sandwich into her mouth, holding it with her teeth, and grabbed a sweet roll in each hand. Turning, smiling, she skipped to the group of girls and plopped down on the ground.

Lyndsy felt suddenly out of place. She gazed longingly at the group of giggling girls, wanting very much to be a part of them. Just then, Marshy looked around, found her, and smiled. Scooting to one side, she patted the ground next to her and beckoned for her to come. Lyndsy blinked. She looked behind her to see if she were the only one Marshy could be motioning to.

Jan pulled his wraps from the cart and went to change. He watched Marshy motion to Lyndsy and saw Lyndsy hesitate and look around. Then her pale face lit with a wide, happy smile as she rushed to sit between Marshy and Tami.

A curly redhead of about fourteen seasons grinned at Lyndsy mischievously. "Wanna hear what Janny done? I r'member. I uz there. He done set the mayor's boat an 'alf the dock on fire!" The girls burst into laughter. "Shoulda seen it! Mayor's fat wench in the boat an all. Had ta jump o'r the side!"

Tami gazed past Lyndsy toward Marshy. "Do ya'll r'member when you an Janny went ta the Firepit Inn an' stole all them blankets?" Tami grinned and met Lyndsy's eyes. "They done threw a rope an' hook at the top window in the middle o' the night an' climbed up. There's 'bout ten o' us waitin' down the alley. Purty soon, they comed back, arms loaded wi' blankets. Jan threw 'em out and fetched more!" Tami smiled reminiscently. "We sure slept warm that winter."

Still watching Tami, Lyndsy saw the red curls bob around the girl's face as she turned her head. Tami's jaw dropped open. All of the girls turned to see what Tami was gawking at. Jan walked through the trees with his clothes in a bundle. He wore a single wrap that tied around his hips. Calling to the boys, Jan walked to the water. Laughing, he picked two of them up off of the ground and threw them in.

"Yay!" one boy yelled. "My turn!"

They watched Jan catch the boy by the wrists, spin him in a circle, and toss the youngster way out into the clear-blue water. Soon, a dozen boys and girls were jumping up and down shouting for his attention.

"I'm next!"

"Me!"

"No, me!"

Tami sighed. "Smokes! I cain't believe that's Janny. Damn, jus' look at that body. He's beautiful!"

Marshy smiled. "Handsome."

Lyndsy growled. "Mine!"

Tami looked quickly at Lyndsy. "I don't mean nothin', but"—she gazed back at January—"I jus' cain't believe it's 'im."

Marshy pointed to a rope hanging from a tree. "Lyndsy, Jan usta swing by that there rope an' do all sorts o' tricks an flips in the water. When he growed up too fast, he couldn't do it no more. Kept draggin' 'is feet an always landin' wrong."

As though he were listening, Jan looked at the rope. He folded his arms across his chest and smiled at it. They saw that look they all knew so well. It could have said, "Mister, you only thinks you still gots money in y'r pockets!"

With a shout, he ran at the rope and flew way out over the water. Swinging back in, he went high up into the trees. Coming back down, he swung way out over the water and did a triple flip before diving smoothly into the lake.

Marshy jumped up and clapped her hands. "Yeah! Come on, girls. Let's go swimmin'!"

"Marshy, how old are you?"

"Don't know. Round fourteen I guess."

"You don't know?"

"No. Ain't never 'ad no daddy or mum ta ask."

Lyndsy ran her fingers through the water as she leaned back against the bank. She gazed at all of the homeless children swimming in the lake. None of them had any family except each other. They were beggars and thieves, taking whatever they could get. "Why aren't there any girls older than you?"

Marshy's large brown eyes became shaded. "They's old enough ta get work." She turned her head, looking quickly away.

Lyndsy caught the scent of resentment, shame, and anger. "What do they do?"

Marshy glanced back in surprise. She took it for granted that everyone knew what street girls did when they were old enough. She said quietly, "They's whores." She looked away again and whispered fiercely, "I ain't never gonna be no whore. I'd kill myself first!"

Jan turned his head, and Lyndsy saw the pain in his eyes. He swam to them, set one hand on Lyndsy's knee, and raised the other to Marshy's shoulder. "My Marshy, you are going to be a respectable lady in Window."

Marshy looked up with a scowl. "I ain't never gonna be no damn lady."

"Yes, you will. You will live in your own house and sell perfume to Lady Reefa."

Marshy seemed to find this incredibly funny. She stood up and squinched her freckled face. "Yes, I's gonna be a lady." Lifting her nose in the air, she offered her hand for some invisible gentleman to take it. "Lady Reefa, I have more exquisite pur' fume for ya ta sell ta all them high-n-mighty ladies in town. Please don't be late wi' y'r payments 'r I's gonna fin' some other distinguished lady o' Window ta do business wi'!"

Looking at Jan, they all three burst into laughter. Lyndsy realized Jan had planned this all along. She gazed around at the children and smiled. "Marshy, January is serious. That perfume you like so much? Jan made it for me. The Lady Reefa said six pence a bottle, five bottles a moon."

Marshy blinked from one face to the other. "You's serious, ain't cha?"

"Yes."

"Thirty pence a moon." Marshy lowered her head.

Lyndsy watched a tear well up and roll down her cheek. It made a small circle of ripples in the water.

"Janny, please don't tease me. Wi' thirty pence a moon, I could feed an' dress ever' damn kid I know."

Jan lifted her chin and held her gaze. Like him, she was streetwise and very intelligent. She'd had to grow up way too fast. Jan remembered finding Marshy in a box in the alley. She hadn't even been old enough to walk.

Carrying his precious find to Lake Side, he had stolen cloaks and blankets to make a bed. Shira, one of the oldest girls at the time, had shown him how to care for a child.

For four seasons, his main concern had been her food and rags. For four seasons, she had been *his* little girl. Then he had shown her places where kindhearted keepers and farmers had their inns and stalls. After she grew too old to find favor as a beggar, he taught her to pick pockets and how to outsmart the guards in the markets.

Jan pulled Marshy into his lap and held her tight. "Marshy, I always tease you, but I would never hurt you. You will learn to make perfume, and you won't have to steal bread crumbs for the children anymore."

Marshy caught her breath, but it didn't help. She couldn't remember how many times she had sat in Jan's lap and cried. Lyndsy gazed at her man. She came closer and gently ran her fingers through Marshy's wavy, dark brown hair. She smiled as she realized Jan was once again holding Marshy in his arms. This time, she hoped he would keep her there until all of her fears fled far, far away.

Jan, Lyndsy, Tami, and Marshy sat by a fire talking late into the night. The other children were either asleep or out prowling Window. Flower decided this was the perfect time to make her entrance.

Marshy leaned back, eyes closed, stuffed with cold turkey and smiled as the night breeze teased a wisp of hair across her face. A shadow passed between her eyelids and the light of the fire. She opened her eyes and gasped.

"Hi! I'm Flower! So, you're Marshy. Jan told me all about you. Said you was gonna grow up to be the best thief in all of Lyre!" Straddling Marshy's thighs, she sat down, and gave the startled girl a big hug.

Lyndsy burst into laughter. "Flower, you're a nuisance!"

Flower turned to Tami. "Hi! I'm Flower. I'm a nuisance!"

Tami reached for the hand and felt the short, soft fur. "In the name of Song! It's a Mythit."

"Yeah," Marshy exclaimed as she gazed into glowing pink eyes, "I think it is!"

Flower turned her nose in the air. "I'm a she, not an it," she said imperially. Leaning forward again, she gave Marshy another hug. "I like hugs!"

Jan laughed out loud. "Flower, you're incorrigible."

Flower looked back up into Marshy's wide, awe-filled eyes. "Hi! I'm Flower. I'm incorrrrrrrrrrigible!"

Lyndsy couldn't resist. She reached out, grabbed Flower, and tumbled her to the ground. "Flower? Do you know what time it is?"

"Yessss!" Flower squeaked. "Time to go!"

"Oh no you don't!" Lyndsy fingers worked mercilessly until Flower gave up all attempts to vanish. "Marshy, come here! It's your turn."

Flower looked at Marshy. "You wouldn't dare. We just met! Oh, no! *Noooo.*"

By the sound of the high-pitched laughter that rang through the trees, Marshy dared much.

40

JAN'S A WIZARD!

Lyndsy, Marshy, and Tami stood beneath a tree in the shade. They grinned, watching the Mythit's antics as she introduced herself to the children. Smiling, they watched and enjoyed the delighted gasps and laughs as Flower disappeared and reappeared. Jan had taken Dolen and another boy to town. He was adamant about going alone. Lyndsy didn't press; she wanted to stay at Lake Side anyway.

After her own amusement faded, she found some rags and started polishing her staff. Marshy came close and inspected all of the little wolves carved over the staff's entire surface. She waited for Lyndsy to finish and then asked, "What's the staff for?"

"I fight with it."

"Fight? Naw, you's just a girl like me."

Lyndsy was about to comment when the smell of alcohol touched her nose. She turned and watched two men walk through the trees. One of them picked up a young boy and started to search him. The other man noticed Marshy and stomped angrily toward them. "All right, which one of ya stole Lady Bray's necklace? Come on, give it up, or I'll give it to ya good!"

Marshy drew a dagger. "We ain't got no damn necklace! Leave us alone!"

The man stepped forward, caught Marshy by the wrist, and twisted. Hard. She dropped the dagger and bit back a cry of pain. The man raised his hand to strike.

It never landed. A blur of white ivory hit him full across the chest. He dropped to his knees, gasping for air.

"Hey," the other man shouted. He pushed the boy away and started running down the hill.

Lyndsy stepped between him and the other children.

"Give me that!" The man made the mistake of reaching for Lyndsy's staff.

Lyndsy knocked his hand away, dropped to one knee, and reversed. His legs flew high in the air, and he landed flat on his back.

All of the children were shouting. Lyndsy walked halfway between the two men, watching them both. "Marshy, is there any reason why they should be treating you like this?"

"Yeah," Marshy said through clenched teeth, "we ain't big 'nough ta fight back!"

The first man jumped to his feet. Lyndsy dropped him with a blow to the side of his head. The other man got up and started to run. Lyndsy chased him, tripped him, and shoved her staff against his throat. "You're not leaving here without an apology to that boy."

"No way."

Lyndsy rapped him up the side of his head—not too hard, just hard enough to make it ring. "Tell him you're sorry and that you will *never* touch him again."

The man looked at the laughing children and felt humiliated. Sudden anger made him stupid. Lyndsy's staff made him smarter. He looked up into the magenta eyes of the strange girl. Cold fear gripped him. "I'm sorry."

"Tell *him*!"

The man turned his head toward the boy. "I'm sorry. I won't do it again."

Lyndsy kicked the man in the ribs. "Get out of here. Now!"

The man pointed at his partner. "What about him?"

"I'm not finished with him. Leave!"

The man got to his feet and hurried away.

Lyndsy went to Marshy's side and inspected the wrist. As the children quieted, Lyndsy found that the bones were obviously broken. Marshy sat still, holding her forearm, biting back tears.

Tami scowled. "What's we gonna do? Ain't no damn doctor gonna help none o' us."

Lyndsy frowned. "Marshy, I have to reset the bones before it swells too badly. Jan can help fix it when he gets back, but right now it has to go back in place."

She turned quickly to Tami. "Take my staff. If that man tries to get up, I want you to hit him. Hard. Think you can do that?"

Tami took the staff and glared down. "You kiddin'? I'll brain the bastard!"

Lyndsy turned back to Marshy and held the limp hand. She caught Marshy's elbow and forearm. "Marshy, on the count of three, I'm going to pull it out and straighten it. Try to relax."

Marshy nodded.

Lyndsy counted, "One," and pulled straight out. With a simple twist, the hand moved back into place.

Marshy gasped. "You tricked me!" She passed out.

Whack.

"Ohhh."

Lyndsy turned to see Tami standing over the now unconscious man with a huge grin one her face.

"What in the name of Song is going on here!?"

"Jan!"

They circled him and told him what had happened. Fifteen kids all talking at once tends to take some unraveling, but Jan got the gist of it.

"What do we do with this one?" Tami asked.

"Take him to the tree and tie him up."

Marshy groaned and opened her eyes. Jan saw her pain as she gritted her teeth. The wrist was already swollen three times its normal size. Jan knelt at her side. "Does it hurt bad?"

Marshy shook her head no. Jan smiled. "I'm going to fix it. I want you to be brave for me, OK? Flower! Where's Flower?" Jan gazed around the clearing. "Tami, blindfold that man. Flower!"

Flower appeared as soon as the man was blindfolded. She sat down and laid Marshy's head in her lap. Jan drew his sword.

"Are ya gonna cut it off?"

Jan looked into the tear-filled eyes of a very young girl. "No. I'm going to use magic. Watch!"

"Marshy," Flower said as she set her hands against Marshy's temples, "look into my eyes."

Jan watched Marshy's face go blank. As the gems flared and the children gasped, he looked into the wrist. Both bones were broken, and some of the tiny bones in the back of her hand had been twisted out of shape. It had been sheer luck that Lyndsy had been there to quickly place the hand.

He let power flow from the gems and slowly filled the hand with his light. He firmly pressed all of the little bones back in place and began the meld that knitted the tissue.

A few rebuilt bone cells held the wrist in place. He worked the cartilage around the tiny bones that allowed the palm to open and close. He tediously renewed tiny muscles, working slowly to make sure he was doing everything correctly. When the back of her hand was done, he turned his attention to the two bigger bones and built row after row of cells.

Lastly, he teased open the tiny vessels and allowed the swelling to recede. He finished and opened his eyes. All the children were just staring at him, wide-eyed in wonder. Tami closed her open mouth. She blinked at the sword and shook her head. "In the name of Song! Janny's a wizard!"

Flower let go. Marshy blinked her eyes. She smiled, reaching as she turned, and caught the Mythit in her arms. Lovingly, Marshy rocked Flower back and forth. Flower returned the embrace as though she wouldn't trade places with anybody in all of Lyre.

Jan saw a sparkling pink-white tear roll down Flower's cheek. He watched, curious. He had only seen this twice before. The tear dropped and landed on Marshy's neck. The tear gathered itself and crystallized. Flower picked it up with her little fingers and enclosed it in one furry hand.

Marshy suddenly remembered where she was. "My hand!" She held it up over Flower's shoulder. She made a fist, opened it, and closed it. "In the name of Song! How?"

Tami grinned down at her. "Jan's a wizard!"

Jan used the tip of his sword to cut the blindfold away. He gazed into the ruffian's frightened eyes and shook his head. "What am I going to do with a terrible, mean, cowardly man who could hurt my beautiful, sweet, innocent little sister so cruelly?"

After a momentary pause, Lyndsy rapped him upside the head with her staff. "My gracious lord asked you a question. I suggest you answer it."

"Lemme go! I swear, I'll never come back!"

"Why do you terrorize unprotected, small, gentle, helpless children?"

Pause.

Whack.

"My wonderful lord asked you another question. Answer it."

"I don't know!"

Jan set one hand by the side of the man's head and leaned close to look in one eye. "Your stinking self makes my skin crawl in loathing." Jan pushed off from the tree and sheathed his sword. Arms folded, he drummed his fingertips on his biceps as he scowled. "You disgust me. First, he is your prisoner.

You decide what to do with him." He paused again as the man realized he was talking to the strange young woman with the angry magenta eyes. A look of dread came over the ruffian's face. Jan nodded. "First, I suggest you let him live." Watching the man sag against the tree, Jan turned on one heel and walked away.

Lyndsy stepped in front of the ruffian and rhythmically tapped the end of her staff against his chin. "Marshy," Lyndsy said, "would you come here for a moment?"

Marshy went to Lyndsy's side, glaring at the man.

Lyndsy inclined her head. "What do *you* think I should do with him?"

"You done beat 'im good already. But if'n he ever comed back, I'd take 'im ta Market Square an make 'im lick all o' our feets clean!"

Lyndsy started to laugh, but it died as soon as it began. Marshy's tone of voice suggested someone had done that to her. Rage filled her. "That's good. Now go back and take the children away. I want to talk to him alone."

The man somehow found the courage to meet Lyndsy's eyes. He hated being humiliated like this! But when the tiny white-haired woman smiled at him, his knees turned to water. Sharp, pointed teeth smiled at him in such a way the simple word *terror* held no meaning.

Lyndsy's eyes were blazing. She wanted to tear him limb from limb. She grabbed his beard and pulled his face up close. "If any of these children even have a nightmare about you, I will find you. You will not like what I do to you, in the night, where no humans can see. I have sworn a vow to protect humans from the likes of you. You have threatened and hurt a human girl. I see very little reason to let you live." Lyndsy slammed his head back against the tree. Twisting her staff in both hands, she had to turn away.

Remembering the lesson she had learned in Virile Swamp, she found a memory to bring her back to calm. After a few deep breaths, she faced him again. "Your scent sickens me. I can and will track you all the way from here to the southern seas if I ever hear about you again." She untied the ropes and pushed him away. "Get out of my sight, *now!*"

Early the next morning, January instructed Marshy in the making of true perfume. They extracted the scent from a pot of wildflowers. Jan showed her how to add oil and enough pure alcohol to keep water and oil from separating.

Flower watched with a critical eye. When they were finished, five bottles sat in a row filled with a light amber liquid. Flower looked up at Jan as she set a small, pink-white crystal tear in an empty bottle. Pouring in a full measure of alcohol, she looked back down at it and nodded to herself. "Marshy, put your finger in the bottle and touch the teardrop."

"Teardrop?"

Jan narrowed his eyes. "Are you sure about this, Flower?"

Flower's glowing eyes became very serious. "You forget who you're talking to. Besides, this tear already belongs to her. Either way, it doesn't matter; everything you ever told me about her is true. She is who she is."

"Still." Jan thought of the temptations he had. To deny ... The sight came on him.

He saw Marshy in a large house. He knew the house well; he had paid for it in gold the day before. Children were everywhere. Marshy stood on the porch. She looked lovely, happy, content. Laughing, she scooped up a small girl and twirled her in the air. They were dressed decently but poorly. Jan gazed past them and saw a table laden with breads and one large round of cheese. A glass pitcher of water stood full on one end. The room was furnished with odds and ends, one broken chair leaning in a corner.

The sight changed. Marshy stood on the porch. She wore a beautiful sky-blue summer dress. Children played in the yard as she watched. Jan saw her smile. It was full, happy, content. She turned and walked in the door. An older woman was waiting. All the children including Marshy gathered before her and sat down in chairs. They were well-made, solid oak chairs.

The woman said something. Jan watched her turn and draw runes on a board. She was teaching them to read. The teacher turned back and asked Marshy a question. Marshy studied the board and made an answer. The teacher shook her head. Marshy smiled ruefully as the children, playfully, made fun of her. Then her eyes lit up as if remembering something. She answered the question again. This time, the teacher smiled and nodded approval. The same girl who had been in the other vision ran to her, clapping her hands. Marshy picked her up, smoothed the folds of the child's new shift, and hugged her close. Jan caught his breath as a tear of pure love rolled down Marshy's cheek. He realized he would do anything to see Marshy so happy.

The sight changed. Marshy, perhaps ten seasons from now, stood behind a counter. Jan realized it was an extension built to the front of the house. She picked up a thin, golden needle and put it in a half-full bottle of bright pink liquid. She pulled it out and set the tiny drop into a perfume bottle. It flashed briefly as the amber liquid turned bright pink. With careful hands, she set it on the counter with a row of other bottles.

Two very richly dressed women came into the shop. One of the women picked up the bottle, pulled the cork, and sniffed. The woman's wrinkled face lit up with pleasure.

She gave Marshy a whole gold piece. Jan watched Marshy's lips say, "Thank you. Come again."

Jan blinked away from the sight. "You're right, of course. Flower, you are a good judge of personality."

Marshy gazed at Jan and wondered at his words, for they seemed to make no sense at all.

"Marshy, put your finger in the bottle and look into my eyes."

Marshy touched the teardrop and, once again, gazed into the soft pink eyes that had no pupil or any whites. Once again, she saw that wondrous place filled with rolling hills, sunshine, and flowers. This time, she looked down and gasped as she felt the cool grass beneath her feet. Flower faded in before her, holding a little pink crystal tear in her furry, open palm.

Touch it.

Marshy touched the teardrop and watched as it turned liquid.

"Marshy, come back."

She opened her eyes. Looking down at her hand, she saw that the tear in the glass bottle had melted and mixed with the alcohol. The whole bottle glowed with a bright pink light. "In the name of Song!"

Flower burst into laughter.

Jan had one arm around Marshy and another around Lyndsy. They walked through town telling Lyndsy stories of their past adventures. Marshy giggled and laughed as though she were walking on clouds. Never in her life had she thought she would walk through Window in a new dress and real leather sandals. She spoke to Lyndsy in a flurry of words every time they passed a place that brought back memories of January.

Jan led them back toward the lake following a muddy, rutted side street. They stopped at the end of the long-deserted lane as Jan turned them around.

"Remember when we used to dream about selling apples and buying this house?"

Marshy grinned, gazing down the path toward the huge two-story home. It sat alone on a large property. In the back field, an old brick smithy sat crumbling in disrepair. "Yeah, said we was gonna bring ever' one 'ere an' never be cold again."

"Come on." Jan walked them up the path leading to the door.

Marshy glanced from side to side. "Jan! It's broad daylight! We's gonna get 'n real trouble f'r sure!"

Jan laughed. "They can't arrest you for being in your own house!"

"Gimme a break."

"I'm serious. There's a deed in city records, witnessed by five people, including the sheriff. It's in your name, and as you know, they all know who *you* are! Sheriff said he would be glad to get you out of his markets."

Marshy swelled with pride. "I bet 'e did."

Jan and Lyndsy followed Marshy as she walked up to the door. She peered inside and shook her head. Impulsively, she jumped up into Jan's arms and kissed his cheek. "I love you, Janny!"

"I love you too. But if you call me Janny again, I'm gonna tan your hide!"

Marshy grinned. "Janny! Janny! Janny!" She ran into the house as Jan chased after her.

Jan awoke in the middle of the night. The house was still. He reached for his sword and drew it. Standing motionless, he wondered why he was feeling the things he was feeling.

"Jan? What is it?" Lyndsy hopped out of bed; walked past him, staff in hand; and peered out of the window.

Jan didn't pay any attention. Curious, he took another step. Once again, he felt that strange sensation. A shudder ran through his body. He glanced down, and for a brief moment, he thought he saw an army camped around his feet. "Lyndsy, tell Marshy we're leaving. Now! No, don't come any closer!" he exclaimed, holding out one hand.

Lyndsy frowned at him for a moment and then rushed from the room.

Flower appeared. "Wow! You sure look funny!"

"Flower? What do you see?"

"Your personality's doing loops," she said in awe. "*Wow!*"

"Flower, what is it?" Jan's eyes opened wide. He did indeed see a small army appear around his feet. A tiny catapult fired a speck of black crystal at his knee. Jan burst into laughter. "That tickles!"

"What tickles? Jan, you really look awesome! Ain't never seen nothin' like it."

"You're no help!"

Flower blinked at the mesmerizing whirl of Jan's aura. "Ain't sposta help."

"Jan?"

Jan looked up. Marshy was walking toward him. "Stop! Marshy, we're leaving right now. I'll miss you. Take care of yourself. Take care of the children. Marsh, I want you to know how much you've always meant to me. I've never forgotten you!"

"Janny," Marshy whispered, "I love you too."

Lyndsy gave Marshy the hug Jan could not.

"Flower, I'm holding some kind of door. Can you see it? I've never … Flower?"

"I'm here."

"Lyndsy?"

Lyndsy knitted her brow in worry. "I'm here too."

"White walls? White walls?"

"Jan, what are you talking about?"

Jan shook his head. His mind was passing through tunnels of rainbows. With great effort, he pulled himself back into the room. Holding his hands out to Lyndsy and Flower, he beckoned. "Come."

They both hurried to his side.

Marshy watched in awe as they vanished. She shook her head. Five days ago, she was stealing breadcrumbs. Today she lived in the home of her dreams. She grinned and swiped at tears that came out of nowhere and whispered, "Jan's a wizard!"

41

WATCHMAKER

The first thing they saw was a glittering chunk of black crystal hurtling straight at them. No time to even move. It detonated five feet in front of them in a shower of fire and flares that spread across their entire field of vision. They felt a vague rumble and heard nothing.

"Awesome!" Flower walked forward and spread her palms flat against the transparent walls. A large army of Vainians stood no more than two hundred strides before them.

"Where are we?" Lyndsy asked.

Only then did Jan realize where he was. "We're inside of the Terror Trail Wizards Watch."

"Here comes another one!" Flower pressed her nose to the wall. The black crystal flew toward her and exploded in her face. Sheets of fire and rainbow flames almost blinded Jan and Lyndsy. Flower turned around. Her smile was that of an elderly scholar who had just discovered all of the secrets of life. Flower's pale pink eyes whirled brighter as she exclaimed in sheer delight. "That's radical!"

"Are we in danger?" Lyndsy asked.

Jan knew of a surety that nothing outside could ever harm this tower. He pulled Lyndsy closer. "No. They have no idea what they're trying to destroy." Glancing around the chamber, he saw stairs leading up to a closed door. "Let's look around. Flower, are you coming?"

"Whoooooaa!"

Lyndsy grinned at Flower's back. "I think she's happy where she is."

They walked up the stairs. Jan called the sword to life and found the red gem pulsing. The door creaked and slid open.

The chamber was huge. Every bit of wall space from the thirty-foot ceiling to the floor was covered in ancient tapestries. In the center of the room was a round table. In its center was what appeared to be a stand-up mirror. They walked closer and realized it wasn't a mirror but, rather, a thin sheet of translucent, milky white crystal. The crystal's frame was bordered in gold etching that met the tabletop and fastened to a disk swivel. A white marble stool, fastened to the table's single leg, extended from a round bar of what looked like pure gold. Jan reached out and turned the crystal. They both jumped out of the way as the stool followed the crystal.

"What in the name of Song is this!"

"You're the wizard. You tell me."

Jan sat down on the stool and gazed into the shimmering pane. He gasped to see the Three Sister Mountains rising up before him. The scene went out of focus even as he recognized what he was seeing.

He pushed off with one foot, and the pane exhibited a blur of colors. As he stopped the stool, the crystal came clear. This time the Veil Wizards Watch came hurtling at him so fast he leapt out of the chair.

Lyndsy burst into laughter. "What was it? It must have been good!" She laughed harder. "Should have seen the look on your face!"

Jan rolled his eyes. "OK, you try it."

Lyndsy sat down. Nothing happened. She stared at the crystal pane and burst into another fit of laughter. "All I see is my reflection. Did you scare yourself?" Lyndsy leaned forward, fell off the stool, and rolled on the floor as tears streamed down her face.

"First! Get off the floor! Come here, now! Kiss me!"

Lyndsy stood up. Still snickering, she wrapped her arms around his neck and smirked up at him. "That an order, my lord?"

"Yes, consider it punishment for laughing at me!"

"Oooo, remind me to laugh at you more often." She pressed forward and pulled him down for an awe-inspiring kiss.

"So! This is how you spend your time!"

Lyndsy stepped right, staff up and ready. Jan turned left, sword drawn before his foot hit the ground.

"Much better!" Pause. "Moonlight? Child, what are you doing here?"

Lyndsy gazed at the strange figure, blinking in bewilderment.

"Ohhh, sorry. *Sleep*, child."

Jan blinked as Lyndsy's head slumped forward. Still poised, she stood motionless.

Jan turned back to the figure before him. The man's personality was so intense he had to blink. He looked young, about twenty seasons. A clean, smooth face sported a thin mustache that drooped to his chin. Light brown hair, cut just above shoulder length, accented a narrow, angular face. The man's eyes were glowing, bright red. Jan gasped as he noticed the brilliant glow. Mythit-like eyes! The pupils were closed—shut doors to the seemingly eternal halls of his mind.

His arms were folded across a lean, strong chest. A sleeveless leather vest hung open to his waist. Three shades of red Mythit silks wrapped his narrow hips and fell in skirts in the fashion of a dancer. On his right biceps was an armband studded with rubies.

Jan realized who he was looking at. "You're dead!"

The Red Wizard, Lori Talon, a Sword Dancer of Lispin Shark, threw back his head and laughed.

A slight rumble shook the tower. Red turned glowing eyes to the wall and looked down. "Dragon's Breath! What are those slither-spawned, three-eyed fools trying to do here, eh?"

Walking to the stool, he sat and tilted the frame at an angle.

Jan watched over his shoulder as the army came into view. Another crystal flew toward them. Red pointed a finger at Jan, and the red gem came to life. Jan's eyes opened wide as the crystal passed through the wall. The glittering black chunk slowed and came to rest on the edge of the table.

Lori Talon released the power of the red gem. Reaching out with fingertips, he inspected the crystal. "Those inbred wads of cancerous growth are getting smarter. Just look at this mixture!" He turned to Jan as if expecting a reply.

Jan felt the intensity of those glowing red eyes. He didn't know what to say.

Lori shook his head. "You don't see it, do you?"

"What?"

The Red Wizard ran one finger under his chin as if thinking. "Look at this." With his other hand, he traced lines through the air. The lines illuminated with a soft red light. Jan realized it was a series of runes and numbers. As it grew, it just baffled Jan more. Then he suddenly realized Red was explaining in runes how a series of cells held themselves together. As the equation grew, Jan was amazed to find he could almost comprehend it. It seemed to be a mathematical expression of a plant. Red finished the equation by touching every cell with a symbol that was always the same. "Do you see what this is?"

Jan gazed at the intricate expression. "Uh, a tree?"

The Red Wizard scowled. "A tree?" he mimicked. "You boneheaded, bumble-brained ... Think about it. Don't guess!"

Jan looked at it again, ears burning. He studied it closely and realized that, even though the expression seemed very large, it was really a very simple plant. He saw how the equation pieced together. He built it in his mind. Finally, he glanced at Red and blushed crimson.

"Well?"

Jan answered, feeling very foolish. "It's a blade of grass." He felt even worse when Red threw back his head and roared with laughter.

Lori Talon came slowly back into his own reality and smiled approval. "I have to admit, you figured that out very quickly once that thick skull of yours started working. How old are you right now?"

"Eighteen seasons."

"I see that, but how old are you really? Wait, don't ... your eyes!" Red's glowing, pupilless eyes lit in wonder. He leaned back against the table and set his face in his hands. "You figured out that was a blade of grass, and you were born eighteen seasons ago." It was a statement. He shook his head and looked back up.

Jan frowned, not knowing what to think or what Red was seemingly surprised at. "Well, how old are you?"

Red turned and looked through the walls. His focus seemed to settle on something far away. "I have watched the seasons change 7,644 times."

Jan whistled under his breath. "I see."

Red's gaze focused back inside of the chamber. He became deadly serious. "I hope you do! You need to get your Mythit to help you study the mind work. You will *never* defeat the Dark Lord without it!"

"So, he *will* come again."

"Of course! Blue said he visited you in a time of—"

"Blue? Visited me?"

The Red Wizard caught himself. He turned and pierced the crystal with his gaze.

Jan felt an almost imperceptible hold forming on his mind. He stilled himself and pushed away.

Red whirled and pointed at the wall. "*Look!*"

Jan felt the command. He took an involuntary step and once again felt Red in his mind. He realized the wizard was trying to erase the memory of what he had just said.

Jan froze and cleared his aura. Feigning innocence, he gave Red entrance. The wizard was caught off guard. Red didn't expect Jan to try and turn the tables. With a swirl of personality, Jan lit Red's mind with a mental burst of confusion. Jan pushed the advantage and pulled memories from the mind of Lori Talon.

A black dragon prowled through a forest, slitted, bloodred eyes glowing in hatred. A purple and pink male Mythit ran, exhausted, through the trees. The dragon blew fire, and the Mythit burned in the flames.

The quick flash faded, and another took its place. Red, in a fit of rage, stood on the ground gazing at the Three Sisters. He leveled his staff and spun in a circle. A stream of water consecrated by Light Lake rose up out of the ground. The water hardened and created a wall around him. Again and again the staff whirled. Levitating off of the ground, the wizard and the wall climbed higher. Jan realized he was watching the Red Wizard build this very same Wizards Watch.

Once again, it was a quick flash of scenes. Jan felt Red's mind relax. He could have broken the hold, but he didn't. A new set of scenes passed before his mind's eye.

The wizard sat on the stool gazing into the translucent mirror. He watched the black dragon that had slain his Mythit. It crept out of the Three Sisters and slithered to the edge of Terror Trail. Red reached out, fingers curled, and twisted the air. The dragon flailed in agony, pounding his tail and flapping huge leathery wings.

Red disappeared from the stool and reappeared in front of the black dragon. He drew a golden-bladed long sword and levitated it above the dragon's head. The black dragon snapped its jaws, but the sword seemed to elude its grasp. It dove at the horned head and pierced its skull. Jan watched the tip of the sword exit beneath the serpent's chin.

Red stood still, arms folded, watching the dragon die.

Jan blinked away and gazed at Red. He expected anger, pain, something, but there was nothing in the red glowing eyes except a hint of amazement. The wizard's next words, totally unexpected, surprised him.

"Not all dragons are evil."

After another moment of silence, Red turned and seemed to suddenly remember Lyndsy's presence. "This is unbelievable. The resemblance is uncanny. I would swear this is a weremaiden named Moonlight." Red's eyes opened wide in surprise. "Child, hand me your staff!" Lyndsy's body obeyed. "This *is* Moonlight's staff. Only yesterday, I placed it in the crystal cave. That old Blue Wizard and his perpetually grinning Mythit told me to." He turned back to Jan. "Did you give it to her?"

"Yes."

Red's eyes narrowed. "Can she use it? I would not have this staff dishonored. The werebitch who wielded this staff was a she-demon as a dancer. I have never seen better, and my own sister was a staff dancer."

Jan grinned. "She can use it."

Red gazed at him, obviously disbelieving. He turned back to Lyndsy and touched her forehead. "Well, I'll be a three-eyed mutant deep fried in dragon grease! She's *were!*" Red reached out and fingered the silver star sash on Lyndsy's arm. Frowning, he turned and peered at Jan. "You obviously call yourself a dancer. Are you?"

Jan raised an eyebrow. He said with total confidence, "Yes."

"Yes, huh? I wonder if there are really any left."

"No," Jan said softly, "there aren't."

"How would you know?"

"I know." Jan shrugged. "I know swords. I also fought a demon named Gembol Slayer. He acknowledged me as a dancer."

This time Red seemed truly shocked. "Who?"

"Gembol Slayer."

Red stepped closer, pushing open palms through his own personality. It was a gesture to calm his own racing heart. In a whisper, he asked, "Show me the slayer. Please, I must *see* this."

Jan frowned at the wizard. Hesitantly, he held out one hand. Setting mind shields and paying strict attention, he opened his mind to the Red Wizard.

Red watched the dance, the sword, and the man. As Jan fed him scenes, Samantha came into clear focus and gave Red the strength he sought. Jan wanted to feel Red's reaction, so he took him through Slim's explanation as well. He was disappointed. The Red Wizard had indeed found his control and seemed only curious—that unique, wondrous curiosity that belongs to children.

Red knew his emotional appeal would win the youth. He smiled as he realized the dance had been performed before the were. Myril the White never really believed in the good of the were. Only through his own relentless persuasion and insistent browbeating had White finally been coerced to show them grace.

Red opened his eyes. "You *are* a sword dancer."

It was said quietly, sincerely. Jan felt a swelling of pride. No one could have paid him a compliment that meant as much as those simple words.

Red turned back to Lyndsy. "They are so strong and so brave. The only good thing that Dagdor the Black and Poison ever did. Even if it was an accident."

"Dagdor the Black?" Jan exclaimed. "But I thought ... I don't know what I thought."

"Yes, Dagdor and his warped Mythit, Poison. The White Wizard, damn the old fool, in the form of Myril, lifted the curse and changed its course. However, they first served the Dark Lord and very nearly caused the death of Lyre. I wonder if they even remember."

"Yes!" Jan said fiercely. "They still take the Vow of Blood Plain!"

A slow smile tugged at Red's lips. "Ah, a man after my own heart. I, too, love the were. This one though ..." He handed the staff back to Lyndsy. "Wake, child!"

Lyndsy opened her eyes and glared at the Red Wizard. "If you call me a child again, I will beat you back into the dust you came from!"

Red's eyes brightened as his jaw dropped open. He turned and gazed at Jan in awe. "I would swear she is Moonlight incarnate! She sounds just like her!" Then he looked back to Lyndsy and said quietly, "I found her after she leapt from the cliff. I carried her broken body back to the top." Still looking in Lyndsy's eyes, he finished, "There is a mound of rocks up there. She sleeps forever next to the Lady and the sweet white clouds."

Lyndsy caught her breath as she smelled the Red Wizard's quiet passion. "You are very kind to give a woman who knew no love such a fine resting place."

Red raised an eyebrow. "Knew no love? Nay, she knew love better than any who has ever lived. Say, rather, that she was given no love in return."

Lyndsy swallowed hard. After a long moment, she nodded. "Yes."

"Aye, that's the way, child ..."

Jan watched the staff that Red seemed so fond of. It passed through the air the wizard had been standing in. Red appeared ten paces away. "I beg your pardon!"

Lyndsy smiled wickedly. "Call me a child again, and you will *beg* much more than that!"

Red threw back his head and roared with laughter. He couldn't wait to go back and tell White about this werechild!

"Wow! Where did that come from? Can I have it?" Flower walked through the door and made a beeline for the black crystal. She seemed to suddenly notice the stranger. "Hi! I'm Flower! Wow, you got nice eyes! You must be a wizard. Red eyes? Ohhh, you're the Red Wizard!" She clapped her hands, delighted at her own power of deductive reasoning.

"Yes, I am. Whose spawn might you be?"

"Spawn?" Louder. "Spawn!" Flower spat furiously. "Lyndsy, hit him!"

Lyndsy laughed. "I tried, but he won't hold still!"

"Oh? Are you a Mythit?" Red asked innocently. "I thought you were a bug-eyed salamander." Red turned to Jan. "Is it yours?"

Flower shook her fist. "*It*! I know when I'm not wanted!" Turning on one furry little heel, she stomped angrily toward the door.

Red reached out and snatched her up off of her feet, "I know what Mythits like."

Flower blinked, instantly curious. "What?"

"To be tickled!"

"No! It's a conspiracy." Her next words were swallowed in a jumble of giggles that turned quickly to mindless laughter.

The Red Wizard concluded the dreaded Flower torture and gazed into the Mythit's pale pink eyes.

After a long moment of silence, Flower sighed. "I will, I promise." She wrapped her slender arms around the wizard's neck and held him tight. Red rocked slowly back and forth, holding her gently.

A bright red tear rolled down Red's cheek. It crystallized like a Mythit tear. Red reached for the tear and set it in Flower's mouth. "You are indeed the *reflection* of Sunder and Jasmine." He smiled. "Flower. It is a charming and very fitting name."

Lyndsy watched Flower smile. It was a picture she would always remember—a soft, beautiful smile, eyes closed, head resting on the Red Wizard's shoulder.

Lori Talon went to the stool and set Flower on the edge of the table. He focused on the Vainian army. "Well, shall we give our little horde of gremlins a surprise?" He pointed at the black crystal, and it disappeared.

They all watched through the translucent screen as the cart carrying the crystals started to glow. The Vainians scattered to the four winds when the cart started to burn. A rainbow display of rockets persuaded the Vainians to run faster. A fireball erupted in the center of the crystals, and then the whole area was lit by one huge flash. This time, the tower rumbled slightly. Then all was dark.

Laughing softly to himself, Red turned back to January. "I have been charged with two messages; one of them is for you. First, though, I want to say this. Be careful how you deal with Gembol Slayer. Do not doubt that he is evil. Yet he has honor. That is, he is honorable."

"You know him?"

"Yes, I knew him. He was the Master of Lispin Shark. I trained under him for ten seasons to become a sword dancer. He was a black cleric and a sword master." Red sighed and touched his hip. A gold-inlayed sheath appeared. He touched the mouth, and a hilt appeared.

Jan watched as Red drew the sword. It was made in the same style as the sword the demon had danced with. This one had a golden blade edged in platinum. Inscribed on the flat of the blade were many intricate runes. The hilt was twined in thin lengths of tightly wrapped gold strings. "It's beautiful. May I?"

Red offered him the hilt. "Gembol gave this blade to me. It is one of five swords made hundreds of seasons before I was born."

Jan's face lit with surprise. "It's so light! No heavier than bleached cottonwood. How? This is obviously gold!"

"I know not. It was forged in black dragon's fire and blessed in a clerical nature. It cannot be looked into or it will destroy itself. That I would not do, not even to discover its secrets. Some things simply cannot be remade. Besides, I have great respect for the dancer who that was a part of the being named Gembol Slayer.

"Now, here is what I have to say. The were will always be your greatest allies but don't forget the Forest of Manshantarrinon. The men and women there are a hardy lot. Find time very soon to go there. Of all things necessary to defeat the Dark Lord, that which dwells in the forest is your greatest need."

With a grin, he took the sword from January's reluctant hand. "Now, I must go. I now believe Blue, for what that's worth." He turned to Lyndsy. "Take care of your man"—Red grinned—"child."

Once again, the ivory staff of Moonlight blurred through the air just after the Red Wizard vanished.

"I want to go Home."

Jan looked to Flower. What had the Red Wizard said to her? What secret did she carry besides Red's tear? "Well, I think that's a good idea. The only way out of this tower is through the red gem. Let's see where it will take us from here." Jan concentrated on the flowing lawns of Mythit Home. To his surprise, the scene came vividly clear. "It seems we will be Home very soon. Come."

42

Take Me, Sir, Be Gentle!

Lyndsy blinked in the morning sunlight. She gazed at her surroundings amazed at the scene. The whole area was covered with soft, short grass—a lawn. No weeds or unseemly plants inhibited the gentle esthetics. She turned in a circle. The lawn spread for as far as the eye could see.

Groups of bright, fragrant flowers stood bunched in clumps in no apparent order. Still, they seemed perfect exactly as they were. The trees were very unusual, although she didn't, at first, understand what made her think so. She saw that they were in a huge ring—apparently planted to produce some unknown design.

Then she looked straight up and gasped. All of the top branches reached toward a common center, creating an oblong, upside down bowl. Leaf-covered nests nestled close to the trunks. The dwellings were obviously woven from the living branches because she could see that the walls of the nests were in green health.

A knotted, silk rope hung from a hole in the bottom of the nearest nest. She walked closer and looked up.

Flower stepped up to her side and grinned mischievously. "Last one up hangs the hammocks!"

Lyndsy jumped up and caught the highest knot she could reach. Hand over hand, she scurried up the makeshift ladder. As she climbed through the opening, she saw Flower sitting by the edge of the round hole.

She looked at Flower in amazement and then with a questioning expression. Then Flower saw *the look* run across Lyndsy's face. "*No!*"

After Lyndsy finished the dreaded flower torture, she inspected the nest. She immediately noticed a fat pile of silks and stared at it in awe. She gazed around and realized the room was simply draped and littered with bright Mythit silks.

"Flower? Is it OK if I get a few new wraps?"

Flower giggled. "Sure, I'll make more. Try yellow and orange. I *like* yellow and orange!"

Lyndsy grinned at the yellow and orange Mythit. "I can't believe you actually make this stuff!" She stripped and decided to do as Flower suggested. She tied an orange wrap across her small breasts and wrapped a yellow strip around her hips. "Well?"

Flower tilted her head. "You look magnificent! Almost as gorgeous as me!"

Lyndsy sat down and pulled Flower into her lap. "Flower, I want to tell you … I uh …"

"I know," Flower said gently. "I love you too."

They held each other for a long time. Neither one wanted to let go as they luxuriated in the glowing feelings passing between them. Finally, Lyndsy lay back, clutching Flower to her breast. "Flower, I need a favor."

"Hmm?"

"My time is coming soon. Can you help me keep Jan away? I don't need to get pregnant right now."

"Why not?"

"Flower please, I need to be ready to fight at any time. I can't take that much time away. I want to be with him, not waiting somewhere fat and pregnant."

"I'll do my best."

"Thank you, Flower. Flower?"

"What now?"

"How come you're the only Mythit here? I thought there would be more."

"Oh. Well, they're just shy. They'll show themselves soon I think." She said a little louder, "After all, you're January's mate. I know if Snow were here, she'd show herself."

Flower! Shut up!

Snow! Come meet Lyndsy. She's my sister now 'cause she married Jan. She's were!

Lyndsy listened, feigning ignorance. She almost choked as Snow asked, *Were? Does she bite?*

'*Course not! Come on, show yourself.*

Snow appeared in front of them. Lyndsy wasn't prepared for it. She hadn't realized what the name implied. She sat up and sobbed as hot tears filled her eyes and rolled down her cheeks.

Snow, one of the few *young* Mythits, stood transfixed. She was startled when the werewoman's personality reached out to embrace her. Snow swiftly realized that Lyndsy was very overwhelmed. A wash of delighted wonder made its way straight into Snow's heart. After a moment, it turned into a powerful feeling of deep, one-on-one companionship. Snow returned the emotion, sensing it was very important to the werewoman but not knowing why.

A quick glow of sadness filled Snow's personality. She instantly reached out to comfort. Lyndsy gladly pulled the little white Mythit into her arms. A flash went through her mind. Snow saw a big, angry female were beating Lyndsy with a stick. The pale, small girl, only five seasons old, tried to run away. The woman reached out and picked the girl up by the hair. Screaming in rage, the woman beat Lyndsy unconscious.

A fierce protectiveness flowed from Lyndsy into Snow. The sensation rocked the Mythit to her core. They both shook as huge, racking sobs burst from the werewoman. Arms wrapped around Lyndsy's neck, Snow cooed and hummed the personality into peace. Then, when Snow thought it was over, a sweet, undeniable, white-hot rush of love filled her to brimming.

"I'm sorry." Lyndsy sniffed. "I don't mean to be so emotional."

"No," Snow whispered, at the moment barely able to speak. She slowly leaned back and placed her small, furry palms on Lyndsy's cheeks. "Emotion *is* life. You are very full of life! Very special! I understand why January loves you."

Flower jumped out of the opening and faded out. She wanted them to be alone to get to know each other. As she faded in on the lawn, she felt a compulsion and went to investigate.

She found January sitting against a tree. As she approached, she thought she saw, for a brief moment, a figure shimmering in the air before him. Jan held out one hand to her, and with hesitant fingers, she leaned closer and grasped it. She had thought he was squared, but as she touched him, he didn't *feel* quite right. With a sudden realization, she slapped him across the cheek, hard. "Jan! Jan! Come back! Don't go there!"

She made a fist and swung. He caught it just before it landed. A knowing smile widened his lips. Motioning to the ground next to him, he said, "Sit."

Frowning, she sat down by his side.

"Flower, each life starts at a certain point. It begins to move and creates its own path. When I came to Mirshol I crossed a path and, not realizing it, stayed on it, following someone else's trail. I'm going to step off of it. Flower, that scares me. I always thought Sunder would do this with me. I know now that he can't. Sunder is following a trail, and it doesn't lead to where I need to go. I don't think he even realizes it.

"Flower, I know better than to try to reach the place where you thought I was. I have to admit; I question the Three's motives. No, I take that back. What I question is their ability to know how I or we will win this war. If they knew, wouldn't they have already done it?

Anyway, the Red Wizard's *mind set* is no more. Sunder and Jasmine hold the keys to the mind sets of Blue and White. So, I can't go to either of those places. Flower, I must make my own place. It's the only way."

Flower bowed her head. "And you want me?"

"Sunder will not do. He will fall into the habit of using past experiences. He will come up with the same answers. I need *new* answers."

"Jan, if you were my Master—"

"No! *That* I refuse. I have lived too long among Mythits, heard too many tales. I have witnessed the faces of those once bound, and I would not do that to you. Flower, I only ask, do you believe I could take that from you?"

Flower stared at her feet. "January, what will you do if I refuse to show or tell you something? Would you steal the thoughts from my mind? Will you just take what you will, leaving me empty and cold?"

"Flower, I will not."

She stood up, straddled his thighs, placed her hands on his shoulders, and gazed into his eyes, *Do you understand what it is that you ask of me? I've never heard of anything so absurd! Legend says that Sunder fought Blue for almost a season before the wizard finally coerced him to give in. Yet, you want me to do this because you love me and trust me. Jan, don't you know that I feel the same way? You are human. I am not. Still, I remember fondly that you said, "If I were a Mythit, I'd marry you!" Jan, I knew this was going to happen when you first came to me. I was truly surprised that it never did. Now you are considerate enough to sit me down and tell me why.*

Flower, if you decide to do this, I will be fast with questions. Right now, I have many.

There is nothing to decide. I will do it.

Are you sure?

Flower grinned, closed her eyes, and spread her arms out wide. "Take me, sir; be gentle!"

Jan burst into laughter. "Flower? Do Mythits really like to be tickled?"

"No!"

In the early summer of the 932nd season of the reign of the kings in Wizards Veil, Flower, daughter of Sunder and Jasmine, chose of her own free will to be bound to the wizard / sword dancer, January. Only once in Lyre's history had this happened—a Mythit freely giving of itself.

Jasmine, the Mythit of the White Wizard, would soon find out!

43

1 Know!

Lyndsy woke up and smiled. Stretching, she growled and laughed nonsense to herself. Rolling to hands and knees, she prowled to Jan's side and leaned down to kiss him. His wonderful scent shot shivers of delight through her senses. Startled, she jerked her head away. Taking a deep breath only made it worse.

Flower?

The Mythit appeared at the opening of the nest. "*Wow!*"

"Shhh!" *Flower, I have to go. Now!*

"In the name of Song! You look awesome!" Flower watched the rainbow effect surrounding Lyndsy's personality. She watched Lyndsy crawl by Jan and pause. Lyndsy took a long, deep breath and snapped back to reality as Flower exclaimed in delight, "Do it again!"

Flower, you're not making this any easier! Quit talking out loud. You'll wake him. If he looks at me with those big, blue, gorgeous, hot, delicious … I have to leave!

Sorry, it's just that you're so, so—hot!

Lyndsy smiled cynically. *That's why it's called being in heat.*

I wish I could do that!

No, you don't! It's the curse of all women everywhere!

Can I go with you?

Lyndsy saw Snow's head peeping through the opening. She smiled gratefully. *Yes, if you think you can stand it. I'll probably do a lot of complaining in the next few days, but you're welcome to come with me. Flower, do you think you can keep him away? Maybe I could just kiss him goodbye. No! I have to go, now!*

Lyndsy scrambled to the rope and slid down. She sighed as she hurried across the lawn. The increasing distance between Jan and her senses cleared her mind.

Snow walked beside her, looking curiously through the diminishing prisms of the werewoman's personality. *I didn't know you could share thoughts. I'm sorry.*

Lyndsy looked down at Snow, puzzled. "Sorry for what?"

Even through the short white fur on Snow's face, she saw the Mythit blush. She didn't know why this revelation delighted her so much, but she was also very surprised. After meeting Snow, she had found out that Snow had not gone through any torment concerning her skin or the color of her fur. After it was explained, Snow understood why Lyndsy had taken to her so quickly. Snow's kind heart had been deeply touched, and she had even told Lyndsy as much.

Now, Snow looked abashed. "I asked Flower if you bite."

Lyndsy smelled Snow's worry. The little white Mythit was prepared to vanish if Lyndsy became angry. Not wanting to frighten this lovely little creature, Lyndsy shrugged the words away. "Oh, I had forgotten. Don't worry about it. Humans wonder the same thing."

Snow was silent for a while as they walked, but her inherent curiosity was playing havoc with her sense of privacy. After at least five whole steps, she just couldn't stand it anymore. "Well, do you bite?"

Lyndsy burst into laughter. "Yes, I bite."

After another split second, Snow thought she would explode. "Are you going to bite me? Why are you thinking of biting if you're not? Can you really turn into a wolf? Can I watch? What's it like? Is it fun? I sure wish I could be a wolf!"

Lyndsy reached down, laughing, and pulled Snow into her arms. "I'll show you how I do it if you promise you won't be scared. I swear, I won't bite you, OK?"

Snow's eyes grew brighter as she savored the uninhibited caresses of Lyndsy's personality. "OK."

Flower and Snow had talked about Lyndsy and Jan all night long. Snow understood that the pain coursing from the werewoman's personality would be intense during the change. As Lyndsy sat back down on the ground, Snow squared, stood on the edge of a fade, and watched.

Lyndsy changed shape as quickly as she could. She didn't understand Mythit abilities, but she was quickly becoming aware of how sensitive their emotions were. When she finished, she blinked at Snow and was pleased to see a look of awe on the small, white face.

"Oh! In the name of Song! Hurt purty bad, didn't it? Can I touch? Wow, your fur is so soft!"

Jump on my back. Let's run!

Lyndsy started off slowly so Snow could feel the rhythm of four feet. Snow wrapped her legs around Lyndsy's body and leaned forward, arms around the wolf's neck. She watched the ground go by with increasing speed until it was a blur. She looked up as Lyndsy jumped a small log, landed smoothly, and kept going.

"Look into my eyes and don't fight it. I've brought you into my mind before, and you thought it was an illusion. The realm of my imagination is a real place. It has substance; it is *not* illusion."

Jan found himself sitting in a field of flowers. He turned his head and looked around. All he could see was rolling hills and bright, multicolored flowers. He smiled as he realized at least half of them were either orange or yellow.

Flower faded in before him and pointed at the ground. Jan followed her finger. A bulb was sprouting. Green sheathlike blades pushed their way through the soil and began to spread. When the plant was knee high, a bud pushed its way through the center of the plant and rose on a thin, dark stem. It stopped rising as the bud began to swell.

Jan watched in amazement as the green cover split apart, releasing the petals within. To his great pleasure, this flower was a rich violet. He watched the petals open, one by one, stiffening, face up to the sky. As the last petals opened, yellow pollen-covered stamens uncurled in a circle.

He gazed at it, shaking his head. Flower reached out and touched it. The sudden burst of fragrance into his senses startled and delighted him.

Flower sat down in Jan's lap and leaned back against his chest. "Now, I'm going to make another bulb. Watch carefully. Look deep into what I do."

Flower cupped her hands. Jan watched over her shoulder as a small speck appeared in her palm. A sudden clarity opened in his mind. He saw the equation grow in expression as she created layer after layer. His unconscious mind made a series of runes and numbers that appeared before his mind's eye for inspection. He didn't know it then, but his realization of the unconscious process would be the second most important thing he would ever learn.

As Flower worked the bulb, the expression became increasingly complex. She paused over one layer for a long time, thinking. Finally, coming to some unknown decision, she wove a series of runes into the equation that lost Jan entirely. When she finished, Jan sat spellbound by all the information lying within a single bulb.

"Plant it."

"No. We're going Home. You need sleep. Besides, I think it would be good to come back and see if you can remember the whole *word*. Now, I want to see if you can find your way back. Go, find your body."

Jan stood up and set Flower on her feet. He gazed around and realized that, if he started walking in Flower's mind, he would quickly lose himself. He also realized just how much of a burden of trust he was placing on Flower's shoulders.

Mythits and emotion are one. A demand, inspired by feeling, was beyond their ability to deny. Access to a Mythit's mind was as simple as a wish or a daydream. And, once shown, any human could reappear in the Mythit realm. Once there, it was simplicity to grasp the essence of the Mythit. This was the way they were bound. A wizard could simply grasp a particular thought and demand the Mythit's presence.

Jan realized, with a surety, he could come here any time he wished, touch any flower or simply be aware of the ground beneath his feet, and demand that Flower appear. Flower must have found him very special indeed to have given him leave to walk freely in her mind.

Now, he saw that he could not find his body. Try as he might, he could not perceive himself. He cleared his mind and let velvety tendrils of feeling reach out. Nothing. The only way to his body was through Flower.

He turned and looked at her. She was waiting. He knew she was testing him. But not just that; she wanted him to know just how easily he could bind her. Perhaps she just wanted to let him know now, and if he was going to insinuate himself in her personality, now was the time. He could hold and *mate* her personality simply by reaching out.

He went to her and knelt down. Cupping her small face in his hands, he gazed into her glowing, pale pink eyes. "I told you I would not do that to you."

"I know."

"I love you."

"I know."

"Your mind is very beautiful."

Flower smiled. "I know."

Jan narrowed his eyes. "You are very ticklish."

"I... No!"

Jan pulled her into his arms. Their mingled personalities made him feel light and content. Flower purred as she rubbed her cheek against his shoulder. "Jan?"

"Hmm?"

"Is this what it's like when humans make love?"

Jan was startled by the question. He remembered Lyndsy's words. "She's only a child."

"Yes, I think this is very close."

The hills and flowers faded away. Once again, he sat on the sunlit grasses of Home. Not wanting to release the glorious feelings within him, he sat back and closed his eyes.

After a long time, Flower sighed. "I love you, January."

"I know."

44

BEFORE THE LEAVES TURN GOLD

Ten days after they left the Knights Alliance, Slim Chance, Sheela, and the high cleric arrived at the School of Prayer.

Among the initiates, the high cleric made small nuances of favoritism toward Sheela. She did not want the young weremaiden to have to deal with the petty initiations that sometimes occurred among the newcomers. She knew Sheela would have enough problems just trying to keep herself in check.

After a few introductions were made, Sheela was shown to a room and told she would live with three other initiates. The young weremaiden walked into the room and caught her breath. Four beds, covered in pristine linen sheets, lay one in each corner. Each bed was crafted with a simple set of drawers built into their undersides.

She stepped cautiously around a beautiful tapestry someone had left on the floor. She had to blink and look away because it was threaded in a zigzag pattern that seemed to move if looked at too long.

Looking up over the nearest bed, she moaned in pleasure as she drifted into a lifelike painting of a deer by a stream. She grinned as her stomach rumbled and simply stood there and admired the full haunches of the doe.

Stomach still rumbling, she felt a cool breeze and smelled the fresh scent of pine. Walking to the window, she gazed outside. Her sense of direction momentarily blurred to confusion. As her thought process realized the tilt of the sun and the shadows of the trees, she blinked. Her sense of direction had been correct. The little forest was definitely in the center of the school.

"Hullo."

Sheela turned and watched a young woman enter the room. As she gazed at the tall blond-haired woman, her instincts said, *Open, strong, innocent.* "Hi."

Pointing to the bed in the corner farthest from the window, the young woman said, "That there's, I mean, that is your bed. Purty small but nice enough. I usta sleep on a old straw mattress at the farm, but now I gots, I mean, now I have a real bed o' my own." The pale cheeks of the young woman blushed crimson, and she looked away, abashed. "I'm sorry, you's probably one o' them rich girls from Veil that's used ta livin' in a huge house an all."

Sheela smiled, wanting to take away the young woman's inferiority scent. "No. In fact, I'm used to sleeping on the ground by a campfire." Sheela's eyes opened slightly wider. She was startled by the young woman's reaction to that statement. She sniffed her scent and realized she had just been judged and instantly accepted. *Just because I slept on the ground!*

The young woman walked closer and held out her hand. "My name's Swan. I'm pleased ta meet ya."

Should I tell her my real name? She decided quickly. After all, Swan had said her name first and she was just too innocent to have any ulterior motives. "I'm Sheela, and I'm pleased to meet you too." She gasped. "Oh no!"

Swan jumped and looked around. "What?"

"You're standing on the tapestry!"

Swan laughed. She finally grinned and said, conspiratorially, "It's a rug! You should see the one in the Great Hall!"

"A rug?" Sheela exclaimed, incredulously. "But it's a work of art!"

Swan smiled knowingly. "I know. Guess what? They put real silk cloth covers on all the dinner tables!"

"No!"

"Yes!" Swan was very pleased to finally have someone she could relate to. She smiled again and looked Sheela over.

Sheela watched Swan closely. She couldn't help it. She found herself liking this Swan very much. Swan's dark blue eyes lit up as though she were thinking of something wonderful. "What?" Sheela asked. "What are you thinking?"

"I just bet you wanna take a good bath."

"Yes," Sheela said, "*that* sounds wonderful!"

"Grab that towel. Come on."

"Towel?"

"Yes," Swan explained as they left the room. "We use 'em, I mean, we use them to dry off with."

"But it'll get wet; it looks brand new!"

"Yeah, I know!"

They walked down the long hall and passed through two sets of double doors. Swan stood back and watched for Sheela's reaction.

Sheela simply stared. A huge, steaming pool of water took up three-quarters of the floor space. Her jaw dropped open as she realized it was the bath.

Swan burst into laughter. "Come on." Walking to the bench, she disrobed and walked down the white marble steps into the pool.

Sheela grinned, undressed, and joined her first human friend.

Samantha stood before a round table within the council chamber. The High Council of Clerics filed in. When they all found their places, she nodded to each in turn, and said, "In the name of our Creator, I invoke the vow. Let thoughts be freely spoken."

"High Cleric, it is rumored that you fought in the battle before the walls of the Knights Alliance. Is this true?"

Samantha turned to the old cleric. "Sterin, that is a part of my purpose for this council. I will now show you something I have withheld, not knowing proper procedure—since there is no precedence." She opened the long, narrow box resting in the center of the table. White light flared into the room.

The clerics gathered around.

"The Scepter of Light!"

"Where did you find it?"

Samantha waited for all eyes to turn back to her. She wanted to impress upon them the importance of the scepter. "It was placed in my hands by a Mythit of Mirshol."

"A Mythit! Then the rumors are true? A Mythit has returned?"

"More than one. I have seen three, and they tell me there are many more within the enchanted forest. Magic has returned in the person of the young man who saved our caravan on the edge of Terror Trail. As you all know, this brings into play the many prophecies concerning the changing of Lyre."

An older graying Cleric named Sister Pency spoke quietly. "This is heavy tidings, High Cleric. The ancient Seer of the North spoke of the Dark Lord's return. We are ill prepared."

"True," Samantha said seriously, "but we have a small amount of time and more allies than you know. I have spent a half moon in the Land of the Were. They are a warrior race, and they will stand by Lyre."

"Were? You mean werewolves?" Brother Sterin gave Samantha a look of disgust. "They can't possibly be trusted!"

Samantha held her peace. "It seems to me their reasons for not trusting us are far more valid. Nevertheless, I say they are a trustworthy people, for I have just spent a half moon living among them. Their culture is vastly different than ours, and their ways are strange. But if they had not helped in the Battle of the Knights Alliance, the keep would now be a pile of rubble, and our greatest protectors would all be dead.

"Now, it is in my mind to ask your permission to wield the Scepter of Light."

"It was given to you. You *are* the high cleric. No leave is necessary; you know this well. I submit to curiosity. High Cleric, why do you ask our approval?"

Samantha smiled kindly at the old woman. "Insecurities perhaps. I wish to know that you approve."

Pency bowed her graying head. "I stand as witness to your humble integrity. High Cleric, it is yours."

Samantha gazed around the room, receiving agreements from the other clerics. Finally, she nodded. "I have another blessed item from the time of our first high cleric. When I stood before you four seasons ago and spoke the Vows of High Clericship, to your collective surprise, I chose the Bow of Myril as my personal symbol. I told you of my dreams—that I had seen myself in battle wielding the bow. It was a gift of sight, for I have now watched that dream in my waking life."

Samantha brought out the bow. "Twenty days ago, I rode into battle followed by a group of wild wolves no less than two hundred strong. In a thousand seasons, I am the first to declare the bow, a warrior's symbol, as my own. The bow is mine; in this matter, I allow no challenge."

"Indeed," Sterin asked as he gazed at the bow in awe, "was this also a gift from the Mythit?"

"No. It was placed in my hands by a maiden of the were."

"A were? Once again you speak of werewolves. I do not doubt your judgment, but they are a curse!"

Samantha thought grimly that, even here, some prejudices never died. She sighed. "Times change. It is written and remembered that, one day, the *were* would walk the land, welcomed as heroes wherever they went. I am the high cleric. I speak true. That day is soon to come."

Pency asked quietly, "Where did she get the bow?"

"She is the wizard's companion. She received it from him."

Sterin scowled. "Do you say the albino girl with him is a werewolf?!"

"Yes."

"And you let it in the school."

"Yes." She paused, gauging Sterin's character. What would he do if he found out about Sheela? "I am the high cleric. My very word, concerning the School of Prayer is law. I *will* do what I will, with or without your approval. However, she entered the school alone, *before* she came here with the young wizard. She walked into the sacred shrine and walked out again. You all, each and every one of you, know well the power of the blessing placed on the shrine. Her soul is special. She does not yet know it, but she is highly favored of our Creator. This young werewoman has been through many hardships in her very short life and, at the very least, deserves your respect in full measure!

"The history shows, in the writing of Myril himself, that the were are to serve a probation. During that probation, they are to serve humankind, which they all but destroyed in the northlands. For almost one thousand seasons, they have faithfully kept their vows. Every single child who has reached puberty has taken the Vow. I cannot even fathom a human social structure, without the presence of clerics, that could retain such strong devotion to any single-minded purpose. I have now seen it with my own eyes. As a servant of the Creator, I feel overwhelming pride to even stand in their presence.

"I invoke the Vow. It is my right as high cleric. I will hear no more prejudice against the were!"

45

A Piece of Past: 5

Jan sat, once again, in the field of flowers. He recreated, in illusionary symbols, the word that lay within the bulb. Jan studied his work and looked up, well pleased. Flower looked down on him in mock disgust. Feeling suddenly very foolish, he blurted out. "What?"

The small orange-and-yellow striped Mythit assumed Jasmine's pose, that said, *'I'm your mother. You are a child. Behold the wisdom of your elders!'* And she started in on a tirade that made Jan wonder if she were being avenged for the same stupidity.

"There are three things that can never be changed. (1) The structure of reproduction must match that of the flower you are imitating. (2) The nectar that attracts insects and small birds must contain the sugars that they find so irresistible. (3)"—she paused, scowling for effect—"You can't forget the green color in the leaves! The green color is very important! It contains the tiny processors that convert sunlight to sug—"

Jan rolled his eyes. "Flower?" He cupped his hands and held them up in such a way that the cup of his fingers was hidden from her sight. "Look at this. I want to show you something."

As expected, she became instantly curious, wondering what Jan held. Walking to his side, she peered into his hands. Jan reached out, flipped her on her back, and performed the dreaded flower torture.

"No! Oh, so unfair!"

After he was finished tickling her and she caught her breath, they changed the missing runes and symbols within the word and sat back to watch it grow. Jan paid strict attention to the equation as the flower unraveled. He was surprised to see the two identically mirrored symbols become two magenta spots on the outside petals.

Flower smiled as she gazed over his shoulder. "Well?"

Jan stared at the white flower. The petals and the magenta spots, along with a pale pink oval center, made the crude likeness of Lyndsy's face complete. "It's beautiful!"

Flower smiled. She loved Lyndsy dearly. It was her deepest wish to see the girl happy. She gazed off into the distance of her mind, and her glowing pale pink eyes filled with sadness. *He's already changing, mind and body turning and tuning to Song. He will live forever. She will swiftly grow old and die. I wonder if he has thought about it.* Flower turned back to watch Jan as he gazed at the flower. *What can I do?*

Four days later, Lyndsy woke Jan with a kiss.

"Where have you been?" His words and thoughts clouded as she smothered him with more kisses.

Afterward, they lay together on the piled-up silks in their nest. Jan knew now where she had been. Her pent-up passion and driving need had shown him that it must be even harder now to stay away. He wondered if he could do it. Once again, he marveled at her strengths. Even her physical strength was so out of proportion to her size it constantly amazed him.

He pulled her close, wrapping her small body with one leg and his arms.

Lyndsy growled, nose full of his wonderful scent, and sighed in contentment.

They sparred at noon. Lyndsy's determination pushed Jan to his limits. He was mentally exhausted; she was loose and ready to roar. He found the strength to come out the winner, but for him it had been a grueling dual.

Lyndsy leaned on her staff grinning and breathing hard. She felt eyes on her back and turned. An involuntary burst of breath issued from her lips as she saw over fifty Mythits standing poised and watching. A few started flickering out. Not wanting them to go and not wanting to scare them, she held herself perfectly still. They were all so different! A literal rainbow of hue filled the lawn of Home.

Snow walked up to her and grinned. Lyndsy reached for the little white hand the Mythit offered.

A sky-blue Mythit with dark blue hands and feet came closer and exclaimed, "You're a good fighter! No wonder January likes you so much."

Lyndsy smiled at the male Mythit. "I hope that's not the only reason he likes me so much!"

A few of the others came closer to get a better look. She watched them in shared fascination. Snow turned to a purple and white Mythit and said importantly, "She's a were. She let me ride on her back."

The Mythit looked up at Lyndsy and tilted her head to Snow. *Does she bite?*

Yes! Lyndsy laughed gaily as the Mythit jumped back.

The purple and white Mythit looked hesitantly at Snow and then back up to Lyndsy. *I'm sorry, I didn't know.*

Lyndsy felt and heard a sudden blurring of words as all of the Mythits seemed to be thinking at once. The burst of words made her feel dizzy. The wave of confusion passed, and she found herself lying on the ground. She looked up into Jan's worried face.

"You OK?"

She nodded. "What happened?"

"Your mind was wide open. All the thoughts pouring in at one time confused your senses." He looked around. All of the Mythits were gathered close, looking at Lyndsy with soft, glowing eyes. Concern permeated the air.

"Didn't mean to!"

Jan smiled at Sky, the blue Mythit. "Of course, you didn't. But we all need to be more careful. She is new to this. Only speak one at a time until her mind grows stronger."

Lyndsy sat up. All the Mythits were very close. She wanted, very badly, to earn their trust, so she remained sitting. The Mythits' irresistible curiosity quickly overwhelmed them, and Lyndsy found herself answering all sorts of questions about the were. How do you change? Why don't you live in cities? How come only a pack leader and a first can have children? What's it *really* like to be a wolf? Isn't it lonely to be One Who Walks Alone?

"Jan."

Jan stood up and frowned at Flower. She looked slightly upset, and he couldn't figure it. Mythits got happy, angry, and peaceful, but they didn't usually feel emotions that were self-inflicted. They didn't feel stress, and that made him wonder what the problem was. Taking her hand, he led her away. "What is it?"

"Mother and Father just entered Mirshol."

Jan looked at her, uncomprehending.

"Jan, they'll be angry when they find out about us."

"Do you regret the choice? I now feel your presence as if you were me, but you are not *bound* to me."

Flower was thoughtful. "No, I don't regret it. I don't know why. I think I wanted you more than you wanted me, but they won't like it—especially Mother. I don't understand her! She curses wizards for what they have done to us but never makes the feeling personal. She even berated Blue, or so I've heard, on Sunder's behalf. But she doesn't seem to feel that way about herself."

Jan realized the truth of Flower's words and also began to wonder why. "Sunder has told me a hundred times, if not a thousand, about his love for Blue. Besides, it's obvious every time he speaks of him. He was willing to take that role in *my* life. Do they think I could be cruel?"

He reached out to Flower, and she welcomed his embrace. She said softly, "They must realize you are different. They must! I don't know," she added in exasperation. "Maybe they're both just so old they think they have to protect everybody. You know?" Flower sighed. "Like parents with children."

Jan nodded. "They will have to accept it. They don't have any choice. But you"—Jan held her tighter—"remember, you can stop and leave anytime you feel you must."

Flower laughed. "I could no more deny you than Lyndsy could!"

January walked through Mirshol alone. He made sure no one followed. A meandering stream crossed his path. He stopped and noticed a large mountain cat playfully chasing a group of squirrels. They stopped when they became aware of him. The cat padded to his side. Jan absently scratched the coarse fur between its ears.

Rose appeared in front of him. He hadn't tried to summon her, but it *was* her he had come to see. The cat left his side and pounced on her. She rolled with the large feline and ended up on top. Jan watched her grab the furry neck with both hands and shake its head from side to side. She was laughing.

His tension and worry had been building. He wanted advice. Was it wrong to sit in peace in Mirshol? Shouldn't he be spying the movements of the enemy? Why did he feel so guilty about enjoying his precious time in the forest?

Rose looked up at him. She was stern and poised. "January, war will come when it will. It is not right to spend one's life sitting on the battlefield waiting to strike the first blow. We see you. You have communications with the schools and the were. You can be summoned at a moment's notice.

"My master fought many, many battles. He often said the best warriors were those who cherished peace, not those who spent wasted lifetimes brooding over what the enemy's next move would be. Do you understand?"

"Yes," Jan said with a smile, "you've said what I needed to hear."

Rose's eyes lit with pleasure. "Good! Now, tell me everything that's happened since you first left. Tell me of the battle that rocked even Mirshol—especially those hardheaded were. Tell me what those stupid, ignorant, lowlife, rat-faced Vainians tried to do!"

Jan looked at her curiously.

She graced him with a childlike pout. "After all, I am a warrior too. I'm eager for news."

Jan laughed softly. "Warrior indeed!"

As January spoke, he watched Rose's reactions. He started with that first fight on Terror Trail. He quickly found that, like her Creator, she was very fond of the were and wanted to hear all about Lyndsy. When he reached the second fight with the demon in its own form, he told her that Lyndsy had not only been unafraid but had sworn by her Fathers to hunt it down and kill it.

"January," Rose asked, "does that really seem so strange to you?"

"Of course."

Rose looked deep within him. Jan felt her penetrate his senses and moved to block her out.

Please, let me show this to you.

Jan became very still and alert as he allowed her to enter his mind. Her thought pattern was almost as hard to keep track of as Red himself.

You have seen the old form that the were had to bear? It is thought among my sisters and I that there must still be a few who can still take that form.

Jan fed her mental pictures of Those Who Walk Alone, Lyndsy standing in the moonlight, the hideous and beautiful form of the old curse.

Rose's cool thought said, *Do you think that creature fears a demon? Behold!*

Jan watched picture memories appear in his mind. The Red Wizard faded in at the mouth of a cave. Peering over the cliff's edge, he watched a handful of silent figures climbing the jagged walls. One by one, they reached the top. The beautiful, wicked figures of the Old Curse reached him and stood in a circle around him. Hot breath and gleaming eyes brought a smile to Red's lips.

The red gem on his staff flickered once. The stone doorway blasted to pieces. The wizard and the were charged through the dust-clogged opening with heart-stopping, bloodcurdling screams. They ran down a long corridor and into a large chamber. Jan saw a woman he already knew, although he couldn't remember ever having seen her before.

Melody the Black stood in front of an iron-bound door. She was dressed in dark blue silks, her black skin contrasting sharply with a head of bright, silver hair. Her terrible beauty made Jan's heart pound in his chest. Soft, sweet tendrils of silky smooth lust assaulted the Red Wizard. She held out her perfectly formed arms. "Come, Lori. I have missed you!"

Red shook off the compulsion with no small effort. He steadied himself, drawing ragged breaths. He knew he had to break her spell and do it swiftly. Even now the were's personalities were turning against him.

He looked her in the eyes and said very slowly, distinctly, "The enchanting fragrance of your womanhood reminds me of hot summer days in the eel markets."

Sudden rage caused her spell to slip. At the same moment, Red set his own spell and placed an illusion around her. It was one of smell.

Eel.

Were love eel.

Were love to eat eel!

Too angry to think clearly, Melody was forced to retreat. She shook her fist and vanished in a flash of thick, ugly colors.

Red approached the door she had been guarding. Dagdor the Black kept a force of demons within the chamber. These bitch-demons were not summoned with specific forms. Dagdor's Mythit, Poison, used these demons to warp the true course of nature. With a human male and a demon, she could create a new form of evil life. Through the mixing of human and demon, Poison had created the were.

Tracing runes and chanting, Red pushed the door open. Jan beheld a group of shape-changing demons that writhed and reformed, defying any single description. Instantly, they tried to attack the Red Wizard.

His were companions were there to perform a deed. Outnumbered five to one, perform they did. The Red Wizard simply watched. One were ripped a growing arm from a demon and beat it back into death. With the same arm, it found its next victim, beat it to the ground, and ripped out its throat.

Another demon jumped on the were's back. Slowly, the were's head was wrenched and twisted in a circle. The were smiled a death's head grin, snapped its teeth, and licked the demon's face. Then, in a fit of rage, it twisted around, slammed the demon on its back, and shredded slimy flesh from everywhere that his claws found purchase. The demon tried to fight back.

But every time a new arm formed and reached from the slime-covered, shape-changing body, the were's awesome, hooked fangs snapped them off. With a final scream of utter delight, the were plunged both long, clawed hands deep into the demon's belly and ripped its guts out.

Jan opened his eyes and wiped at the cold sweat on his brow. "In the name of Song! I didn't understand."

Rose held his gaze and frowned. "If your feelings for your lover have changed because of me, I will kill you and never forgive myself."

Jan took a deep breath but offered Rose a slight smile. "You don't need to worry over that. I swear, she can do nothing to make me love her less. They are so different now. How can the were of today even be considered the same?"

"The were have always been the were. Come, show me more."

Jan started his thoughts with eating raw eel in wolf shape. To his delight, Rose burst into musical laughter. He showed her the first meeting with Sha, and she stopped him.

"That man, the one with you. He was the one you sent us to heal."

"Yes. We call him Slim Chance. You first told me you watch me, but you don't know about him. Why?"

Rose looked both defensive and sad at the same time. "You have to understand that our lives are bound to the gems. We know when you use us—I mean, them." She paused and then said very carefully, "We cannot see through your eyes. We can only guess what you do. We know every time you use the gems, every time. I know that you have used the destructive powers of the red gem many times. I know that, for a few hours, seven days ago, in the middle of the night, the red gem passed from my sight. I will not ask, because I already know. I ramble. Please continue."

Plunging back in, Jan took Rose through the conclusions that led them to believe the Knights Alliance would come under attack. She watched the battle with a veteran's critical eye, intent on every move. At the end of the battle, she scowled. "You are very brave and very lucky. That battle was a fine display of stupidity and incompetence on both sides! Your thick skull should have been split twenty times over!"

Jan didn't argue. As he played all of this over, he could only agree. Nevertheless, they had been victorious. Not only had they won, they had suffered very few casualties while inflicting severe losses on the Vainians.

As he reached Virile Swamp, Rose slowed him down. She replayed Slim's description of the werechildren's battle over and over.

The older children had placed the infants in watertight containers and buried them in the swamp. Air tubes made from animal intestines let them breath.

Thirty large bags of oil had been tied with slipknots and buried in a huge circle. Mud-covered, they were simply lumpy patches of ground. As three werechildren led the Vainians into the circle, other children pulled the ropes. Oil spilled and quickly covered the surface of the thick, muddy swamp.

The six children, buried up to their chins and covered with oil-soaked weeds, waited until every last Vainian was trapped in the circle. They all lifted their arms at the same time, ripped open the waterproofing, and ignited the weeds in front of them.

The older children waited to see the first flames and then immediately hauled on the ropes and pulled the children across the surface of the swamp.

All of the surviving Vainians were chased to the edges of the marsh. A handful of the older children had circled around with bows while the Vainians were first led in. Now, surrounded on all sides, the Vainians did not stand a chance. None of them made it out of the swamp alive.

"Now that is a fine display of cunning and teamwork! I wish I could have been there! A fine battle, fit for many songs!"

Sisters, I have had my way with him. Come, ask your questions.

Sapphire and Star appeared. To Jan's surprise, Sapphire pulled him to his feet and hugged him hard. "Oh, but it's good to see you again!"

Star stood back and looked him over. She seemed to see something that startled her. Gazing into his eyes, she easily penetrated his senses and all of his barriers. He knew he could call on the power of the white gem and control her, but something in her gaze, perhaps longing or hope, stopped him.

She played his memories of Samantha. When the high cleric charged into battle carrying the Scepter of Light and the Bow of Myril, she gasped. Jan watched again as Samantha met and was unconditionally accepted by the were.

At Lyndsy and his joining, he felt overwhelming sensations of excitement and awe coming from the white specter. She seemed to watch the scenes as though she were weighing some secret decisions. But the biggest shock for Star was when Samantha blessed the weremaiden Sheela.

Star broke contact and looked away. Rose looked from Star to January and scowled. "Well, *sister*, are you finished picking his bones?"

Star's reply, obviously guarding the issue of Sheela, didn't really surprise him. "He is joined to the weregirl, Moonlight, blessed by the high cleric in the presence of the Creator himself!"

Once again, Sapphire embraced him. She held him as she would her own child, stroking his hair and humming a peaceful tune. "I'm very pleased with you. Take care of your lady were for she is the key to all that comes after."

"Sister!" Star shouted.

Sapphire's eyes made it clear she had already thought about, and decided, to say what she had said.

"Why?" Jan asked. "Why is Lyndsy the key?"

The Three Sisters stood silent. Jan thought again to use the sword to gain his answers, but the scared look on Star's white face made him pause. He wanted to know; he wanted to know now. What could possibly involve Lyndsy other than himself? She had no power except to change shape. The way of magic was closed to the were. He didn't know why, but he did know it was true. Why Lyndsy?

Sapphire again spoke through Star's protest. "You once said in jest that we should join the Riddlers of Wizards and Mythits. I would say this—"

"No!"

Sapphire looked at Star. "There are *still* things singularly understood by each of us. It is my place to speak of this. Trust me." She turned back to Jan and smiled. "Here is a riddle for you to ponder at your leisure: Why did the Three never take mates?"

Jan watched Star shake in fear. What could she fear about wizards taking mates?

Jan looked back at Sapphire. The Blue Lady's warm, kind smile made him wonder.

He walked back Home. His heart was light. He found great comfort in the familiar sounds and smells of Mirshol. He stopped several times, visiting places where Sunder had given him various lectures and instructions in sword dancing and mind work. This was truly his home.

No Mythits were in sight as he stepped onto the short grass. He reached his rope and looked up. A full group of shimmering personalities were all huddled together in his nest. Climbing to the top he looked in and saw Lyndsy asleep on a rainbow mass of silks. She held a Mythit in each arm, her head resting in Snow's lap. Many other Mythits were curled up next to her, resting against her legs and ribs.

Jan knew they didn't sleep. He also knew from long experience that, in touching her, they could see and share her dreams. They could even appear in a dream if her mind was properly framed. She giggled and smiled in sleep, mumbling something.

Jan sat down next to her sleeping form, set one hand on her thigh, and closed his eyes.

46

REFLECTION

"**S**tand up and face me like a man, human!"

Jan opened a sleepy eye to see Jasmine's wrathful face.

"How dare you! You would rape your own sister? I thought you loved us! You're a filthy, stinking liar, and I would kill you myself if I could!"

"Mother!"

Jasmine turned on Flower. "And you! You would sell yourself so cheaply? Did you even try to run and hide?"

Jan sat up. "Jasmine, listen to me. We—"

"*Silence!*" Jasmine screamed. "Sunder was prepared to *give* you this. I would have done it myself. But no!" she said scornfully. "You have to destroy she who loved you most!" Jasmine's swift hand slapped Jan across the face.

Jan reached out and pulled Jasmine into his arms. She fought back furiously, but his embrace forced her to stillness. She raged as Jan's affection penetrated her personality. She hated it! But as all Mythits must, she was slowly forced to partake of the sweet, peace-filled emotion. Flower came to them, put her hands on Jasmine's shoulder, and reinforced the emotion between January and her mother.

All at once, Jasmine's rage stopped. With a final, "No!" she gave in. Jan held her close as luminous, bright red tears crystallized around his legs. *I love you, my mother. Please don't hate me.*

Jasmine wept, now quietly, against Jan's muscled chest. No, she could never hate him. But not Flower—not her only child! Slowly, she opened her mind, thinking perhaps the bond wasn't too strong. Perhaps, she could break it and take Flower's place. Yes, she would do that willingly.

Trying not to let Jan know her thoughts, she felt for the written memory of the place in Flower's mind. She couldn't find it. Giving up all pretense of stealth, she plunged headlong into Jan's mind. Nothing, nothing at all!

Flower? Child?

Mother, you're acting like a fool!

Jasmine felt as though she had been slapped. In effect, she had. She came back to herself and looked around. Like a clear, cool mountain stream splashing gaily down its path, comprehension filled her. There was no bond. Flower had done this of her own free will. No one could have understood this better than she. A memory came to her from long ago.

The Blue Wizard had found her sitting by a little pool. She had, the day before, used all of her wit to try and shame him for having bound Sunder. She had been furious. To the bruising of her pride, he had laughed at her! Now he sat down by her side and silently shared the quiet surroundings with her. He had looked at her and waited for her to turn her head and meet his eyes.

Giving in, she'd met his gaze. His bright blue eyes held the little specks of white fire that she recognized as the sign of the individual feeling strongly about the moment. His glowing, blue orbs held her silent as he smiled and wilted all of her reservations. "Little Princess, it has been over three thousand seasons since Sunder and I first became bound. You probably don't understand this, but I am just as bound to him as he is to me. Nevertheless, Princess, I will offer you some hope. From time to time, I am able to see the truth in an individual. A truth that is within *you* is that you will bear a child that will change everything as you now know it."

As she sat, now silent and still, in January's lap, she remembered this. She who held more secrets than any living creature never thought there were things the White Wizard didn't already know. Sudden shame filled her. Just as suddenly, she felt Jan and Flower wash her shame away.

I'm sorry, I have no right.

Compassionately but firmly, Jan thought, *Your right is that of a mother worrying for her child. The child must someday grow up.*

His sweet, gentle personality overwhelmed her. She turned her face to see Sunder and Lyndsy standing together. Sunder thought, *I'm glad you're taking this so well.* He smiled. *I couldn't bear to see my family taken away. Again.*

Sunder knew many things. Quite a few of them were understandings that Jasmine thought she bore alone. He too had secrets. Was he not the Mythit of the Blue Wizard? Even though he didn't understand the implications of a Mythit's free will, he had known of Jasmine's choice. Blue had secretly told him that he would have a daughter who would be the Mythit of the man in legend. This was why he'd never bound himself to Jan.

The one thought that had never occurred to either of them was that, through Flower, Jan's growth would be square the ability of either one of them. She was their daughter. What was a Mythit child if not a reflection of both of its parents?

Jan stood next to the old dammed creek gazing off into the trees. Flower's laughter made him turn. Lyndsy was holding Flower over the pool by one ankle. Lyndsy smiled, mischief sparkling in her bright magenta eyes. "I believe the Flower is in need of watering. What do you think?"

Jan grinned. "Most definitely."

"No!"

Splash.

As he watched Lyndsy dive in after her, he thought about all the things he had learned in the last two moons. The one thought that kept returning was something the Red Wizard had said. *Don't forget the Forest of Manshantarrinon. The men and women there are a hardy lot. Find time to go there. Off all things necessary to defeat the Dark Lord, that which dwells in the forest is your greatest need.*

"What do you two think about a trip south?"

Lyndsy, flinging Flower back into the water, heard the suggestion and, startled, forgot to let go. Jan laughed as Lyndsy and Flower tumbled head-over-heels into the creek. Lyndsy came up sputtering. Flower exclaimed, "That's a great idea!"

Lyndsy frowned. In truth, she wanted to stay with the Mythits. She knew in her heart Mirshol was the only place she could ever find complete acceptance. The Mythits were wondrous. They didn't care if she were were. They made no issue over the color of her skin. Jan and Flower had to drag her away from Home just to go for a walk!

Flower smiled. *Methinks Lyndsy of Mirshol has found a home.*

Jan wrinkled his nose. *Methinks you're right.*

Lyndsy of Mirshol?

"Of course!" Flower exclaimed. "You are the first of January of Mirshol!"

"Lyndsy," Jan said soothingly, "from now on, this will always be your home."

Lyndsy's heart settled into place. She didn't know why she had felt apart, but she had. Now she realized she need never have worried. Truly, she would forever after consider Mirshol her home.

"Lyndsy of Mirshol," she said to herself. Remembering the blissful nonsense of her first morning after, she laughed. "A trip south? Why not."

"Can I come too?"

Jan looked from Snow to Lyndsy. He knew there would be times when he and Flower would need to be alone. Snow could be company to Lyndsy. Besides, just how much trouble could one Mythit be? Jan flinched and shuddered at his own thought. Way too much! Well, they were only going on a short trip, right? They weren't expecting any trouble.

"Snow, you can come. But if you cause any problems, I'm sending you home!"

Wide, innocent magenta eyes looked up at him accusingly. "Problems? Me?"

Here ends *The Young One*, Book 1 of Through the Eyes of Children.

Made in the USA
Coppell, TX
20 October 2023

23102409R00208